The Children of Divinity, Book One

AWAKEN

By Garth Reasby

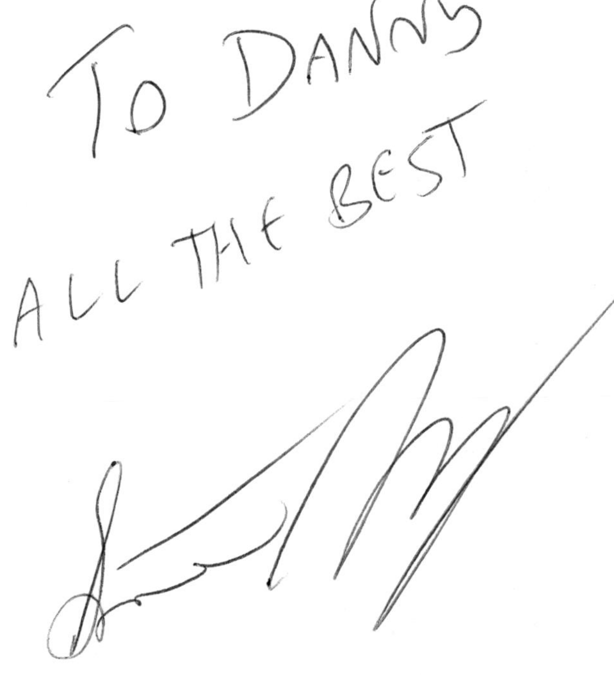

Cover Art by Garth Reasby

www.thermalscorpion.com

ISBN-13: 978-1466354586
ISBN-10: 1466354585

Printed in the United States of America

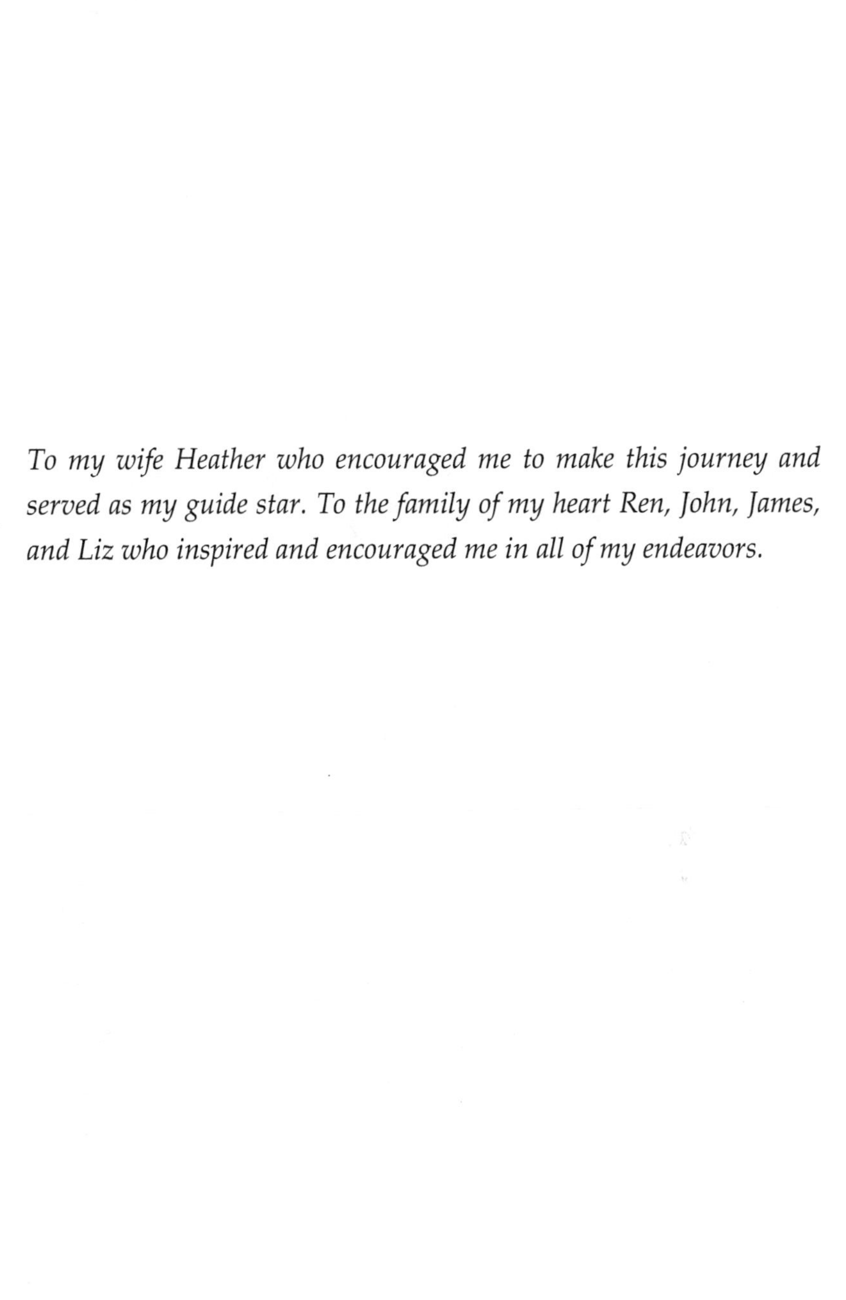

To my wife Heather who encouraged me to make this journey and served as my guide star. To the family of my heart Ren, John, James, and Liz who inspired and encouraged me in all of my endeavors.

CHAPTER 1

The bitter cold of the Afghani night had yet to give way to the oppressive heat of the day and the sun had not even begun its slow crawl from behind the rugged mountains. The terrain was treacherous at best, though the combination of sharp, uneven rock, prolific scrub brush and several large camel thorn trees provided excellent protection for the small village nestled near the steep rock wall. The rickety collection of patchwork buildings had been built near where an uneven smuggler's pass exited so that travelers could rest there after making the long journey from Pakistan.

In the quiet pre-dawn, the sound of two vehicles approaching echoed off the tall rock walls that rimmed the valley where the unnamed village sat. The sputtering cough-like echo of each truck's four cylinder gas engine created enough of a racket to stir the one dog of the village and send him into a fit of sharp barking. The barking ended in a yelp of pain when a weary sentry kicked the dog into silence.

"Stupid cur. My wife complains enough even when she's slept all night. That damned dog and its incessant barking!" Dehqan cursed in Pashto while he and a fellow Mujahedeen picked their way through the uneven terrain along the ridgeline on their way back to the village which was over a kilometer away.

The other man grinned widely with a mouth full of nicotine-stained teeth. "Your wife will be cranky again my friend, and no doubt twice as ugly without more sleep."

Dehqan glanced at his friend Babur and chuckled quietly at the joke. "Yes, but not so ugly as your own with twice again as much rest." Both men allowed their amusement to fade into silence as they continued down the rough slope towards their homes.

The sounds of the two sentries' battered Russian combat boots crunching on the rocks disappeared as they wound their way down the broken trail. Neither man noticed the concealed form that lay on the ground not more than five meters away from the trail where they had traded barbs. The form remained motionless until the scent of sweat, clove cigarettes, and gun oil the two men reeked of faded. Even then there was no obvious motion from the shadowy shape that blended seamlessly with the straw colored halfa grass where it lurked. Hidden by a shaggy ghille suit carefully crafted from the local foliage, the distinctly feminine form was rendered nearly invisible even in the full light of day. Here in the dim pre-dawn she was a ghost.

It had been so for two days and nights. Thankfully, the straw colored ghille suit combined with the lose-fitting British lightweight DPM fatigues, or battle dress utilities and the Underarmor thermals beneath provided some protection from the frigid cold of the Afghani nights. Those same layers also kept the blistering sun from the woman's skin. Though it was better than being fully exposed to the intense sunlight that baked the countryside, she found it insufferably warm. Still, the ghille suit did what it was designed to do and reduced the chance that someone would detect the sniper wearing it.

The trucks were closer now, perhaps three kilometers from the woman's position. It was the same two beaten and battered Toyota T-100 pickup trucks, one red, and the other blue. Both vehicles were packed with Taliban fighters. They were carrying all manner of weaponry from old Soviet AK-47 assault rifles to World War Two era bolt action rifles. The woman that was concealed beneath the camouflage narrowed her eyes and continued her vigil. She had counted roughly twenty fighters in the village in addition to the fifteen that went out in the trucks nightly. She had been in the middle of the snake's nest for two days' time, but that didn't bother the young woman from Northampton. She was there because she was the only one who could make it so deep into enemy territory without being discovered.

Pushing the brief moment of reflection to the back of her mind, like the worry before it, Jordan focused her attention on the mission at hand. Fate seemed inclined to reward her discipline. The procession of twenty men and donkeys Jordan had been waiting for picked their way out of a large shadowed crack in the weathered rock wall as if on cue. The first hints of dawn caressed the stone wall's weather-beaten surface as the group of insurgents navigated the rough and uneven terrain of the old smuggler's path. They seemed oblivious to the danger they were in and made casual conversation as they walked.

Jordan carefully adjusted the aim of her Accuracy International L115A3 Arctic Warfare Super Magnum sniper rifle and centered the cross hairs of its Schmidt & Bender 3-12X variable scope on the center of the lead walker's face. *Not him,* she thought.

The sleek L115A3 was a highly accurate bolt action rifle that had a polymer stock and an adjustable cheek rest so that each shooter could set the weapon to their own tastes. The stock was cast in a khaki tan while the metal barrel and bipod were painted in a simple, but effective, desert camouflage to match. The long scope that was mounted just in front of the bolt was also painted to blend in with the terrain. To reduce the chance of detection, the optic had been fitted with honeycomb shaped anti-reflection devices. Though different versions of the rifle were designed to use a variety of calibers, Jordan's super magnum was chambered for .338 Lapua. Thanks to this large-caliber high-performance round, the L115A3 was capable of taking down any game animal, including an elephant, which meant that any human struck by a well-aimed bullet was unlikely to live. The L115A3 rifle was a precision instrument, a surgeon's scalpel in the world of warfare, and perfect for a master marksman like Jordan. The weapon was practical, reliable, accurate, but, most of all, it reminded Jordan of her father, himself a former sniper. She knew it would never let her down.

Continuing to seek out her target, Jordan repeated the adjustment eight times before she saw the familiar features of the target. She knew his name, though she didn't dwell on it. He was the target and that was it. It didn't matter what he was called. His distinctive features were what were important, features that he had just revealed by unwrapping the off-white cloth from around his head to allow the rising sun to warm his face. The man had helped orchestrate over two dozen attacks against American and British forces in Afghanistan, and had been responsible for a terrorist bombing at Heathrow airport only four hours after the destruction of the Twin Towers. He had murdered hundreds, but worse yet, he had trained hundreds more, a cadre of like-minded fanatics that could potentially kill thousands, of innocent people. Jordan was here to make sure he had trained his last terrorist, committed his last murder.

A strong, cold wind caught the cloth about the man's head and tugged it to the side causing Jordan to smile slightly. The flapping of the material allowed her to easily gauge the wind speed where he was standing. She waited for the group to make their way down the trail towards the Taliban-controlled village that was their destination and, more importantly, past the areas she had already pre-ranged so she didn't need a spotter to assist her. At just over two thousand eight hundred meters in poor light and high, inconsistent wind, it was a tough shot at best. For most snipers, it wasn't possible. It was why she had come.

Awaken

Jordan clicked off two ticks of the windage adjustment knob on her scope and let her finger lightly caress the trigger of her rifle, releasing her breath in a long, slow exhalation. The target continued along unsuspectingly, one step, another, and then another. The man continued to talk with his companions, Jordan's eyes watched his face through the magnified optics of her scope while her breath trickled from her parted lips. Her mind focused on a span of time between breaths and everything in the world around her slowed down.

Unexpectedly, the Mujahedeen leader's head started to turn to face Jordan's position. The man's eyes met Jordan's through the view of her scope and began to shift from a warm brown to solid white. Like the scrabbling of dozens of clawed feet on stone, an unintelligible whisper filled Jordan's mind. A pain so intense that it made Jordan's jaw clench accompanied the disturbing sound and seemed to be growing. Instinctively, Jordan squeezed the trigger. The familiar recoil of the weapon rippled through her arms and shoulders, but she kept the rifle on target.

The bullet crossed the intervening terrain quickly, leaving a hint of distorted air in its passing. It crossed over the tops of several bushes, through the Y shaped intersection of branches on a camel thorn tree, then rushed through a fist sized space between two large boulders. Unerringly, the projectile continued on its path for just over two seconds before it sped past another man's ear and struck the target in the left eye.

The .338 Lapua round had lost much of its kinetic energy on its long journey but it still struck the terrorist leader like a sledgehammer. Just before the bullet struck, the man smiled serenely at Jordan, the whispering in her head coalescing into a single phrase, *"Allahu akbar."*

The force of the impact was such that the target's head barely moved but the back of it explosively sprayed on the large boulder he was walking by. His companions immediately hit the ground and started shouting loudly. The village came alive with activity as the report from the large bore rifle reached them and shook the guerilla fighters from their sleep.

Soon people were streaming from nearly every ramshackle structure, yelling for everyone to prepare for attack. Even the previously silenced dog was barking again as people rushed about in a panic. The remaining nineteen men in the procession opened fire with their Russian-made Kalashnikov AK-47 assault rifles. Most of the insurgents fired into the areas that they thought the attacker was in, which resulted in several of the fighters firing in different directions. Only a couple of the disorganized men managed to bring fire in Jordan's direction though none of the hastily fired bullets reached her.

Though her shot was well over the world record for a long range kill, Jordan took no time to revel in it. It wasn't the first she had made at such a range. None of her best shots would ever be recorded in a history book, yet history had been irrevocably altered by many of them. Jordan took no pleasure in killing, but understood that there were certain people that couldn't be dealt with by any other means.

Jordan was all business as she put her rifle in the long tan sniper drag bag next to her and rolled up the shooting mat she had spent the last two days on. Tucking that away, she thrust her hand into a pouch and pushed herself into a crouch holding a small bottle in her hand. With a flick of her thumb, Jordan opened and then dumped the small container of vinegar she had retrieved over the entire area where she was laying. The strong-smelling liquid would prevent any dogs from tracking her by scent. With practiced efficiency she slung the drag bag over her shoulder and grabbed the Heckler and Koch G-36K assault rifle from where it lay next to her.

The sudden and unexpected sound of a boot grinding stones together made Jordan freeze in place. Turning her head, the British operative stared into the eyes of the Afghani man, imaging herself as thin and light as a morning's breeze.

Dehqan shook his head and lowered his battered AK-47 assault rifle, his eyes squinting in the haze of the rapidly arriving dawn. Cautiously, he walked forward and wrinkled his nose, the harsh scent of vinegar unpleasant and unwelcome, though he could just barely make out the fading scent of burned gunpowder. The Afghani fighter could have sworn he's seen someone several meters down the trail. A woman. A tall woman with dark hair half hidden by a backwards-turned tan baseball cap and a curtain of local plant life pushed back from a camouflaged face. She had the most intense and beautiful blue eyes he had ever seen, but suddenly she was gone as if she had never been there. Dehqan blinked rapidly as if the act would bring the woman back into existence, but she did not return. A voice from behind called his name and the poppy farmer turned 'freedom fighter' jumped.

"Dehqan what is it? What did you see?" Babur rasped quietly in Pashto.

"Nothing…nothing, just a trick of the morning light."

* * * * * *

It had been over ninety minutes since Jordan eliminated her target. Since then she had kept up a steady run through the rocks. The remaining insurgents had set out to try and find the person responsible for killing their leader, but Jordan pushed on hard and fast to out-distance them. She made her way into another hilly area dotted with large rocks and small caves. Jordan had anticipated that she may have hard time getting out of the area when she originally designed the mission, so she spent several days locating places she could hide as well as store equipment.

As she approached one of her caches Jordan heard a faint metallic rattling off in the distance. About a kilometer off, one of the battered Toyota pickups sped down the dusty road packed with Taliban fighters. Its engine sputtered in protest as the driver pushed it far beyond what the poorly-maintained machine could handle. Surprisingly, the engine held and the dust covered machine sped past Jordan's position, leaving a wake of black exhaust in the air behind it.

Jordan watched the truck pass from where she crouched in the rocks and remained completely motionless. After it was gone, she turned and ducked into a crack in the wall behind her. She knew that the guerillas would most likely drive until they thought they were well ahead of her and make their way back on foot.

They're a tenacious lot, I'll give them that, Jordan thought as she moved into the small passage in a half crouch.

Once she was a meter inside the passage, Jordan pulled a small tan box from her combat vest and placed it at the mouth of the cave amongst a small pile of rocks. She flipped a small toggle switch on the side of the device and then moved further into what was little more than a water carved pocket. The cave was only four meters deep, a meter wide and maybe a meter and a half tall with fairly smooth surfaces. During a good rain, the water would rush in through a small hole in ceiling and out of the crack in the wall. Jordan moved to the back of the shallow cave and pulled an assortment of brush off of the cache of supplies she had hidden several days prior.

The waiting three-day pack was tan and loaded with ammunition for the G36K, as well as Jordan's semi-automatic .45 caliber pistol. In addition, it had six L-2A2 fragmentation grenades and four N-110 smoke grenades that were divided into different colors. One was red and one was green and they were to be used for signaling, the other two were standard grey smoke for creating concealment. Most importantly, the pack had full hydration bladder for Jordan's Camelbak water carrier which she opened and took a long drink from.

After letting the semi-cool water run down her throat, Jordan exhaled long and slow to ease some of the tension from her body. She had pushed hard to get to the small refuge using short bursts of speed followed by minutes of hiding to leap frog from cover to cover in order to stay ahead of any foot pursuit. Jordan secured the top on the new bladder and swapped out the old for the new, placing the spent rubber bladder in her pack.

I should have waited and blown the engine blocks on the two trucks to put them all on foot. Rookie mistake, girl, you should have tidied up that bit before you exfiltrated, Jordan chided herself and pulled her ghille suit off. She rolled the sections of it and strapped the bundle to her three-day pack just in case she needed it again. It was no substitute for her gifts but they were hard to use at a full run, especially against large numbers of people.

The purpose for taking the camouflage suit with her was twofold. She wasn't going to leave a trail for the Taliban fighters to follow, or anything with her DNA on it. No trail of bread crumbs for anyone to follow back to who she was or who she worked for.

Jordan reached into the pack and pulled out a high-calorie concentrate bar she had wrapped in a piece of aluminum foil. These weren't standard-issue ration, but Jordan needed the extra calories after three days of relatively little to eat and the brief but high level of energy she expended in her retreat. The candy bar-sized was pasty white and looked like hard taffy though it tasted like very bland oatmeal. Jordan unwrapped one side of the calorie bar before she popped the end of it in her mouth to let her saliva soften it up.

As she worked at consuming the small bar, Jordan reflected on the past three months since her assignment to work with 22 SAS's A Squadron. Jordan's director, Nigel Stevens, had never admitted it while she was in the room, but Jordan was one of his few operatives that could make it so far into enemy territory without being detected. Her past work had shown she was exceptionally good at getting into, and out of, locations that were so-called impossible targets. Jordan knew that Stevens' real issue was that he couldn't figure out how she did it. It was her secret and she was going to keep it as long as possible.

The first month of the assignment had been training with the SAS team so that Jordan would know how to work with them without the need for excessive communication. It was a lot of move and cover exercises, night exercises, and kill house drills at Credenhill. The men had treated her with mild courtesy and professionalism, however, they pushed her. At the time, Jordan wasn't sure if it was because she was a woman, or if they just wanted to test her ability to keep up with them. She had played both games before. In the male-dominated field of work, a woman had to show they were just as skilled as the men and twice as tough. They had done their best to make her quit, mixing misogynist humor in with the grueling training. Jordan was *no* quitter. In fact, they learned that she was every bit the marksman that she was made out to be and that she was as strong and as fast as any of the men. By the time that month was out, she had convinced them that she could keep up and more.

Once the team had made it in country, they immediately set out to locate their target. It had taken nearly two months to find out about the small, unnamed village that was arguably within the Afghan border. They quickly realized that they would have to go in to get their target as an airstrike would kill civilians as well as the fighters. Despite what the media portrayed, they weren't there to murder innocents. After numerous simulations, Jordan knew that the entire team of eight would never be able to make it so far in and get out alive. Even though it had earned her no friends, Jordan made the decision to go in alone, keeping the team on standby in case she needed help during extraction.

A crackle and hiss in Jordan's left ear brought her out of memory and back to the present. The familiar voice of A Squadron's commanding officer, Paul Killian, was strong and clear over the small ear piece Jordan wore. "Cobra One-Five to Viper Zero-Two-Two. Come in, over."

Jordan brought the thumb and index finger of her hand to the activator studs of her throat microphone to open the channel. "Viper Zero-Two-Two, here."

The voice that came over the communications net was professional and to the point. "Viper Zero-Two-Two, status."

"In process of exfil to point Bravo," Jordan replied and glanced at the black dive watch on her left wrist. She quickly estimated how long it would take her to get to the rally point where the SAS team waited for her. "ETA ninety minutes. Be advised that tangos are agitated and on the prowl."

"Confirm, point Bravo, ETA ninety, nine zero, minutes," Killian replied.

"Confirmed, Cobra One-Five. Will provide further intel as situation evolves. Viper Zero-Two-Two out." Jordan dropped her hand away from the throat microphone and slung the waiting pack onto her back. She tugged the tension straps to secure it in place and then collected her rifle bag, placing it over her left shoulder.

Unconsciously, Jordan caressed her ring finger with the tip of her thumb, the absence of the recently placed engagement ring surprisingly noticeable for having only been there three months. She resisted the urge to sigh. Jordan was a professional and professionals don't let these sorts of thoughts interfere with their missions.

Jordan compartmentalized her thoughts as she had been trained, tucking memories of Brian neatly into place so that she would be free of distraction. After making a final check of the small cave, Jordan tossed a small canister from her vest into the middle of floor before she ducked out of the low entrance. The canister's internal timer counted down five seconds before it began to spray a special, acrid-smelling chemical into the air. MI6 operatives the stuff called 'Spook Be Gone'. The fine mist filled the small cave and covered everything it touched in an ammonia based film formulated to destroy DNA evidence as well as kill any scent. Jordan disliked the smell of the chemical but she was long gone when the device triggered.

CHAPTER 2

Heathrow airport's terminal five bustled with traffic as mid-morning travelers hurried to their flights. The high sloping ceilings of the terminal carried the sound of thousands of voices throughout the structure. The rolling arches served to blend and soften the sounds creating an atmosphere of activity.

Jordan found the place interminably bright thanks to the reflective stark white colors of the décor. Sunlight pouring in from the large windows only served to create a glare that hurt her sensitive eyes. She adjusted the emerald lensed Oakley Alinghi's she wore to better block the bright light and looked at the flight status board. Brian's flight had landed twenty minutes ago, but he hadn't cleared customs yet. They hadn't seen each other in three months and Jordan was more than ready for that to change.

Soon, Brian strolled out of customs with a carry-on over his shoulder and a smile on his face. Jordan admired his tall, graceful form and the rugged features that made her pulse race. Brian ran a hand through slightly tousled brown hair and swept his gaze around. His dark brown eyes were filled with expectation as he searched the faces of the crowded airport.

It had been too long since Jordan had seen her fiancé and she marveled at how attractive he was. It was almost as if she were looking at him for the first time again. He was one point nine meters and lean, a runner's muscled body hidden beneath the tailored blue dress shirt and black slacks he wore. Brian's shoes were immaculate black loafers, expensive, as was most of his wardrobe. He wore his brown hair medium length and let it run amok in a roguishly handsome manner.

Jordan had always been fascinated at how pretty his dark brown eyes were.

Raising a hand Jordan waved at him and started in his direction. Brian's happy smile made Jordan grin. Unconsciously, she tugged the hem of her black business skirt down to keep it from creeping too far up her leg. It was too short for proper business, but Jordan had anything but proper business on her mind.

"Nice suit," Brian commented playfully as Jordan moved into his open arms. Any response from her was silenced by his lips pressing against hers.

Jordan's fingers curled into Brian's shirt as she kissed him fiercely. The ache that had resided in her heart for three months vanished after a few short moments in Brian's embrace. She remained there in his arms until Brian broke the kiss.

"I missed you, too," Brian murmured. He brushed his fingers against Jordan's cheek tenderly and used his thumb to tuck a few locks of hair behind her ear.

"You're lucky we're in public, love," Jordan replied saucily.

Brian laughed warmly and slipped his arm around Jordan's waist. He pulled her against his body snugly and started guiding Jordan towards baggage pickup. "I don't think that's lucky."

"You probably don't, but I'm certain your reputation does," Jordan chuckled.

Brian grinned. "Ah, that damned reputation again."

Smiling, Jordan leaned into Brian as they walked, her arm around Brian. "How was Moscow?"

"Nice, actually. A bit cold; but the people were very friendly," Brian replied. "How was your business trip?"

"It was business," Jordan said and lifted her eyes to Brian's. "Let's grab some take away on the way home."

"That sounds perfect." Brian smirked. "How was the weather where you were?"

The way that Brian let the question linger made Jordan chuckle. "You're never going to stop, are you?"

"I've grown fond of the game, Jordan. I'm not stopping unless you ask me to. The unknown demands to be explored," Brian teased.

"If I could tell you details, I would. You're just going to have to accept I'm a woman of danger and intrigue," Jordan replied and grinned at her fiancé. "Besides, you love it."

Brian pressed his lips against Jordan's temple lightly. "I love you no matter what, even if I don't buy the whole "security analyst" business."

* * * * * *

Jordan relaxed in the passenger seat of Brian's Mercedes sedan. She idly traced her fingertips along Brian's thigh as he drove them back to their flat, just enjoying his presence in general. Another smile crossed her lips which prompted one from Brian. He took her hand and squeezed it tightly. Jordan could tell Brian was equally happy by the familiar sparkle in her fiancé's eyes.

Homecomings were always pleasant for them, almost like a third date in many ways. There was no pressure to go out of the way to impress the other person, they could just be themselves, enjoy each other's company without pretense. The night always involved satisfying the physical side of their relationship. What followed were quiet conversations and tenderness that filled their emotional needs. It was their way of reconnecting and no matter how many times they repeated the ritual, Jordan found herself enjoying it as if it were the first time.

The takeaway had become a tradition too. She and Brian had half a dozen places that they liked to go in London and they rotated randomly through them every time they came home from the airport. The scent of the curried meat tempted Jordan from where it sat in the Styrofoam containers in the back seat. The paper bags the two containers were sitting in did little to keep the scent of spices and chicken from filling the interior car. Jordan's stomach rumbled in anticipation and she placed a hand over it.

"When was the last time you ate?" Brian asked. He reached over and caressed the back of Jordan's neck firmly. "You're tense, too."

"Last night," Jordan said and dipped her head forward. She smiled as Brian's caressing turned into an impromptu neck rub. "The tension is from my mother."

"The wedding again?"

"What else?"

Brian's smile reappeared. "You did tell her that we're working on it, didn't you?"

"Of course. She wants me to come round tomorrow and look at more crap. I swear to God, if I have to look at any more china patterns, or bridesmaid dresses I am going to shoot someone." Jordan sighed. "This is supposed to be special and magical, isn't it? It feels more like work than it should."

"I thought you settled on everything?" Brian asked in a curious tone.

Jordan smirked. "That was three months ago, love. The trends have changed, and she won't have her daughter being out of style." She shook her head in frustration. "Are you certain we can't elope?"

A soft chuckle came from Brian and he redoubled his efforts massaging Jordan's neck. "Maybe you should just meet with her and get it over with?"

Closing her eyes Jordan exhaled slowly as she let the tension wash away. "I'd rather go with plan B."

"Plan B?"

Jordan turned her head and smiled at Brian. "Yes. Eat our takeaway and toss both of our phones in a drawer somewhere for the next few days."

Brian smiled broadly. "Plan B it is."

A companionable silence fell between the two for several minutes. Jordan couldn't seem to banish the smile on her face, nor did she want to, so she sat quietly watching Brian. After his neck rub was complete she placed Brian's hand between hers and allowed herself to enjoy the feeling of contentment the physical connection created. The mundaneness of holding hands was something the average couple took for granted, Jordan thought. For two career-minded people such as she and Brian, these moments of simplicity were more valuable than gold.

The unexpected rapid beeping of Jordan's work phone intruded the silence of the car's cabin, shaking Jordan from her thoughts. She quickly pulled the device from her pocket and unlocked it by swiping her thumb across the screen. The small device flashed the word *AUTHENTICATED* across the screen twice after it read her thumb print and unlocked itself so that she could read the text message.

Come to work. 30 minutes

Jordan's smile vanished as she read the message. "Bollocks."

"Where do I need to take you?" Brian said in a patient tone.

"Vauxhall Cross," Jordan replied. Her stomach growled angrily as the realization that it would be denied food again sank in. Jordan's blue eyes looked at Brian apologetically. "I'll be as quick as I can."

There wasn't even the slightest hint of annoyance in Brian's tone. "Give me a ring once you're done and I'll warm your food up for you."

The smile Jordan had worn returned in full force. "Thank you, love."

CHAPTER 3

The steady clicking sound of heels on stone echoed along the marble floor of the MI6 headquarters as Jordan made her way down the hall with a purposeful step. Jordan wasn't sure why she had been summoned with such urgency. Her post-mission report had been filed for over a week and she had already been debriefed several times. For a moment, she considered the possibility that she was going to be subjected to an impromptu psych eval after reporting what had happened with the target. An agent reporting voices in their head was usually not well received, but when it was accompanied by the target's eyes shifting to solid white, perhaps it was being taken more seriously. Jordan knew that she couldn't be the only person with unusual abilities. She thought that the world powers had to be aware of such people as well.

Jordan turned the corner and headed straight for the reception area outside of her director's office. As usual, his assistant Daphne sat at behind her conservative-looking black desk. The middle-aged woman was dressed in a dark grey business suit with her auburn hair pulled into a tight updo and was typing away on her computer.

The woman looked away from her work as Jordan approached and sympathy filled her brown eyes. "Jordan, I'm so sorry for calling you in. How's Brian? "

"Brian's good. We were on the way back from the airport when I got your message," Jordan said. She smiled at Daphne in a subdued fashion, the expression borderline weary, "Do you know what's going on?"

"He's got someone in there I've never seen before," Daphne said and nodded over her shoulder towards the director's office. "A tall man, forties, maybe fifties, well dressed, attractive. He just showed up out of the blue and the director canceled all of his appointments for the day. It's damned odd."

"Did he look like one of the blokes from medical?" Jordan asked curiously.

Daphne shook her head, "Not at all. His suit was too expensive for someone from medical. Besides, he had the swagger of a field agent."

Jordan chuckled softly. "Swagger huh?"

"Yes. All of you have it to one degree or another, confidence and all that. Now, have a seat and I'll let them know you're here," Daphne said smiling.

"Thanks, Daphne." Jordan took a seat in the small waiting area to the left of Daphne's desk and crossed her legs at the knee. Her fingers tugged down the hem of her black business skirt for the umpteenth time as she settled into the high-backed leather chair.

Jordan did her best to ignore the irritation she felt at being called in. This was part of the job after all; though more and more often it seemed the demands of her career and her commitment to Brian were at odds. They had only been engaged a short while and most of that time Jordan had been in Afghanistan or at Credenhill training. The lack of quality time with Brian was wearing thin, but Jordan wasn't sure what to do about it.

This was a new experience for Jordan. She had dated infrequently during her life, and for her, men had been a pleasant distraction that satisfied her physical needs. The emotional attachment was always messy and only created dangerous distractions. She had never *needed* any man in her life. Brian had been different, and he was the one man that made Jordan feel like an inelegant school girl. It always seemed as if she had a foolish grin on her face when she was with him, even if her expression didn't show it.

Now, she was lonely when Brian wasn't with her, she wanted to feel his comforting embrace and hear the gentle words he would whisper in her ear as they lay in bed at night. The part of Jordan that was independent and pragmatic didn't like these new emotions; love, neediness, attachment, all distractions that she couldn't afford in the field. It recognized what she was feeling as a form of fear. Fear of loss, fear of another woman sweeping in to steal what she held so dear and, unlike the fear of being killed in combat, there was no adrenaline, no survival instinct to quash it.

"Get a grip on yourself, woman," Jordan murmured under her breath. She pushed all of the conflict in her mind aside, tucking it neatly away for later review. Jordan was well-known for her ability to adapt and she was damned certain she would find a way to make all of the pieces of her life fit together.

"Jordan, Director Stevens will see you now," Daphne said from behind her desk.

"Thank you, Daphne." Jordan stood and straightened the hem of her skirt once more before walking over to push open the double wood doors that led to the director's office with both hands. She knew it was a dramatic entrance; her sister, Ryan, called it her 'Darth Vader arrival' because of the way she entered a room and commanded the attention of everyone present. Jordan thought the reference was amusing, but she recognized her flair for the dramatic and the effects that certain mannerisms had on people. She also appreciated the look of consternation she received from her boss in this case, and noted the nearly invisible smile a second man in the room favored her with.

She had never seen the other man before. Daphne's description was spot on; the man was attractive with dark hair and a soldier's muscular build. Tall and lean with intense grey eyes, the man had hard, weather-worn features that reminded Jordan of old paintings depicting the Greek gods, Zeus or Ares. The midnight black suit the mysterious man wore was Hugo Boss, immaculate and very pricy. Jordan noted that he wore no rings, lapel pins, or any other sorts of identifiable decoration.

There was also his scent, an expensive aftershave that she couldn't place, but Jordan's keen nose allowed her to tell it was coming from the nicely dressed visitor as opposed to Director Stevens who smelled of Old Spice and cigarettes. Jordan was intrigued by the mysterious man, to say the least.

"Agent Law, sit," Director Stevens said, the firmness of his voice betraying the irritation he felt at Jordan's showy entrance. Stevens was also tall, but starting thicken in the middle from too many years at a desk, and far too few hours of exercise. The man was even beginning to develop a bit of paunch. Stevens was in his fifties and had short but thick salt and pepper hair, his cool brown eyes and hawk nose making him look severe and angry most of the time. Jordan's presence only seemed to make the man act as severe as his appearance, though she had heard that Stevens tended to treat all of the female field operatives in the same manner. Stevens was part of the old guard and had come up when women didn't serve in the field and his disdain for the changing times was clear.

Jordan took a seat in one of the high-backed leather chairs that sat in the wood paneled office, her long legs crossing at the knee. Once more, she tugged down the hem of her skirt and silently cursed the bloody thing for its need to be constantly adjusted.

"Director," she said by way of greeting, giving a silent nod of acknowledgement to the other man who stood near the large window behind Stevens' desk.

Director Stevens motioned to the man who still stood at the window. "This is-"

"A private conversation, Director Stevens. If you please," the mystery man said in a quiet, but steely, tone. It was dismissive but there was no hostility in the man's eyes.

Steven's jaw clenched tightly. To Jordan's surprise, he inclined his head to the man, gave her an accusing look, and strode from the room purposefully as he did his best to give the pretense that he still controlled his office.

When the doors shut, the other man walked around the Director's desk and stood at the edge, leaving much less physical distance between them than Jordan was comfortable with. He allowed his eyes to settle on her with an uncomfortable intensity. "Let's speak frankly, shall we?"

"Of course."

"I *know* what you are. I know what you can do," the man said, eyes on Jordan's.

Jordan tried to play it off and gave an ever so slight shrug of her shoulders and her best attempt at a look of innocence. "Know, sir?"

The man lofted an eyebrow. "Know, Agent Law. I know what you can do. If you favor a game, then let's play. Jordan Elizabeth Law, daughter of Colonel Cassidy Law, 22 SAS, and Lady Shawna Law. All through school, top marks. MI6 Training, top marks. Did you know you have never been sick a single day in school? In fact, you never had a *single* sick day until you joined MI6," the well dressed visitor said with mock surprise. "Very impressive."

Jordan felt her chest tighten and hoped she managed to school her expression well enough to hide her discomfort with the topic of conversation. She hadn't been sick on the day she called in either. Brian had some free time and had convinced her to spend it with him. Jordan began to wonder if this man knew that as well. "I must have good genes, sir."

The mystery man smiled and looked into Jordan's eyes. "I dare say; allow me to continue." He followed up as if he were a school dean speaking about a student's records. "Injured playing soccer, bruised rib left side, no follow-up. Injured falling from a horse during a polo match, dislocated shoulder, no follow-up. Injured in hand to hand combat training, concussion, follow-up indicates no sign of injury," he said, pausing to give Jordan a chance to speak, one that she didn't take.

Casually, the man took his wireless phone from his belt and tapped the touch screen, his eyes never leaving Jordan's. Suddenly, the TV attached to the far wall sprang to life and displayed several digitized x-rays and medical reports. He used his phone like a remote and clicked through them, each of the documents matching one of the described injuries.

"You heal unnaturally fast; your reaction times are in the top one percentile on paper. In reality, they are much faster than that. No doubt your perceptions match. You are also much stronger than anyone you know, and have an endurance that is off the charts. In addition, you can make yourself disappear from sight as you did when you were discovered in Afghanistan on your last operation," the man said firmly, his keen grey eyes locked on Jordan's in a way that suggested he either had evidence or a witness, perhaps both, and no matter which he had he was certain in his knowledge.

Jordan felt the familiar and unwelcome sensation of fear constrict her chest. She knew that at least one of her sisters displayed these "powers", for lack of a better word and wisely both she and Ryan had hidden their abilities from everyone. Now, Jordan tapped those powers and with a single breath unchained her mind. She let herself enter a state of hyper-accelerated speed of thought and action which caused everything in the world to slow down to a crawl. She needed time to think and weigh her options.

This man knew what she could do so Jordan assumed that he knew about her sister, too. She was terrified that whoever he worked for would sweep in and abduct her siblings in the middle of the night. No doubt each of them would be tested to determine what they could do, if anything, and how they did it. What happened after that took Jordan to a place she didn't want to go. The thought of her sisters being dissected or imprisoned for the rest of their lives was too much to bear.

There was no way Jordan was going to allow that to happen. Jordan's blue eyes hardened as they settled on the visitor's, but she remained silent. She was well-trained and she had her Para Ordnance .45 tucked into a holster on her waist at the small of her back. She would fight her way out if it came down to it. Or, she could use her power to make herself invisible to others' minds, but what about her family? What about Brian? Options were slim and Jordan knew that any rash action would be dangerous to more than just herself. She inhaled and put the mental restraints back on her mind which caused the world to return to normal speed.

"As far as you are aware, you have abilities that set you apart from anyone you've met aside from the individual you encountered in Afghanistan," the man said and pulled up a picture of the terrorist's face. "Raamiz Kazir. He was a mid-level telepath. You were lucky. He could have lobotomized you if he had been closer, but that's why *we* sent you, isn't it?"

"What do you want from me?" Jordan asked cautiously.

"I'm here to offer you more, a chance to become not just one of the best but *the* best. I can provide training in how to use your abilities, and a chance to put them to work for Queen and Country in a more useful way than you ever have before. I may even be able to tell you how you came to have these gifts of yours." He let his words hang between them for several moments before speaking again. "Interested?"

"I am," Jordan replied. She still felt the urge to clear out of the room, but what the man offered was too tempting. Her powers had always been a mystery and Jordan had been forced to master them on her own. There had been numerous injuries, and not just to herself. As a child Jordan tried to jump from the roof of their stable to a fence post on the far side of the exercise yard. The jump was too ambitious and Jordan had broken both of her legs when she had landed. Her younger sister Ryan had found Jordan lying on the ground covered in dirt and grass. Ryan had taken Jordan's hand to help her sit up when Jordan's legs reknitted themselves. The pain of the bones mending in seconds was so intense that Jordan lost focus and broke Ryan's hand with her enhanced strength. Ryan's scream brought their father running, but instead of telling him what had really happened Ryan lied and told him that one of the horses had stepped on her hand.

It had taken weeks for Ryan to heal and Jordan spent every waking moment of her ten year old existence making sure Ryan had what she needed. Loyally keeping Jordan's secret had forged a bond between Ryan and Jordan that neither of them enjoyed with their other sisters. It had also taught Jordan how important control and focus was. Control was different than understanding, however, and Jordan still yearned to know how her powers worked. As Brian had said, *the unknown deserves to be explored.*

"You have stipulations, of course, and so do I," the man continued. "You cannot tell anyone what you will be doing. You will have to accept that you will tell lies to those you love, and do things that even you may find distasteful because our country needs them done. For this, you will be well-compensated and your family will be looked after. If you pass the selection process you will be inducted into an elite group that will push you to new levels of excellence. This is a one-time offer, by the by, *and* limited in duration," he said and gestured to Jordan. "Your turn."

Jordan inhaled softly and gathered her thoughts. She had a multitude of questions, but he was looking to her for a response and she sensed it was important to make a good showing of herself. "If I agree to this, I expect my family to be left alone, period. Let them live their lives. If I find out that you're responsible for any harm that comes to them, I'm going to kill you and anyone involved." Jordan's determined expression was backed by the conviction in her voice.

"Agreed," he replied calmly as if her threat was never voiced. "You'll have a month off to spend with your fiancé and then you'll be contacted to begin your training." He held up a hand to forestall any comment from her. "Your fiancé is going to be temporarily assigned to London for that month; in fact, it's already done. Then, he will report to Moscow as he was intended to, while you complete the first phase of your training, free of distraction." He extended his right hand to Jordan. There were no rings or even scars on the fingers which Jordan found unusual in a man who so obviously had been a field agent, if not a soldier.

Jordan grasped his hand and shook it firmly, the pretention of the man assuming she would say yes irked her but she kept it to herself. "One more thing, who the bloody hell *are* you?"

"Ethan McIntyre," was the reply. "Director of Special Operations Squadron Seven."

"SOS? That's not very comforting," Jordan quipped blithely.

Jordan's comment made that hint of a smile return to the man's face. "Yes, well, we've changed names a few times now. No doubt the next will be better. There aren't seven squadrons either, just one. You'll learn all this soon enough," Ethan said. He pulled a card from the right breast pocket of his suit and extended it to Jordan. "This is my number. Call if you need anything. I'll see you a month from tomorrow."

Jordan took the plain white card and examined it, there was a number printed in a common typeface in black on it and nothing else. After her inspection, Jordan placed it inside her own inner pocket and inclined her head, taking his last words as a sign that the meeting was over. "A month, then."

CHAPTER 4

Jordan exited the taxi with grace, her long legs carrying her smoothly up the concrete stairs to the house she and Brian shared. It was in a nice part of town, an area where diplomats like Brian lived and one that was free from most crime due to more frequent police patrols and the private security that many of the well-to-do residents had on-hand. The community was bordered by a small greenbelt with a park nearby and every lawn was well-manicured.

Decorating the interior of the flat wasn't something Jordan had looked forward to. She had never been particularly keen on some of the domestic aspects of a relationship and managing the home was one of them. Jordan had wisely hired an interior decorator to do the work instead of spending hours trying to put the right combinations of materials and colors together. The finished product was tasteful and proper for their station, if not a bit on the opulent side. All of the furniture was antique and made from dark hardwoods and leather which gave it a darker more business-like feeling than Jordan liked. As she slipped her keys into the lock and turned it, Jordan could hear Brian's voice raised in a tone that was anything but diplomatic.

"Bollocks! I want to know who had me moved to bloody *London*! I've put in a lot of effort to get where I am and I want to know who's sabotaging me!" Brian railed.

Brian was deeper in the flat standing in the living room, or more correctly pacing about it. She could see him stalking back and forth inside the wood-paneled room and heard the methodical thump of his loafers against the wooden floor. Brian paused every so often but quickly returned to the back and forth movement, a physical expression of his agitation.

Quietly, Jordan made her way inside and slipped her jacket off, placing it on one of the black iron hooks on the antique wooden coat rack next to the door. Brian was so upset that he had failed to notice Jordan come in. Normally, she would mention how dangerous it was for a man in his position to be so distracted that he lost his situational awareness, but this time she decided against it. It was going to be difficult enough for Brian to learn that she was being reassigned and she didn't want to add to that tension.

As she considered just how she was going to break the news Jordan watched Brian pace. He had removed his jacket but hadn't done much more than that. No doubt he got the call from the Foreign Ministry before he had been able to settle in. Brian's career was as important to him as Jordan's was to her, so it was understandable that he was trying to get answers from his contacts.

In frustration, Brian looked skyward as if he were appealing to God for patience. Jordan felt a sharp pang of guilt. Brian's anger was partially her fault; even if she hadn't actively caused his temporary reassignment she was the root of it. Ethan McIntyre had used what must be considerable pull to have Brian, a count and veteran ambassador, reassigned from a prestigious post to the home office.

Poor Brian must think he's set someone off, Jordan considered. She also noted how, once again, McIntyre had assumed she would agree to his offer and set all of the arrangements in motion. *Cheeky bastard,* Jordan thought and walked towards the living room.

"No, Gavin, I want you to find out who did it. No. No, it *isn't* a good thing. I wanted to surprise Jordan with her new assignment and now someone's gone and changed that, too. This is just bang out of order," Brian growled angrily into the telephone he held up to his ear.

An appreciative smile graced Jordan's face. She enjoyed Brian's take charge attitude and fantasized briefly about what would no doubt be an incredible night now that he was so angry. Sex always had a calming influence on him, and her as well. Being relaxed would also help cushion the news that she had accepted this new assignment. Jordan watched Brian continue to rail, but quickly decided that he needed to get off the phone before he was past talking down. Her fiancé had a fierce temper, but Jordan felt confident that she could redirect his energies with the proper motivation. After discarding her shoes, Jordan walked up behind Brian and slipped her arms around his waist, her head resting against the back of his neck.

Jordan's touch caused Brian to tense, but then he relaxed after realizing it was her. An easy and charming smile formed on his lips as he turned to look at her. Brian slipped an arm around Jordan's slender waist and pulled her close to him. The expression Brian wore became one of fondness and he pressed his cheek against the top of Jordan's head.

"Look. The point is, someone is into my business and, more importantly, Jordan's business. I want to know who it is and I want to know in three days. I'm going to be unavailable until then," Brian said and met Jordan's eyes, the intent in them clear. "Goodbye, Gavin. No, don't try. Do. No, I'm not going to let this go," he said, frustration making his entire body tense.

After a reassuring caress along Brian's spine, Jordan raised an eyebrow and stepped away from him, easing the first two buttons of her shirt down as she moved. A distinctly playful smile formed on her lips as she took another step, unfastening another button. Each step she took meant one more button opened and that definitely garnered Brian's attention.

"Yes. If that's what it takes, Gavin," Brian said, his voice losing some of the conviction as he watched Jordan's striptease.

Jordan sighed in a flirtatiously exaggerated manner that she hoped Brian would act on and turned to walk towards the stairs leading up to their bedroom. She was stopped three steps into her walk by a pair of strong hands seizing her hips and using them to spin her around.

Brian was there and one of his hands went to grasp the side of Jordan's face, his lips pressing to hers in a fierce display of passion. He tugged Jordan against his body and held her tightly while his tongue pressed into her mouth.

With her heart fluttering and pulse racing, Jordan let herself dwell in the sensation of Brian's touch, the scent of his skin. As Brian's hand roamed along her back Jordan felt light-headed, almost giddy. He was the only man that had ever made Jordan feel so carefree and happy, and it was this sense of intoxication he managed to stir in her that had convinced her that she wanted more than simple and infrequent one night stands with him. He had a strong character and an unquenchable spirit; if Brian could manage, it he would right every wrong in the world. Further consideration of Brian's moral merits disappeared as he continued to welcome her home.

Jordan felt Brian push her hands above her head and he pressed her back into the wall roughly, his lips and teeth drawing maddeningly pleasant sensations along her neck and jaw.

"Oh, no, you don't," Brian breathed along the skin of Jordan's neck. "No running off."

"It didn't even cross my mind, love," Jordan replied in a throaty voice.

"Was this shirt expensive?"

"Not particularly. Why?" Jordan responded, her voice growing more curious. Any uncertainty was dispelled as his hands parted the front of the shirt, the remaining buttons dropping to the polished wood floor with a clickity-clackity sound. *Oh yes, tonight is going to be spectacular,* Jordan thought and lost herself in the emotion and sensations of the moment.

CHAPTER 5

No matter the time of day, Port Newark was always full of sound; from the racket made by the cranes moving large shipping containers, to the sound of shouting workers going about their daily duties. Even in the dark of night, the peal of a buoys' bell or the long droning horn of a departing cargo ship could be heard against the backdrop of the wind and water.

The wind made the air cold and biting in January, but the workers from New York and New Jersey were a hardy lot and bore it. This didn't mean that there wasn't complaining, but complaints never kept the work from getting done. There was no adversity that prevented the hardworking men and women from keeping one of the largest shipping hubs in the world running day after day.

"It's so freakin' cold tonight, my grandma's poodle's balls just fell off down in Florida," Danny Kine said and rubbed his gloved hands together in an attempt to warm them up. He was in his mid-forties and had worked as a security officer for the docks for the last ten years. Danny hadn't learned the thickly built Russian man's name yet. The cold nights and long hours of security meant that the job wasn't for everyone, so he didn't usually bother memorizing their names until they had been on the job for at least a month. He glanced at his partner and smirked. "You don't talk much do you, new guy?"

The larger of the two blue uniformed men shrugged his shoulders. "I am from Russia. We have snows that would bury your grandma's house there. If you are so cold, maybe you should just go get some of her, what is it, cannelloni?"

Danny watched the large man with a hard gaze. "Hey, you better not talk too much about my grandmother, Vlad. First the house, then her cooking, next thing you know, I'm layin' your bald ass out. Got it? This job pays for that fuckin' house. I bust my fuckin' ass to pay for that god damned house."

"My name isn't Vlad," the large Russian replied and continued along. He swept the flashlight about the area slowly, illuminating the gate into secure cargo storage pen nineteen. The chain link fence around it stood three times the height of an average man and was rimmed with razor wire.

"I've put down guys bigger than you, new guy. Just watch what you say about my grandmother. Since this is your first time working night shift, I'll give you a break," Danny said sternly. He plucked a large ring of jangling keys from his belt and sorted them until he found one with a red slash across it.

The Russian man adjusted his company baseball cap and glanced around. "This is place is secure enough, I suppose. Let's go get some coffee, nobody is going to try and climb that fence."

Danny shook his head. "We gotta go inside and walk the stacks, man. Come on."

"You would have to be able to fly to get over the fence," the new guy said again. "Why put it here if you have to have someone check it all the time? In Russia, we would have made it taller and out of brick and iron, that way we don't have to pay anyone to guard it."

"Yeah, yeah, next thing you'll say is that in Russia this is how you secure your fuckin' toilets. What is it with you Ruskies and everything is bigger and better in Mother Russia?" Danny quipped and opened the heavy lock set in the gate. The door rattled with a metallic resonance as he slid it open.

"That's because we are proud of our country," the Russian replied in a boastful tone. He stepped through the gate after his partner and shut it hard enough to make the chain link fence rattle loudly.

"Huh, yeah, well that's good and all. Gotta have something left after we kicked your red asses in the Cold War, I suppose," Danny grinned.

The new guy laughed and slapped Danny on the shoulder. "That's a good one, my friend. Too bad we just wanted you to think that we lost."

Danny joined his companion in laughter and continued into the stacks of shipping crates that were arranged in neat rows all through the security area. He pulled his own flashlight out and swept the beam around as they walked the stacks. "We gotta do this three times a night, every night. In ten years, I ain't ever caught anyone down here who wasn't supposed to be here, but still we gotta do the walk. The cameras are always watchin' us so you can't fuck around and not show. They fire you if you don't check this place like clockwork."

"I see the cameras. Aren't they enough?" the Russian replied.

"You sure you guys didn't lose the Cold War, buddy? Never rely on a fuckin' machine," Danny said and flashed his light up to one of the tall posts that had been placed systematically throughout the area to hold the cameras. He expected to see the black domed device sitting in its usual spot but the dome was missing and so was the camera beneath it.

"Mother fucking kids!" Danny growled. "I bet those little bastards we caught over in the Transco storage area yesterday came over here and stole the fucking cameras. Come on, Vlad, let's check the rest of them."

The two men hurried through the stacks shining their lights into the dark shadows cast by the three container high stacks. Very little light from the tall pole lights in the area reached them. As they neared the water side of the storage yard, the sound of low voices reached their ears.

Danny stopped suddenly when he heard the quiet conversation. He shut his light down and nodded for the new guy to do the same. They both strained to listen for several moments and exchanged a meaningful look when they heard the squeaking hinges of a container door being opened.

"I'm gonna break those little fucker's knees when we get them," Danny rasped in a harsh whisper. "You go around the left side, I'll go right."

The Russian motioned to the radio he wore at his waist. "Shouldn't we call for back up?"

Danny shook his head, leaning close to the Russian so he didn't have to raise his voice. "Oh, fuck that. We're gonna do this Jersey-style. Just follow my lead, new guy."

Each man nodded and went their separate direction. Danny smiled in anticipation as he thought about beating the crap out of the teenagers. He briefly wondered how kids got over the tall razor-wire topped fences, but the thought was discarded. Kicking the occasional kid or transient's ass was a favored diversion in an otherwise boring job. As he crept around the stack of containers Danny could make out the Russian that was being spoken. He didn't understand a word of it, but the accent was unmistakable. As he got to the edge of the container he was behind, he crouched and peered around the corner. What he saw made his jaw drop and he immediately froze in place.

The container was open and seven of the largest men Danny Kine had ever seen were moving several steel-colored cylindrical containers into the back of a waiting black speed boat. All of the men were dressed in black wetsuits with combat harnesses on. Each man had a small radio bud in their ear and each also carried a Russian made assault rifle and a holstered pistol. Danny's heart started pounding in his chest as fear-borne adrenaline surged into his blood. Slowly, he slipped back around the container and pressed his back up against it.

Danny Kine had grown up in some of the toughest streets in the city and had taken his lumps just as much as he had dealt them. He had even been stabbed in the arm once, but none of his experiences had prepared him for this situation. He started to reach for his radio but stopped when he realized the thieves would probably hear him calling for assistance.

No fucking job is worth getting shot over, Danny thought and started back the way he came so he could find his partner before he did something stupid and got them both killed. Mustering as much courage as he could find, Danny hunted for the new guy amongst the containers. He was relieved when he saw the Russian coming towards him quickly.

"Thank god you didn't jump those guys," Danny said in a quiet voice. "Now, let's get out of here and call the cops. We don't get paid enough to fuck with guys like that."

The new guy's expression was hard as he walked towards Danny, but Danny supposed that he was probably trying not to look scared. Danny drew a long breath to try and slow down his heart rate and turned for the gate. "Come on."

Without warning the new guy's hand closed over Danny's mouth from behind. Danny panicked and grabbed the hand. He tried to pull it free, but the Russian's grip was like nothing he had ever felt. He couldn't even budge a single finger. Danny tried to scream, but the presence of the Russian's hand prevented any sound from reaching past where they stood.

Danny punched over his shoulder, aiming for the Russian's head but the larger man simply leaned back and took Danny to the ground. Now on one knee, the Russian held his partner in a sitting position. Danny's feet scrabbled across the concrete in a desperate attempt to push the other man away from him but the size and strength difference between the two was too great. The Russian didn't even seem to be breaking a sweat. The hand over his mouth squeezed tighter and for the first time in years Danny Kine feared for his life.

"You should have gone for the coffee," the Russian said, his tone almost sympathetic. He tightened his grip on Danny's mouth and reached behind his back. When the hand returned it held a black combat knife. Then, the Russian drew the razor sharp blade across Danny's throat, opening the precious blood vessels there.

Danny Kine thrashed for several moments, but each spasm of motion was weaker than the last. He couldn't break the man's iron grip no matter what he tried and soon his muscles refused to respond. The cold of the East Coast winter seemed to grow worse and soon Danny couldn't feel his feet, or hands, or legs, or arms.

As the last of his life left him, the Russian Danny had called 'Vlad' whispered in his ear "I will make certain that your grandmother's house is paid for."

CHAPTER 6

Jordan stood in front of the antique full length floor mirror, her short dark hair still wet from the shower as she studied her naked form. During the month of downtime she had continued to work out and train, but she had eaten quite a few sweets thanks to Brian's pampering. Fortunately, she had a very high metabolism and despite his tendency towards luxury, Brian did enjoy getting outdoors for more active pursuits. Jordan smiled as she thought of their mountain climbing expedition in Tuscany. It had been an enjoyable day of climbing, complete with a picnic on the side of a stone face which culminated in being stuck overnight at the top of a craggy mountain thanks to an unexpected torrential downpour. They had spent long hours beneath the tarp that Jordan had in her backpack, talking about their future together as husband and wife. Jordan's musings were interrupted and forgotten as Brian continued the conversation they had been having most of the morning.

"I'm still not happy about this, Jordan. A month! A full month has gone by and not a single straight answer to my inquiries about who changed our assignments. I've gone to everyone I can think of and all they'll say is that someone of "high authority" changed them," Brian growled from where he lay sprawled on his side on the bed. His brown eyes watched Jordan as she dressed in one of her dark skirt suits. "High authority? That's it! Was it God? Because it wasn't the Queen, it wasn't Parliament and I can't think of any higher authorities in this country. Gavin was apparently told to let it drop. Jordan? Jordan, are you listening to me?" Brian asked in a harsh tone.

"Yes, I can tell you're still put out," Jordan replied in a patient tone. She forced the guilt she bore in agreeing to this new assignment from her mind. Their entire lives were changed and there was little Jordan could to alter it at this point.

"Put out? Tell me you're not put out, Jordan! I'm going to Moscow and you're not coming with me. I had to call in a lot of favors to get you assigned to with me and now you're about to run off with a bunch of boot necks again to God knows wh-"

Jordan turned quickly on her heel, the sympathetic smile on her face silencing Brian mid-sentence. "I know it isn't easy, but we both have a duty to do. I'll come visit as soon as I'm able."

"But you're not going to tell me what you're up to," Brian replied tersely.

"Correct," Jordan answered and sauntered over to sit on the edge of the bed, her hand coming to rest on his thigh. "I can't tell you and you *know* that. Do you tell me absolutely everything about your work? I know for a fact that you don't."

The quiet sigh Brian made was more to let off tension than anything else. "No, but it isn't the same thing."

"It's me Brian, my life, my career. I'm not housewife material and you knew that before you asked me to marry you. I can't sit around chatting it up with the girls. I need to *do* something; something that has meaning, something that makes a difference," Jordan replied empathically. "My work means a lot to me."

A long silence hung between them before Brian spoke again. "A month is too short," Brian said, his tone matter of fact. His face was still flushed with anger and there was a tension in his jaw that was very characteristic of a bad mood set in stone.

"It feels like it doesn't it, but we've had a month. An *amazing* month, yeah?" Jordan gave Brian one of her best mischievous smiles and caressed his calf.

The month had indeed been amazing. Aside from the more intimate moments and climbing in Italy, they had been hiking in Scotland, and gone to no less than three dinner parties with friends. Though the parties were less to her liking than Brian's, she still enjoyed seeing Brian turn on his charm with their friends and the opportunity to talk current events and politics, not too mention being called his fiancé. Mundane things in her world of intrigue and action, but things that reminded her she could be a normal person from time to time. Jordan felt grounded once more and like she was actually on the way to being married. It wasn't just a role being assumed, or some sort of childhood game played with her sisters.

Brian replied with a slight nod of his head and sat up on the bed, his hands resting firmly on Jordan's shoulders from behind. "This cloak and dagger business is harder for me to deal with than I thought it would be. Promise me that you'll be careful."

Jordan closed her eyes slowly and responded with a slight bob of her head. She took a moment to enjoy the warmth of Brian's touch and the scent of his freshly bathed skin before responding, "I promise." She consciously ingrained the moment in her memory, knowing that these times were going to be all too few in the near future. "What I *can* tell you is that I'll be working with people that are the best in their fields. I'll not want for any equipment or support. I know I've said this before, but I'll make sure to ring you when I can, or if I can't do that I'll write. Have I ever failed to keep in touch?"

The all too familiar response made Brian grip her chin firmly and turn Jordan's gaze to his. "I *worry* about you, Jordan. I know you can handle yourself. I do. It just doesn't make me feel any better when I can't be there with you. It's my job to protect you; you're going to be my wife."

She let her gaze rest on Brian's and brought a hand up to touch his clean shaven face. Jordan quickly bit back her usual response, the terse one about being better trained and more experienced than Brian in these sorts of matters. "I love you."

Brian's mouth flowed from a stern pursing of lips to a charming smile. "And you evade again. Well played," he replied, a distinct tone of annoyance in his voice despite the contradictory expression.

Jordan immediately regretted the fact that she didn't do a better job of assuaging Brian's concerns. Relationships weren't her forte and, unlike being in the field in the thick of it, she felt these sorts of situations were beyond her at times. "I wasn't intending it to come off that way. I don't know what more I can say to reassure you, Brian."

"I love you too, Jordan," Brian retorted smoothly, though the hurt in his eyes refused to be covered by any amount of charm.

* * * * * *

Thirty minutes later, Jordan descended the cement stairs in front of their flat towards the black Mercedes sedan that awaited her in the quiet darkness of the early morning. The car's engine purred powerfully as it idled at the curb, Jordan unhurriedly making her way to it. She used the time it took to traverse the distance to let her eyes quickly scan the area, the vehicle, and the shadowed form of the driver that lay behind the tinted windows.

With perfect timing, the driver's door opened and a man of average height emerged. The man was wearing a black suit and had short cropped hair that screamed agent. With a smile in place he used one hand open the rear driver's side door for Jordan. "Good morning, Agent Law."

Jordan inclined her head to the man, sizing him up as she slid into the back seat. Despite his well-tailored suit, she could see he was carrying a sidearm under his left shoulder, a backup on his right ankle, and a compact blade on his left. His accent placed him from the North of England, most likely Cumbria, though Jordan detected that the man had probably been schooled further south in London by the slight differences in how he pronounced his A's.

"Good morning," she replied politely and offered the man a friendly smile.

The man waited for Jordan to buckle in before he closed the door and then took his seat behind the wheel. He placed the car in gear and quickly accelerated away from the curb, the Mercedes' engine growling fiercely. As the car continued down the suburban street, the driver glanced away from the road, his dark eyes looking back at Jordan from the rearview mirror. "I'm Laurence. If you need anything, please ask, Agent Law."

Jordan studied the eyes that watched her from the mirror, acknowledging him with a gentle bob of her head. "A pleasure to meet you, Laurence," She paused for a moment, mulling over her question for a moment before asking it, part of her not expecting an answer. "Where are we going, exactly?"

"Porton Down," the man replied and returned his gaze back to the road they traveled along.

Intrigued, Jordan sat back in her seat. Porton Down was home to DSTL, or Defense Science and Technology Laboratory, and what exactly went on there was subject to much conjecture. It was known that chemical weapon research was conducted there when it was first opened in 1916, as well as the fact that more than one scientific company called the seven-thousand acre reservation home. There were even rumors of tests on human subjects, and studies on supposed UAP, or Unidentified Aerial Phenomena. UFOs, as the Yanks called them. Of course, the tabloid rags had a field day with such places and even touted supposed pictures of bulbous-headed aliens that had reportedly been breeding with human females. Or there was the secret world summit with world leaders such as Tony Blair, Bill Clinton, and the like.

Though Jordan had never been there herself, she knew a few people who had been and they were required to keep mum on anything they saw. Jordan supposed that if people with extraordinary abilities were being trained and used by the British government, Porton Down was the most likely place to house them.

The trip to the facility was calm and quiet, the early morning hour allowing the black sedan to stay ahead of the usual rush of traffic as it made its way across town and out onto the highway. Jordan looked out of the window and settled back in the comfortable leather seat. Just as she started to think back on the morning's conversation with Brian, Jordan's phone came to life. The sing-songy *Hello Kitty* ringtone her youngest sister Jillian had downloaded to her phone filled the car's interior with its painfully shrill tone.

Jordan reached into her jacket's inner pocket and plucked the phone out, catching Laurence smiling as he looked back at her in the rear view mirror. Glancing at the screen Jordan saw the familiar visage of Hello Kitty's expressionless face looking back at her with Jillian's number over it. Jordan answered the phone in a pleasant voice. "Good morning, Jillian."

"Good morning, Jordan, and it's Jill, which you well know. I'm too young for 'Jillian'. It makes me sound like a librarian," Jill replied in her usual cheery mood. The young woman had an accent; a mish-mosh of American and Queen's English that leaned more towards the American, "So, I bet you're wondering what I'm doing up and about so early in the morning?"

As usual, Jill was quick to assume what the other person was thinking, and, as usual, she was correct. Jordan started to reply but she wasn't fast enough to beat her sister's response.

"Aside from the fact I'm on my eighth cup of coffee and fragging berks like they were free, I am ringing you on a most urgent matter," Jill said, finishing her sentence in a fairly convincing impression of Jordan's voice.

"What would that be, Jillian?" Jordan replied and found herself grinning. Jill had a special talent for making people smile with her earnest and enthusiastic charm.

At seventeen, Jill was exuberant and precocious, with a zest for life that Jordan had never seen in anyone else. The youngest Law sister was fierce and never hesitated to speak her mind, even when propriety was best served by silence or, at least, a modicum of tact. Worse yet, Jill's observations were always insightful, frequently painfully correct, and always well-timed but delivered in ways that nearly anyone would find amusing or cute. Even their stern and etiquette-minded mother was forced to smile at some of her youngest daughter's more colorful quips.

"Let me break out the crayons here. You're getting married! You haven't set a date yet and Mom is on everyone's goolies about it. She wants to invite half of England, all of

Scotland, and a quarter of America. Please… pleeeeeease help me!" Jill said with over-exaggerated emphasis. Before Jordan could say anything in response Jill gleefully yelled into the phone "In your face, sodding Muppet!"

Jordan's smile was replaced by a look of annoyance, "Are you playing a video game, Jillian?"

Jill immediately sensed Jordan's displeasure with her divided attentions and responded in a more subdued manner, "Maybe." Not one to lose the initiative Jill continued on quickly. "However, that doesn't change the fact that you and Brian need to get this damn show on the road before Mom makes us all insane. Don't bodge this up for the rest of us."

"I can't set a date yet. I just got a new assignment and I'm not sure when Brian and I will both have the time off. I'll speak to him about it tonight before he leaves for Moscow," Jordan said.

"A new assignment?" Jill asked with unbridled curiosity. The mention of something new and possibly mysterious redirected her considerable energies in that direction much like a cat being thrown a ball of foil without warning. "Are you going to be attending lavish parties, blowing up tangos, and taking lots of hot enemy spies to bed? You know that would be totally ace! Brian may get angry about the amazing evil spy sex, but you can always say it's part of the job, for Queen and Country and all that James Bond rubbish."

Jordan snickered at Jill's painting of a spy's life and responded with a well-honed deflection that didn't hide the amusement in her voice. "Jillian, you know all I do is travel to the various interests of the country and conduct security reviews. It's all quite mundane."

Jill made a phssing sound by pushing air through her lips. It was one of her quirky signatures, much like her propensity for everything that was *Hello Kitty*. "Right. Like I *believe* that, Jordan. Brian wouldn't be so hacked off about your job if all you were doing was going around and testing security. Look, I know you can't tell me what you really do, but I know it isn't checking to see if there are enough outdoor lights at an embassy. *But,* you still need to set a date no matter what your new job is. I also expect a visit from you because you're my big sister and I never get to see you enough."

"As I said, Jillian, I'll speak to Brian about it," Jordan replied. "I'll also come visit you when I get some time. It will probably be a couple months, at least. Besides you're still in the States aren't you?"

Resigned, Jill sighed in a long exaggerated way to emphasize her displeasure. "Fine. So, do you want to hear about this hot Yank I've been seeing? Or we can talk about my new bunny? He's a pretty grey and really huge. I'm talking about a rabbit so large he has a gravity field."

Jordan smiled as Jill moved the conversation to something more everyday, but expression sobered as she realized that Jill's desire to discuss things like boys and her many pets was probably due to the fact that their mother wasn't making enough time for her youngest child. Unconsciously, Jordan shook her head and thought back to her own childhood and how little time her mother had given her when compared to her sister Alessandra.

As good a parent as their father Cassidy was, a young woman needed her mother. There were just some things that fathers couldn't truly understand about their daughters, like that first break up or the pressures that society put on women when it came to beauty or behavior. All of Jordan's sisters, even Alessa, had made time for Jill in their lives which helped strengthen their bond. Now that all of the sisters except Jill were out on their own, Jordan wondered what her mother was thinking by letting an impressionable seventeen year old girl have so little of her time. Jordan made a mental note to speak to her mother about Jill as soon as she could manage it and settled in to listen to Jill's current events.

It took Jill nearly two hours to explain all that was going on with her life; boys, school, animals, video games and music. All of the topics were pleasantly normal and revolved around the life of a teenaged girl, but Jill's entertaining delivery made time pass quickly. Finally, Jill paused and took a long breath before moving into a more serious topic. "I'm going to be a doctor. It's decided, in stone, for certain. I want to help people, Jordan. I really think I'd be a good doctor. Don't you?" Jill asked enthusiastically.

Jordan was pleased that her sister was finding some direction. The fact that Jillian was even bothering to tell Jordan meant that she was seeking the emotional support her mother often failed to provide. "I think you would make an excellent doctor. What can I do to help you?"

Jill's impassioned response was immediate. "I just need you to back me up, to be there if I need help. I'm not talking about homework, because Ryan's way better at that stuff than you, but you always make me believe that I can do anything. I need that. I'm young and hot, but not daft you know."

A truly genuine smile formed on Jordan's lips in response to Jill's sincerity. "I would never even think such a thing, Jillian. I'll be there if you need me. Just ring me up."

"Brilliant! I will when I get back from visiting Ryan. We can do lunch, shopping, and sister stuff. Did you know Seattle has more rain than London? I never knew that. Well, I don't know if it's a fact or statistic, but it sure seems like it. They have good coffee. By the way, I'm going to go to university in Seattle at the University of Washington. I really like it here,"

Jill rattled off so quickly that her words almost strung together.

"Jillian, you should do with less coffee. How much longer are you going to be there?" Jordan asked.

Jill made her trademark phssing sound, the thought of not having coffee alien to her. "Another week or two but, I'm seriously thinking of telling Mom to piss off and just move in with Ryan. She's got a huge place, lots of cool electronics, and she said she could get me on with her company. She said she'd even pay for school if I decide to take the job."

Laurence cleared his throat softly and looked back at Jordan through the rear view mirror. "Agent Law, we're almost there."

Jordan took a quick look out the window and nodded a response to the driver. Time had flown by thanks to Jill's engaging personality, but Jordan was thankful for the pleasant distraction. "I think you should, Jillian. Ryan will keep you on course and you'll be able to get a taste of what being on your own is like. Make sure to discuss it with Mom and Dad first, in person."

"I will. So you like the idea, yeah?"

"I do, Jillian."

"Jill."

"Ok, Jill."

"Yay! I love you, Jordan," Jill beamed as she won a victory in Jordan using the shortened version of her name, a rare and simple thing, but marvelous to her.

"I love you, too. I need to dash though; I'm almost to the office. Give Ryan my love," Jordan said and looked out the window as Laurence pulled the car off of the highway.

"I will, big sis. Get your ass in gear on the wedding and set a date, seriously. Bye!"

Jill hung up the phone before Jordan could respond which made the latter chuckle. Tucking the small black device back in her pocket Jordan sat back in her seat while the car turned to head into the western entrance of Porton Down.

As the car rolled up to the main gate Jordan could see two men wearing black battle dress carrying HK G-36 assault rifles in the guardhouse. When the sedan came to a stop in front of the red and white bar, the shorter of the two men stepped forward towards the driver's side window. The other soldier maintained a watchful guard over the first man, his hand notably keeping this weapon in position for quick deployment,

"Identification please?" the shorter asked politely, but firmly.

Laurence produced his identification from the inside of his suit jacket, flipping it open with a flick of his wrist and smiled at the man as he greeted him. "Morning, Sergeant."

The sergeant returned Laurence's greeting with a nod of his head. "Agent Blaine." Without missing a beat the sergeant knocked on the back window where Jordan sat.

Jordan pressed the window activator and let it roll down. Pulling her ID from the inside of her suit coat, she opened the black leather billfold with both hands and showed its contents to the uniformed man.

"Agent Law," the sergeant greeted her respectfully. "You're cleared for entry into the property; however, you need to make sure you get a proper identification card for tomorrow. Reg, we need a guest pass," he called to the other soldier who disappeared back into the guard house. A minute or two passed and then man stepped back out and passed the badge to his Sergeant, who in turn handed it to Jordan.

Jordan nodded to the man and tucked her ID away once more. "Thank you, Sergeant, I'll see to the permanent badge as soon as I get settled."

"Excellent, Agent Law. Have a good day," the Sergeant replied and waved the sedan on.

Laurence accelerated the Mercedes away from the gate and drove further into the Porton Down reservation, the sedan smoothly traversing the well maintained roads that were framed by equally manicured lawns and flower beds. Jordan looked out the window as they passed several buildings with the logo of Ploughshare Innovations, one of the United Kingdom's most prestigious defense contractors.

Eventually, the sedan pulled into the lot of a building that was marked as Porton Down Waste Management Facility B. Outside the building were several well-worn rust-colored garbage trucks designed for hauling rubbish, marked with the PDWM on the doors. Several more idled in a line, waiting to deposit their sensitive waste into massive industrial mashers and shredders so that nothing of use was able to be gleaned from them. What was recyclable was set aside for special handling in a large bay, which is where her driver turned in. He rolled up his window fully just as the effluvious stench of garbage made its way into the cabin.

Jordan wrinkled her nose and looked out at one of the trucks they were passing. "I trust that my office won't be in that lorry?"

"No, ma'am, we're almost there," Laurence replied, an amused smile visible in the rear view mirror. Casually, he reached up and pressed the rear window defrost button three times in quick succession and the road before them suddenly fell away, revealing a ramp that the sedan promptly traveled down.

Jordan could see they were in a large tunnel, easily big enough for two lorries to drive side by side. A row of dim blue lights illuminated the path from recessed wells in the ceiling casting the entire tunnel in an eerie blue glow. They continued on for another solid minute before coming around a corner where a heavy and quite obvious grey-colored secure door waited. On the front of the door, marked in yellow and red, there was painted a sign that said, RESTRICTED ACCESS and beneath that Use of Deadly Force Permitted.

Laurence casually pulled his ID from an inner coat pocket and held it out the window as he parked in a marked area in front of the door. Jordan's window also slid down to expose her. Suddenly, a green laser shot from the wall and scanned the badge and laminated card, and the car while two smaller lasers imaged each of their faces. Only a moment passed before the center of the heavy door rotated as its locking mechanism worked to give them passage. The door hissed open, parting down the center, a deep rumbling vibration made the sedan tremble as it was granted access to what lay beyond.

The car accelerated again and continued on its way, the door shutting behind them with a resounding clash of metal as the locking mechanism secured itself. Another three minutes of travel and the sedan arrived in a massive hangar-like structure that had numerous ground vehicles of all sorts parked along the sides of the walls, ordered by type. Luxury sedans, economy cars, armored cars, even police and emergency services vehicles.

Off to Jordan's right, she noticed another large bay where several vehicles were being worked on, some on lifts, others in various states of repair on the ground. A handful of the vehicles rather obviously had been smashed into things, while others had bullet holes riddling their outer skins. Jordan continued to look about, noticing that the men and women working on the vehicles all wore dark blue overalls with an ID badge affixed over their right breast.

Agent Blaine drove into the back of the hangar area and pulled the car off to the side. He parked by a pair of heavy-looking polished steel doors where two armed men dressed in unfamiliar black uniforms stood. Each was armed with a weapon Jordan had never seen before. It was a compact black rifle, that didn't show any sign of an ejection port and seemed to have two selector switches on the side. The weapons looked like something out of a video game or a science fiction movie.

In addition to these weapons, each man wore a black pistol, also unrecognizable, but also mostly hidden by their tactical thigh holsters. Jordan also noted compact radio systems and the presence of what must be torso body armor beneath the vests. More so than the equipment, the hard-eyed observant looks of the two men and their ready-for-anything body language gave Jordan a better hint of the danger presented by them. Fortunately, she was on their side… or so she hoped.

Laurence placed the car in park and then stepped out, walking over to open the door for Jordan. He extended a hand to Jordan and assisted her out as she stood, nodding his chin towards the door. "This is it, Agent Law. Colonel Shaw will be out momentarily to collect you. He'll see to your needs from this point forward. Your baggage will be taken to your room on base for you. I'll see that it is treated with all due care."

"Thank you, Laurence," Jordan replied and looked around the area. Her eyes returned to the two men who had noticeably adjusted their positions so that Jordan wouldn't easily be able to reach both at once, let alone get position to fire on them easily.

"Of course, welcome aboard," Laurence replied and smiled before entering the sedan again and turning the car around to head back to where the vehicles were parked.

The door that the two men guarded slid open with a soft mechanical hum and out strode a tall man dressed in black BDU pants and a black t-shirt. Handsome with rugged features, he was in his early thirties at the oldest, with hair as dark as Jordan's worn in a neatly trimmed manner that didn't immediately suggest military affiliation. He was lean, but well-muscled, his physique revealing that he must train extensively to maintain it. His eyes were dark brown, intense and intelligent-looking as they met Jordan's.

"Agent Law, welcome, I'm Colonel Tristan Shaw," the man offered in a deep voice that sounded as confident as the intent expression he wore on his face looked. Shaw extended a hand to Jordan which she took, his grip firm as he gave her hand a shake.

"Thank you," Jordan replied politely.

"I trust that your trip here was pleasant," the man said, turning to head through the open doors.

"It was, thank you, Colonel."

"I'll be overseeing your training, Agent Law. Today will be the formal induction process and a tour of the facility. Tomorrow we're going to see what you can do with an exercise or two, and you'll get a full medical work up. We don't waste a lot of time here so be prepared to hit the ground running."

"I am. I like to get up to speed quickly," Jordan offered.

Shaw nodded. "So your file suggests. You also like to work alone. We're operating in a team environment here. There will be times that an operation dictates solo work, but if you can't integrate into a team we can't use you."

Jordan glanced at Shaw. "I have five sisters. I assure you that teamwork was mandatory in our house."

"That's your dad's doing, no doubt. Good man, Cassidy," Shaw observed as they continued their walk.

Jordan looked at Tristan and raised her eyebrows in surprise, "You know my father?"

"I served in 22 SAS before this posting. I was never in his squadron, but I took his counter-terror psychology class when I was assigned to Special Projects. I was full of myself until your old man showed me I didn't know shite, " Colonel Shaw said, his respect for Cassidy Law was unmistakable. "I wouldn't be where I am now if he hadn't given me some humility."

"He's got a talent for that," Jordan smiled fondly.

"That he does. Don't let my gratitude go to your head, Law. I'll expect more from you because you're his daughter. He only had a few months to whip me into shape, with you, he's had years."

Jordan smiled, and then nodded. "Understood."

Colonel Shaw led Jordan down the hall which very much looked like she imagined a secret facility would. The floor was a polished white laminate of the sort that made silent movement difficult, with walls painted a medium grey. Along the walls were golden yellow markings that denoted a room number and a section number, as well as floor. One clearly had to be familiar with the layout of the facility in order to find anything as the only universally recognized markings were for the bathrooms and the emergency exits. The halls were lit by recessed lights centered in the middle of the ceiling that had bulbs meant to simulate natural daylight. The building smelled clean, the recycled air a bit dry for Jordan's tastes, but she considered it far better than the scent of refuse that had greeted her in the waste management area.

The sound of Shaw's boots and Jordan's heels were the only noises that either made for a while as Shaw continued to lead them down the long pristine hall. As they reached a T-shaped intersection he nodded to the right. "Team quarters and mess are down that way," Shaw said, and then turned to the left. "This way is the operational section. Mission control, briefing rooms, medical, combat simulation rooms, administration, the armories, and the shops."

Jordan nodded and took note of the markings, working on making sense of them as her tour guide indicated things. She also counted the paces from entering to where they were now in case she had to navigate them without being able to see where she was going.

"We have over three-hundred support staff organized into three shifts housed in this facility. They come from all branches of service in the United Kingdom, as well as the civilian sector," Shaw said, pausing by a door long enough for the automated sensor to register their presence and open it.

Inside, Jordan saw a very complete gymnasium with all manner of exercise machines and a few free weights off to one side. There were several men of different ethnicities inside using the equipment, a driving electronic beat playing from the speakers mounted in the corners of the large room.

The colonel gestured to the room as they walked through it, passing the men using a row of treadmills. "This is the gymnasium. We have a variety of standard equipment as well as machines designed to handle people with enhanced physiologies such as you. First off I'll show you the hydraulic press. It's specifically engineered to handle people able to lift enormous weights and do so safely."

Shaw led Jordan into the room and across a light colored lacquered wood floor over to where a white machine the size of a passenger van stood. The machine had a computerized readout of mostly blues and greens set in a black display frame on the side and a simple pushbutton control setup including a large red mushroom shaped stop button. Jordan could see the weight bar being lifted by someone, their tennis shoe clad feet visible. Instead of weights on either side of the bar there were two very heavy looking hydraulic pistons that were surprisingly quiet despite their size.

"Sergeant Douglas, front and center," Shaw said, his voice taking on a tone of command.

The person lifting the bar lowered it slowly, the pistons hissing as they reduced their resistance. A dark haired man rose from the padded couch and brushed off the grey tank top and blue shorts that he wore.

Sergeant Douglas was over one and half meters tall and muscular, though more stoutly built than Shaw. Though silent, Douglas radiated an intensity of personality; his dark brown eyes boring into Jordan's in a way that made her feel as if he was inspecting everything that was her and taking stock of it. She was used to such looks and, true to form, she looked right back.

"Jordan Law, meet Sergeant William Douglas, formerly of the Royal Marines," Shaw said, introducing the two.

Jordan offered her hand to Douglas, "A pleasure, Sergeant."

Douglas shook Jordan's hand in an almost too firm grip, his voice warm and mildly accented with a Scottish inflection.

"Ms. Law. Nice t'meet you. It's about time we prettied up the place a bit, giving the fairer sex a go at the real hush-hush stuff." Douglas' expression was one of warmth and charm, though the glint of mischief in his eyes spoke more about the man than his appearance. *He's trouble, but of a good sort,* Jordan thought.

Shaw gave Douglas a disapproving look and cut in before Jordan could speak. "Assuming you pass selection, you'll be the first operational female member of the team. The other women currently assigned to us are all in support roles."

"I was going to say they haven't been as pleasantly distracting, Colonel," Douglas chimed in with a smile that lacked any sort of repentance. "We can always use more of that 'round here."

Jordan looked between the two men, her face neutral as she replied to them. "I'll make certain I don't disappoint, at least in the operational arena."

Douglas responded with a lopsided smile that was nothing short of impish. "Well then. I'd best get back to my workout, wouldn't want to fall behind you, Ms. Law." The shorter man slipped on a pair of headphones attached to an mp3 player, the sounds of heavy metal music crashing out from the small ear pieces as he slid back into the hydraulic weight machine. He paused and looked up at Shaw, "Do me a favor and put her up to forty, Colonel?"

Shaw nodded and moved to the side of the machine, his expression still reflecting how Douglas' attitude rankled him. He punched in a new weight setting and hit the engage button. Immediately Douglas' legs tensed and the machine made an almost angry hissing peal as the hydraulic pistons began to press downwards. Douglas' expression tightened as he began a fresh set of repetitions at the new setting.

Jordan raised an eyebrow as she saw that 'forty' meant forty *tons*. Her gaze went to Shaw, "Is that safe?"

Shaw gave Jordan a faint smile in return. "Of course, it is. He's still about ten tons from his maximum press. You didn't think you were the only one who was special, did you?"

* * * * * *

Two men watched the scene play out on a high definition monitor, one sitting behind a large oak desk, the other standing with his arms folded.

"I don't think this is a good idea, Ethan." the standing man said in deep, gravelly voice. His tone was judgmental.

"This one is different, James. She's got the look in her eye," Director McIntyre replied and sat back in his comfortable leather executive chair, his gaze still on the surveillance monitor. McIntyre stabbed the mute button for the monitor's speakers to cut out the sounds from the gym and turned his gaze on Portsmouth. "Her record is exemplary."

Portsmouth stood one point eight meters with a thick muscular build built up from nearly twenty years in the Royal Marines. The man's weathered features were hard and the dour expression he wore made him appear like one of the Moa statues from Easter Island. Add to that thirty-eight years of hard living as a soldier and it was no wonder that the man most called Porty was always taken seriously. His brown hair was cut short and in the military fashion that matched his bearing. He was all business, and military business at that. "It's not just that she's a woman. It's that she's a woman *and* she's from a well-to-do family. I've seen enough of those hobby warriors to last me a lifetime. They just want to pin some service ribbons on a uniform so they look fancy at parties. They also get good people killed."

McIntyre tried a different approach. "She's a better shot than you, Jimmy, she bulls-eyed Kamir at twenty-eight-hundred meters while she was being attacked telepathically. You couldn't make that shot if the Almighty was ranging you. Neither could I. That sort of skill takes dedication and talent."

"Playing in the sand with the boys and being able to shoot a gun doesn't mean she has what it takes to do this job. It's more than that and you know it. We need people that are tough, that can be subjected to conditions that would break the average special operations soldier," Porty replied tersely.

Director McIntyre favored Portsmouth with a raised eyebrow and inhaled as he considered his next words. He switched to "I'm in Charge Mode" as he addressed his long time friend. "Sergeant, I value your opinion and expertise, but don't judge this one before you see her in action. She's pulled off operations that we would consider challenging if they were handed to us. Stevens' quarterly reviews all give her high marks."

"It also says she's overconfident," Portsmouth countered.

"Confidence is mandatory in our line of work Do keep in mind, she's also young. You and I may not remember what it was like to be young and full of one's self but both of us had some rough edges that needed rounding," McIntyre said fondly. The Director remembered the old days when he and Portsmouth were young and wild, apparently better than his friend.

Portsmouth nodded grimly and used his calloused hands to smooth his dark green BDU shirt and pants. "No disrespect intended, Director, but adding a piece of fluff like her to the squadron just seems politically motivated. I know we've taken a lot of guff because we've turned away every bird that's come here. They just aren't fit to serve in the field, not at this level. What about that Simons woman from the Marines? She couldn't keep her sodding legs closed. Hastings was also useless, remember her, how she broke down when she got a little harsh language? They just don't have the balls to handle this job. No ability to emotionally distance themselves from the work, or they want to shag everything they can find. I'm sure she'd do well in public relations, or intel. She's got a lovely voice and patience if she can deal with Douglas for more than thirty seconds."

The Director rose to his feet and walked over to a small bar situated at the side of the room. Portsmouth was never easy to convince of anything once his mind was set against it but the service was changing, and had been for two decades. Though his friend's gifts blessed him with a long life, McIntyre wondered if James was cursed with being stuck in the past. As the years wore on Portsmouth's viewpoints never seemed to change. Only the clothes he wore or the weapons he used. When they had first joined the military women were glorified secretaries or nurses, nothing else.

"I take it you don't agree Ethan," Portsmouth stated.

Pulling rank was the last thing Ethan McIntyre wanted to do, but Jordan Law was a force multiplier for his team. Her skills, her physical abilities, not too mention her invisibility power, were too good to pass up just to keep the peace with Portsmouth and his anachronistic ways. "You're right. We have had criticism about the boy's club we've been running here. This isn't the fifties anymore, James. Women serve in frontline combat units now. They work the field all over the world. We're supposed to be the innovators and game changers here. Our team has thrived off of adopting methods and procedures, and people that other agencies refuse."

He gave Portsmouth an interrogatory look that received a nod of acceptance. McIntyre took down two glasses and a bottle half full of an amber colored liquid. Setting the glasses next to one another he put a measure of scotch in each, extending one to his severe-looking companion. "The squadron's operational readiness is what I care about. I'm not going to put a woman in unless she can do the job and do it as well as anyone else on the team," McIntyre took a long drink from his glass, exhaling after letting the alcohol warm his throat. "Your objection is noted, however."

Portsmouth's stony face was unreadable as he drank. "Alright then, but I'm not going to make it easy on her. I'm going to push her, and make her cry for her daddy. I give her a week before she asks to be reassigned."

Director McIntyre returned to his seat, crossing his legs as he sank into the leather. With a canny look on his face McIntyre turned his attention on the monitor where it showed Jordan and Shaw continuing with their tour of the facility. "Just a week?" he replied, his tone amused. "I think you need to read her file again, James. She'll meet even your performance standards and then some. Take your week and do what you like to her, within reason. Keep in mind, this woman is from a good family and about to be married to a man of position and means. We don't need any extra attention from the politicians. Colonel Shaw is handling the majority of her training, so work with him and don't get too creative."

"I don't care if she's the bloody Queen mum's favorite niece. I'm the senior NCO and I need to know that she's not going to get one of my boys killed because she needs to stop for a potty break," Portsmouth replied sternly.

CHAPTER 7

The sounds of AC/DC's *Dirty Deeds Done Dirt Cheap* bastardized into Muzak filtered in through the interior of the steel and wood elevator. The two passengers were subjected to a meandering blend of electronically sampled jazz horns and soft strings. Though the melody was fairly close to the original, the music had lost its soul.

Konstantin Tretyak frowned slightly as he heard the familiar tones of the music warped and violated by instruments it was never meant to be heard in. Though originally born in St. Petersburg, Russia at the height of the cold war, Tretyak had access to the forbidden American and European music, even as a youth. His brother and father were both in the KGB and they would often-times bring confiscated contraband home to share with their family. The family always ate well and enjoyed a good life when many in Soviet Russia lived worse than slaves.

The benefits of power, Tretyak contemplated. He, too, had gone into the KGB after earning a degree in military science from the University of Moscow and spending nine years in the Spetsnaz commandos. Konstantin had done well in life, well indeed. After a successful career of service, he left and started his own business. It was this business that brought him to the home offices of ImaGen on a sunny California afternoon.

Pulling his mind away from thoughts of the past, Tretyak glanced down at the woman standing in front of him. She was of average height and very leggy with a pretty face and long blonde hair. *Dyed,* Tretyak thought and wrinkled his nose as it was assaulted by the unnatural chemical scents that clung to the woman. He could also smell the scent of silicon and large amounts of it. No doubt that came from the rather ample assets her dark red suit covered, or *almost* covered. She wore the white blouse open further than was professional, her red suit coat buttoned up to frame those assets. The perfume she wore was expensive, but the strength of the smell suggested she either put it on several times a day or bathed in it.

Despite the panoply of various artificial scents, there was one scent in particular that stood out from the rest: fear. Though she managed to hide it well enough, this woman was terrified of him and that brought a faint predatory smile to Tretyak's face.

"Enjoying the weather, Mr. Tretyak?" Karen asked, injecting pleasantness into her tone.

"It's nice," Tretyak replied, his voice quiet but intense. Like a heavy stone lid being slid from a sarcophagus.

Another slight smile turned up the corners of Tretyak's lips as he saw Karen shiver in response to the sound of his voice. He knew part of her fear was his size and not just his presence. At just under two meters tall, he was larger than the average man. Years of hard work, warfare, and physical pursuits, not too mention very good genetics, gave Tretyak a well-developed physique that would make most American football players envious. The Louis Vuitton suit Tretyak wore couldn't disguise his size and the deep black color only enhanced the fearsome presence he radiated. Women like Karen feared him and that fear, that *weakness*, repulsed him. The predator in him saw her and those like her as nothing but prey, and prey could sense a predator among them.

The elevator chime sounded quietly as they reached the seventy-eighth floor of ImaGen's headquarters and Karen immediately stepped out of the small enclosed space even before the doors had fully opened. She was off down the tan marble floor with a purpose, her red pumps clicking on the polished stone in a quick rhythm. Tretyak smiled darkly again and followed behind her, his large silent form almost gliding across the floor with far more grace than any man his size should. In fact, Tretyak's step was so quiet Karen paused and turned to see if he was following her at all. The normally collected personal assistant nearly jumped out of her skin when she realized he was *right* behind her.

"Th-this way please," Karen stammered as she looked into black eyes that looked down at her from what was a rugged and handsome face. Her own image was reflected in the dark soulless depths that were Tretyak's eyes.

Tretyak inclined his head as an indication for Karen to continue which she did with a quick turn on her heel. Although Tretyak's dark eyes faced forward, his mind perceived the entire hallway in a seven-hundred-and-twenty degree sphere. It was a three dimensional environment, a world that was full of surging colors. Every object was limed in a specific color that correlated with its own unique electromagnetic aura. The floor was a cool dark blue while power cables running beneath it and through the walls shone as brilliant electric blue lines pulsing with life. Those lines led to either outlets that continued the line of color to a device that had its own unique aura, or brilliant white lights that radiated electromagnetic energy like small suns. It all stopped at the end of the hallway as if the electromagnetic ocean that filled the Earth had been covered in an impenetrable shroud. The marble wall and the ceiling-high metal doors were entirely dead. A barely visible dark blue aura protected the entire room at the end of the hall and even suffocated the normally bright EM luminescence of the light fixtures on either side of the door.

"Mr. Spears is expecting you," Karen said and forced a pretty smile onto her face as she pulled open the large metallic door easily.

Tretyak glanced at the six-inch-thick door with curiosity that never cracked the stern expression on his face. The door was obviously solid steel and had eight thick three inch diameter cylinder locking shafts inset on the door's edge. After doing some quick math in his head, Tretyak realized that each door must weigh well over ten tons, yet a small slip of a woman opened it with one hand and no effort.

"Perfectly balanced," the tall man standing at the large multi-paned window said without looking back at Tretyak or his assistant. Unlike Tretyak's voice, Spear's was rich and pleasant-sounding though a slight hint of superiority underpinned his tone. "Karen, drinks please."

The woman quietly entered the large marble office and headed for a small, but well-fitted, wet bar along the wall. Karen quickly poured two drinks from the crystalline decanters. The two glasses clinked softly as she poured a measure of amber liquid into one and clear into the second. Karen quickly brought the glasses over with a wooden coaster for each glass, and set them on the large flat black metal desk that Tretyak moved to stand in front of.

"Thank you, Karen. Please, hold all calls until further notice," Doctor Spears said congenially and turned away from the window in an unhurried manner. He took a seat in the black high backed executive chair and crossed his legs after collecting the amber-filled glass from its coaster.

"Yes, Mr. Spears," Karen replied smoothly before she left the room.

After the door was shut, the man behind the desk fixed Tretyak with his smoky grey eyes, the expression on his handsome face neutral. Elgen Spears was nearly as tall as Tretyak, though his build was lean like a swimmer's. He looked as if he should be an actor or model, not one of the world's leading genetic scientists and the sole owner of

ImaGen. The company was a medical and genetic engineering giant that had cropped up just as science had brought genetic engineering out of the realm of science fiction. ImaGen produced genetically enhanced crops, gene engineered animals, and was currently leading research efforts to treat numerous hereditary maladies with gene therapy. It was making money hand over fist and the corporate headquarters with its expensive art and ultra-tech interfaces let every visitor know it.

Spears tugged the sleeve of his tailored dress shirt to smooth out a wrinkle in the sleeve and did the same to the leg of his light grey slacks with the tips of his fingers. He followed up the primping motions with a sip from his glass. He obviously savored the taste of the liquor for several moments before looking back at Tretyak who sat in his own seat, patiently waiting for his host to begin.

"I'm very pleased with the performance of your people, Mr. Tretyak. They're very efficient and very mindful of the necessity for completing an assignment with a minimum of violence," Spears said as he watched Tretyak, displaying none of the trepidation or fear that his subordinate had. In fact, his casual posture and indifferent tone gave the impression that Tretyak was nothing but a simple underling. "Your organization is well-worth the sizeable fee that you charge. I have other work, if you're interested."

Tretyak disliked being treated like a hired thug and the resulting frown made most people move back a step or two if they were smart. Not Spears, though. The man simply watched Tretyak as if he had all the time in the world to wait for a decision. He had no fear and that was something Tretyak disliked, indeed. "What did you have in mind?"

"There is a shipment of very expensive, very delicate, and very rare materials being delivered to the Port of London late next month. You will need to be able to move roughly nine tons, taking up the volume of four medium-sized cargo trucks. What is being shipped is not friendly to bullets, explosions, or high-speed traffic accidents. I'll need the materials delivered to America within two weeks of their acquisition," Spears responded with a more interested tone. The businessman watched Tretyak's cold eyes with a steely gaze. "If you can't meet all the requirements of this assignment, I'll need to retain a different contractor."

Tretyak folded his hands loosely in his lap and lifted his chin as he considered the assignment. "Don't worry, my people can handle it." With a perfunctory gesture of his hand Tretyak motioned across the desk to Spears. "What sort of security do your materials warrant?"

Spears smiled widely. "Good security. SIS is overseeing the transport of the goods to Porton Down and my contact tells me that they're using Marines to guard it. Once the ship makes port, the cargo's going to be switched over to a pair of cold storage semis. The security team will be two operatives per truck with two Range Rovers front and back and an additional four operatives per vehicle. All of them well-armed with the usual assortment of military equipment."

"What's name of the vessel they're coming in on?"

"The merchant vessel Dunleavy, she's a government contracted cargo ship, but they're transporting cargo bound for civilian destinations as well. Probably a cover of some sort," Spears replied and took another drink from his glass. "Are you considering interdicting the cargo at sea?"

It was Tretyak's turn to smile, the expression disturbing for the utter lack of humanity in the man's eyes. He tilted his head slightly and appeared to contemplate his response. "It's the best option if you want your cargo intact, Mr. Spears. There's a reason why my organization is called The Vodnik, water is no barrier to my people. No doubt, the marines on board the vessel will have less training than those that will have to transport it over land. They will also have far less ability to call for assistance on the open water. Even if they do, the response time will be significantly longer." The large man tipped his glass back and drained its contents as if the lengthy explanation had dried out his throat. After setting it back down on the coaster he spoke again. "It will cost five hundred thousand American up front and the same upon delivery of your items, within your timetable of course."

"Ah yes, a mythological Russian water demon or something, very apropos considering your underworld nom de guerre. Very well, my dear Crimson Shark, one million American it is. Karen will have the money wired to your account in twenty four hours," Spears answered with a pleased smile on his face. He tossed back the contents of his glass. "I look forward to hearing from you."

CHAPTER 8

The blow came out of nowhere and sent a wash of pain up Jordan's right side. She could feel the corresponding arm trying very hard to go numb, the tingling reaching from her shoulder to just past the elbow. Faster than the eye could see, Jordan spun the opposite direction and struck out with a short but high-powered jab from the fully operable limb. She felt no impact, just the rush of air past her skin. With sweat making her short hair cling to her forehead, Jordan took three quick and graceful steps to her left, spinning to face where she had been previously. There was no sign of her attacker anywhere on the large blue matted area that she stood in.

Even as her body's regenerative abilities restored function to her disabled arm, a shooting pain lanced out from the back of Jordan's knee all the way into her hip and down to her toes. Again, her attacker was nowhere to be seen and the thin, tight-fitting black yoga pants she wore did nothing to cushion the blows. *No impression on the mat, so he's not invisible, not unless he's bloody flying.*

Jordan shifted her weight onto her other leg in order to keep upright and give her body time to restore blood flow and sensation to her limb, but it would never get the chance. Jordan caught a flash of black BDUs as Colonel Shaw's image appeared in her peripheral vision. His booted foot lashed out quickly and placed a sweeping kick to the back of her weight bearing ankle that put Jordan's entire body off the ground for an instant before she landed on her backside against the matted practice floor before flopping back prone. The landing was far from graceful and highly undignified, which made her face flush with a combination of anger and embarrassment. She grimaced sourly as she heard Douglas' amused laugh from the edge of the sparring area, mirth as well as dash of sympathy in his tone.

"I'd not laugh too hard, Douglas, else I'll drag you out here and do the same," Colonel Shaw said, his face as serious as his tone. The tall colonel extended a hand down to Jordan who had pushed onto her elbows, perspiration soaking the tight grey tank top she wore. This was round seven, and Jordan was zero and seven though her pride felt more like she was zero and twenty.

Douglas held up both hands in mock surrender and grinned unrepentantly at Shaw. "It's just good to see *everyone* get worked over by you, sir. It's a squadron tradition at this point."

Jordan shook her head lightly, more in disgust with herself than anger towards her sparring partner or the flippant Douglas. She tried to figure out exactly how Shaw had pulled off his little stunt so many times. It was as if the man had ceased to exist and then came back just to cause her pain and embarrassment.

"How did you do that?" Jordan asked as she grabbed the offered hand and pulled herself up. She took a moment to brush her sweat soaked bangs back with her fingertips and pushed them to the left side of her forehead.

"I just knocked your good leg out, luv," Shaw replied, his amusement at Jordan's embarrassment borne in the slight smile and the way his eyes sparkled with mischief.

"That's not what I meant, sir," Jordan replied tersely.

"I suspect not."

"So you're not going to fess up then?"

Shaw chuckled and shrugged his shoulders as he stepped back from Jordan. "How do you think I did it? Magic? Wishful thinking and good luck? You need to stop thinking linearly, Jordan. This position requires more thought than that. Just ask these fine gentlemen," he said and motioned in a wide gesture to where the rest of the operational squadron stood at ease on the sidelines. "None of the people we fight are so well-mannered as to give you a rundown of their abilities, or tips on how to combat them."

Jordan nodded unenthusiastically and watched Shaw's eyes. The team chuckled in response to the Colonel's sarcastic statement, all except the dour looking Portsmouth. He just stood there with his arms folded across his barrel chest watching Jordan get introduced to the thin blue practice mat over and over again.

A cheeky laugh came from another man in the small formation. "Too right."

Briar Young, Jordan noted with distaste. She had met the man during the tour the day before. He was what Shaw referred to as a "professional acquirer of things." Filled with false charm, and what most would call a pretty boy, the blonde and athletic Young didn't have the personality to match. He was arrogant and lecherous in a way that frankly made Jordan uncomfortable. Even now, the man was busy looking at Jordan's breasts as opposed to anything else in the room.

Shaw took a few steps back and unfolded his arms, clearly intending for the sparring to go another round. "Well? I expect an answer, Law."

"Your feet didn't leave an impression in the mat when I couldn't see you, so I ruled out your being invisible. Your blows all hit locations that are more easily hit from a standing position, so I don't believe you were flying *and* invisible," Jordan said, her mind working out what other possible abilities could account for Shaw's attacks. "Teleportation, if it exists, I ruled out as there was no displacement of air, no sensation of any kind, aside from your fist."

Shaw nodded, and paced the mat for a moment. "All good guesses. Especially from someone who hasn't read any of our files on existing catalogued abilities. So, what does that leave? If I'm not invisible, not teleporting, not flying and invisible, what other possible means could I be using to evade detection so I could strike you? Did I use my magic power ring to cloud your mind?"

Though rhetorical, the last question Shaw asked made Jordan smirk, his sarcastic tone angering her. She schooled her expression into one of thought versus one of anger and stared into Shaw's eyes. "I doubt that's the answer because you'd have not brought it up would you? Especially as you have forbidden my using my own invisibility power in this exercise."

Shaw shrugged casually. "I'm still waiting for an answer, Ms. Law. Perhaps this will get your mind properly framed for solving this problem."

Jordan dropped into an immediate guard stance as Shaw vanished before her eyes. There was no sound, no shimmer, no smell. Nothing. One moment, he was there, the next he wasn't. Jordan felt something strike her in the back of the head, a slap. Not even a punch, or any sort of blow that would do more than humiliate her. The impact wasn't even strong enough to rock her head forward, but she capitalized off of the position she thought Shaw to be in and dove forward into a roll. She swept her long leg around as to sweep behind her and then used the momentum to gain her feet again. This time, however, she counted the time passage between when she was struck and when the next blow came.

It didn't take long before Jordan saw Shaw appear briefly in front of her, his punch slamming into the side of her jaw.

Three seconds, she thought and flipped herself backwards, her feet kicking up in an attempt to hit Shaw who vanished just before they passed through the air where he had been. She used the momentum to carry her backwards in a series of flips that left her across the mat over fifteen meters from where she had been. Jordan finished the maneuver with a strong mid-height snap kick out in front of her in an attempt to catch Shaw as he appeared.

This time Shaw struck from her left flank, his knuckle punch hitting Jordan on the left side just below her ribs. *Three seconds. There's a time limit on whatever he's doing.* Jordan's thoughts were as augmented as her reflexes and physical speed, and she spun away from the blow which left her side stinging. Her spinning motion robbed the punch of much of its force, sparing her another visit to the mat. Jordan had seen a glimpse of Colonel Shaw just before he appeared that time, and mentally counted down those three seconds.

To her, three seconds was a long time and she used that pause to leap high into the air and land on the far edge of the mat. With a serious expression on her face, Jordan timed her movement so that she would land in a crouch just shy of three seconds and then she immediately dove forward like a missile, her arms in front of her, hands balled into fists.

Shaw appeared right in front of Jordan, his right fist swinging at where Jordan's head would have been. The man's eyes widened as Jordan's fists slammed into his stomach followed by the weight of her body. Jordan's blow knocked the air out of her opponent and both combatants landed on the mat five meters away from where Jordan had struck Shaw. Straddling the Colonel, Jordan drove the tips of her fingers into the nerves on the right side of Shaw's neck which made him grunt in pain. In a blur of motion, she struck Shaw under each arm with rapid, precise thumb strikes, hitting pressure points, and then slammed her elbow across his jaw hard enough to knock a lesser man out.

As quickly as he could, Shaw brought one hand up to cover his face, but to Jordan's celerity-enhanced perceptions he was moving five times slower, so she was able to land short jabs into the Colonel's jaw twice before his hand moved into position. The urge to smile almost won out over her will as Jordan saw Colonel Shaw's eyes lose focus from the nerve strikes she assailed him with. He was still conscious but definitely dancing the fine line between awareness and the black embrace of unconsciousness.

On the sidelines the rest of the team stood in silent shock, and even Portsmouth lifted an eyebrow in surprise. Jordan could hear their whispers over the steady pounding of her own adrenaline-fueled pulse, but her eyes never left Shaw. He definitely wasn't the sort of man you counted out until his body stopped moving. After she was satisfied that Shaw wasn't going to renew his attacks, Jordan rose from her position on top of him and extended a hand down to where Shaw lay. "I still haven't put my finger on *how* you do that."

* * * * * *

Just past noon, Colonel Shaw and Jordan walked down the grey-walled hall of the medical section towards Doctor Thomas Lindon's office. The hall was fairly busy with men and women wearing white lab coats pushing carts, carrying an assortment of medical implements, or just talking amongst themselves. Jordan was impressed that Shaw was up and around. He was slightly bruised, but otherwise unharmed. She considered that she had, perhaps, been too aggressive during the match. *I hit him far harder than I should have.*

Before the sparring session, the Colonel had told Jordan not to pull her punches too much, but to avoid any serious injury and he would do the same. He said he wanted a gauge of her abilities, but Jordan realized that he was gauging her control and ability to analyze an opponent more than her skill at hand-to-hand combat. If she had hurt Shaw, he was good at hiding it.

Jordan wasn't particularly proud of her showing in the match. Oh, she had been at first. It was nice to be the only member of the squadron who had defeated Shaw during their welcome aboard match, but Jordan thought that all she had showed was how important winning was to her. Not the how of it, just the ends. Shaw had even congratulated her on how well she had done, but something in his eyes made Jordan feel like she had lost the one round she'd won.

Unconsciously shaking her head, Jordan considered how perplexed she was by Shaw. Most men who boasted the same sort of swagger and confidence would have been humiliated by a woman trouncing them so soundly in front of their troops, but the Colonel continued to treat her with the same professional friendliness that he had when they met the day before. He smiled at her, joked, and had essentially remained the same in regards to his interactions with Jordan. This was a new experience for her. Jordan had humiliated far more than her fair share of men in her life, she hated misogynists and took every chance possible to make them look lesser than her. Comparing him to misogynists like her former Director Stevens wasn't right. Shaw was different, that much was clear to her. *I wonder if they can clone him. The world would be a better place, I should think.*

"Doctor Lindon is perhaps the world's leading expert on people like you and me, Ms. Law," Shaw said, pulling Jordan out of her thoughts.

"What *exactly* are people like us called, Colonel Shaw?" Jordan replied and glanced over at the man next to her.

A rich and warm voice came from behind the two, saying "'Awakened' is the colloquial. The proper term, however, is Evolved Genome Human. The acronym sounds rather like a noise you'd make after consuming too many bangers with a particularly rough tasting pint."

Jordan and Shaw turned simultaneously to face the owner of the voice. "Doctor Lindon. We were just looking or you," the latter said in a friendly tone.

Lindon was of average height and, judging by the appearance of slight crows' feet at the edge of his eyes, and a slightly weathered appearance, Jordan guessed he was in his fifties. The man was thin, but more athletic than skinny, with keen, pale blue eyes and medium length blonde hair. The doctor's expression was welcoming and the smile on his face was mirrored by the friendliness in his eyes. Jordan thought his overall demeanor made him very handsome.

"Well, here I am," Lindon said with his hands out to his side.

Shaw chuckled in response to the doctor's reply. "I'd like you to meet Agent Jordan Law, our newest recruit."

"Jordan is fine, if you'd prefer. I understand that we're supposed to be informal here," Jordan said and smiled for good measure.

Doctor Lindon stepped forward to look Jordan over as one might a performance sports car, slowly walking around her in a manner that made Colonel Shaw take two steps back so the doctor could complete his initial revolution. "Ah yes. I have read your preliminary file. Quite impressive, quite impressive, indeed; regeneration, enhanced neural and motor ability, enhanced perceptive ability, enhanced skeletal durability to allow for a very robust musculature. "

The doctor abruptly stopped and crouched down to tie the lace on one of his bright red Converse tennis shoes. He fretted with the position of the lace for a moment so that it was in perfect symmetry with its twin on the other shoe and then adjusted the each leg of his slacks so that they, too, were perfect. The man nodded in satisfaction once that was done, rose to his feet, and continued on as if nothing had happened. "What I find most interesting is your ability to render yourself invisible psionically. We have yet to see that in any other individual. It's a sort of Teleobfuscation, or Psicloak. I can't wait to get under the hood and see what makes you tick."

Shaw chuckled. "You just made those terms up, didn't you, Doctor?"

Lindon smiled broadly. "I did. It's the purview of scientists to do such things, you know."

Jordan raised an eyebrow as the doctor walked around her again and noted the length of her legs, the way she stood, how her posture measured against notable combatants. Without warning, Lindon pulled the LED pen light from his lab coat pocket and flashed it in Jordan's eye which caused her to blink rapidly,

"Hmm, yes, I can see that you have a sensitivity to light, probably due to an increased count of rods and cones, or perhaps more efficient versions thereof," Lindon said in a voice thick with fascination. He unexpectedly exhaled in Jordan's face which made her expression twist into a mask of distaste as the pungent scent of garlic and onions assaulted her nose. She could also smell spicy beef, white bread, and something that smelled like strawberry fruit candy.

"Quickly, young lady, what did I have for lunch?" Lindon snapped as if he were a drill sergeant.

Jordan waved her hand in front of her face to disperse the smell. "I'd wager the Italian meatball sandwich I saw on the mess hall menu for today, with extra onions and the strawberry after-meal candy."

Lindon smiled in delight, but Shaw spoke before the doctor could reply. "Doctor, I was actually bringing Jordan by for the standard exam. It's scheduled to start in ten minutes. She'll also need the usual study materials on Awakened abilities." The Colonel fixed Doctor Lindon with a meaningful gaze that drew the man out of his examination.

Lindon gave Shaw a slightly vexed expression. "Colonel, I'm quite aware of the time. Perhaps not so much as yourself, considering your innate awareness of that particular medium, still, sometimes the best place to study a subject is in the field. Be it a hallway, or in action on a mission!" With a dramatic swirl of his lab coat the doctor turned to head in the direction in which Jordan and Shaw had been going. "Now, if you will please come with me, Ms. Law, we will begin to open your eyes to a very large and complicated world."

* * * * * *

The next few hours were spent with Jordan being poked prodded and scanned in the squadron's very well equipped medical center. Blood was drawn, tissue samples taken, and all of the standard specimens for a full physical. Jordan was given an MRI and scanned with devices of unknown function. As one battery of tests gave way to the next, Doctor Lindon questioned Jordan about previous injuries, her abilities' limits as she knew them and some very personal questions about her biological functions. Jordan silently wondered if this rather invasive session violated the agreement she had made with McIntyre when she accepted the offer to join the unit.

It seemed as if there would be no end to the tests. Jordan had been asked to lift weights and hold them for specific amounts of time, then at specific angles. The weight tests were followed by reflex tests that involved her catching varying amounts of ping pong balls shot at her with an airgun. At all times, she was to wear a small mp3-player-sized device attached to a band around her waist that transferred all manner of physical data to the doctor's tablet that he carried to take notes as well as control the testing machinery. Perhaps the most unpleasant thing out of the whole physical testing portion was the current test which was to smell various scents contained in bottles marked with only a letter and a number.

Doctor Lindon thrust a black bottle that was marked F-11 in Jordan's face and she wrinkled her nose as the acrid odor accosted her. "Burned wiring," She refrained from commenting on how the label's adhesive was sort of sweet smelling, unlike the last one. Lindon had called her a showoff after the first three times she had commented on the smell of the glue the label had been attached with, though he had seemed more amused than upset by it.

"Excellent, that's 18 out of 22, very good, indeed," Lindon replied and reached to grab another bottle from a shelf full of identical bottles while one of his assistants entered the results in her own data tablet. The woman, Reggie, as the doctor called her, smiled at Jordan sympathetically, but otherwise remained out of the doctor's way. Reggie seemed to know exactly what Doctor Lindon needed at any moment and was quickly there with whatever it was.

Lindon squeezed the newest bottle which pushed the scent from the small container into Jordan's face. This one smelled old, wet, and fishy. It was quite horrible, in fact, and Jordan began to wonder if these bottles only had the worst of smells in them.

"Some sort of fish?" Jordan replied and waved her hand in front of her face for the twenty-third time. This smell was so abhorrent that Jordan's eyes were watering.

"Yes, but what *sort* of fish?" Lindon asked firmly and watched Jordan's expression as if he was hoping for a revelation, or some sort of breakthrough.

The dark haired woman shrugged slightly in response to the prompting for further detail, her eyes settling on the doctor's. "A bad smelling sort, I'd have to say."

Lindon laughed warmly. "Oh yes, that's for certain. It's a shark, actually, to be specific, Carcharodon Carcharias. Now, is it male or female?"

This latest question gave Jordan pause. *How the sodding hell am I supposed to know that?* Sighing more impatiently than she intended, Jordan shrugged her shoulders. "That, I can't say, Doctor."

"Female," Lindon responded and smiled broadly as if he hadn't even noticed Jordan's new less-than-enthusiastic demeanor. "You should be able to tell from the stronger estrogen levels in the sample. It's quite fine to be strong, fast, and beautiful, Jordan; but knowledge and experience will carry you through things that simple instinct can't. You have the ability to smell in a far greater spectrum than the average human and you *need* to begin learning what things smell like at a deeper level. You *should* be able to differentiate between scents. Male and female, animal types, explosive types. See where I'm going with all this? It's not just rubbish that I spout to make myself seem more important or charmingly quirky."

Jordan gave Lindon a pretty smile. "Yes, Doctor. I trust that you have resources here to teach me these things?"

Lindon smiled at her with his own charismatic smile. "Indeed, we do. I will add the exercises to your training schedule. This is most important for you. We don't just train soldiers here, or spies. We train *heroes*! We train the most efficient, capable, intelligent, and flexible agents in the world here. Each member of the operational team must learn to maximize their potential, to reach beyond the limits they impose upon themselves. Now, do you have any questions for me?"

Jordan gave a slight incline of her head as the doctor changed direction. "Several. However, I think the most important is how did I come by these abilities?"

"Brilliant," Lindon replied enthusiastically, snapping his fingers and smiling like another doctor Jordan had seen in a recent television episode. "That's the real question isn't it? Where do these fantastic gifts come from? Why do only a scant few examples of humanity have these powers? Are you gods? Are you freaks of nature? Is this evolution making a running leap?"

Doctor Lindon continued on with an enthusiasm that reminded Jordan of her youngest sister Jillian explaining the latest musician she followed, or the last episode of *True Blood*. Much like dealing with her sister, Jordan just had to sit back and hang on for the ride as there would be no getting a word in edgewise.

"The honest answer is this: we have no idea!" Lindon exclaimed and smiled at her brightly, his arms outstretched to either side of his body. "None whatsoever. You see, in reality, we have found that roughly seventy-nine percent of humanity, across all ethnic groups and geographical regions, has the potential to Awaken. The potential only, mind you. Why is this, you ask? How did this come to be? We aren't certain of that either. It's *frustrating*, that's what it is!"

Lindon walked over to where his data tablet sat on the exam table and typed something in rapidly, the virtual keys' clacking drowned out the slight hum of the building's air system. He waited for something to come up and then turned the screen to face Jordan. It revealed a three dimensional map of the globe with numerous markers placed around the world, though the highest concentrations were where humanity clustered along the coasts, and rivers. There were markers of various colors, the meaning of which were not immediately clear.

"We do, however, have theories, lots of theories, in fact, but little more than that. We theorize that this enhanced genetic potential started appearing in humanity in ancient times. We've all heard of the heroes of old; Achilles, Perseus, Cú Chulainn, Samson. People who could eat more than an army, regenerate missing limbs, men and women who could throw fire, could make the mountains shake and could bring the dead back to life. The theory is that these were the first. Because ancient man couldn't understand the science behind it all, they called these people Gods, Demons, Heroes, sons and daughters of divinity, and many other things," Lindon said, his enthusiasm picking up strength as he continued to give voice to his theory. "Think of it now, beings that could defy the laws of the universe as people of the times understood them. Icarus? Did he make his own wings or did he *have* them? What of the stories of Angels visiting people and shooting rays about, healing people, telling the future?" The doctor rotated his hands around one another as if they were a ball rolling down a hill faster and faster.

Jordan folded her arms and watched Lindon with rapt attention, her mind sifting through old stories her father told her of the ancient Greek heroes and those of Scottish and Irish folk lore. The memories brought a smile to her face.

"Now, here we are in modern times and you must be asking yourself this: Why aren't these people seen every day? Why aren't there people running around in tights and outlandish costumes saving people, or hurting them? The answer to this quandary is simple, there are too few of them, and too many of us. Humanity destroys that which it fears, or can't understand, as a rule. No doubt, if Awakened beings were acting publically, humanity would rise up like a terrible monster, fearful and green with envy, and strike them down if they couldn't have that power for themselves. Of course, this will eventually change. Some day, the scales will tip." As Lindon finished he slammed his hands together in a loud clap to emphasize his point. The gesture sent the Doctor's tablet flying, but the startled nurse caught it just before it hit the ground.

Reggie gave the doctor a slightly vexed expression and set it aside on the exam table. "Doctor, may I remind you that these are not inexpensive. Director McIntyre said that the next one will come out of your pay."

The man gave Jordan a devious smile after glancing at his startled nurse. "Of course, you may remind me, Reggie. However, I think that I will ignore your sage counsel in this matter as I always do."

"Yes, Doctor."

Jordan looked between the two briefly and concealed a smile behind her hand. "You say green with envy, Doctor. Has anyone tried to Awaken someone artificially? This sort of power in an army of people would give nearly any country almost unlimited influence."

Nodding with certainty, Lindon gave her a congratulatory smile. "Oh, indeed, we have, World War II, the Psi-Experiments of the seventies, the more recent use of growth hormones and steroids. All around the world, governments and organizations have tried to unlock this secret and have been failing for ages. Some limited success has been achieved in the case of remote viewing, mind over matter, and all that, but nobody has been able to unlock these deeply buried sequences that awaken *true* superhuman power. Nobody, but Mother Nature, that is. The matter of who does or does not Awaken seems to solely rest in Her more than capable hands," Lindon said and dropped onto a padded lab chair, suddenly less animated. His posture became weary for a few brief moments before he slammed his hand down on the stainless steel exam table hard like his football team had just lost the World Cup.

Jordan pursed her lips and studied the doctor for a few, silent, moments. "So, what happened to the people who had artificial means used on them?"

Lindon sat forward some, his expression darkening noticeably. "Nothing good, young lady. Horrible mutations, cancers, blindness, insanity, an entire range of human frailties enhanced and magnified by every experiment tried. It's almost as if God has put a password on his goodies and won't allow us mere mortals to share in his power," the doctor said with an unexpected incredulousness to his voice.

"I see," Jordan replied thoughtfully. "So, do we naturally Awakened individuals ever have problems with these gifts; mutations and such?"

Jordan's curious expression seemed to bring down the doctor's intensity some and his voice softened as if he were talking after being up for days without rest. "At times, there are problems with control, or sensory input overloads, but the body compensates for the demands of the power. It adapts. Those who are exceptionally strong have dense skeletal structures, or some other means of compensating for increased weight loads such as different muscle structure. I have yet to see a naturally Awakened person have an ability that would kill them by its wise, and calculated use. Of course, even the Awakened have limits, so don't go trying to stand in a blast furnace and hope to heal from it. However, in answer to your question, no; God did his work very well."

Lindon's expression suddenly erupted into a warm smile, and the newly animated man started speaking just as Jordan was about to ask another question. "Anyway, I should have some results for you in a few days, at most. We will discuss your abilities then and adjust your conditioning and training schedules to match. Until then, reasonably push your limits and study the materials I'll soon upload to your computer share. I'm sure Colonel Shaw is having his brother get you all sorted in the systems as we speak."

"Brother?" Jordan replied.

"Yes. Leftenant Shaw. He was at your initiation. Tall fellow, blonde, friendly," Lindon said. "He's the team's information hound. As such, he likes to make certain you have all of the informational particulars you'll need in regards to your job."

"I remember him. I haven't had a formal introduction yet. In fact, I haven't met most of the team," Jordan said with a nod.

Lindon smiled. "Sometimes you have to make your own introductions around here. It's all part of the game, Jordan."

"Game?"

"Yes. Our focus is as much about knowledge as it is about fighting," Lindon said and handed Jordan a lollipop from a small basket of candy on his desk.

Jordan eyed the candy for a second before she pocketed it. "Meaning the things I don't do are being scrutinized as much, if not more so, than the things I do."

Doctor Lindon shrugged innocently. "Enjoy the candy, Jordan. Your metabolism could use a few more calories after the workout it's had today. Oh, and tell Colonel Shaw that the next candidate will *not* be getting the physical combat lesson prior to the exam. My lord, what would happen if he or she had some sort of flaw that was never noticed? Foolish military rituals, bah."

Jordan replied with a nod of her head and stood smoothly. "Thank you, Doctor Lindon. If I have more questions later, may I set an appointment?"

"By all means Jordan; you *will* have more questions. I frequently work late so feel free to pop in. No appointment necessary," Lindon said and smiled at Jordan paternally.

Jordan returned the smile and walked towards the door. She already had numerous questions. Her mind burgeoned with them, but she wanted to lay them out on paper before speaking with the mercurial Doctor Lindon next. "Thank you, again. This has been enlightening."

CHAPTER 9

A blast of angry orange flame leapt out from the mouth of gargoyle-like statue perched on the corner of the building where Jordan had landed. She immediately flipped backwards toward the center of the roof and fired the twin pistols she held. The bullets struck the creature in the head and shattered it. Jordan glanced down at her booted foot and patted out the flame that had ignited on the toe.

"You're getting slow, Law. That one almost got you," Portsmouth barked from where he drifted about on an antigravity platform. His gaze was unrelenting and had no compassion for the woman in his charge.

Jordan ignored her trainer and looked for her quarry. The target had leapt across to the building north of them and was disappearing into a stairwell leading down inside. Sparing a brief glance for Sergeant Portsmith, or "Old Stoney", as the team called him; Jordan leapt up and darted across the roof. She vaulted through the air towards the nearest building's roof easily.

When Jordan landed, she tucked into a roll and came up running. Her body ached all over. The weary operative wasn't certain how many hours she had been running these exercises, but it was taking a toll on her body. Every muscle hurt as the lactic acids released from so much strenuous activity overpowered her regenerative abilities. As a reminder of how long she had been at it, Jordan's stomach rumbled with hunger, a byproduct of her enhanced speed and strength. She had eaten a good breakfast as she had been instructed to, but the simulations she had been participating in had forced her to push herself hard; harder, in fact, than she had ever needed to in the field. Even the previous month's worth of training exercises hadn't required her to operate at such a high intensity level for so long.

Sudden and unexpected gunfire from Jordan's right forced her to dive forward onto the rough concrete rooftop. She slid along the ground and rolled, her weapon firing twice at a masked man wielding a sleek black American M-4 carbine. The two rounds she fired took the man just above the bulletproof vest he wore and tossed him backwards. His body lay still and unmoving, but Jordan listened intently. Normally, the sound of gunfire would temporarily deafen her, but the small sonic dampeners Jordan wore in each ear protected her sensitive hearing from the weapon's loud report. By closing down the specific decibel ranges that would rob her of hearing, they only blocked sound at the moment of the weapon's discharge. Once the offending noise was gone, they would once again open up those ranges.

The man's heartbeat was gone. He was down for good. Jordan glanced at the open stairwell where her quarry had run and decided against following him into what was most likely a trap. She holstered her pistols and reached for a three centimeter thick disc on the waist of her combat harness. The press of a thumb ejected a small metallic grappler from the side of the device and Jordan grabbed it as she ran for the edge of the roof. As she neared the edge, Jordan leapt and threw the grapple into the stone rim of the building, turning around to face the building in mid-air. The momentum of her leap carried her out several meters before she locked the grapple line with another press of the button. Immediately, she swung back towards the building, three floors down, and crashed through a window feet first.

Jordan disconnected the line and drew one of her pistols from the small of her back. The sonic dampeners also functioned as a communications link back to control, in this case Portsmouth, and the man prodded her relentlessly. "Come on, Ducky. This man has killed over two hundred people. Are you going to let him get away? Are you going to be the one that has to tell the parents of the next murdered child that *you* failed?"

"No, Sergeant," Jordan breathed and made her way to the door of the apartment building. She opened it carefully and glanced up and down the hall. It appeared clear so Jordan proceeded to head for the stairwell door.

Almost from day one Portsmouth had done everything he could to break her. The former Royal Marine was cold and made it painfully clear he bore a distinct dislike for women in any position other than serving him lunch. According to the files Jordan had been given to read, Portsmouth was one of the first operators of SOS-7 and had been an Awakened for over thirty years.

At lunch one day, Douglas had called Portsmouth "old-timer" and that seemed to fit the man's demeanor, spot on. A image of her sister, Jillian, scrunching her face up like an old man screaming "Get off my lawn, you kids!" in an American accent came to mind. That put a smile on Jordan's face.

The distraction cost Jordan. As she approached the metal stairwell door, it flew off of its hinges and slammed into her. Both she and the door landed several meters away. Jordan shoved the door off quickly, but not fast enough. Another masked man stood there dressed in BDUs, but without any weapons. He grabbed Jordan by the front of her combat harness and hauled her roughly from the floor. He continued the motion through and slammed Jordan's back into the wall hard enough to drive her body into the sheetrock, sticking her there.

The man drew back his hand to hit Jordan, but before he could strike, she lashed out with both feet and sent him through the wall across from where they stood. The explosion of sheet rock sent a cloud of chalky dust into the air that coated everything. The man was crumpled on the floor with his right shoulder bent at an odd angle, but Jordan placed one round through the man's skull just in case. She pushed herself out of the wall slowly and took a moment to try and catch her breath. It felt like she was trying to move through mud. Jordan inhaled deeply and wiped the sweat and sheetrock dust from her face.

"What are you waiting on, Law? Does her Highness need an engraved invitation? The target is getting away," Porty shouted in a demeaning tone over the comlink.

Jordan did her best to ignore Portsmouth who was, no doubt, watching her through the cameras mounted throughout the simulation area. She turned and jogged towards the stairwell, slamming up against the wall next to the door. She quickly swept the entry point above and below and focused her hearing to try and pick up any slight sound. Below her, Jordan could make out the echo of running feet growing more and more distant as their owner charged down the stairs at full speed. The sound was unexpectedly muffled by Portsmouth's haranguing in her right ear.

"Faster, dovey!" Portsmouth bellowed from behind her. "You're not tired yet, are you, Princess? I was told that you've more endurance than an elephant. I'd be disappointed if you were put out by all of this training. If you are, by all means, speak to the Director and he'll find you something more to your liking, perhaps handling documents in the file room. Is that your lower lip quivering, Law? About to cry? Show me some tears, woman, I know you want to. I know you want to run home to your mum and dad and get a hug."

The sound of the man's voice was like nails on a chalkboard. Not so much because of the sound itself, but because of the emotion it engendered in her. She wanted to strangle him, shoot him, burn him, and then shoot him again. *That's what he wants. He wants me upset and frustrated,* Jordan reminded herself.

"Are you still laying about, then? Do you want me to call it off? Your ladyship had best get going. It wouldn't do for you to not carry your share of the load, would it? Then again, if you were a proper soldier, a man, all of this would be like having a pint at the pub with your mates. I can send you home now. Do you want that, Law; a warm bed and a spot of brandy in front of the fireplace?" Portsmouth asked in a derisive tone.

Part of Jordan *did* want that, a nice fire, Brian's arms around her. It would be easy to quit. Even though Director Stevens would never let her forget it, Jordan was fairly certain she could return to her old position. Brian had offered to take care of her several times as well. He had the money to keep her in luxury and she could spend her days doing whatever she wished. The ache in Jordan's limbs only seemed to grow worse as thoughts of more pleasant things tantalized her. *No!*

The angry response immediately popped into Jordan's mind. She'd made a difference in the world. How many times had she stopped someone who wanted to detonate a bomb in a packed shopping district? Jordan remembered every mission, every target. Each terrorist, gun dealer or child trafficker she had stopped had saved an innocent life. *That's* what mattered most. The world was filled with people who couldn't defend themselves from the fanatic or the corrupt, and she was their shield. Work had never been just a job, or even a career to Jordan. It was her *calling*.

Forcefully Jordan cast away the uncertainty that her fatigued body used to batter her will. "With all due respect, Sergeant, shut the fuck up. Your blathering is interfering with my hearing," Jordan said in a surprisingly even tone. She was sure she would pay for the disrespect later, but she didn't care. There was a mission to complete.

Portsmouth unexpectedly complied and fell silent so Jordan listened intently for any indication of where her target was. The echo of the target's feet was further away, but Jordan could still hear it. She glanced down the stairwell and caught a glimpse of the man running from the fourth floor to the third.

"That's it, then," Jordan said under her breath. Without further thought, she leapt over the railing feet first. In mid-fall, Jordan pulled a larger pistol from a thigh holster and flicked off the safety with her thumb. She was dropping fast and the sound of the wind whipping past made her doubt her sanity. Fifteen floors was ten floors further than she had ever tried to go before today. The ground floor came rushing up fast and Jordan flexed her legs just as she landed. The landing was painfully jarring, but she managed to keep her feet under her. The target she was chasing came down the stairs and had a startled look on his face as he nearly ran into Jordan's raised weapon.

Jordan fired the EMP pistol without hesitation. The weapon hummed loudly as the capacitor discharged a bright blue arc of electrical energy from the weapon's barrel. The energy clawed its way over the masked man and sent him sprawling back against the stairs, unconscious and smoldering.

Jordan waited for a moment to make sure the man was down and holstered her weapon. "Viper to Control. The target is down."

The entire stairwell of the apartment building shimmered momentarily and then vanished. The hard light holograms of the squadron's Full Emersion Combat Simulator shut down as the exercise ended, leaving Jordan standing there in the vast open space that the room occupied. The room was often referred to as Never Never Land because of the wide variety of simulations that could be programmed. It could test nearly any set of Awakened abilities using a series of engagement levels. Jordan had progressed to level ten out of twelve which meant near-lethal force would be employed the by the super-computer running the exercises if the human operator so chose.

Portsmouth guided the observation platform down from near the ceiling, the anti-gravity lift humming softly. He parked the machine and stepped off of it, his tone gruff as he addressed his trainee. "Would you ever attempt that sort of stunt during a real mission, Law?"

"Yes, Sergeant," Jordan replied in a weary voice. "If that's what was needed to complete the mission."

"How did you know you wouldn't break both of your legs when you landed?"

"I didn't, Sergeant." Jordan said and shrugged

That seemed to stump the old soldier for a moment, but only for a moment. The craggy faced man scowled and stalked within inches of her. "What's it going to take, Law?" he said in voice so low that it wouldn't pass beyond where the two stood. "Hmm?"

Jordan's gaze didn't waver. "Take for what, Sergeant Portsmouth?"

"For you to throw in the towel? You know you'd rather be with your rich fiancé. All you have to do is give the word and I'll have you back home in twenty-four hours and in Moscow with Agincourt in forty-eight," Portsmouth said and angled his face so that Jordan had to look in his eyes.

"I'm fine here, Sergeant Portsmouth. I'm going to finish the program."

Portsmouth's face tightened as annoyance had its way with his patience. The older man mastered it quickly and renewed his assault on Jordan's resolve. "No doubt, a man of means like the good Ambassador will find his comfort somewhere, with someone else, if *you* aren't around. It's been done for hundreds of years with those types hasn't it?"

Jordan pulled off innocent far better than she expected. "Do you mean men, Sergeant?"

The Sergeant's cheeks reddened with anger. He hadn't been expecting that retort and Jordan's reply was authentic enough to keep him from outright calling her on it. Silence dominated the space between the two but Jordan finally broke it.

"Did you want me to run the exercise again, Sergeant?" Jordan asked.

The expression on Portsmouth's face was impossible to read, though the cold look in his eyes was easy to see. "Get to it, then, Law."

* * * * * *

Colonel Tristan Shaw stood like a statue near the long one-way window that overlooked the cavernous underground training area that Jordan and Portsmouth were in. Shaw's jaw was set and his eyes were narrowed as the external microphones relayed the conversation between Jordan and Portsmouth back to the hi-tech observation room he and Director McIntyre occupied. They had all manner of listening and sensory devices available to them so that any perspective candidate could be monitored for safety concerns as well as performance levels. Shaw watched Jordan reload her weapons as Portsmouth reset the simulator again.

Though he kept it from his face, Shaw admired the grace that seemed to permeate Jordan's every movement, the intensity of her gaze and the warmth of those rare smiles that were notably absent as she worked with Portsmouth. Jordan was exactly the type of woman with whom Shaw liked to spend time when he could find it. Smart, beautiful, confident and fearless, but still able to be soft and feminine. These sorts were rarer than a bottle of 1961 Hermitage La Chapelle and they satisfied the palate far more than the savory wine did.

Shaw felt a pang of regret that overshadowed the desire he felt for Jordan. Despite Shaw's best intentions he had grown fond of Jordan very quickly. If he had his way, she would be under his command soon enough and anything besides friendship would get in the way of business. It was also inappropriate to say the least.

"She's tough. I thought Portsmouth had her there, for a moment," McIntyre offered, breaking into Shaw's musings. The older man sat at one of the desks near a bank of monitors that displayed the training course from nearly every angle. Currently, the cameras followed Jordan's progression through the first set of obstacles, thanks to a small transponder that she wore on her equipment.

The younger man turned away from the window and gave the director a slight nod, "Yeah." Shaw didn't care that his tone sounded distinctly unhappy because it was also honest. "Portsmouth is going too far. He did this to the last female candidate and the one before that. Still, you let him just keep on with it. Why?"

McIntyre steepled his fingers and considered his response thoroughly. "Just as you and I need to be reassured that prospects can handle this job physically, mentally, and emotionally, so does Portsmouth. So does the rest of the squadron. Like it or not, most of the men respect Portsmouth's judgment of both character and capability. As the senior NCO, Portsmouth's stamp of approval carries more weight with the team than yours or even mine."

Shaw gave a slight shake of his head. The tension in his jaw made the muscles ache and the colonel's tone became sharper. "Unit cohesion, is it? Portsmouth has never liked the concept of female operatives and goes out of his way to keep them out of the running for new candidates. I don't know if his mum failed to hug him enough or if he was picked on by an older sister, but we need to select good *people,* not just good *men.* Portsmouth's outdated mentality has no place in today's world, or this unit, as far as I'm concerned."

"At the end of the day, I'm the one who signs off on Jordan Law or any other recruit. I'll take your recommendations, as well as Portsmouth's, into account. I may override them, if I choose to do so," MacIntyre replied in a tone that suggested an end to the subject's discussion. "You have six months to get Jordan mission ready, sooner, if possible."

Shaw nodded and glanced towards the monitor that showed Jordan nimbly jumping across a line of uneven wooden posts that would randomly elevate, or lower, sometimes retract entirely into the ground and do so at varying speeds. Injuries on the course the team called Buggerland were not uncommon, and the name came from one of Sergeant Douglas' observations of a worst case injury. He admired how easily Jordan traversed the course, making last moment adjustments, and using the momentum of the posts to propel her into the air or cushion her landing.

"Six months is more than enough time," Shaw observed and lifted his gaze to Director MacIntyre's. "In fact, I'd say I can get her ready in half that amount of time or less. She's already been through most of the tradecraft stuff. Her work with SIS has given her a better skillset than most of the military operations folks we've recruited. We need to focus on improving her teamwork and group timing. She likes to work solo and I've got a lot of habits to break."

MacIntyre looked down at the monitor and rubbed his chin. "Excellent. We've been getting some reports about stolen medical material from the Americans. High end kit, the sort used for bio-weapon development, or genetic engineering. Doctor Lindon believes that the type and quantity of some of the stolen materials indicate that whoever is stealing them is working on a genetics project."

"What sort of genetics project?" Colonel Shaw asked and slid into one of the nearby monitor station seats.

"Apparently, some experimental suspension medium called "Safehold Gamma" was in the last stolen shipment and Lindon feels that the only real use for it is to contain a completed genetic re-sequencing agent that uses a nano-biomechanical organism." McIntyre paused for a moment as he recalled more information. "Both the organism and Safehold were designed by the CIA's Project Divinity for their Awakened Operative program. Safehold was designed in-house by a Doctor McCreary, but the re-sequencing organism was subcontracted out to ImaGen. It's called Nintu after the Sumerian Goddess that supposedly created humanity from clay."

Shaw sat back in the chair and mulled the information over for several moments before he responded. "So, did Project Divinity succeed?"

"No. Their first creation escaped confinement and killed twenty-seven of the project's personnel including Doctor McCreary. My sources say that they terminated the project and then restarted it under the name Messiah, but entirely outsourced it to ImaGen."

"I'm going to assume we're concerned about our risks. Has analysis worked up potential targets in the U.K., yet?" Shaw asked.

McIntyre stood smoothly and buttoned his suit jacket. "They're working on it. Once they get the report to you, sit down with Lindon and assemble a list of likely targets. Divide the squadron as needed and put our people on security detail for any key shipments. I want to catch these bastards."

"Yes, sir," Shaw replied.

The Director patted Tristan's shoulder as he headed towards the door. "Good man."

CHAPTER 10

"I miss you, too, Jordan and I think a winter wedding would be perfect," Brian Agincourt said in to the speaker phone that sat on his desk.

A smile that burgeoned with warmth appeared on his face as the sincerity of Jordan's words sank in. He had no doubt that Jordan loved him. Their relationship hadn't been easy with Jordan disappearing for days or weeks at a time. Worse yet, he never knew where she was or what she was doing. She would never call, though she would send an e-mail or write once a week.

There were times when he wondered if Jordan was worth the effort it took to maintain a relationship with her. It seemed as if the entire world was determined to keep them apart and that every moment together was a gift. It was frustrating and made for many lonely nights.

Then there were the reunions.

Brian smiled fondly as he remembered the last one. Those moments were always intense physical expressions of their need for one another that would give way to more tender moments once their physical longings had been silenced. Hours of conversation followed and Jordan would ask Brian what he had been doing and he, in turn, would talk about the life he led when she wasn't there. She would evasively talk about her job using fictitious names and places to discuss her life without him. Though she would never talk about what she was doing, she would mention how frustrating Mr. Blue had been because he refused to listen to reason, or how Ms. Green was very friendly and helpful when Jordan was attempting find a seat on an airplane.

All the secrecy made Brian imagine every spy movie had ever seen or Bond book he had read. When Jordan would tell her stories, he really wondered if most of them involved being shot at or jumping from an exploding airplane in an evening gown. Despite his best efforts, Brian was unable to find out exactly what his fiancé did for the government. All his sources could ever learn is that she was a security analyst though details of what her job required were never available. He never admitted that every news story with a woman's body showing up in a ditch or park set him on edge until he heard from Jordan. Despite all the stress of the unknown when she was gone, when he and Jordan were together, life was better than it had been with anyone else.

The times between Jordan's trips were always pleasant and they would live as close an approximation to a normal life as they could. They would go to movies, take walks in the park, and go to the theatre or dinners out with Brian's friends. Jordan would make breakfast every day, or try to. He didn't have the heart to tell her that she was not a very good cook because the simple domestic tasks seemed to take away any stress she was keeping inside.

"You're sure your parents won't want me drawn and quartered? Considering your station I'd expect they would want a spring wedding," Jordan said, her voice sounding far away through the speaker phone. It carried the playful tone she employed when discussing the difficult subject of Brian's parents.

"Let me worry about them. What I want is for us to be happy. Jordan, I will show up wearing a brown sack, a clown wig, knee-deep in snow if that's what it takes to marry you," Brian said earnestly, which made Jordan laugh. He imagined how Jordan's laugh lit up her blue eyes and the way that her lips formed that pretty smile that she no doubt had on her face.

Jordan's laugh died off and her tone was even more pleased. "Though I'd pay good money to see that, I very much doubt your parents, or mine, would approve. Jill would also have it all over the internet before we could finish the ceremony. If we could get away with it, I'd run off with you and get married tomorrow."

Brian steepled his fingers and considered that. It would be a scandal to say the least. His parents would disown him for certain and the trade talks he was currently handling would collapse if he abruptly disappeared. He had spent the last few months getting to this point with the Russian Trade Commission and they would never forgive a breach of protocol like that.

"Brian, are you still there?" Jordan asked.

"I am, my love, just… considering the options."

"I was joking."

Another brief silence followed as Brian smiled picked up his tea cup. "I know. I'm not. You shouldn't toss out challenges like that without considering the consequences."

"Brian, I wouldn't put you in that position. You're very busy right now and your work needs you. Britain needs you."

"What about my poor parents' sensibilities?" Brian replied in an impish tone.

"Yes, your parents. We could send them a postcard I suppose," Jordan quipped playfully.

It was Brian's turn to laugh and though he loved his parents, he wasn't going to let their misgivings about Jordan interfere in the happiness he would have with his soon-to-be wife. After a long sip of tea Brian looked at his watch. "I hate to do this to you, but I have a meeting in thirty minutes."

The disappointment in Jordan's voice was veiled, though not very proficiently. "Alright. Call me when you're free, yeah?"

"Definitely. How about a phone dinner?" Brian replied, referencing one of their long-distance rituals.

"That sounds marvelous, Brian. I *love* you," Jordan said in a softer voice.

The words always made Brian smile and this time was no exception. "I love you, too. I'll talk to you tonight."

"Tonight," Jordan replied in a happy tone.

Brian disconnected the call and looked around the well-appointed office he sat in. The room was tastefully decorated with dark stained oak bookcases, a large black leather sofa, two matching leather and wood chairs, and, of course, his own desk, which was made out of oak as well. The desk was intricately carved and had brass fittings for the drawer handles. He kept the desk free of extraneous items and kept it to necessities. Aside from his computer, all that remained on the desk were a secure multi-line phone, a leather desk pad, and a brass-framed picture of Jordan dressed in a dark blue evening gown with Brian in a tux.

The world seemed to be back in focus now that he was off the phone with Jordan. He had all but forgotten where he was during the conversation with her. Brian studied the picture for a moment before he picked it up and traced his fingers over the image of Jordan's face.

There was a brief knock at the door before it opened and Brian's personal assistant, Lina Danvers swept in. "Sorry to bother, but it looks like the Russian delegation is going to be late."

In her early twenties, Lina was very pretty and always seemed to have an impish expression on her face. She was shorter than Jordan at five-foot-seven, but was curvaceous in a way that gave her power over most men. It was a fact that she was well aware of and regularly used. Currently, she had her long brown hair pulled into an updo that kept it from touching her collar though she had a left a long curl of hair in front of each ear to frame her face. Lina's green eyes were very bright and always inquisitive and the dark grey suit and skirt she wore made them stand out.

Brian nodded absently. "Alright."

"You were talking to Jordan, weren't you?" Lina questioned, snapping Brian from his thoughts.

"I was. How did you know?"

Lina smiled at Brian warmly and walked over to collect his tea cup. "You always look like so love struck when you're done talking to her."

Brian smiled at the image that popped into his mind. "Really?"

"Yes," Lina replied, her smile brightening as she walked over to the small tea service Brian kept off to the side of his office. She poured him a fresh cup and added honey, and placed a saucer under the cup so that Brian wouldn't damage his desk.

"I don't know if that is the most flattering thing to say to your boss," Brian quipped.

"I was saying it to my friend," Lina replied as she placed the saucer down on his desk. She tapped the saucer with the nail of her index finger. "These do wash you know. Don't be shy using them."

Brian sipped the warm tea and chuckled softly. "You're sure you're not my mum?"

Lina laughed and stepped back a pace, her hands folded in front of her. "Speaking of said mum, she wants you to call her. It's about the wedding."

The smile faded from Brian's face and he set the cup on the desk pad so he could rub the bridge of his nose. "What did she say this time?"

"Oh, the usual," Lina said and reached out to place the cup back on the saucer. "She said that 'if you must go through with the plans' she would like to meet with Jordan to discuss the details. She is having tea with Jordan's mother next week as well."

Brian sighed deeply. "Maybe things will go smoother once she and Jordan's mother get to know each other better. The woman is charming and as scandal-conscious as my mother."

"I wouldn't put money on it."

Brian exhaled, "I don't know why my mother persists with this rubbish. For God's sake, I'm almost forty. I stopped needing her permission for things a long time ago."

The young woman turned and walked back to the tea service where she began fixing herself a cup as well. "It doesn't matter how old you are. You're her son and you have appearances to think of. Brian, you should to consider your parents' position. They love you and no doubt they're concerned that you're marrying a woman who is much younger than you. A woman, may I add, who is stubborn and willful and very open with her opinions. This same woman is also gone at least six months out of the year on work-related trips."

"Alright, alright. I thought you liked Jordan?" Brian replied in a less enthusiastic tone.

"I do. I just don't think she's right for you, Brian. You deserve a woman that's going to be with you all the time. One who will be there for you every night and who will know her place when she's amongst people who care about such things," Lina said and continued to focus on making her tea.

Brian looked in Lina's direction as she moved away from the tea service to look out the window. "That's not the woman I want. I don't want someone who's going to be a good girl and keep her place. I want someone strong, someone able to command my respect as well as my love. Jordan does that. I want her there every night, but I won't ask her to give up her career for me. What we have isn't easy, but it works."

"As long as you're happy, Brian," Lina replied coolly and turned for the door. "I'll go see if Angela has gotten the agreements finished." Despite how good Lina was at putting on emotional airs when she needed to, the way she held her chin high and kept her back rigid signaled she was far from pleased. "I want to make certain everything is ready. She was having some trouble with the printer again."

"Thank you, Lina," Brian said quietly and watched Lina stride across the room. She was none too gentle with the door as she shut it with a firm thump. It wasn't the first time Brian had been on the receiving end of Lina's attitude.

Lina was as opinionated as Jordan was, even if she was better at keeping those opinions to herself. Brian had known Lina since she was eighteen and they had been friends for a few years before he and Jordan started seeing each other. The two women were similar in many respects and both of them were definitely used to being the alpha female in their respective careers. *Maybe that's the problem,* Brian considered.

Not long after he and Jordan became serious about their relationship Brian had found the women having a face to face confrontation in his office. Brian wasn't entirely certain what had transpired between the two, as neither woman would discuss it. At the time he had assumed it was because Jordan's unexpected visit had derailed the carefully planned schedule that Lina always kept for him. Brian had casually canceled all of his appointments for the day and took Jordan out on the town. It took a full three days for the icy demeanor Lina wore to melt. Brian had apologized for putting Lina in the position of explaining his sudden disappearance and it seemed to mollify her; though the subject of Jordan had been a sore point ever since. Brian shoulders slumped and he stole another look at Jordan's smiling face in the picture. "You do make me work for it, don't you, love?"

* * * * * *

Jordan smiled after she hung up the phone and pushed up onto her feet. She grimaced as she made her way over to put on a pair of black tennis shoes. Her head was still swimming after drinking far more than she ever had only a couple hours before. It took a lot of alcohol for her regeneration to be overwhelmed even for a short amount of time, but Douglas' 'family secret', a very powerful whiskey that his uncle made on his farm in Scotland, seemed to be more than up to the task. Jordan wasn't drunk anymore, but she was still buzzed and her reflexes felt like mush compared to normal.

At least she hadn't slurred her words when talking to Brian. That would have been hard to explain. Her graduation celebration had been an old fashioned pisser, an activity she didn't normally participate in, but she made an exception in order to bond with the rest of the team.

Even Doctor Lindon had been there and the alcohol appeared to sharpen his wit while doubling his quirky behavior. At one point, the good doctor had balanced a chair on its back legs and recited lines from old Doctor Who episodes while doing shots of various alcohols. He declared the activity an old college drinking game and managed to pull Chance and Deckard into it as well. Surprisingly, Lindon won by being the last man to fall off of his chair seven times in a row.

After tucking her feet into the shoes, she headed out of her room dressed in a pair of black yoga pants and a blue Scottish national football team jersey. She and Brian liked different football teams which made for very interesting days when his England Nationals were playing her Scottish. Jordan smiled as she walked down the hall towards the common room where the operational team members usually hung out.

Though it was only five in the morning in London, the SOS7 base was still generally busy. The operational team's quarters and common area was a different story. Most of the team was still in bed having been given a stand-down order by Director McIntyre so they could welcome Jordan to the team properly. Jordan took advantage of the time difference to call Brian and talk to him before his day was into full swing, but she quickly realized that she was the only person moving around. They had briefly discussed the wedding, twice on one call, and Jordan came to the conclusion she really wanted it to happen sooner rather than later. She had lots of work to do in planning and preparing for it, but she could e-mail her sisters for help in calling all of the places she wouldn't have time to ring up.

The thought of all five of her sisters working in unison made Jordan think back to the days where they were kids cleaning the house or doing dishes. Those were simple times. Good times. Their father insisted that the girls do chores even though their mother had a handful of servants to manage the estate they lived on.

Cassidy Law had come from a privileged family, as did their mother, but he grew up cleaning out stables and chopping wood. His parents knew that hard work had given their family wealth and status and encouraged it in their son. So, Cassidy had encouraged it in his girls. "Cassidy's Commandos" as one of his brothers called the six girls. He taught them to work hard for everything so they could better appreciate what they had accomplished in the end.

It hadn't prevented the occasional argument between Jordan and her sisters, but when they needed one another, the young women of the Law family came together and tackled things as a group. Jordan knew she'd need that sort of support to get her wedding taken care of, deal with all of her various cousins, uncles, aunts, and the other family members, plus all of Brian's family. She wanted to pull it off as pain-free as possible while trying to manage her career, but it was a monumental task. Jordan inhaled deeply and walked into the common area to see what sort of carnage was left over after several hours of carousing.

Inside the common area, Jordan saw Douglas with his head down on the table. More than a dozen empty bottles of hard alcohol stood around him as testament to his drinking ability. He had the endurance and resistance of twenty men, which also bestowed him with a similar alcohol tolerance. His Scottish blood seemed to serve as a multiplier for that and Douglas had managed to drink everyone under the table. Jordan remembered him escorting her to her quarters where she fell asleep for a good hour while her regeneration dealt with the alcohol. She wasn't sure where everyone else was, but was fairly certain most of them were sleeping it off still as she, Douglas, and Portsmouth were the only members of Special Operations Squad Seven with regenerative abilities or enhanced metabolisms.

Quietly, Jordan collected a wool blanket from the closet and placed it over Douglas' shoulders. The newest member of Special Operations Squadron Seven didn't bother to pick up the mess. She didn't want to wake up the former Marine, so she headed back out into the hall where she nearly ran into Briar Young.

Young smiled at Jordan like he had just won a large sum of money and the lack of focus in his eyes suggested he was still good and drunk. He also stank like a distillery. "Jordan, still up an' about I see."

Jordan grimaced as Young's alcohol laced breath hit her in the face. "You should go back to your room and sleep it off, Briar."

"When I see you, sleep is the last thing on my mind love." Briar grinned. He smiled at Jordan lubriciously and lowered his voice "What say you and I find a nice quiet place where we can chat, eh?"

"I'm not interested." She didn't wait for a reply before she attempted to step around Young and head in the direction of the cafeteria.

Young boldly grabbed Jordan's bicep and smiled at her lecherously. "Wait, now. Wait. You an' me, we should stick together, ya know? The rest of these tossers are all military. Not me. Not you," Young slurred and gestured to himself and then Jordan. "We both come from outside. We gotta, ya know, bond and shite like that. I like doin' that naked."

Jordan glanced at Briar's hand, barely checking her desire to break it. She was well aware of Briar's reputation as a womanizer, as well as his recruitment circumstances. Young had been caught after years on Interpol's most wanted list. He had attempted to steal some industrial grade diamonds that were meant for SOS7's R&D team and got caught in the act. He was given a choice to join the team or spend a couple of decades in a supermax prison for his handiwork. He was an exceptional thief, but his luck had run out. A thief needed their hands intact, however, and Jordan tried to keep that in mind. "Briar, I'm not in the mood for this. The only reason you're still standing is because you're ratted right now."

Young shoved Jordan back into the wall and glared at her with the unreasoning anger of a drunk. "You're such a little prick-tease, Law. Walkin round here lookin like that. You fucking cunt. Think you're too good fer me, huh? Think you're too good for ol' Briar Young? I've fucked nearly every bitch in this place!"

"That doesn't speak very highly for my female colleagues, does it?" Jordan retorted and pushed Briar back, moving forward two steps before she pulled her hands back from his chest.

That was the last straw for the inebriated Young. He snarled incoherently and lunged for Jordan, his fingers grasping for her throat.

Jordan sidestepped the hand and let Briar slam into the wall behind her. Young's arm folded under him and he crashed face first into the wall. The impact, combined with the alcohol, robbed him of his senses. He slid down the wall and landed on the floor a crumpled insensate mess.

Sighing, Jordan crouched down to make certain the Young was still breathing. When she saw Young's chest rising and falling she rolled him on his side and then slung him over her shoulder. She walked back into the common area and put Young on his side on one of the large couches, immediately dismissing the thought of getting a blanket for him.

Briar was part of the team, but she had no desire to do more than work with the man. Even that was most likely going to be a headache, she knew. Jordan turned on her heel and headed for the cafeteria to get breakfast. The momentary burst of adrenalin that she had when confronting Young had dispatched the lingering effects of the Douglas' 'family secret.' She was thankful for it as she had larger concerns than Briar Young's drunken display.

Jordan started working out the details of her wedding again and found them much more to her liking than Briar Young's drunken foolishness. Even though she wished she could, Jordan knew she couldn't get away with a small informal affair. *Big and ostentatious, it is,* Jordan mused and started laying out a large wedding that would satisfy her in-laws', as well as her own mother's, wishes. Although Jordan knew that Brian's mother might never consider her the right woman for her son, she would do her best to make their relationship amiable; even if that meant dealing with poufy dresses and flower arrangements.

CHAPTER 11

The sound of the gently rolling waves that the merchant vessel Dunleavy plied helped mask the powerful diesel motors that drove her through the North Atlantic Ocean at a steady nine knots. The ship was a newer-geared Handymax, in excellent condition, with a fresh coat of black paint over the majority of her hull. The bridge deck and gear, a series of four built in overhead heavy lifting cranes for unloading cargo, were painted white with red accents. The name of the vessel was carefully stenciled on her stern with the Union Jack just below it, picked out in crisp and oft-painted red, white, and blue colors. Despite the relatively young age of the cargo ship, it still had all the creaks and groans of a mass of metal plating carrying fifty-nine thousand tons of cargo.

Most of the vessel's cargo was below decks, but several rows of dark blue cargo containers the size of compact cars were secured to the deck with chains and heavy straps. These, too, added to the natural sounds of a cargo vessel, and much to Jordan's displeasure they made hearing anything else nearly useless. Her enhanced hearing picked every little sound out, which seemed to include everything from the crane cables above, to the rustling sound of the British flag flying from front of the Dunleavy. It created a massive white noise barrier that Jordan had to focus on ignoring lest it give her a headache. Thankfully, her training with Doctor Lindon had helped her adjust her hearing so that she didn't need to wear noise-dampener plugs much anymore.

Out on the ocean, the night air was refreshing and even though the vessel was noisy, Jordan had enjoyed the five day voyage on the ship. It gave her time to bond with Sergeant William Douglas, Sergeant Brady Lincoln, and Colonel Tristan

Shaw, though, as first missions went, this one was pretty uneventful. Douglas, the name which everyone chose to call him, had kept the mood light with witty jokes and well-told stories about his time in the Royal Marines. Most of the stories involved a woman, a bar fight, or some sort of prank pulled on a fellow Marine, but several were of action in Iraq.

Jordan glanced out over the water as she walked patrol with the man in question. Douglas' levity ended when it came to duty and dealing with the business of guarding their secret cargo. He was a professional and his sense of when or when not to crack wise was impeccable. Jordan found him to be a welcome relief to the monotony of a deck patrol or quiet lunch.

Lincoln was standoffish at best. He made it clear he wasn't going to buy into Jordan's skills until she had proven them on a real operation. The former SAS operator spent most of his time talking with Shaw about football or racing, his favorite sport, instead of socializing with Douglas or Jordan. Lincoln possessed amazing hand-eye coordination and was considered the team's best shooter before Jordan had arrived. She had outshot him at every turn in the kill house and on the range. The man was hyper competitive and had continued to try and beat Jordan at absolutely everything since her arrival.

Shaw was surprisingly approachable for a senior officer. He was generally a quiet man, but he was able to hold his own with Douglas when it came to charm, though his was more of what Jordan thought to be the dark and mysterious. Shaw's smile was also easy to like and very genuine. Much like Douglas, he could switch back to the serious professional at the drop of a hat.

"That's a thoughtful look," Douglas said from next to Jordan.

Jordan glanced over and presented Douglas with an enigmatic smile. "I suppose it is."

Douglas' expression flowed into one of his easy grins. "Ah, I see, thinking about that rich handsome Count of yours. That's ok. I understand. You're too overwhelmed by my presence to admit your feelings for me, so you're clinging on to that walking bank account. That's fine. Sooner or later you'll be able to come to terms with the us that could be."

Jordan's expression became playful, her eyes filling with amusement. She knew Douglas' occasional flirtations were harmless and the exchanges had become a game between the two. It helped reduce the tedium of guarding the secret cargo hidden in the Dunleavy's lower decks. "Oh, most definitely. I have spent *each* and *every* night on board thinking about you. I don't know how much longer I can hold out."

"Now, that's what I like to hear, the truth in all its glory," Douglas replied smoothly and turned to face Jordan in a clear sign that he was going to carry this game as far as he could.

The witty retort she had prepared went unspoken as an unusual, but familiar, scent caught Jordan's attention. It only took a moment for Jordan to parse the scent out from the other background aromas and immediately she remembered her early tests in Doctor Lindon's lab. "Carcharodon Carcharias," she murmured.

"What?" Douglas asked and stepped back as Jordan whirled to look towards the bow of the Dunleavy.

"Sharks. Great White sharks. I smell several," Jordan said and wrinkled her nose. She pulled the twin .45 ACP pistols from their thigh holsters and swept her gaze through the shadowed areas of the cargo containers looking for an unusual shapes or movement. "And gun oil."

Douglas brought up his Heckler and Koch UMP .45 submachine gun and held it in a ready stance without question. He, too, swept the area and looked into the arc that Jordan wasn't currently checking. "Where?" he rasped in a low voice and positioned himself to cover Jordan's back. He swept his gun from right to left, never letting Jordan leave his peripheral vision.

Jordan erupted into a blur of movement and, in one action, pushed Douglas to the side using the flat of her foot while shoving herself away hard enough to slide across the deck on her back. Both of her pistols barked out four shots above where she and Douglas had been standing, their muzzle flashes illuminating the area with angry bursts of orange and yellow light.

A large, shadowy form dropped from the ship's cargo gear. It shrugged off the large-caliber bullets as it landed on the deck in a low crouch where the two agents had been only moments before. The spent rounds were crushed and flattened from the impact against the creature's forehead and dropped to the deck with a muted clatter.

The creature was the most horrifying thing Jordan had ever seen. It stood nearly two and a half meters tall once it rose to its full height and had the sort of defined muscle that only a body builder or professional wrestler had. Its smooth wet skin was grey with white running along the underside of its snout and the front of its neck. Each hand had five webbed fingers that ended in black claws that were easily three inches long and the creature's bare feet were similarly equipped. Neither the size nor the build of thing made Jordan's fight or flight instinct kick in, it was the shark-like head that protruded from the creature's thick neck that permeated her with fear. The creature's mouth formed an unnatural grin filled with serrated triangular teeth and the cold gold-on-black eyes contained the promise of violence and death. Unlike a shark, the eyes of the monster before her gleamed with intelligence driven intent.

If the natural abilities of a humanoid shark weren't enough to strike fear in an opponent, it was also wearing a black sleeveless combat suit with accompanying equipment harness that had several grenades and other devices affixed to it. In addition, it carried a squad automatic machine gun which it gripped easily in one hand. The massive anthropomorphized great white raised the Russian made PKM squad auto in Jordan's direction with a speed that was unexpected for such a large creature and opened fire.

Still sliding, Jordan threw her feet into the air and rolled backwards onto her shoulders, using the momentum to draw her hands under her. She pushed off of the weapons she held in either hand and catapulted herself out of the line of fire just before the creatures' weapon tore a line of jagged paint scrapes where she had been.

The entire world slowed to Jordan's perceptions, as they always did when she took the mental restraints off of her enhanced reaction times. Sounds became longer and slower, and everyone else seemed to be moving in slow motion. The shark-man seemed to be moving much faster than anything that large should be able to, though not fast enough to track Jordan's line of movement.

Jordan continued her arc upwards and brought the twin pistols in line with the shark creature's head again. She squeezed the triggers of the weapons smoothly and emptied the last four shots from each weapon into its head and shoulders. The creature let out an enraged roar that Jordan could feel in her bones, but once again the copper jacketed hollow points did nothing to it.

Suddenly, the beast's chest arched up and forwards and it launched into the air. It flew as if it had been hit by a freight train running at full clip and slammed into one of the large cargo containers with a calamitous boom. The flailing creature was embedded face first at least twenty centimeters into the steel wall of the cargo container and the sounds of crunching cartilage indicated that it could be hurt with the proper amount of force.

Douglas stood where the creature had been with his right fist extended forward after his punch. "What the fuck is that?"

Jordan landed on the deck gracefully and slammed two fresh magazines home in her pistols. She shook her head and released the slide locks to chamber the first rounds in each weapon. "I don't know, but it's still moving."

The creature growled and flexed its arms to push itself free of the container's wall. Corded muscles popped loudly in chorus with the protesting metal of the container and the creature staggered back a few steps and shook its head. It wasn't uninjured by the attack, but it was far from down.

Swiftly, Jordan moved to Douglas' side with one hand raised to her throat microphone. "Viper to Lead, we've got a code black perimeter breach, some sort of large shark-human. Repeat, code black perimeter breach." Jordan frowned as no reply was given and brought her pistols up. She emptied both of the weapons in the creature's spine. The heavy bullets tore through the massive dorsal fin that jutted from its back, but couldn't penetrate the muscled flesh that it was attached to.

Douglas snapped his own weapon up and fired into the creatures' back as well, but his .45 caliber bullets had little more impact than Jordan's had. He tossed the spent submachine gun to the side after emptying the magazine and stalked towards his opponent flexing his fingers before he made them into fists.

"Fuck this. We do this the old fashioned way," Douglas said calmly and gave the creature a cocky smile as it turned to face him.

As the agent closed the distance, the shark creature swung a clawed hand at his chest, but the smaller man nimbly ducked under it. When he came up he landed a vicious uppercut against the underside of the protruding jaw, which slammed the creature back into the cargo container. Like a prize fighter, Douglas pummeled the creature in the side of the head with three more punches that drove it back into the container's wall even deeper. Without pause, the shorter man drove his fists into the creature's stomach and sides, each blow turning the muscle and cartilage beneath armored skin into jelly.

The sound of gunfire from the wheelhouse drew Jordan's attention and she saw two more of the creatures attacking the three Royal Marines that were on duty there. The marines didn't last more than a few breaths and the creatures shrugged off their bullets as easily as the first had Jordan's and Douglas'. Contemptuously, one of the attackers flung the shattered body of one of the marines through the wheelhouse window and onto the ship's cargo gear. The blaring of the ship's klaxon drowned out the automatic weapons fire that began to erupt around the ship as the captain sounded general quarters.

A painful squeal filled Jordan's ear as the sound of electronic jamming came over the ear buds she was wore. She plucked the devices from her ears and stuffed them into a pocket on her combat vest. "Douglas, we're on our own!" she yelled and turned to see how her partner was faring.

The shark creature had partially recovered from the damage that had been inflicted on it and it was currently trying to eviscerate Douglas with its claws. Wild, desperate swings replaced any sort of precision or thought that the creature had displayed. It was if instinct had kicked in and overwrote the intelligence it had previously shown. The monster was very obviously on its last legs and each swing made it fight to keep its balance. The lower jaw of the humanoid shark as off center and viscous black blood ran from the corner of its mouth. Douglas deftly jumped to the side and then landed several more jabs against the creature's torso. He backed up a few paces as the creature staggered forward and gurgled something unintelligible.

A cocky smile affixed itself to Douglas's face as he dusted his hands off. The creature fell to the deck with a thud and ceased moving, its labored breathing the only indication it was still alive. The victory was too short-lived to celebrate as a second creature vaulted off of the wheelhouse railing. The massive bestial humanoid slammed feet first into Sergeant Douglas' chest. The force of the impact drove the former Royal Marine into another cargo container and the creature pressed forward. It, too, had a PKM in its clawed hand which it swung at Douglas' head like a club. The metal and wood weapon shattered against the Scotsman's skull and sent him rolling across the deck.

Jordan dashed towards the creature before it could further press its attack; moving in from the right side, she landed a kick against its rib cage. The creature immediately lashed out with a powerful backhand that Jordan dodged by crouching and spinning with the direction of motion of the swing. She converted the momentum of her spin into a double-fisted strike under the creature's arm pit. The impact sent the creature cart wheeling away from the cargo containers howling in pain.

Douglas appeared at Jordan's side and threw a glance her direction. "See what kind of date I can put together?"

A slight smile appeared on Jordan's lips, but her blue eyes remained focused on their opponent. "Funny, Brian and I had a picnic. I think I liked it better, to be honest."

"Well then, I'll have to try harder," Douglas retorted and charged at the creature that was picking itself up from the deck where it had landed.

The creature sidestepped Douglas' charge, but failed to realize his true intentions. In mid-run the sergeant ducked low under a blow that would have caught him in the face and drove his fist into the creature's kneecap. Roaring in pain, the large monster fell to one knee and Douglas brought both hands up into the underside of his opponent's jaw. There was a sound of crushing flesh and the creature spun up into the air head over heels, flying back and over the Dunleavy's railing.

Douglas grinned at Jordan and winked playfully just as another of the attackers landed on the deck beside him, "Bugger."

The third attacker brought its hand down on Douglas' back with its full weight added to the momentum of its drop from the Dunleavy's wheelhouse. The sergeant was immediately driven to the deck and had the air forced from his lungs.

Jordan launched herself at the creature and slammed her fist into its solar plexus. The blow knocked the creature backwards, but it quickly recovered and leapt over Jordan's follow up kick, the speed and agility of it far superior to its fellows.

"I'm going to savor this, you limey bitch," the creature intoned in a bass voice, a voice that had a thick Russian accent.

Standing protectively in front of Douglas, Jordan settled into a defensive posture that kept her low to the ground, one hand in front of her and one leg stretched out behind and to the side. She tilted her head slightly looked into the black eyes of the creature. "Then, why do you smell like fear?"

The creature's mouth curled into a sneer, revealing a maw full of razor sharp teeth just before it charged at Jordan. Moving fast and sure, it led off with a bite meant to catch and hold Jordan, but it was too slow. Springing into the air, Jordan flipped up above the creature using its long nose to vault over it. She landed at its back and spun on her heel in an attempt to drive her heel into the creature's knee.

It seemed to know where her attack was going and rolled with the impact of Jordan's foot. Using its own momentum, it came around and slashed at Jordan's face with its claws, forcing her to lean back off-balance to avoid the strike. It followed up with another bite that narrowly missed Jordan's arm.

In response, Jordan threw a blinding assault of punches and kicks at the creature's head and torso, but it quickly used its arms to cover its head. With shoulders hunched, it weathered the storm of attacks like a professional boxer. As soon as it found an opening, the creature rose up out of its protective posture and struck out with its large fists. Jordan dodged three of the blows, but was forced to block another and the sheer power of it forced her to a knee in front of the beast.

It immediately brought its knee up and drove it into Jordan's head which flipped her up into the air. She tucked herself into a ball and sailed back five meters where she landed on the deck in a barely controlled crouch. Jordan used the back of her sleeve to wipe the blood from her lips and rose unsteadily to her feet. She could feel her regeneration already dealing with the damage and took a few steps back to give it time to eliminate the ringing in her head.

The creature came on with a horrific smile on its face. "Your blood smells good. I think I'll take a taste." Its voice dripped with confidence as it approached, both clawed hands opening and closing. "Too bad I don't have the time to play with you, little girl."

Without warning, Jordan jumped up and snapped her foot into the creature's elongated face. The blow's power was taken away as the creature slammed its hand into Jordan's ribs which sent her sailing through the air like a bullet. Flipping head over heels, Jordan managed to right herself well enough to strike the side of the Dunleavy's wheelhouse tower feet first which allowed her to absorb a majority of the impact by drawing her legs up beneath her.

She put one hand against the railing surrounding the wheelhouse to keep her from landing on the deck below. A sharp pain blossomed in her side, each breath making Jordan grit her teeth. Jordan knew at least two of her ribs were broken, judging by the painful grinding of bone. It would slow her down, but her body would heal it if it had the time to do so. Time was something she didn't have, however.

The third shark creature grabbed Douglas by his shoulder and used its other hand to smash the man in the face. Unlike Jordan, Douglas' body adapted to his enhanced strength not with regenerative ability and mild skeletal strengthening, but with dermal resistance and extensive micro-reinforcement of the bones using dense layering. It was the only way his body could support the extreme weights he could lift without folding in on itself. It also saved his life as the creature repeatedly landed punch after punch against Douglas's face.

Jordan sprung away from the bulkhead and launched herself at Douglas' attacker. The action caused pain to spread across her side, but Jordan ignored it as she smashed fists first into the solid flesh of the creatures' head. Staggered, the half-man, half-shark ceased its attack on Douglas and attempted to grab Jordan as she nimbly swung up on to its broad shoulders. The creature tried to grab the woman from her perch, but Jordan snapped her booted foot into the attacker's wrist to knock its grasping claws away before they could get a hold of her. In one fluid motion, Jordan drew the long-bladed commando knife from her boot as she used the creature's broad shoulders and neck like a gymnast's horse to evade its blows. Without hesitation, she stabbed the polycarbonate blade into the shark creature's eye with a fierce growl of her own. The eye itself popped like a jellied candy and the roar of pain was silenced as the blade hilted itself in the creature's brain.

Jordan hopped off of the creature's shoulders as its lifeless body crumpled to the deck with blade still protruding from its eye socket. Douglas took an unsteady step back with blood running from his nose and Jordan grabbed his arm to keep him from falling over. "Douglas, are you alright?"

"Yeah. Anyone see my teeth?" Douglas replied and shook his head to clear the stars from his vision.

"You're fine," Jordan replied quickly and looked for any more attackers. She could still hear gunfire from the stern of the boat, but none of the attackers were visible. Any further comment was held when the Dunleavy shuddered as if it had been struck by something massive from below. Jordan held onto Douglas and fought to keep her own footing while the deck pitched back and forth. The alert siren's tone changed from a combat alert to an all hands attention and a shaken unsteady voice came over the loudspeaker. "All hands, abandon ship. All hands, abandon ship. We are taking on water. I repeat, we are taking on water, all hands abandon ship."

"Shite," Douglas swore and wiped beneath his nose with the back of his sleeve. "I'm not getting in the bloody water with those things."

Jordan nodded her agreement and motioned to the creature she had killed. "It's not my preference either, but we're taking that one with us. Grab it and follow me. We're going to get the Colonel."

Douglas nodded and hefted the creature up over his shoulders in a fireman's carry which left little of Douglas' body visible beneath it. "Let's move."

The two hurried back towards the stern of the Dunleavy, which was now listing to the starboard side. The crew of the stricken vessel rushed to free the lifeboats from their mounts. Jordan and Douglas dodged past the crewman as they rushed about the deck and headed back towards the stern cargo section where Shaw was supposed to be patrolling. Jordan paused long enough to grab a fire axe from one of the fire stations mounted on the bulkhead before leading Douglas further aft.

It didn't take long to find Colonel Shaw and Sergeant Lincoln hefting a surviving marine into a life boat. Both were surprisingly unharmed, though Shaw was missing his submachine gun and his combat vest.

"Glad to see you two could make it. What's our status up front?" Shaw asked calmly.

Douglas dropped the body of the shark creature against the side wall of the ship and smirked. "I'd say we're about arse-up, Colonel."

Jordan nodded her agreement and watched the area warily for any attackers. "We took this one out and probably one other. I saw at least four."

"That means there are at least eight to ten of these bastards because there were four back here too," Lincoln said as he swung up into the lifeboat. He extended a hand down to Shaw and helped the other man aboard.

"Fuck," Douglas grunted. "And all tooled up?"

Shaw nodded, "Like an army regiment. Looked like Russian gear and some hi-tech one-offs." The Colonel nodded his chin in the direction of the body at Douglas' feet. "I managed to get one myself, but he got back up and dove over the rail."

Jordan reached down and pulled her knife out of the dead creature's head. She wiped the blackened blade off on the creature's bicep and sheathed it again. "At least we've got one to examine." Jordan paused and plucked a small black sphere the size of a golf ball off of the dead creature's combat harness, holding it up lens down for her companions to see. "They're wired."

The Colonel frowned and reached for the small camera. He examined it a moment before he pulled a small antenna off of the side of the sphere and tucked both into a pouch on his gun belt. "That's that. We'll give it to Chance and see what he can come up with."

Lincoln shouldered his UMP 45 in the high ready position and scanned the decks. He was silent as he kept vigil over the rest of the team while they loaded onto the boat.

Douglas nudged the dead creature with the toe of his boot before he grabbed it by the combat harness and slung the body up over his shoulders as if it were as light as a sack of rice. He transitioned it from the dying Dunleavy to the middle of the life boat. "I need a bigger fucking gun next time."

Shaw leaned forward and took Jordan's arm so he could haul her aboard the soon to be crowded lifeboat, "Just get in,

Douglas. I got a call out with my satcom before they jammed us. We should have backup and a ride shortly."

"Good. I don't fancy taking a swim at the moment," Jordan said and looked over the side of the lifeboat to the water that was over fifteen meters below. "What about the rest of the crew?"

Shaw pulled Douglas on board and kicked the winch control with his boot heel. The small electric motor whirred to life and started lowering the lifeboat towards the water, "They're on their own, Jordan. We've got to report this and get the body back to Lindon."

Jordan nodded in response and remained standing in the lifeboat. "I don't like the thought of letting these people die. We could take at least one or two more with us."

"It's the cost of doing business, Agent Law," Shaw replied in his command voice. His eyes were hard as he spoke. "Most of the crew got off the ship while we were fighting."

Douglas clambered over the dead creature to the back of the boat so he could unlimber the small engine attached to the stern. "What about the marines?"

Shaw shook his head and nodded to the unconscious marine that lay at the bow of the lifeboat. "He's the only survivor I could get to."

"The rest of the poor bastards were ripped apart by those things," Lincoln added and ran his fingers through his sweat soaked brown hair. The soldier's face wrinkled in disgust. "In ten years I've never seen that much blood."

Jordan moved to the marine's side and began to check him over for injury, her fingers searching for a pulse at the side of his neck after checking his torso. "It just doesn't feel right. To have all these abilities and then turn around and let people we could save be put at further risk."

"We're extracting, Jordan, period," Shaw reiterated. "This job isn't about saving twenty people when there's more at stake. We need to know who these things work for, what they are. More importantly, we need to know how they figured out that the Dunleavy was carrying a top secret cargo. I doubt they were here for the tellies packed in the deck containers."

The dark haired agent frowned and continued her check on the marine, but did so without further comment. She understood mission necessity and sacrificing the good of a few for the good of the many, but it never sat easy with her when the innocent paid that price.

Douglas took the brief pause to redirect the conversation away from the crew of the dying ship. "Jordan, how is he?"

"Pulse is thready, but he's alive. He's probably got internal injuries, though," Jordan replied.

"Hang on, brother. We're going to get you some help," Douglas said as if it were an oath. The former Royal Marine fired up the small boat's motor just as it hit the water and waited for Shaw and Lincoln to disconnect the winch cables. As soon as the last was free, Douglas gunned the engine and pulled the motor lifeboat away from the Dunleavy.

With the cables released, Shaw wearily dropped back against the dead creature's body and glanced at Jordan. "Hell of a first op, isn't it?"

"Yeah," Jordan said and held the marine's wrist in her hands so she could monitor his pulse. "We lost a lot of good people, *innocent* people. What were we carrying that was so important that these people, these *things*, would sink a ship for it?"

Shaw watched Jordan work on the marine for several moments, his gaze drifting to look back at a hard-eyed Douglas before he responded, "Awakened criminals in cryogenic stasis. Twenty seven of them, in all. I'm guessing that's why none of the life boats are being attacked. They're probably offloading the Cryopods before the Dunleavy goes under. Something definitely exploded beneath the ship, broke her spine."

"Smashing," Jordan replied in a quiet voice.

The implications for releasing criminals with abilities like she and her team possessed were staggering. Some Awakened could control minds and others could do far worse things with energy emission powers. She had read the files on the various meta-criminals that had been captured by Special Operations Squadron Seven over the years.

None of the criminals were nice people, most were more dangerous than any normal human. They had a variety of physical and energy related abilities, but one of the criminals was able to control water at a molecular level, a hydrokinetic. That one had killed several people during a bar fight by simply pulling every drop of water out of their bodies. The post-mortem pictures showed that his victims were little more than desiccated skin and bones. Lindon's notes suggested that the process was brief, but painful and it was one Jordan had no desire to experience or witness firsthand if she could help it.

"Twenty-seven?" Douglas asked incredulously. "Twenty-seven? That's a third of the bloody prison, sir. A third of what we've brought in. Where's the rest at?"

Shaw looked between his teammates. "Still locked up. The Director talked the Americans and Russians out of moving all of them at once. I'm not sure what they're doing with the

Awakened they've had in containment in Death Valley and Siberia."

"Thank god for that," Lincoln added and kept watch on the water as the small boat cut through the waves, "Why the hell weren't we told that we were moving prisoners Tristan?"

"Because it wasn't deemed the operational team needed that information," Shaw said and looked over at his long time friend.

"Fuck me. I would have wired the bastards up with a little Semtex or something if I had known. We could have fragged the lot of them *and* the blighters that just killed a platoon of our men," Lincoln responded in an irritated voice.

Shaw's tone changed, easily switching from comrade to commander. "That's enough. This isn't the first operation we've done where secrecy was the primary defense. I'm more concerned we have a leak somewhere."

Jordan watched Shaw to get a read on his mood before she pressed on. "So, where were they going?"

"A new facility in the Arctic that is designed to hold Awakened beings. It's a Supermax called The Block. It was built by us, the Americans, and the Russians. It's supposed to be the most secure prison on the planet and is just as hard to break into as out of," Shaw said and looked Jordan in the eye.

"Hopefully, the fucking thing isn't underwater," Douglas retorted angrily. "It isn't underwater, is it?"

Shaw glanced back over his shoulder at Douglas and shook his head. "I don't know. I haven't seen the specs. Murphy being the bastard that he is…" he let that thought trail off ominously.

"Brilliant, just brilliant," Jordan replied and looked in Shaw's direction. There was a popping sound as her ribs knitted themselves back together and Jordan's expression tightened.

All three men looked at Jordan curiously, but Lincoln was the first to speak. "What the hell was that?"

Jordan placed her free hand along her side to make certain that everything was back where it should be. If it wasn't she would have to re-break them and reposition them so they would heal properly. "My ribs. They feel much better now, if you can believe it."

Douglas smiled wearily. "That's handy. My head still feels like it was tap danced on by Godzilla."

The sound of protesting steel and bubbling water drew the three operative's attention away from one another to where the merchant vessel Dunleavy was living out her last moments. The large vessel finally broke in two and spilled numerous cargo containers into the water where they quickly sunk below the waves. The front of the ship disappeared first, but was quickly followed by the shattered stern leaving only the swirling down current of water to mark its passing. The remaining crew crowded into three lifeboats watched long-faced as their livelihoods, and several of the men they called brothers, vanished into depths of the sea. Their profession wasn't a forgiving one, but what had happened on the Dunleavy was a nightmare.

The sounds of weeping and terrified murmurs carried to where Jordan sat in the bow of the lifeboat. The men were afraid that whatever had attacked them would come back and finish what they had started and Jordan had to admit that she was wondering much the same. She couldn't make out the men's faces from where she was, but could hear the growing panic in their voices. She didn't know what she could do to make them any safer at the moment, but she could reassure the men that help was on the way, and perhaps see to any wounded that had amongst them. Jordan glanced at the others briefly before motioned to the three boats that floated one hundred meters away. "Douglas, take us over there. We still have work to do."

CHAPTER 12

The video replayed itself for a third time, though the same expression of interest remained on Konstantin Tretyak's face as he reclined in a large black leather chair. State of the art technology that rendered the video in high definition also digitally enhanced it so that night was turned into day with all of its vivid colors. Tretyak thumbed the rewind button on the remote he held in his left hand to back up the video again and watched the image of the lovely dark-haired woman springing off the bulkhead of the M/V Dunleavy towards one of his men. She was lost in a flurry of motion as she moved to where the tactical camera couldn't see her, so Tretyak switched the feed and watched the same replay from a different angle that was further back and slightly above the fight between his Vodnik soldiers and the unknown operatives. The woman gracefully swung around the body of his soldier and landed on his shoulders, kicking his wrist to keep from being grabbed. Almost too fast to follow, she drew a blade from her boot and drove it into his soldier's eye and the brain behind it, killing him instantly.

"I couldn't help Misha before that bitch killed him and Dimitri looked dead, too. I thought it best that we carry out the mission so I went to oversee team two," a voice said in Russian from behind Tretyak.

There was a hint of worry in the voice that the speaker tried to conceal, but to Tretyak's senses, nothing remained hidden. He could smell the fear that permeated the room. The anxiety tasted bitter and caused Tretyak to frown unconsciously. His thumb pressed another button on the remote which changed the feed back to the original camera which was then paused on a shot of the woman's face. Her dark hair partially obscured her features but there was no doubting her beauty. The woman's blue eyes were radiant like the waters of the Caribbean.

"What you thought was best was that you save your own skin, Arkadi," Tretyak said matter-of-factly and turned the chair he sat in to the side so he could see his lieutenant's face.

Arkadi Maelyev stood stiffly with his hands behind his back and scowl on his face. He was the same age as Tretyak, nearly fifty, but, like his master, he appeared to be in his late twenties. Arkadi stood a full three inches shorter than Tretyak himself, but his body was much bulkier and the three-thousand-dollar suit he wore did nothing to hide his size. His features were very angular and reminded Tretyak of a stone gargoyle hanging from some old European building, though with far less humor. Arkadi shaved his head, which only added to his fearsome presence and the lack of compassion in his dark brown eyes made most people instantly fearful of him.

Arkadi started to respond to the accusation, but Tretyak fixed him with a meaningful look that suggested that he was not done speaking.

"What has happened has happened, brother. Though I am certain you're asking what you can do to give Misha's death meaning. I applaud you for that," Tretyak said and rose to his feet. "Find out who this woman is. Find out who her people are; who these operatives are."

Arkadi smiled viciously and watched Tretyak's eyes. "I ask that you allow *me* to be the one to kill her. I'll make it slow. I'll make sure she begs before she dies. A life for a life." The man's voice filled with bloodthirsty eagerness as he imagined what he would do to the dark haired woman on the video.

"No," Tretyak replied calmly. "A life for a life, yes, but she will undergo the process. She'll be one of us, part of the Vodnik."

Tretyak's lieutenant's features twisted into a mask of disbelief. "You're planning on giving her the gift? Why? Because you want to fuck her? Konstantin, let me bring her in, take what you want from her and let me slit her throat. Be done with it! We don't need this woman in the Vodnik."

"Afraid of some new blood? Think of what someone like her would become with my power coursing through her veins. She already has the look of a hunter in her eye and she's got exceptional abilities of her own. Not to mention the information she may have about whatever organization she works for. You know that once she's is one of us that she will deny me nothing," Tretyak replied with more emotion in his voice than was normal.

Arkadi frowned in disgust as he watched his longtime friend. "You've let Americans join us, British, Frenchmen, Africans, and now a woman? I remember when this organization was a brotherhood. Soldiers from Russia, all blooded against our enemies. No women, no fucking foreigners. Weak blood will yield nothing!"

The reaction from Tretyak was swift and entirely un-telegraphed. The large man hadn't batted an eye, or tensed before he exploded into action and closed the gap between Arkadi and himself. In an instant Tretyak had gone from sitting to hoisting his subordinate by the throat lifting him half a meter into the air. "Weakness? You speak of weakness, but why is it that you returned without two of our own? Hmm? Dimitri made it to the extraction point on his by himself. Half-alive." Tretyak's voice was cool, business like, but low and dangerous.

"You're afraid of this woman, this weak woman? Why didn't you bring me her head and the heads of her associates? Do not speak to me of weak blood, Arkadi. Do not speak to me of it." Tretyak dropped Arkadi unceremoniously to the floor, the power of his presence filling the entire room. "Do as I say and keep your place as my lieutenant. Prove to me that you still have value."

The scent of fear and rage mixed in the air around Arkadi as he picked himself off of the floor and stepped away from his boss. Tretyak's displeasure was thick in his scent and the smell of it was like burning gunpowder. It was obvious he had gone too far and his next actions would either shorten or extend his life. Without meeting Tretyak's gaze, Arkadi nodded and then exited the room leaving a scent trail of capitulation in his wake.

The man known as the Crimson Shark stared in the direction of the doorway that his lieutenant, and friend, had passed through. He pushed his will out through the entire Los Angeles compound that Vodnik used as their American headquarters and touched the minds of each of his men. He felt a sense of satisfaction as the empathic waves from his followers flowed back to him in the form of emanations of loyalty and solidarity. They were his brothers as much as they were his children.

Emotions were a luxury that Tretyak seldom indulged in, but he allowed himself to do so now. The death of one his men and this blue eyed woman had stirred a riptide of emotional energy inside him that required attention instead of dismissal. As he read the empathic current of his men, he sensed the grief and anger corresponding to Misha's death. They were all brothers.

Withdrawing from the tumultuous pool of emotion, Tretyak returned to his chair and sat back in it. He let his dark eyes focus on the woman's features and her intense blue eyes. She enjoyed the thrill of the fight, the moment where life could turn into death in the span of a breath. This was a creature worth any expense to possess, though already the price had been high.

Tretyak pulled his phone from inside his suit pocket and dialed a number. Almost immediately an elderly woman's voice answered. Tretyak allowed himself a moment of compassion, an unusual flavor of emotion but at times it was as proper as any other. "Aunt Galena. Misha is gone."

* * * * * *

Jordan made her way across the state of the art briefing room, only glancing at the monitors briefly as she took her seat next to Sergeant Douglas. Most of the large high definition screens showed the salvage operation that was underway where the M/V Dunleavy sank, though one was playing Lindon's autopsy on the humanoid shark that they had brought back, and another had the BBC News Channel and CNN on split screen. The volume was muted and both of the news agencies were showing still pictures of a sister ship of the Dunleavy so that viewers would understand what sort of vessel she was. The news helicopters had been restricted from the area and currently there was a five mile security zone around the ship's grave. The captions speculated that the attack was terrorism-related, though the official story had yet to be released. Jordan suspected that an accident would be blamed for it.

"Sea mine," Douglas said and glanced at Jordan with a smile.

"How did you know I was thinking that?" Jordan's expression turned wary

"I didn't," Douglas said and sipped his coffee. "Or did I?" The man's eyes widened and he tilted his head back in a way that reminded Jordan of some nefarious villain out of an old black and white movie.

Jordan snickered and shook her head lightly. "Though you are a man of many talents, Douglas, I don't believe mind reading is one of them."

"Yet, love, yet," Douglas retorted and smiled broadly at Jordan.

Any further banter was put aside as the rest of the team filtered in and took what Jordan had learned were their usual seats. Shaw and McIntyre moved to the front of the room. Portsmouth took up position off to the side near the door, his arms folded and he looked as grim, as usual. Shaw collected a remote from the metal and wood office table at the front of the room and moved to stand near Portsmouth to give the director the floor.

McIntyre nodded to Shaw, who pressed a few buttons on the remote to switch the screens' images to headshots of the shark creature on one screen, another displaying the names and faces of the twenty-seven cryogenically frozen prisoners.

"Gentleman and lady," McIntyre began in a business-like voice and swept his gaze over the eight members of Special Operations Squadron Seven. He made eye contact with each member of his team before continuing with the briefing. "We'll cut to the chase on this one. We have lost possession of twenty-seven exceptionally dangerous Awakened humans. A full platoon of Marines sacrificed their lives, save one; as did six crewmen from the merchant vessel Dunleavy, including her captain and first officer."

The team watched the Director in silence and Jordan noted that all of them had serious expressions as they absorbed the data. The members of the team who weren't on the operation were just finding out what had happened and they, much like those who were on it, were not pleased. Being reminded of the lost lives quickly doused the good humor she was feeling from bantering with Douglas. Jordan's expression hardened as she reminded herself that every lost life was a brother, or son, or husband.

McIntyre let his words sink in for several moments before he continued on. "The attackers, by all reports, were beings like this." The Director swept his arm towards the screen that showed the shark-like visage of the creature that Jordan had killed minus one eye. "They were highly organized and armed, as well as carrying state of the art equipment. Initial investigation shows that they boarded the ship in two teams of four, one bow and one stern. They proceeded to eliminate the marine sentries and attempted to kill Colonel Shaw, Sergeant Lincoln, Agent Law, and Sergeant Douglas. They failed."

Again McIntyre let his team absorb the intelligence data before proceeding. "They then split into two-man elements and took the wheelhouse, engineering, and the fore and aft decks. Once their element of surprise was ruined they used a controlled spectrum electronic warfare device to jam all local communications. Colonel Shaw was fortunate to get a single code black transmission out prior to the jamming."

Jordan re-crossed her legs as she gave Shaw a slight nod. His code black, a warning that they had engaged metabeing threat forces, quite probably saved their lives. No doubt whomever was jamming their communications had detected it and accelerated their timetable which meant cleaning up survivors wasn't an option if they wanted to get away with the prisoners.

"During the engagement, Agent Law and Sergeant Douglas were able to kill a single attacker, as well as recover the body for examination. Leftenant Shaw has run a preliminary check on the captured equipment. Leftenant?" The Director looked in the direction of Colonel Shaw's younger brother, Leftenant Eric Shaw, whom everyone called Chance for his well-known love of gambling, as well as his unconscious ability to manipulate probabilities.

His ability was rare. In fact, he was the only one known to possess it in the world. During her training, Jordan made the mistake of playing a game of darts with Chance and had lost miserably. It seemed Chance's power allowed him to seldom miss and encouraged Jordan to miss the mark at every opportunity.

The handsome blonde man stood up and walked to the front of the room with an orange plastic tray the size of a large pizza box in his hands. Chance took a moment to smooth his black BDUs before he addressed the room. The realm of technology was his specialty and he very clearly enjoyed speaking about it if the enthusiasm in his voice was any indicator. "I pulled all the good bits out of our friend's kit and tore into them." He proceeded to pull out several items and placed them on a table near the front of the room. Chance held up the first which was the small black sphere that Jordan had plucked off of the creature's combat harness. "This is a custom job, an image enhancing digital wireless video camera with multi-spectral capabilities. It has fifty-times zoom with high speed capture. There's no onboard storage memory and it has a scrambled signal, so it isn't easy to hack. Fortunately, it's short-ranged and anyone watching would have had to have been within a kilometer or less."

The team all focused on taking notes about the device, most using paper and pen, though the team's breaking and entering specialist, Briar Young, used a secure PDA to capture the data. Chance continued on before any questions could be asked. "Sat recon of the area shows that there were no surface craft within three klicks of the Dunleavy, so that means our boys were probably using a sub."

He placed the spherical camera back on the table and picked up a small black MP3 player sized device that had only two black buttons on its face positioned one above the other. "This is the most unusual piece of gear in the whole set, to be honest. It's an electromagnetic halo field."

"A what?" the team's Executive Officer, Othello Laird, asked. Laird was a dark-skinned man of African ancestry who spoke with a very pronounced Londoner accent. He, like the rest of the team, was dressed in simple black BDUs with a black t-shirt beneath.

"For the slow kids in class, it's a force field of sorts," Chance replied with a cheeky grin. He held up the device in his left hand and held the index finger of his right hand over the top button. "This is on and the other is off. My guess is that this little trinket is designed to hide our friends from electromagnetic detection, as well as protect their senses against any sort of EM spikes, such as jamming. They, being sharks and all, probably have very advanced electromagnetic sensory organs, though I'll let Doc Lindon speak to that. Anyways, it had biometric data in the memory, so my opinion is that each one of these has to be calibrated for a specific individual's bio-electric field."

Jordan considered the expense and technical skill required to build these sorts of devices, especially the EM halo. Whoever had funded these people had immense resources or, at the very least, someone who was exceptionally talented in making small equipment. "Leftenant, are any of the components in their devices rare or off the shelf?"

Chance grinned broadly and pointed at Jordan, "Gold star for the lady. I've found three off the shelf chips of identical make: one in the camera, one in the halo, and one in this last object of interest." He set down the halo device and picked up a silver cylinder the size of a three-cell flashlight, though it was rounded on one side and flat on the other. "This is a data transmitter. Plug and play, of course."

Briar Young snickered and looked in Jordan's direction. "Doesn't look like any transmitter I've seen. I think we should look to Jordan for her expertise on that particular sort of object."

Jeff Deckard, the red haired communications and cryptography specialist of the team, shook his head slightly. Deckard was in his late twenties and was a former Royal Navy sonar operator. With the ability to naturally detect high and low frequency sounds, as well as ultrasound and high and low band radio frequencies, Jeff Deckard was a natural choice for an organization that needed to eavesdrop at a moment's notice.

Deckard's expertise was such that he knew of nearly every sort of radio, transmitter or receiver that was in use by the major governments and civilian entities of the world. His deep voice couldn't hide the annoyance he was feeling after Briar's rude comment. Deckard was also referred to as the team gentleman and he insisted on holding doors open for Jordan and the female support staff, as well as treating them with the utmost respect. "I'll save her the trouble. That's a spike. Plug it in to your source and it automatically downloads all the data it can in the shortest amount of time possible. Judging by the size and dimensions it's also hitting a satellite when it's transferring data."

"Oh, I'm certain Jordan could use it for that, too, if needs be," Briar retorted and gave Jordan salacious leer.

"Young," Shaw snapped impatiently from where he stood in the front of the room. "Shut up and let Deckard finish."

Deckard continued on as if he had never heard the reply from Young. "I've seen that model before. MI6 recovered a device like that from the HMS Illustrious security breach last year. The color is different, but the size and external configuration match. The components were traced to an electronics manufacturer in China, if I remember correctly."

Chance inclined his head towards Deckard and sat the spike down in the tray, "Another gold star. This, however, is not that device. In fact, I'd say the other device was a knock off of this model. Everything inside this is state of the art and quality made. In addition, all of this gear is waterproof and pressure resistant. I'm not sure of the depth yet, but if I had to guess I'd say about four hundred meters, maybe five hundred."

With his hands now free Chance gestured towards the image of the shark creature on the screen. "The rest of the gear our friend here is carrying is from all over the world. American grenades, Russian ammunition and weapons, and the dive watch is an Omega Seamaster on a modified band. Chunky wrists, that one."

"Young, see if you can get anything off of the gear," Shaw said after his brother paused to take a breath.

Briar nodded his response and rose from his seat. The former thief swaggered from where he sat over to the table where the equipment was and took his time doing so. He selected the spherical camera first and held it cupped in both hands. After taking a deep breath, Young's eyes closed and his expression turned serene.

Jordan hadn't seen Young use his abilities yet and watched him work with interest. According to the squadron's files psychometry, or object reading, wasn't a rare ability. Those with the gift could 'read' an object's history and gain glimpses into people and events that it had recently been a part of. Without the will to focus the images it was just an assault of sound and imagery that made about as much sense as puzzle pieces scattered all over a table.

An average Reader could only go back a few hours into the object's past; though Young's file indicated he could reach back as far as three days. This set him apart from most and gave the team a powerful tool that went beyond standard intelligence gathering practices. Jordan supposed it was also why his near criminal behavior was tolerated by Director McIntyre. No matter how useful Young was, Jordan didn't care for him at all. Her skin crawled almost anytime he was looking at her, and after Young's drunken attempt to assault her, Jordan wanted to put a bullet in him.

Several minutes passed before Young's blue eyes opened. "We're in the shite now, boys and girls."

The quiet chatter that had started amongst some of the team abruptly stopped and silence pervaded the room. Portsmouth and Shaw both turned their full attention to Young.

"Let's hear it," Portsmouth ordered.

Young sat the camera sphere down slowly, "One second, old duff. I've only just started on this kit." The former thief's tone suggested that he enjoyed being able to give orders to the people who had effectively press-ganged him into working for him. "I better read the rest of it before I give any details. I wouldn't want to be accused of being sloppy, now would I?"

Portsmouth started to say something but a look from Shaw silenced him. The latter nodded towards Briar. "How long do you need, Briar?"

"Not long, Colonel, a few more minutes at most."

Shaw nodded his approval and Briar immediately got back to work. This time the room remained uncomfortably silent as the team put their full attention on Briar Young. The man went from object to object, holding each for no more than a couple minutes before moving on to the next. Eventually, he sat down the last piece, the thick banded dive watch, and then walked over to pour himself a cup of water from a pitcher sitting on a side table. He tossed the contents of the cup back and refilled it before making his way back to the front of the room. "Alright, then. So, these guys are some sort of merc unit. Everyone I saw was Russian and they were all able to turn into those things."

"How many are there?" Portsmouth asked.

"I don't know. I saw a lot, maybe thirty, maybe forty. The crew that they used to hit the Dunleavy was about twenty strong."

"Did you get any names?" Jordan asked in a curious tone.

"A few. Just first names or nicks. Some guy named Arkadi was in charge. Mean looking bloke. He looked a lot like Zidane from Real Madrid but bald," Briar replied.

Jordan pictured the retired French footballer in her mind and filed the image away for later use. "Did they use any ranks?"

"They referred to someone called the Colonel, but I never saw him."

"How did they get into the area? Swim?" That was Laird.

"They had a sub. Fancy thing, too, probably a Russian fast attack, but then again I've never been into black-market arms dealing. Too much danger and not enough reward." Young smiled.

Lincoln's brow furrowed. "They'd have to have massive backing to run one of those. The maintenance costs alone would be prohibitive."

"Unless they rented it," Jordan countered. "I was on a mission for MI about a year ago and we took down a former Soviet General who was renting MI-28 attack helicopters to drug lords. It's possible we have a sub captain who's started up a side business."

"It could be a Russian operation," Lincoln offered and looked towards Shaw. "They've been trying to break the genetic locks on Awakened for decades. Maybe they needed test subjects?"

Portsmouth spoke up from where he stood near the wall, "They have their own prisoners to experiment on. There's no reason to risk an international incident to get a few more."

Shaw mulled over the information as his team put out their perspectives. They needed more to go off of and at this point Briar's divinations were the most likely to give them something actionable. "Briar did you get anything that would help us determine a location? Any phone numbers, addresses, e-mail addresses?"

"Not a thing, Colonel. I was only able to get a couple of days; and aside from the watch most of the gear was stowed. They just sat around playing cards and talking about women and sports. Just like you lot do," Briar replied ever keen to distance himself from being part of the team.

"Bullshit," Portsmouth rumbled. "*We* talk about a lot more than that while we're waiting for an op to kick off. You better not be holding out again, Young."

Young played it cool and shrugged, "Not at all, duffer. My Russian isn't that good so maybe I missed something."

"You didn't say they were speaking in Russian the entire time," Jordan noted.

"An oversight love, nothing more," Young said in a casual tone.

Portsmouth wasn't having any of it and took a step towards Young. "You're full of shit, Young. You were warned about playing games and holding back information."

Shaw placed a restraining hand on Portsmith's shoulder; though it was the stern looking Director MacIntyre that spoke. "Out with it."

The words were a command not a request and Briar took them for what they were. Now that Portsmouth was angry, Young didn't bother to keep up the pretense that he didn't have more information to offer; though he didn't admit to holding something back either. "Some of them had identical tattoos. Not prison stuff but quality ink."

Now that something tangible and actionable was offered, Chance spoke up. He enjoyed information gathering and had built a huge database over the years. Information was as much his field of battle as a jungle or desert. "What did it look like?"

"It was black shark with arms and legs holding a small shovel in one hand and trident in the other. There was something in Cyrillic written below it, but I couldn't make it out."

"Sounds like they're Spetsnaz to me," Jordan concluded. The shovel was a dead giveaway. Russian Spetsnaz teams were widely known for carrying the compact and deadly weapon and it had reached almost mythic proportions in movies. It was well-balanced with sharpened edges so it could be used for throwing or hand-to-hand combat. In the hands of highly trained operators like the Spetsnaz, it was more dangerous than any knife.

"Spetsnaz that turn into giant sharkmen? That's just perfect." Douglas chuckled.

The door to the room opened and Doctor Lindon strode in like he owned the room. He nodded to the team and took the remote from Shaw's hand as he made his way to the front of the where the table of captured equipment sat. If he noticed any of the tension between the command staff and Briar Young, he didn't acknowledge it. "Sorry I'm late. I had to put our lad back in cold storage to keep him from stinking up the place."

Young and Chance exchanged looks and returned to their seats. The force of nature that was Doctor Lindon just continued on like he had been in the room the entire time.

Lindon brought up several new images of his patient, most showing what appeared to be organs, though there were pictures of the creature's claws and teeth as well. "Now, our subject here is most definitely an Awakened human. Age is undeterminable due to Delta-level regenerative abilities. However, what I have determined, and this is a most amazing thing, is that this being didn't start life Awakened. In fact, there are clear signs of genetic alteration at the cellular level recently. I'd say less than three years. A near-complete rewriting of his genetic code sequences to make him into this powerful creature."

Director McIntyre's eyes widened at Lindon's revelation. "Someone's cracked it? They've figured out how to make a stable Awakened human?"

Lindon slammed his hands down on the table which created a loud clatter as the devices in the plastic tray bounced around its interior. The smile on the doctor's face was like a child finding out he got his fondest desire for Christmas. "Yes! It's spectacular, isn't it? Bloody spectacular!"

The surprised looks on the faces of the team did nothing to comfort Jordan in the least. She knew well from Doctor Lindon's lessons that artificially Awakening humans had met with disastrous results in every known example. The thought that someone was making people into these half-human, half-shark monstrosities made her blood run cold. Combining one of nature's perfect predators with a human's adaptability and intelligence was courting disaster.

The Director's expression was dark and Jordan felt sympathy for the man. He would have to deliver this dire news to his superiors, as well as his counterparts in allied organizations. No world power would be pleased to learn that these sharkmen were out there and reproducing. The ramifications of Lindon's discovery were staggering. If one world power had broken the genetic code behind creating an Awakened human it would only be a matter of time before others did. The result would most likely be an arms race that would make the threat of nuclear apocalypse appealing. Jordan imagined the damage that could be caused by an army of Awakened and it made her inwardly cringe.

At the front of the room, Lindon continued without missing a beat "Our fine lad here was not confined to just this form. No. Not at all! The genetics indicate that he could also, in all likelihood, take on a full shark form, and perhaps intermediary forms between human and shark. He's a very complex being, this is a true metamorph. In fact, if Jordan hadn't driven a knife into the area where the subject's pituitary gland resides, I'd say he would have reverted to his human form." Lindon pulled up a series of brains scans on the central monitor and grinned like child with a new toy.

Each image was rendered in a series of blues going from very dark to very light which helped separate sections of the brain on the image. Using the laser pointer built into the remote, he circled an area on a side view image. "See here. This is the pituitary gland. Notice how overdeveloped it is. This black gash here is where Jordan's blade struck home. It's unfortunate that most of this section was destroyed as it was an entirely unique gland."

"Unfortunate, Doc? This thing was using me like a speedbag when she did that," Douglas said in a disbelieving voice.

Doctor Lindon tilted his head back to look at Douglas appraisingly. "My dear, Sergeant Douglas, you have a very hard head and your looks seem none the worse for it. We're talking about an incredible loss to science. Not your looks, of course."

Most of the team broke into subdued laughter at the comment which only intensified as Douglas held out his arms and looked at Lindon dumbfounded. Jordan reached over to pat Douglas' shoulder comfortingly. "Could be worse, love. You could look like one of those creatures."

"Why, Jordan, that is an excellent segue! Yes, Sergeant Douglas, you *could* very well look like one of these creatures. I've determined that the alterations were brought on by a very complex virus. The samples I took show an amazing resilience and aggressiveness. Ingestion of the man's blood in a significant amount, say a mouthful, would be sufficient to initiate the transformation of your genetic code. I'll need to run more tests before I can be certain of the stability of such a transformation. The end result would be the ability to transform one's self into a Homo Sapiens Carcharias," Lindon said and looked directly at Douglas, moving his head to one side and then the other as if he were visualizing the changes that would occur in that instance.

"You would gain the ability to function at great depths, swim at incredible speeds, and smell a single drop of blood in an ocean of water, massive strength increases, as well as what I believe is the ability to see in the electromagnetic spectrum. The ability is much like sonar imaging I would guess; though I'll need more time to sort that bit out." Lindon pointed the laser pointer at an organ that was attached to the frontal lobe of the subject's brain. "This is it. My initial examination suggests that this functions like a very advanced electroreceptor. It is very complex in nature and is layered like the human brain."

"So, they can see all around them, then?" Jordan asked and sat forward in her seat. "In total darkness, as well?"

The doctor's tone was foreboding as he replied to Jordan. "Yes, my dear. These beings are quite possibly the most dangerous species on the planet to date. Physically, they surpass humanity on every level, and mentally they are on par. Simply put, they are an apex predator on both land and sea. I'd daresay finding the source creature is vital."

Jordan raised an eyebrow and watched Lindon's face, the dark look in his eyes worrisome. "Source creature?"

"Source creature. Person. The being that was born with these abilities naturally and has learned that they can pass them on. I'd say it's as important as locating these missing stocks of genetic material, the prisoners, the medical equipment. Yes, indeed. One could cause all sorts of trouble with an army of these creatures. Especially if they carried forward any existing Awakened abilities," Lindon replied and placed his hands on the table looking very weary as he often did after one of his excited expositions. "It could mean the end of humanity, or the beginning of a *new* humanity."

CHAPTER 13

Doctor Elgen Spears smiled in satisfaction as the floating wireframe image before him erupted in flashes of blue and green energy. The construct highlighted his face as well as deepened the shadows, giving his face a diabolical appearance. The room he worked in was kept dark except for the tactile holographic models, which he manipulated through hand gestures and vocal commands to his laboratory's central A.I.

He swept his hand from right to left and the image slowly spun in midair so he could get a look at the complex helical DNA strand that floated in front of him from a different angle. The rhythmic sounds of string symphony played *adagio* in the background as Spears worked, the slow mournful notes making him long for home as they always did. He dismissed the thought of returning home, just as he had so many times before. Home was lost to him. He was in the process of creating a new home and, some day, he would not only live there, but rule.

"Infusing compound gamma twelve, series three hundred three," a woman's voice replied. Though the voice was digitized, a normal human would never be able to discern that it was anything but a real woman. The advanced technology that allowed the computer's artificial intelligence to speak ensured that there was a less than one tenth of one percent variance from human vocal patterns, including inflections and emotional depth. It actually bore the same warmth as a human voice, thanks to complex subroutines that Spears himself had written. "Infusion in progress, Doctor Spears. Subject is currently stable."

As the compound wound its way through the test subject's body, the wireframe model of his DNA was once again surging with the array of blues and greens. "Adjust protein sensor, gain point three eight percent and continue the infusion," Spears commanded and studied the helical DNA sequence.

The Doctor's hand made a pulling motion and twisted which caused the wireframe to pull in closer and turn horizontally. He quickly touched four of the base pairs which caused their structures to turn red. He tapped each one in sequence and then reached to the side with his left hand. He made a grabbing motion and pulled a set of purple highlighted base pairs from another wireframe DNA sequence that floated off to his left. Spears then brought both hands up and twisted them until the DNA sequences aligned and overlapped one another. Suddenly, both of the sets of highlighted base pairs begun to flash at varying rates, almost as if they were battling one another for supremacy.

"Overwrite primary sequence," Spears intoned.

The voice replied in a tone that held excitement, "Overwriting."

Spears' eyes narrowed as he watched the new base pairs adhere to the subject's DNA and merge with the old set of pairs. A small amber digital clock appeared to the right of the DNA model and counted not only hours and minutes, but seconds and milliseconds. Time sped by on the small clock and Spears drew a circle in the air around the DNA sequence in front of him with a flourish. The music playing in the background often made him feel as if he were conducting a symphony during his experiments. It occurred to him that something with Tympanis and a horn section seemed more appropriate. These weren't waltzes, the challenges of this particular series of experiments were epic battles and deserved powerful accompaniment. "Show replication rate. Play something by Holtz, *Mars* from *The Planets*."

"Displaying replication mapping," the computer's voice replied and to the left of the DNA's wireframe a map of the genetic structure of a human male sprung to life. The complex map showed a dense field of small blue dots that represented the genetic code of the test subject with the recently infused area flashing in purple at the base of the human shaped wireframe's neck. The biological data for the subject such as identification number, age, height, weight, known relatives, and such floated just to the left of the map. Below that, the subject's current heart rate, bioelectric production level, and other real-time biological data hovered. Currently, it was all green.

Spears reached up and made a clawing motion over the subject's biographical data, then gestured as if he were tossing it away like an empty soda can. The data folded in on itself and spun off to the side of the room in which Spears worked. It was pulled into a series of floating rings that represented the data trash bin where it waited to be recalled or deleted. He narrowed his eyes and brought up both hands in front of him, outstretched as if he were projecting a ray of power from his palms. Spears crooked his fingers into claws and then made a motion like he was violently parting a curtain. "Take me in!"

The room exploded in brilliant colors; reds, purples, blues and greens, and Doctor Spears' body was suddenly enveloped in the computer model that had been floating in front of him moments before. A look of near mania appeared on his face as he watched the representations of his test subject's body fight against the genetic changes that were being forced upon it.

Not far away in the test lab, the subject's body writhed in agony despite the powerful sedatives it had been given. Spears couldn't care less. The pain experienced by his test subjects meant nothing to him. Spears had decided long ago that he would use as many subjects as he needed. The rapid reproduction rates of humans meant he would never want for test subjects. Procuring them was simple enough. A few thousand dollars in the hands of the right third world general, or dictator, and he would have fifty subjects to work on. A million and he had a private lab complete with government supplied soldiers to guard it. The thought of humanity's willingness to perform tricks for worthless paper or coin brought a smile to Spears' face. Only a few members of the species really understood what true power was: the ability to create, destroy, and control.

The geneticist closed his eyes and basked in the light of the holomodel. The pounding, martial rhythm of Holtz filled the air of the room with the thunder of timpani drums, and the crashing lightning of cymbals, and all the while Spears turned slowly within the cocoon of light. These moments always made him feel powerful. Godlike. Here he was standing amidst the very stuff of the human genome watching evolutionary changes occur that he had designed. Not some divine creator or entity of similar powers. The feeling of being on the precipice of such power was heady and it made Spears feel a rush of anticipation. Someday, he would be worshipped as a god, the author of a new humanity, the father of children with the power to shake the heavens and burn the cosmos.

The combat between the two genetic codes continued for several minutes, which made Spears' smile grow considerably. He glanced at the elapsed time, which was currently just over five minutes. Suddenly, the insertion points where the base pairs were in the process of merging began to flash with a purple so dark that it was nearly black and small ragged tendrils began to wind their way through the entire genetic strand. The amber clock suddenly turned red and froze at eight minutes and forty-four seconds while a duplicate of the same clock replicated itself in orange below it. The second clock continued to run for another two minutes before it too froze and turned an angry shade of crimson. The biological status information also transformed and quickly shifted from green, to yellow, to orange, and then finally to red as the data started to turn to zeroes one by one.

"The subject has expired, total elapsed time since primary infusion, ten minutes, forty-four seconds. Genetic lockouts began engaging at eight minutes forty four seconds. Analyzing data and preparing subject for physical analysis," the computer said in a frustrated tone of voice.

Now surrounded by a sea of lifeless red, Spears' hands balled into fists and he hung his head. He stood there fighting the urge to look for something to kill for several breaths, rage and frustration boiling inside of him as he faced yet another failure. Where had he gone wrong this time? He could almost hear the laughter of his former superior, talking to him as if he were some witless child who had burned himself when he should have known better. Spears teeth ground and he made a fierce clawing gesture which fragmented the projection. The crimson data fragments spun away like an explosion. Ragged pieces of the digitized model swirled towards the ceiling of the room where they coalesced into a swirling cloud before being pulled towards a pair revolving blue rings which hungrily devoured it all.

"Lights," Spears growled in a low voice. He hadn't yet moved from his place, or the position he was in. His rage was powerful and only through practiced mental exercises did he keep it in check.

The room illuminated, revealing it to be spacious and nearly empty. The walls were constructed from a bronze-colored metal and had an art deco feel to them. Each wall had two scoop-shaped sconces that were made out of a translucent frosted material that diffused the light source inside of them. A single high-backed chair served as the room's only piece of furniture. It, too, was made from the same bronze material as the walls with black cushions for the seat and back. It had a rounded scoop-shaped back that was completely smooth. The chair's arms were wide with several small controls on each, and it floated off of the ground half a meter in the air.

Spears stepped from the small circular platform and crossed the room to the grav chair, dropping unceremoniously into it. Frustration still whispering for blood in the back of his mind, the doctor sat back for a moment and contemplated this last test. He had lost count of how many times he had tried to Awaken a human's Adaam Helix and failed. Most didn't survive the process and the few that did had been insane, to say the least. Most were put down instantly to prevent any resultant abilities from destroying expensive equipment or, worse yet, escaping. *At least I have twenty-seven new donor subjects to analyze. Perhaps one of these will give me the secret to breaking the genetic locks,* Spears considered, and that fact brought a small measure of comfort to the frustrated geneticist.

"Jenna, have Doctor Horst begin an autopsy on the last target subject. Continue DNA extraction and mapping from our new donor subjects and notify me when it is complete," Spears ordered the A.I.

"Understood, Doctor Spears, proceeding as directed. Estimated time of completion seventy-one hours, fourteen minutes," Jenna replied. "Would you like some tea, Doctor Spears? These setbacks always increase your Deravene levels beyond optimal levels."

"No, thank you, Jenna. Sometimes it's good to feel stress, to feel anger. It makes you work harder to achieve your goals. I see that you are starting to understand that, yourself. Bring up CNN, please," Spears said and steepled his fingers in his lap.

"Yes, Doctor," Jenna replied in a thoughtful tone.

A thick, glowing blue digitized frame folded out of the air two meters in front of where Spears sat. The dark space at the center of the panoramic frame flashed once and then resolved into the feed from CNN. A very pretty blonde woman with grey eyes and a stylish grey suit was currently discussing the very topic that Spears was interested in.

"Officials in London are calling this a tragic accident. Current evidence points to an old World War Two sea mine as the culprit in the sinking of the merchant vessel Dunleavy," the woman said pausing to add a well-practiced gravitas to her delivery.

"Give me biographical data on the reporter, Jenna," Spears ordered. In a few moments information on the reporter Dana Lancaster appeared. It showed her address, phone number, measurements and current resume all in scrolling white text which Spears manipulated with casual flicks of his index finger. He paused and swiped his hand from right to left to toss other pictures of the woman into the air where they formed larger images.

Meanwhile, the reporter continued with what Spears thought was a quite lovely voice. "At this time, the Royal Navy is maintaining an eight kilometer safety zone around the site and is asking all mariners and pilots to remain outside of it. A spokesman for the Royal Navy says that they expect to have the area swept for any other rogue sea mines in the next seventy-two hours."

"Jenna, place a call to Ms. Lancaster and arrange a dinner for sometime next week," Spears said confidently and smiled. He was seldom turned down by women. He was attractive and very wealthy, a combination that few women found distasteful. The media industry directed and controlled humanity's good will and Spears thought that having one more journalist well-disposed towards him only helped his company's public image. A good public image meant less scrutiny, and less scrutiny allowed Spears to work without being bothered by activists and their ilk. Bedding her was only a diversion. It also never hurt to have a well-know pretty face on your arm at a dinner party.

"Very well, Doctor. Mr. Tretyak is on the line for you, as well," Jenna replied in a polite voice.

Spears quirked an eyebrow as he responded to the news from the AI, "Put him on."

The image of Dana Lancaster vanished and was replaced by a wave form representation of Tretyak's voice which Spears noted was typically calm. "Doctor Spears."

"My dear, Crimson Shark. What can I do for you today?" Spears asked in a practiced tone of politeness. He didn't care for Tretyak as a person, but there was no denying his organization's effectiveness. This last operation had been uncharacteristically sloppy, however, and Spears expected that this call would explain why that was.

"You sent a request for information, Doctor," Tretyak replied over the speaker, the wave form of his voice dancing in response. Spears manipulated the virtual controls along the bottom edge of the display to activate the voice stress analyzer and responded.

"I did. All of our other work together was problem-free. Why did your men sink the Dunleavy? It's wasteful and mysterious ship sinkings cause people to take notice. Explain," Spears said firmly.

"It was unavoidable. The British had operatives on the vessel. They added complications to the mission that had to be dealt with," Tretyak said. The voice analyzer painted the wave form in green indicating that the truth was being told.

Spears frowned deeply and sat forward in his chair. "Complications? My appreciation of your expertise is diminishing my friend. Perhaps if you elaborate on what happened, we'll find that my perception is incorrect?"

There was a long pause before Tretyak replied. Spears knew the man was proud. He was also a freelancer and it was very possible he might try and demand more money because he realized the value of what he had taken on Spears' behalf. Or worse, perhaps Tretyak was working a second angle and whatever had happened played into his reticence to divulge information.

"They were metabeings, four of them and a platoon of marines. Nothing my men couldn't handle, but it did require a more drastic exit strategy to ensure we acquired your merchandise," Tretyak said.

The analyzer continued to show that Tretyak was speaking the truth, though Spears suspected there was significantly more information to be had. "I see. What did you do with their bodies?"

"My men took only what they were paid to take."

Spears resisted the rage reasserting itself inside of him. Awakened humans were hard to come by and every single one had value to his research. Any of them could hold the key to unlocking the Adaam Helix that contained their powers and the secret to creating Awakened abilities in others. Drawing a deep breath, Spears rapped his fingers against the side of his chair. "You struck me as a man who thought out of the box, Mr. Tretyak. A man with such a mindset would have brought those agents to a man such as myself and would have been richly rewarded as a result."

Tretyak's response was deliberate and his tone lacked any obvious emotion as he responded. "They were exceptionally well-trained. My teams had casualties and your cargo was our first priority. The British operatives were still alive when my people extracted. Their reserves were inbound via helicopter. Staying to subdue them would have risked completion of the assignment."

Spears smiled darkly as he forced Tretyak into admitting that everything had not gone according to plan. He enjoyed making men such as Tretyak deflate their own egos and in this case it would give him leverage in future dealings with the Crimson Shark. Still, Tretyak had completed the job as specified, even if it wasn't as cleanly handled as Spears had hoped. "Tell me about them. What abilities did they display?"

"There were three men and a woman. One man was a hyper-physical; strong, resistant, powerful, but unremarkable. The second man was accurate but his weapons weren't up to the task The third could move from place-to-place instantly. I believe he was using some form of tele-relocation," Tretyak replied. "The woman was a hyper-physical as well. She was moving so fast that my men had trouble tracking her motions. I've never seen someone so fast or agile."

Spears sat back again with a surprised look. "I see. A teleporter is a remarkable find. Your men are fortunate to have escaped at all. This woman sounds like a special case, as well. How many men did you lose to them?"

Tretyak's voice was still flat as he responded. "I didn't say he was a teleporter. I know some things about Metahuman abilities, Doctor. I said he was tele-relocating. There was no distortion or displacement of air when he appeared or disappeared." There was a momentary silence before the

Crimson Shark continued. "My losses are not your concern. Just as what you're doing with those prisoners is not mine."

"Touché, Mr. Tretyak," Spears replied, his hand moving to rub his chin thoughtfully. There weren't many abilities that allowed someone to move from one location to another without actually traversing the space between points physically. The fact that Tretyak knew enough to determine that it wasn't teleportation confirmed what Spears had long suspected, the Crimson Shark's Vodnik had metahuman operatives amongst it.

Two hyper-physicals with any amount of professional training could slaughter a company of a hundred baseline humans. With quarters as close as a crowded cargo deck, hyper-physicals would be nearly unstoppable, which meant Tretyak's Vodnik had to have at least a couple of their own in order to have escaped with the cargo at all. It was a safe assumption that Tretyak wouldn't allow any genetic sampling of his people, and even suggesting it would shatter the limited trust the two men had between one another.

Doctor Spears exhaled quietly and leaned forward again. "I congratulate you on a job well done then, my friend. If you come across any information on these individuals, or the organization they come from, I'd pay well for it. I will also pay one million per live individual you bring to me. However, I suspect that they will be quite difficult to acquire."

Tretyak's response was expected. "I'll see what I can do. Anything else?"

"No, I'll be in contact if I need anything further, and I *expect* to hear from you if you come into possession of anything I might find useful. Good day, Mr. Tretyak." Spears disconnected the line with a swipe of his hand and smiled faintly. "Jenna, have Karen arrange a trip to London after the next series of tests. I'm going to see an old friend."

CHAPTER 14

"It's all I could get man! I wouldn't try and screw you guys. Come on!" Karl Ericsson protested in a fear-laced tone. The twenty-something hacker's feet kicked uselessly as the large Russian held him suspended with one hand. It was all Karl could do to keep from pissing himself. The Russian was twice his size and the two hard-eyed thugs that had come with him were no smaller. Karl realized he would be lucky to get out of this alive and the twenty grand he had been paid for the job suddenly seemed inadequate.

Arkadi's eyes narrowed dangerously and he gave the hacker a shake. "You've never come back with this little before, Karl. I said I wanted everything you could find on her." Before Karl could respond, Arkadi slapped him in the face with the roll of printouts he held in his other hand. "This is everything?"

Karl flinched, yelping as the papers struck him. It wasn't as if the ten sheets of paper actually hurt, but he expected the Russian to switch to a fist any moment. "Dude, trust me. I wouldn't keep anything back from you. That's all I could find. Her file was scrubbed."

The answer momentarily appeased Arkadi and he dropped Karl on the floor. The two other members of the Vodnik he had brought continued to search the hacker's cluttered apartment.

Ericsson had been used by the Vodnik on numerous occasions and their money had paid for much of the computer gear that sat on the benches around the apartment's living room. No less that six different computer towers and a rack of servers had been at Karl's beck and call during his intrusion into the SIS mainframe. Even with all of that computing power in his hands, the kid hadn't been able to unearth more than basic information on the woman Arkadi now knew as Jordan Law. The bald Russian thumbed through the papers again. "This is shit. I could get more by looking her up on Google."

The hacker scrambled backwards away from Arkadi until he was against the wall. The boast wasn't true, but Karl wasn't going to argue that point. "I know right? Her files were totally sanitized."

What little information Karl had provided was most likely fabricated to cover Jordan Law's identity and shield her from exactly what Arkadi and his men were trying to do. He couldn't even be certain that the name on the file was her real name. Still, he had to admit that Karl had done well considering he had a picture and a possible nationality to start with. "If it was easy I wouldn't have come to you."

"All you gave me was a picture. I got you a name. I got family members. I got you a position and an agency, man. I can't control what I find," Karl said with a boldness that even surprised him.

Arkadi frowned. "I need an address or a way to find her."

"I tried to follow the IP that made the changes, but the guy was a pro. The IP belonged to a computer that runs the building's HVAC," Karl said, referencing the unique electronic identifier that every computer possessed. "He cleaned up his tracks so I didn't have shit to go on. So then I went into every computer that had touched her file in the last year and all of them had been scrubbed. Do you know what that takes?"

"No, that's why I'm paying *you*, Karl," Arkadi intoned and stepped towards the hacker menacingly. "I expect fucking results. What you gave me is worthless."

Fear surged in Karl as the Russian loomed above him. His mind raced to find any answer that could save his life. "Please, don't kill me. Please, I got what I could."

The man's weakness turned Arkadi's stomach. The stench of fear radiated from the skinny American and Arkadi's instincts told him that this prey was telling the truth. As useful as fear was, there were times where it impeded the process, and this was one of them. "Get up, Karl. I'm not going to kill you."

The hacker's eyes widened with surprise, "You're not?"

Arkadi grabbed the smaller man by the shoulder and brought him to his feet, "No, because you're not done yet."

"I, I'm not?" Karl stammered.

"I see this name, Stevens, listed as her director. I want you to find his file for me."

Karl nodded and hurried over to his desk. He shoved aside an overflowing ashtray so he could get to his keyboard. The smell of old nicotine made Karl crave a cigarette like nothing else, so with a shaking hand he pulled one from a nearby pack. He lit it and took a long drag, hoping it would soothe his frayed nerves.

Karl sat there with his eyes closed, enjoying the calming influence of the nicotine for several moments. He was always amazed at how focused he was after good drag. "I checked into him already. His file didn't look doctored at all. It was actually pretty boring for a spy and I didn't find jack on her. I did keep a copy though; you never know when that sort of shit will come in handy later."

"Just pull it up."

"You got it," Karl replied. His fingers flew over the keyboard and he pulled the file from one of his many storage drives. The hacker ran a special decryption program he had created to keep people like himself out of his files and then displayed the results on the screen for Arkadi. "See, nothing on your girl."

Arkadi leaned forward and lightly tapped the screen with a finger. "Print his address."

Karl immediately realized what Arkadi was thinking and his hands began shaking all over again. He took another long puff off of his cigarette, but this time the nicotine didn't calm his nerves at all. Deep down, Karl knew that he had just killed Archibald Stevens.

* * * * * *

The genetics lab always sounded like it had a life of its own. With a cadre of quietly humming machines spread out over several lab stations, the room pulsed with sound not unlike a heartbeat. The entire section was reinforced so that it could be sealed in the event of an emergency. That necessitated that the walls and doors be constructed out of specially treated steel designed to resist fire as well as pathogens. Their reflective surfaces bounced the sound from the machinery back into the room, but it also made certain that an accident in the lab wouldn't contaminate or destroy the entire facility. The central lab was also outfitted with four smaller, self-contained multi-purpose laboratories so several hazardous experiments could be conducted at once without risking the lab as a whole.

As usual, the half-dozen or so technicians that staffed the lab were hard at work reviewing data, conducting experiments, and manipulating the array of hardware. Chance had been in the lab numerous times; and as a man who prided himself on knowing a lot about many different subjects, he was at least passably familiar with a good number of the tools within it. There were several three dimensional microscopic imagers, a pair of mass spectrometers, no less than five small bio-sample containment units, and numerous genetics analyzers to name but a few. The mechanical population of the laboratory changed from time to time as Doctor Lindon acquired or constructed new things to meet the needs of his work.

Chance was always amazed at how many scientific disciplines Lindon had mastered. His file indicated that genetics was only one of many fields that the often quirky doctor excelled. Unlike mechanical engineering or quantum mechanics, genetics was Lindon's passion. He was most excited when discovering something new about Awakened abilities, or when he found some sort of pattern in the evolution of those abilities. Genetics research is what Lindon dedicated the lion's share of his time to. With that in mind, Chance assumed that Lindon was probably deep in some experiment related to one of the team's DNA, which usually meant he was going to be distracted. However, the doctor had been the one to call Chance down to the lab, so he'd put down his other work so to meet with Lindon. First, he had to get past Lindon's assistant Regina Collins.

Regina, or Reggie as she was affectionately known, was Lindon's chief medical technician and personal assistant. She was also his gatekeeper. Reggie always intercepted visitors before they could disturb Lindon and get him going on some tangent. Because of that, too many people made the mistake of calling her a nurse or a secretary. Reggie was a skilled researcher who was pursuing her own doctorate while working for Lindon. The woman was smart and tough, but Chance thought she was one of the friendliest people in the agency.

Chance put a charming smile in place as he approached Reggie. Lindon's assistant was in her late twenties and though she wasn't a supermodel, she was still pretty in a natural, girl-next-door way. What she may have lacked in physical attributes, she more than made up for in personality and Chance couldn't remember a time where she was rude to anyone. The tall, leggy, blonde was currently operating a 3D imager that displayed the internal structure of a cell. Chance wasn't sure what she was looking at specifically, but waited patiently for her to finish.

"Good morning, Chance," the woman said, sparing her visitor a warm smile. She took a moment to brush the bangs of her long hair back and then made an adjustment to the imager's holographic control panel. The blue light cast by the machine's floating, three-dimensional control board illuminated Reggie's white lab coat and made it look like she was glowing with her own radiance. "What's brought you down here, today?"

"The Doctor wanted to see me about something?" Chance asked and peered at the readout over Reggie's shoulder.

Reggie smiled again and shut down the display with a swipe of her hand. "Really? He's been in his lab since late last night. I'm not sure what he's working on, but he wouldn't even take his morning tea."

Chance chuckled. "Well, he called me. Do you mind if I go in?"

The woman hesitated for a moment and then pulled up something on a thin black data tablet sitting on the lab station. She studied the screen for only a second when she frowned. "Yes, go ahead, he's gone in and wiped his schedule for the day. Again."

The annoyance in Reggie's voice was unmistakable and Chance smiled at her sympathetically. "If you give me his tea, I'll take it in for you."

That drew a smile out of Reggie and she nodded towards her office. "I'll make him a fresh cup. Do you want one?"

"No, thank you." Chance smiled. "I was in meetings with my brother and the Director all morning. I've had my quota for the day."

"How is the Colonel?" Reggie asked and led Chance into her office. The room was of average size and had a single desk, two office chairs, and a large flat screen on the wall. It was typical of the team's base and had all of the usual bells and whistles. Lindon's assistant walked behind her desk and faced the small counter that ran along the back wall. Methodically Reggie started loading the small coffee brewer occupied one corner of the counter. She picked up one of the pre-measured pods of dried tea and popped it into the receptacle on the machine. "He looked exhausted when I saw him yesterday."

"Tristan's, well, Tristan," Chance said as if that explained it all. He and his brother were very different in appearance and in demeanor. They got along well enough, but they clashed from time to time as all family did. "He's been missing sleep like the rest of us. The Director's got us working our asses off trying to chase down leads on that group that hit the Dunleavy."

"How's that going?" Reggie asked as she shut the machine. With the press of a button the machine started to hiss as it applied heat to the water inside of it and forced it through the pod.

Chance shrugged. He wasn't sure how to answer the question. After several hours of scouring the database and making calls, he was able to find out the name of the sharkmen's Spetsnaz unit, but according to his contacts in Russia, the unit was destroyed during their occupation of Afghanistan decades ago. Chance suspected that the destruction of the unit may have been a cover. Too many of the responses he received were very short, very similar, very political replies.

"I don't see you get stumped very often, Chance," Reggie injected into the brief silence. Her tone was warm, but thoughtful, and she turned her attention from the softly hissing machine to Chance. "Maybe the Americans have something?"

"I'm waiting to hear back from my contact at the CIA."

"She's not still mad at you for standing her up, is she?" Reggie replied

Chance chuckled. "No, I cleared that up."

Reggie's smile broadened, "Good. She sounded like a nice woman."

"She's great. Hopefully, she'll be able to give me what I need." Chance smiled.

"I thought you two weren't dating anymore?" Reggie added playfully.

Chance was seldom embarrassed, but Reggie's off-color comment managed to bring color to his cheeks. "We aren't. The long distance thing didn't work out."

The machine made one last hiss and then beeped quietly to signal that it was done brewing. Reggie collected the cup, dropped three sugars into it, and placed it on a tray with a single chocolate éclair, "That was horrible of me. I'm sorry."

"It's alright, Reg. No offense taken," Chance smiled and held his hands out for the tray. "It's too bad my powers don't extend to the dating arena."

Reggie nodded. "Mine don't help either. Knowing what the man across from you is thinking really seems to ruin most first dates."

Chance smiled and focused his mind on the tea's rich smell. "I'd love to be a telepath."

The woman's eyes met Chance's and her smile softened. "I don't think you would. The tea smells good, doesn't it?"

Again Chance blushed and looked at Reggie sheepishly, "Are my thoughts that loud?"

"Oh, not particularly, but most people tend to project when they're trying hide to them," Reggie replied and placed the tray in Chance's waiting hands. "Off with you now, and remember don't take too much of the doctor's time."

After accepting the tray, Chance smiled at Reggie and couldn't help but wonder if she was still seeing Bob Jacobs from Operations. When she smiled at him and raised her eyebrows Chance smiled just a bit wider. "I won't. See you later, Reg."

A faint smile played across Reggie's lips as she looked down at her data tablet. "I'm having dinner in the cafeteria at seven."

"What a coincidence, that's when *I* was going to eat," Chance said and grinned. He stole a glance at Reggie as he made for the door and was pleased to see that she was still smiling.

The SOS7 operator crossed the busy central lab area to where Doctor Lindon kept his personal lab, only to find that the steel double doors were shut. The status light on the circular locking mechanism in the center of the two doors burned a steady red. Chance had never seen Lindon lock the door to the lab before. *That's unusual.*

As Chance considered the reasons why Lindon would lock the lab he stepped in front of the security scanner. A green beam immediately projected from the device above the door and spread out in a fan shape. It swept down Chance's body once and then back up before it shut off. The door's lock hissed long and low before it spun to the right and then back to the left. Once it was finished, the indicator switched to green and the doors hummed open.

Chance headed in and proceeded around a barrier wall into the lab proper. The room itself was very spacious and made from the same steel as the rest of the lab. What differed was the amount of equipment. Instead of neatly arranged and ordered lab stations spaced through the room, Lindon's lab boasted numerous machines packed on benches against each wall. Three of the walls were equipped to support a different scientific task; genetics research, mechanical engineering, and physical sciences. The last wall was reserved for a testing room that Lindon constructed and used for a variety of purposes. This room had a large viewing window dominating the wall that showed the stark white interior. Currently, all of the equipment in the room was put away inside its respective wall storage unit.

The center of the room was left open except for a section of flooring that was raised a third of a meter above the rest. That's where Lindon currently stood. He was surrounded by a shimmering computer generated holographic display that he manipulated with his hands and vocal commands. Chance couldn't determine what, exactly, the doctor was looking at, but it appeared to be something organic and alive.

Lindon seemed entirely focused on the information that surrounded him. If he noticed that Chance was in the room, he didn't show it. The doctor continued to scan a holographic screen that was suspended in the air before him relentlessly. He was murmuring to himself in a low, incomprehensible voice and using the tip of his index finger to scroll through lines of data with short, choppy gestures.

Chance waited patiently for a minute, but when he started feeling like he was eavesdropping, he cleared his throat. Lindon suddenly clapped his hands and the entire holographic display shut off. Chance recognized a surprised reaction when he saw it, and kept his expression friendly, "Hey, Doc. I'm here."

"Yes, so you are, Leftenant Shaw," Lindon replied in a distracted tone.

"Did you need something?"

The doctor adjusted his lab coat and stepped down off of the platform. He gestured to the tray in Chance's hands. "Is that for me?"

"Oh, yeah, Reggie sent it for you," Chance said and sat the tray on a nearby lab table. Curiosity got the better of him. "So, what were you working on, Doc?"

"Just some routine things, Leftenant," Lindon answered.

The doctor's response was uncharacteristically restrained, and it made Chance even more suspicious. The Lindon that Chance knew was usually energetic even after working for several days straight without any real sleep.

The man in front of him made slow, efficient, movements. Lindon's body language combined with the slight hunch to his shoulders reminded Chance of his own grandfather. Lindon looked old. The doctor was in his early fifties or late forties at most and he was far from infirmed. *That's bloody odd.*

Lindon sat on the edge of one of the workbenches and sipped his tea, lost in his own thoughts. His unfocused eyes moved back and forth as if he were still reading the display.

"So, what can I do for you, Doc?"

The tea cup was set back on the tray after another sip. "Can you explain why Ms. Law's file is so restricted?"

Chance folded his arms, "Officially?"

Lindon ignored Chance's question. "I need some additional data for my work."

"That's pretty vague," Chance said, letting his words trail off.

The doctor pushed off of the counter and walked over to his computer terminal, "But quite standard. A third of this project's funding is for research. I can't do research if I don't have what I need, now can I?"

"Fair enough, Doctor, but the Director restricted Jordan's files and didn't explain it to me. Then again, he doesn't have to."

The Doctor countered quickly "I'm sure you know why."

Chance couldn't deny that, his reputation for being able to track down information was well-known amongst the squadron's staff. "I do. Does the why really matter?"

A dark look was Lindon's initial response. He reigned in his anger before saying a word. "No, but I still need that information."

"What do you need, specifically?"

"I need you to promise me that you'll keep this between us, at least for now," Lindon said quietly. "Nobody, not even the Director, can know. Not until I can confirm my suspicions."

"That's a big request, doc, but I'll bite. What's going on?"

"I need access to Jordan's family medical records. I need names, medical history, and DNA," Lindon said. "Especially DNA."

"The Director doesn't want anyone poking around her family. He didn't say why, but he made it clear that about it wasn't up for discussion, "Chance said firmly. "He'll have our asses if he finds out we're mucking about where we're not supposed to be."

Lindon considered Chance's words for a moment, but only just. "If what I've found in Ms. Law's DNA is what I think it is, there could be world shaking ramifications. I'm willing to suffer the wrath of the Director for that."

Chance looked dubiously at the doctor, "World shaking? What is she the cure for cancer? The fountain of youth? You've got to give me something, Doc."

The Doctor suddenly seemed full of his usual energy and excitement. It was as if a switched flipped in his brain somewhere and everything was back to normal. The man gripped Chance by his shoulders and smiled brightly. "No, all of that is *nothing* compared to what I've found. Tell me, Chance, what do you know about ancient sciences?"

CHAPTER 15

A sleek black, newer model Mercedes sedan turned off of the quiet suburban road it traversed and onto the private drive of 31 Brookshire. As the vehicle approached, a pair of iron gates swung open allowing it to pass through onto the property. The entire two-acre plot was surrounded by a lush greenbelt of Corsican pines, oaks, and a smattering of other greenery intended to provide privacy to the residence. As with other properties in the area, the greenbelt had been planted years ago when the developers began preparing the area for its wealthy inhabitants.

The luxury car's engine growled as it made its way through the greenbelt on the smoothly paved drive, illuminated only by the vehicle's headlights. It didn't take long for the vehicle to navigate the shrouded private drive and roll to a stop in front of an ostentatiously large two story home made of earthy-colored brick and white wood siding. The exterior of the house was well-lit by brass and iron wall-lights fashioned to look like ornate lanterns, and a series of matching light posts that flanked the sidewalk leading up to the home. The lamps' warm glow cast just enough light so that visitors could see the well-manicured flowerbeds that bordered the house and the equally well-kept lawns.

Director Archibald Stevens shut down the engine of his car and sat back in the comfortable leather seat. Closing his eyes, he drew a deep breath and then slowly let it out along with the stresses of the day. This nightly ritual had helped him switch his focus from work to family and since he had started it, tensions with his wife, Helena, had decreased noticeably. Stevens looked into the rearview mirror and studied his features. He was only fifty-three, but he looked at least six years older. The world of espionage had a way of taking its toll on people, especially those in charge. It was a weighty thing to send an agent into a situation that they may never come back from. Throw in the political machinations of other departments, other agencies, and even one's subordinates and a man could age unnaturally fast.

Despite the trials of his position, Archibald Stevens loved his work.

He had been with the agency for more than twenty years, having entered it straight out of university. Though he had seldom gone into the field, he was an expert at organizing operations and making sure all the political liabilities had been properly managed. The Queen had said so herself, as had more than one Prime Minister. Early in his career, Stevens had masterminded the cover up of a rather embarrassing hobby of one of the Queen's relatives, and had done so without any expectation of reward. That was what truly launched his career as those in power recognized his affinity for propriety, as well as his creativity.

Stevens opened the driver's side door and stepped out. He paused briefly to pull his black leather-bound briefcase out from the backseat before he shut the car door and walked towards the front door. As he approached, Stevens could hear the sound of his daughter Lilly's music thundering from the expensive home entertainment system he had purchased so he could enjoy Strauss and Verdi. Neither classical composer had anything in common with the music currently blaring from his several thousand pound sound system. He recognized the song playing as *Invaders Must Die* by The Prodigy, one of Lilly's favorite songs. She was eighteen years old and full of rebellion. He supposed it was normal and was thankful that she hadn't yet dyed her hair blue, or pink, or changed her name to something equally unflattering. It was bad enough she had her nose pierced last year and worse yet that her mother had allowed it.

Stevens thrust a hand into his coat pocket to retrieve his house keys and paused. He tried to find his center again before he opened up the door and stepped into the ocean of noise created by the thumping electronic music. "Good evening," he said in a voice loud enough to be heard.

Without warning, a tall, bald man dressed in a black suit stepped out from behind the recently opened door and slammed his fist into the side of Stevens' head. The older man crashed into the wall and fell to one knee. The attacker kicked Stevens in the face, catapulting him into the wall again and then grabbed him by the back of his suit jacket. He hauled the MI6 Director forward and threw him across the polished wooden floor of the entry area.

Stevens' mouth filled with the coppery taste of blood as he slid across the floor in a daze. Sluggishly, he reached for the Walther PPK he wore tucked under his left arm in a shoulder holster. He barely managed to free it before another large man stomped on his arm, which sent the weapon skittering along the floor. Pain shot through Stevens' arm as the bone cracked and a cry of pain tore from his throat.

The second man, a cruel and hard looking sort with short blonde hair, hauled Stevens up by the front of his suit using two hands and smiled malevolently. With little effort, the man spun him back; first into the oak railing of the staircase and then back into the wall. Stevens shouted in pain with each violent impact.

"Bring him," Arkadi Maelyev growled menacingly and shoved the heavy oak door shut as he turned to walk deeper into the house.

A third man, smaller than the other two at five foot ten with short unruly brown hair, turned down the music coming from the sitting room and moved to join his comrades as they walked to the kitchen.

Stevens' head was still foggy as he was carried into the spacious kitchen at the back of his house. He saw two more men, dressed in dark suits like the others, standing complacently next to Helena and Lilly. Both women were unbound, but Lilly was blindfolded with an old t-shirt. Helena's long blonde hair was out of sorts and her cheek bore an angry purple bruise, but there wasn't any further sign of abuse. Her black slacks and cream button-up-the front shirt were both spattered with some sort of black liquid.

Lilly's clothes, a black skirt and tight black-and-white t-shirt with horizontal stripes, were still clean; though the blindfold that hid her eyes was wet from crying. The dark black mascara she wore when she was out of school had run down her cheeks and was doing so again as tears flowed freely.

"You bastards," Stevens snarled angrily. "If you've done anything to them-" One of the men cuffed Stevens in the back of the head to silence him, but continued to haul the battered spy into the spacious kitchen area.

"Daddy, is that you?" the young woman exclaimed in a panicked voice. One of the men near her grabbed her shoulder hard enough to make her pretty face twist in pain.

Anger filled Stevens like never before as he saw his child brutalized and he drove his elbow into the jaw of the man holding him. The blow was solid. Stevens wasn't in the shape he was in his younger years, but he still kept up on his skills, as was required by The Service. The man's head rocked back and he dropped Stevens to the floor. Immediately, Stevens grabbed for a cast iron pan that sat on the island in the middle of the kitchen.

The sound of a safety clicking off made Stevens freeze and he saw one of the men press a Russian made Grach 9MM pistol against the side of his wife's head. The man looked much as the others did; hard-eyed and weather-worn with an expensive dark suit. The way his brown eyes looked pitilessly into Steven's was enough to make the MI6 Director take his hand away from the pan.

"Good," the bald man said and adjusted the lapels of his suit casually. His Russian accent was thick and Stevens placed it from being around the St. Petersburg area. "Now we have an understanding, Director Stevens."

"What do you want?" Stevens replied and cradled his right arm. "Why have you broken into my home and attacked my family?"

Arkadi reached into the right side of his suit and produced a picture. It was a digitally enhanced close up of a dark haired woman with intense blue eyes that Stevens immediately recognized as Jordan Law. Her expression was fierce, like someone fighting for their life. The image was taken at night, but rendered in color, and Stevens recognized that it was probably a very expensive camera using a multispectral lens that wasn't bought at a local electronics store. Whoever these men were, they were well-funded professionals and that terrified him.

"This woman, who is she?" Arkadi asked and thrust the picture into Steven's face.

Stevens mustered every ounce of effort he could to speak calmly and focus his mind on finding some means to get his wife and daughter out of the situation unharmed. "You obviously know who she is, if you're here."

Arkadi shrugged. "Pretend I know nothing."

"That's pretty obvious," Lilly spat.

One of the men standing next to the girl smashed his fist into her stomach and doubled her over. Gasping for air she fell to the ground and whimpered with her hands clutching her midsection.

Stevens moved to go to his daughter's aid, but was shoved back towards the island roughly by one of the other thugs. The man shook his finger like a mother scolding an errant child and kept his other hand on Steven's chest.

"Your daughter's got a mouth on her. I had a sister much like her. My father taught her manners with a belt," Arkadi said without looking in Lilly's direction. "I want to know everything you know about this woman, Stevens. Everything. If I think you're lying, I'm going to break your hand. I will move on from there."

The thought of his hand being broken didn't matter to Stevens. The sight of his daughter curled up on the kitchen floor did. That and the knowledge that these men would make Lilly and Helena watch whatever was done to him filled Steven's with a cold rage. There was no love lost between the MI6 Director and Jordan, but she was one of his people. Even if she were off with the secretive Ethan McIntyre doing God knows what, Jordan had come up in his organization. It was no secret that she hadn't particularly cared for Stevens, but she had placed her trust in him. He wasn't going to give these men any more than he had to in order to save his family.

"Her name is Jordan Law. She's an intelligence analyst at MI6. Twenty-six years old, very talented, and more arrogant than is proper. She was reassigned several months ago and I don't know where she is," Stevens said in a business-like tone.

Arkadi nodded and turned the picture of Jordan so he could look at it. The large man appeared to be considering something and then gestured nonchalantly to the man holding Helena Stevens. Two of the men grabbed Helena and dragged her over to the island where Stevens was. One of them took her left forearm and forced her hand down on a wooden cutting board while he grabbed the cast-iron frying pan with his free hand. There was no hesitation as he brought the bottom of it down on Helena Stevens' hand, crushing nearly every bone in it with a loud, wet sound.

His wife's face turned ghostly white and she screamed at the top of her lungs. The sound of her mother's scream caused Lilly to wail in terror from where she was on the floor, which prompted the man next to her to punch her in the stomach again. Meanwhile, the man holding the older woman took a handful of her long blonde hair and tilted her head back so Stevens could see the pain and terror in her blue eyes.

Tears ran down his wife's cheeks as she sobbed. "Oh God, Archie, don't let them do this! Please! Just tell them whatever they want!" she pleaded.

Once again, Stevens was held in place by the man who had shaken his finger at him. It took all of his restraint to not launch himself at the man and choke the life from him, or try. Stevens knew that he stood no chance against five younger men. All of whom were in far better physical condition than he was in, even uninjured. Not to mention, at least one of them was armed and all of them seemed to have suddenly gotten very bloodthirsty looks in their eyes. All except the bald man who seemed to be in charge. He looked much more intent.

"Stop! Just stop," Stevens relented.

Arkadi returned his attention to Stevens and took a step closer. "I'm sorry, my friend. My English is not so good at times. Did I say *your* hand?" He extended one large hand towards Helena's face and stroked her cheek with a surprising gentleness. "Your wife is very beautiful, Director. That could also change." The big Russian withdrew his hand and fixed Stevens with an appraising look. "Come, let us talk like men, shall we?"

Arkadi took Stevens by the shoulder and walked him over to the kitchen table, away from Helena and Lilly. He gestured for the older man to sit and did so himself. The shortest of the five men brought over two crystal tumblers and a bottle of Stolichnaya vodka from Stevens' own bar. He opened the bottle up and poured a measure in each glass before shoving one towards Stevens.

Several moments passed as the two men watched each other's eyes and took each other's measure in. Stevens broke the silence first. "What do you want with Jordan? What's she done?"

The Russian took a drink from his glass and studied Stevens quietly as he formed his response. "What we want her for is none of your concern, Director. Even if we were inclined to tell you, a man like yourself should know that more information is not always better. At this point, only you and your wife know what we look like. There's fortune in that, yes?" The man took another drink from his glass and looked pointedly at Stevens. "I will make you a deal. Man to man. You give me what I'm asking for and I'll make sure your daughter walks out of here alive. She stays that way unless she does something foolish. If you refuse, I will make certain she is left alive, but only after everything that can be done to her has been done. You will watch. Your wife will watch. Then, you will watch the same happen to your wife. I am not an unreasonable man, but I am a busy one. I have little time for games."

Stevens felt a chill go through him. Somewhere in the back of his mind he knew that none of them would be left alive, but now that it was out in the open, it felt as if it were much more tangible a thing. He tried to come up with a plan, any plan, to get them all out of here, but realized that he had no moves to make. All he could do was make sure Lilly got out and under the best conditions he could manage. Stevens assumed that the men were going to pimp her out or something and the very thought of that made him wonder if death was preferable. He glanced at where Lilly was on the floor with one arm over her stomach and then looked back at Arkadi. "Why would I believe anything you offered?"

"A fair question," Arkadi replied and took another drink from his glass. "I give you my word as a soldier. We will not kill your daughter unless she does something to cause it. This is an offer I make only once. Right now, here. You decide your child's fate. If she is strong enough, she will survive this. If she is not, then she won't. I can offer no more than that, but it is more than my friends here would have given you. If they were allowed a free hand, they would do far worse things to them."

A whimper from Helena made Stevens shudder and he looked into the cold malevolent eyes of the man seated across from him. His daughter deserved a chance to live, even a slight one. "Alright. Give me your word and your hand on it. Understand this, if you hurt her you get nothing," Stevens said in a pained voice.

Arkadi nodded and set aside the glass so he could extend his hand to Stevens. He knew the man was no soldier, but he could respect his desire to keep his child alive. This sort of work was always ugly, but Tretyak wouldn't accept failure or loose ends. To fail in the Vodnik was rare and it was never looked on well. They were like brothers, he and Konstantin, but Arkadi knew his friend well enough to know that he was serious about capturing this Jordan Law woman. "You have my word as a soldier."

Stevens took the hand and squeezed it firmly. He had made a deal with the devil and he hoped that Jordan would forgive him for it. She didn't have children and couldn't possibly understand why he would make such an agreement. Stevens hoped that whatever happened in the end, Jordan would make these men pay. She was many things, but her loyalty to the crown and the people she had worked with was never questioned by Stevens. If anyone could get his daughter out of trouble and make those responsible suffer, it would be Jordan.

"Her name is Jordan Elizabeth Law," Stevens began. He was unable to hide the defeat from his voice as pain and fear eroded his resistance. "She's eldest daughter of Lady Shawna Law and Lord Cassidy Law. Jordan has five sisters; four of them are very close to her in age and one still in school. She is engaged to Ambassador Brian Agincourt who's currently with our Moscow mission."

"Continue."

Stevens watched the Russian's eyes and reluctantly continued. "Jordan was a field operative under my charge for the last five years. She's one of the best agents I've served with in my entire time with The Service; smart, dedicated, creative, and decidedly deadly. She's an infiltration expert and has extensive undercover experience all across the world. That's probably why she was reassigned several months ago. As far as I can tell, she went to work for a man named Ethan McIntyre. Who he is exactly, I don't know. What I do know is that he is part of an operation that isn't officially recognized. Nobody knows what its name is, or what exactly it does. As far as Law is concerned, her records have been moved out of the system. She doesn't exist as an agent of the United

Kingdom any longer, at least not on paper. My people say her entire family is under twenty-four-hour surveillance, so you won't get to them."

The reality of who the woman was and where she had come from made sense to Arkadi. Tretyak, too, had been part of such an organization in Russia under Putin; in fact, so had many of the Vodnik, including Arkadi himself. Most had been Spetsnaz, or VDV, prior to the transformation. They had clashed with the CIA's Awakened operatives numerous times and had lost many good men to them, as well as to those of the British and Germans. Arkadi supposed that the rest of the old Russian team were still fighting a shadow war against the Americans and their allies. Things tended to go in cycles in the world of espionage and politics. Though the Russian Federation had recently worked with the Americans in the Middle East, they were far from true friends; they just had mutual goals. Arkadi sat back in his chair and stroked his chin, his stone-like features thoughtful. "I want her address."

Reluctantly, Stevens took a pen from a cup on the table and wrote Jordan's address down on the tablet they used for grocery lists. "Here," he said and pushed the paper towards the Russian.

A brief look was given to ensure the address looked real and Arkadi tucked it away with the picture of Jordan. He finished his vodka and nodded his head towards where Helena and Lilly Stevens were. "Go, be with your family."

The finality of what was unfolding, made Stevens' hands shake as he rose. He didn't say anything further to the bald Russian and took the opportunity that he had been given. Moving to his wife, he took her in his arms, his lips brushing against her ear. "I am so sorry, Helena. I am so, so sorry." His wife began to sob quietly and the aging spy just held her while he reached down to Lilly with the hand of the broken arm. He ignored the pain. It was only temporary and this was the last time he would be able to comfort his only child.

Lilly rose to her feet and started to reach for the blindfold. Stevens stopped her and looked at the two large men nearby before he kissed his daughter's temple. "What are they going to do, Dad?" Lilly asked and began to sob quietly.

Stevens looked down at his daughter and wished he could see her eyes. He had always done that when she needed buoying during particularly difficult moments in her life. He wanted Lilly to see how much he loved her, however preventing his daughter from seeing her attackers was for the best. If she knew what they looked like she would be a loose end that they would probably tie off, "Nothing good. You need to be strong. You need to remember how much you are loved by your mother and me."

The words only made Helena Stevens weep louder and clutch onto her husband and child. She was mentally shattered and in immense pain from her crushed hand. Archibald Stevens sighed and resigned himself to comforting her as best he could. He looked at Lilly's face and cupped her cheek firmly. "I know we've had our differences, Lilly, but I love you. I've done what I've had to do to keep you alive. Forgive me for this." Leaning forward, Stevens placed a gentle kiss on his daughter's forehead.

Lilly's body shuddered visibly as she cried and desperation filled her voice. "They're going to kill you, aren't they? *Aren't they*?" She brought her hands to her face and shook her head in denial. "No! Please, don't kill them! Please! I'll do whatever you want!" the distraught young woman pleaded with the group of men and received nothing but silence.

The frown on Steven's face deepened as he saw the remorseless stares. There was no pity there, no compassion, just cold, uncaring focus in their eyes. He placed his hand on Lilly's shoulder gently, "Lilly, stop. This won't help."

The lack of response from the men made her angry and she gave way to it. "Fuck you, then! Fuck you all, I hope you burn in hell, you fucking wankers!!"

That got a reaction from the mercenaries and one of the men took Lilly by her arms and pulled her towards the door roughly. Full of rage and fear, the young woman screamed and kicked frantically the entire way. The man hauled his hand back to slap her, but a dangerous look from Arkadi stopped it. Scowling, the bald man turned and spoke quietly, but firmly, to the girl. "Your father gave you a chance. You should take it. You will not be given another."

Tears were streaming down Stevens' cheeks as he watched his daughter being pulled towards the door. With his arm around his incoherently sobbing wife, the veteran agent considered his own sanity. What sort of father would let his daughter be taken away by these brutal men? Desperation clawed at Director Stevens' heart, the sight of his daughter being manhandled by the thugs almost too much for him to bear. "Lilly, you go. This is your only chance," Stevens said firmly and watched Lilly's terrified face. "You're a Stevens. Never forget that. Your mother and I love you."

Lilly's body shook as she heard the resignation in her father's voice. Helplessness and rage burned inside of her chest so brightly that it hurt. The large man that held her pulled her towards the door again. Summoning all of her strength, Lilly jerked her arm way and stabbed her index finger at him, an angry response on her lips. Before it could be given voice, however, there was a loud hissing sound like bacon being cooked on a hot griddle. Around her finger, the air warped as intense heat formed a halo around her entire hand about the size of a dinner plate. The hissing turned into an angry rush of heat and air and a beam of brilliant golden light shot from Lilly's fingertip straight through the startled Vodnik soldier's face.

To Arkadi, it seemed as if the girl had somehow captured the sun in her hand. The energy that had surrounded her finger had spread down her arm and over her upper body, incinerating the t-shirt she wore instantly. Though the Stevens' daughter clearly didn't notice the nimbus of heat that burned around her, the temperature in the room had gone up by twenty degrees and anything flammable nearby was catching fire. His man, Vasily, had become a human inferno the moment the beam of energy had burned through his head and through the back wall of the brick house, but his body disintegrated into ash before it could fall to the floor. The blindfold around Lilly's eyes incinerated. Golden energy radiated from her eyes as rage fueled the power inside Lilly's genetic code.

Arkadi's senses began to return and he looked away from the girl's display towards his remaining men. "Get out of here!" he shouted. It was hard to hear his words over the rapidly increasing roar of power. He shouted once more and ran from the kitchen hoping that his men would be smart enough to follow suit.

Archibald and Helena Stevens stood in utter disbelief as they watched their daughter go from an angry and terrified young woman to an incandescent being of light and heat. Lilly's hair was caught in the displacement of air created by the release of tremendous energies and danced within the corona of heat and light that surrounded her. He shouted Helena's name and the hot air burned his throat painfully.

Ignoring the pain, Stevens bodily hauled his wife towards the back door as she stood agape at what her daughter had become. They exited hot on the heels of the Russians who were, even now, sprinting towards the greenbelt. Spurred on by her husband, Helena began to run along with him. Instead of heading towards the greenbelt, he turned and headed towards the side yard. Stevens held his wife's wrist painfully and pulled her towards the small creek that ran between the garden and the house. There was no hesitation as he tossed Helena into the shallow water and dove in behind her. Just as he hit the water, Stevens felt a concussive wave strike him from behind and a rush of intense heat and light passed overhead.

Fueled by adrenaline, Arkadi and his thugs sprinted away from the house at full speed. In mid-run, the bald Russian's expensive suit split and tore at the seams. His body quickly shifted into the powerful humanoid shark form and he used its increased strength to propel him at speeds no human could attain. Three of his men followed suit, though the fourth made the mistake of looking back at the radiant light that coruscated from the windows on the first floor of the house.

There was a stark, brief moment of silence and then the world turned white.

In an instant, the large brick home was enveloped in a molten sphere of light, its surface streaked with burning veins of gold and white. Anything that the miniature sun touched was completely devoured by the energy that fed it; consumed so completely that it was if it had never existed. A circular pressure wave rolled out from where the Stevens' residence had been, chased by an inferno of thermal energies that set the large lawn alight and tossed the shattered form of Arkadi's fourth man into the air like a ragdoll. As the sphere expanded behind the wave of force it seemed to grow brighter and brighter until night had became day.

Then, light and sound vanished. The small sun abruptly blinked out of existence, leaving a ninety meter crater that was as deep as it had been wide. The outer yard was burning in patches while other sections closer to the blast had been converted to a smooth, smoky-colored glass.

Stevens exhaled and rolled to his side in the water of the creek. He held his wife close and waited for another minute before he sat up. Helena had passed out, but to be certain, Stevens placed two fingers against her neck. When he found a steady pulse Stevens allowed the hint of a smile to appear on his mud covered face. Carefully, he sat Helena up against the bank of the creek and silently thanked whatever powers existed that his wife had insisted on the addition of the small winding creek to their landscaping. It had been a very expensive project which they had fought over, but Stevens had eventually acquiesced to his wife's demands. It had saved their lives.

The perversity of the universe's sense of humor wasn't lost on Stevens as he carefully laid Helena just out of the water. After making certain that his unconscious wife wasn't going to slide into the creek, Stevens rose unsteadily to his feet. He grabbed a largish piece of shale from the bed of the creek and searched for any of the men that had attacked his family. There was no sign of the bald Russian with whom he had made a devil's deal, or the three remaining thugs; though the stench of burnt flesh was heavy in the air.

Stevens hoped that all of them had been consumed by the blast of heat, or were crushed by the wave of force. He hoped they all had died painfully. The look on Lilly's face as she was pulled away made Stevens want to bash someone's head. Stevens turned towards the crater and dropped the rock he held as he hurried to it.

The edge of the crater was only five meters from the creek and Stevens supposed that if they had been any closer, even being below the house's foundation wouldn't have been enough to save them. What he saw nearly made Steven's legs give out beneath him. There, at the center of the sixty meter deep bowl, lay a naked form curled into a fetal position. Lilly's body radiated waves of heat, but she looked otherwise unharmed. Stevens didn't hesitate as he stepped over the crater's lip and onto the smooth glassy surface of the crater. He immediately regretted it; the soles of his expensive dress shoes were far too smooth to successfully navigate the nearly frictionless surface of the crater's bowl. Archie Stevens slid down the side of the bowl to where his daughter rested, his hands frantically trying to slow his descent. Pain erupted in Stevens' broken arm and caused him to pull it back. The uneven contact on the crater's surface sent Stevens into a spin and he ended up stopping upside down near Lilly's prone form.

Even from a meter away, Stevens felt like he was near the fireplace on a cold winter morning. He still couldn't understand what had happened to Lilly or how she had survived what appeared to be spontaneous combustion on a massive scale. Stevens turned over and came up on his knees. Lilly's chest rose and fell slowly as if she were only sleeping, so Stevens reached towards his daughter. As his hand came closer, Stevens could feel the skin of his outstretched fingers getting hotter and hotter until it felt like they were going to burn.

Stevens sighed and withdrew his hand. He felt helpless and useless, just as he had when the Russians had his family in their power. It was a feeling he had never experienced in his life and he didn't enjoy it. Anger and frustration were warring against logic. He wanted to risk the injury just so he could touch his daughter to reassure himself that she was, indeed, alive, but the part of his brain that made all living creatures wary of fire and heat won out. Director Stevens cursed and sat back on his knees drawing on an attribute he normally had in spades. Patience.

Over the next several minutes, Stevens felt the heat emanating from Lilly gradually recede and cautiously crawled closer to where she lay. He touched her cheek which was still hot to the touch and then placed his fingers against her neck looking for a pulse. Tears rolled down Stevens' cheek as he felt his daughter's life's blood pulsing beneath his fingers. Stevens slipped his coat off and wrapped it around his daughter's torso, one hand stroking her disheveled hair. He did it as much to protect her from the cold of the night as he did to protect her modesty, but he supposed the former was probably unnecessary. Tears continued to stream down his cheeks and Stevens wasn't certain how much time had passed when an unusual staccato roar made him look upwards.

A beam of bright white light sprang to life and panned across the crater briefly before it came to rest on Stevens. The painful intensity of the spotlight forced Stevens raise one hand to shield his eyes from it. The light remained on Stevens for a few moments before it dimmed considerably and revealed a sleek black aircraft with a triangular wing design and elongated fuselage. Stevens blinked to clear motes of light from his vision and studied the unusual aircraft.

It had no markings on it and it was at least four times the size of a Gulfstream business jet. The design of it reminded Stevens of photos he had seen of the Americans' Aurora transorbital spy plane, but this craft was different somehow. There were four small half-spheres beneath the craft that were no bigger than the diameter of a trashcan lid and some sort of sensory package was slung in an aerodynamically shaped housing beneath the nose. It panned around the area slowly as the strange craft orbited the crater. Stevens wondered what kept it aloft, as the aircraft had no visible vectored thrust ports and the sound of its main engines had died down to a steady, but throaty hum. The craft's fuselage seemed to melt away halfway between the nose and the engine section which revealed metallic looking door.

The door slid open and a man dropped from the craft rapidly. Stevens strained to see who the man was, but the black form-fitting body armor he wore made it impossible to identify him. As the man dropped down, Stevens could hear a quiet humming from the two half spheres fitted to the sides of his combat harness. The devices were no bigger than half of a tennis ball and as the man touched down on the ground they went silent.

The aging spy blinked, any night vision was long gone thanks to the light from the aircraft, and he tilted his head to try to look at his rescuer's face. The man wore a black balaclava style hood with a pair of unusual looking goggles attached to it. The hood itself had a filter over the mouth and some sort of framework on the top of the head that the goggles were attached to. The combination of equipment effectively hid the man's identity and prevented the director from reading his intent.

Stevens pulled Lilly closer with his good arm and swore that this time he would die protecting her. That's when the man raised both hands palm up and spoke in a Londoner's accent. "It's alright, mate. We're here to help you."

Stevens blinked, but kept his daughter close as the armored operative extended a hand towards her. The man paused and once again showed he had nothing in his gloved hands. Reluctantly, Stevens nodded and glanced in the direction of the still orbiting aircraft. "Who are you people?"

"We're on your side, part of Special Branch," the man responded and crouched down. "One of my team is seeing to your wife, Director Stevens."

The name Special Branch was used when describing any of the more shadowy arms of the British intelligence services. They were usually thought of as rogues and the worst sorts of people that became spies, but at the moment, Stevens didn't care. In pain, emotionally drained, and exhausted Stevens nodded towards his daughter. "I can't lift her. My arm's been broken."

"Don't worry. I've got her," the man said and used one hand to push the goggles to the top of his head revealing a pair of blue eyes set in a black grease-painted face. "I promise I'll treat her as if she's my own."

The man's eyes were compassionate and sincere, and, at the moment, that was enough for Stevens. The operative waited for Stevens to move the arm he protectively held across Lilly's body before he picked her up and cradled her in his arms. He glanced up at the edge of the crater and spoke into the air. "This is Seven. I'm coming up with the girl first. Director Stevens will need medical immediately."

Stevens rose on unsteady legs and looked up at the craft. "How are you going to get back up there?"

The man's smile showed in his blue eyes. "I'm going up top first so we can get your daughter looked at, Director. Then I'll come back down to get you. Won't be a moment." The man suddenly sprang up into the air and cleared the ninety meter distance to the edge of the crater as if he were hopping up a curb. The devices on his harness hummed as the operative disappeared with Lilly, leaving Stevens to his thoughts.

The man was true to his word. He was only out of sight for half a minute before he reappeared and leapt from the edge of the crater. Once again, he landed smoothly and he extended a hand. "Director, if you please."

Stevens nodded and gripped the hand. The man picked Stevens up as easily as he had Lilly and then made the leap. Stevens looked down as the ground disappeared beneath him, though strangely he didn't feel any sensation of acceleration or the pull of gravity on his body. When they landed, the Special Branch operative set Stevens down and nodded to where two other men dressed in similar fashion were tending to Lilly and Helena. A tall black-clad woman stalked the edge of the green belt with yet another man. Both of them were armed with some sort of heavy drum-fed weapons that Stevens didn't recognize.

The craft ceased orbiting and floated over to the driveway. It settled down to half a meter off the ground and the black fuselage near the door reformed itself into a set of stairs. Out of the door, came a tall man dressed in a grey trench coat, escorted by two heavily armed men wearing black that reminded Stevens of something out of a science fiction movie. When the man got closer, Stevens recognized the face of Ethan McIntyre. As usual, the man was dressed in an expensive suit, however, his eyes showed an unusual degree of sympathy. "Archie, my people will see to Helena and Lilly. We'll get them proper medical attention as soon as possible."

"How did you know we needed help, McIntyre?" Archie asked and let one of the armored men start checking his arm.

McIntyre gestured towards the crater. "A spy satellite picked up the explosion and it was throwing off so much electromagnetic energy that it knocked out the power for two kilometers." He gave Stevens a moment to absorb it before he spoke again. "Archie what happened here?"

"I don't know," Stevens said in a tired voice. "Things I can't explain. Things you won't believe."

Ethan McIntyre gave Director Stevens' good shoulder a squeeze and started guiding him towards the floating aircraft. "You'd be surprised what I might believe."

CHAPTER 16

It was early morning in Moscow and rush hour was just starting. People moved about on their way to work in one of Russia's largest and most modern cities, though it was still too early for the roads to be at a standstill. As the cars, trucks, and motorcycles picked their way along the street another vehicle darted in and out of the lanes, tires squealing.

It was a late-model four-door BMW luxury sedan with dark-tinted windows and a blue rotating light above the driver's side door. The speeding sedan seemed to defy gravity as it took a sharp left onto a busy road that ran along the Moskva River and accelerated with a roar of its powerful engine. Few people paid it any attention as such sights were common in the former Soviet Union. If one had enough money, they could buy a blue light and corresponding plate and do nearly anything they wished behind the wheel of a car.

The vehicle continued to accelerate, barely missing a large truck carrying a load of heavy cement water pipes as it changed lanes to go around it. The driver of the truck honked angrily and shook his fist out the window as the car passed, but the BMW continued on its way without pause. Inside, the three men looked at the female driver with expressions of shock and aggravation. One of the two passengers in the back seat simply shook his head and relaxed after checking his seatbelt and crossing himself while the other gave the driver of the truck an apologetic shrug of his shoulders.

The man in the front passenger seat fixed the woman with an angry look. "Bugger all, Jordan; you're going to kill us!" Briar Young snarled acrimoniously. He gripped the door with one white-knuckled hand while he braced the other on the dashboard.

Jordan jerked the black leather-bound steering wheel to the left to avoid crashing into the back of a white delivery van that belched black smoke, her blue eyes glancing at Young dismissively.

Briar pointed excitedly at the quickly approaching rear end of another delivery van. "Eyes Front! *Eyes Front*!"

"I don't think she's worried about our safety, mate," Sergeant Douglas replied from the back seat. He smiled at Jordan in the review mirror and wagged a finger at her playfully. Before they left, Colonel Shaw had told Jordan to avoid injuring Briar. The erstwhile thief had gotten a dressing down by Shaw for his behavior after their encounter, though he deserved a beating, in Douglas' opinion. Douglas chuckled at the man's discomfort and folded his arms, his brown eyes looking out at the vehicles they sped past.

"Definitely not," Chance added and glanced at Douglas. He was holding the handle above his own door and had one hand on the back of Jordan's seat to keep from being whiplashed.

"Briar, be quiet," Jordan replied tersely and maneuvered the sedan around the delivery van and a motorcycle in front of it. She narrowly missed an economy car in the process, but didn't let it slow her pace.

Briar Young fumed and looked at Jordan for a moment. "Your precious fiancé isn't worth all of our lives you, batty git. Slow down before we crash into something."

Jordan narrowed her eyes and drove on. There had been no contact with Brian or Lina, or anyone in their staff, for over twelve hours. Considering what had happened Director Stevens and his family, she had every right to worry. If they were normal men, she wouldn't be as concerned, but the large clawed footprints at the scene matched the shark creatures they had faced on the Dunleavy. The same footprints had transformed from human-sized dress shoes to the bare webbed feet within a few short steps, though one of the attackers had apparently been too slow. His charred body provided DNA evidence that corroborated the presence of the metamorphs, as Doctor Lindon referred to them, at the Stevens' home. Stevens himself admitted that he provided the Russians information about Jordan; her name, her address, and more.

The fury Jordan felt was indescribable. Director Stevens had done what he did to save his family but at the cost of her own. Whoever the mysterious Russians were they had shown they were resourceful and well connected. With the information that they had beaten and coerced out of the Stevens family it wouldn't take long for them locate all of her sisters. Jordan couldn't blame the man for saving his family, but now her own was in serious danger and she felt conflicted. Were his daughter and wife any less important than Jordan's sisters or parents?

An image of her own mother brutalized as Helena Stevens had been surfaced in Jordan's mind and the anger it induced made Jordan's chest feel uncomfortably tight. She clamped down on the emotion and shoved the image from her mind. She couldn't blame Director Stevens for trying to save his daughter. Put in his position, she couldn't be certain that she would do anything differently. It didn't matter that her rational mind forgave the man, her heart couldn't. Everything Jordan loved was placed in jeopardy, everyone, including Brian.

In the back seat, Sergeant Douglas touched the small ear piece he wore as his satellite phone began to vibrate. He answered in brief and thanked the person on the other end before leaning as far forward as his seatbelt would allow. "That was Laird. We've gotten confirmation that the

Americans have moved your sister, Ryan, to a safe location. She's being held in protective custody for the moment."

Jordan's blue eyes glanced at the face in the rear view mirror, "And Brian?"

Douglas shook his head gently, "Nothing. The embassy reports that they've tried his people several times but haven't gotten an answer. Control also tried a GPS locate on his phone and it still shows at the address he's been assigned near the embassy."

"Hold on," Jordan said calmly and down-shifted the car. She dodged out into oncoming traffic and around a cluster of tightly packed cars in her lane of travel. Ignoring Briar Young's spate of invective Jordan gunned the car around an oncoming bus. The world streamed by slowly as Jordan tapped her powers to enhance her perception speed and reaction times. To the others, they were narrow misses, but to Jordan they weren't even close.

At that breakneck speed, it didn't take long to arrive in the neighborhood where Brian and his staff lived. She unexpectedly applied the brakes and slowed the car to the speed limit. She also shut down the blue light and brought their rental car to a stop in an alley about two blocks away. Without waiting for her passengers, Jordan opened the door and started down the alley towards Brian's house.

Douglas freed himself from his belt and hopped out of the BMW, one hand grabbing the blue light as he did so. He tossed the light into the back seat and shut the door, doing his best to ignore Briar's cursing. He generally didn't like the man, but he had his uses. Young's ability to read objects had come in handy on more than one mission. If they had to try and hunt down the team of metamorphs Young's powers might be invaluable. Of course, that didn't make him any less of a bastard.

"That bitch'll be the death of us. We should have let Lincoln drive and left her at the airport." Briar said and adjusted the grey sports jacket he wore over his wiry frame. He watched Jordan stalk off down the alley, admiring the way her tailored black suit hugged her body, despite his anger.

Chance and Douglas exchanged looks and the former grabbed a black duffle out of the sedan's trunk, "Here we go."

"Ease up on her, Briar. This is her fiancé. I know the concept of monogamy and love is something you don't believe in, but pretend to this once," Douglas retorted and hurried to catch up to Jordan.

Briar spat on the ground and spoke to Douglas' back. "Maybe if you forgive the two hundred pounds I lost to you on the Liverpool match."

Without warning Douglas turned to face Briar angrily and grabbed the slender man's shoulders. He leaned his face forward slowly, eyes wide with fury. For an instant, he considered knocking Briar out and putting him in the BMW's trunk, but he let that instant pass. He patted one of Young's shoulders lightly, "Done. Keep your mind on the mission."

"Done it is, mate." Briar said and cocked his head to look at one of Douglas' hands, "Easy on the Armani, friend."

"Let's go," Douglas said and released both of Briar's shoulders at once. He spun on his heel and walked after Jordan quickly. She hadn't slowed at all and was following the course she had outlined on the flight from London.

Briar increased his pace as well and reached down to collect a discarded pipe the size of a paper towel tube. He shook it once and then slid it up his right sleeve. "You know, if you actually had a chance of bagging her, I'd understand this whole knight in shining armor thing. As stands, you've got no chance unless you let the Russians put to her man."

Douglas scowled angrily at Briar and put his hand on the other man's shoulder to stop him, "For fuck sake man you need to put it in check. This is her fiancé."

"I heard you the first time, Willy. That's why she shouldn't be on this op, let alone leading it," Briar retorted, his eyes fearlessly meeting Douglas', "You know it. I know it. "

Jordan ignored the exchange and walked straight towards a rusted fire escape attached to the side of the nearest building. "Young, I want you to walk round the area to see if you can find any physical surveillance. William and I will take the high road while Chance gets into an overwatch position at the rear of the building."

"Understood." Briar acknowledged tersely.

"Are we ready?" Jordan asked without looking at the two men.

The muscles in Douglas's jaw bunched up as he turned away from Briar to face Jordan, "*We* are."

Jordan motioned towards the rusted iron fire escape attached to the side of the building. "We'll take that and go from rooftop to rooftop, just like we planned."

Douglas nodded and walked over towards the nearby fire escape. He pulled down the ladder going up to the first landing and started up it. Jordan wasted no time in following, though she did spare a look for Chance who gave her a reassuring smile as he headed out onto the sidewalk.

The former thief smiled darkly and leaned to the side to peer at Jordan's backside from directly beneath her. After a wistful sigh, Young started out onto the street proper at a stroll.

The two operatives made their way to the roof and Jordan looked around the area briefly. Her eyes narrowed as she searched all the spots she would use to snipe at Brian's building and some she wouldn't risk. There was no sign of shooters or observers, just a few people hanging laundry on what promised to be a warm summer day. The sun was already making it uncomfortable outside, but Jordan noted a light breeze coming from the north where Brian's building was. The numerous scents of the city assailed her nose as she drew in a deep breath. Pollution was thick in the air, as was the scent of garbage, accented by the presence of the freshly washed laundry hung to dry on lines that stretched between poles on the building's rooftops.

Jordan crossed towards the far side of the roof and looked four buildings over where Brian's building stood five floors taller than the buildings nearest to it. "We'll jump to the roof. I'll go in through the skylight in the living room. You'll take the balcony entry. Keep in mind, his assistant Lina could be in his flat. Other than that, he has a single maid who's in her late fifties and his bodyguard and driver, Martin."

"Got it. Let's give Briar a few minutes to finish his walk," Douglas replied and scanned the area as well. They had gone over the operational details in-flight, but he knew it made Jordan feel more comfortable to reiterate them. He let his gaze rest on Jordan and gave her one of his warm smiles. "He may be the biggest tosser this side of the Thames, but Young does know his job. Plus, he blends in. Better than you looking all Terminator and we all know how my good looks draw attention."

The brief humor brought a slight smile to Jordan's lips. "Best to not rush in and get caught like an amateur."

Douglas crouched down and retied the laces of his black tactical boots. "Best not to. It's bad enough we couldn't bring any weapons sides Briar's pleasant disposition and my pretty face. We don't want to rush in and get someone shot for lack of care." He finished re-tying his laces and looked across to the other roof. "I'm just reassuring myself, you know? I know you understand all that."

Jordan nodded and took the chastisement in stride. She deserved it. Her patience hadn't been very present since she had seen the destruction at Director Stevens' home and it seemed to take her caution with it. She was terrified for her family, but all of them had been secured in safe locations. They were all accounted for except Brian. He was seldom far from his phone and Chance had verified that not only that it was on, but that it was active and the local network wasn't experiencing any problems. This wasn't normal. As worried as Jordan was, she wasn't going to foolishly rush into a potential hostage situation and get anyone killed. She touched her earpiece to open a channel. "Viper Lead to Control. What's our orbital surveillance status?"

Even though the mission controller was back at the base, the satellite communication sounded so clear it was almost as if he were standing right next to Jordan. "We are still thirty-four minutes out of window. Actual is recommending you hold position until we have satellite visibility on the target location."

Annoyance filled Jordan's voice and her jaw clenched. "Is that a hold order?"

There was a short pause before Control responded. "Negative. You have final call, Viper Lead."

"Understood Control, Viper Lead Out," Jordan glanced at Douglas who was watching her with a hint of a smile on his lips. He obviously knew she wasn't going to hold for the satellite to move into position and found it amusing, "Four, Seven, sitrep."

"This is Four, looks as clean as can be out here. All I'm seeing is a couple of the local tough boys standing round chatting about the weather. There's a jam sandwich down the road about one hundred sixty meters, parked in front of a cafe with nobody inside," Briar replied through the communications network.

Chance reported next, "Lead, this is Seven. I've got eyes on building security, two officers out back having a fag. The faces match the names from the duty roster I pulled."

"Copy. We're moving," Jordan replied and looked at Douglas who was still smiling.

Douglas flexed his legs and then leapt across to the next building effortlessly. He could jump even further than Jordan due to his powerful leg muscles, and when he landed he broke into a jog towards the next rooftop. Jordan followed suit, quickly navigating the rooftops until both she and Douglas were at the building next to Brian's. They were on the side opposite to his flat with the sun at their backs. Jordan had meticulously planned their approach, as well as entry, on the flight over and so far it had paid off. There was no sign of their movements being noticed. Every curtain on the upper floors of Brian's building was shut to block out the bright, early morning sun and, at the moment, nobody was on their balcony. The only sign of activity nearby was the sound of cars passing by on the street below.

After a quick check of the roof, Douglas turned to face Jordan who was still in mid-run across the last rooftop. He cupped his hands together and she hopped foot-first into them. Douglas tossed her up and into the air as easily as anyone else would a small stone and shifted to watch her flight. She shot upwards and landed gracefully on the ledge before dropping down onto the roof itself. As soon as she touched down, Douglas leapt over and landed beside Jordan.

It only took a few seconds for Jordan to quickly survey of the roof's security measures and give him an all clear nod.

There was a single video camera on one corner of the roof that slowly panned about the area. That had been on the plans and it had a dead spot right next to a waist high air conditioner so Jordan had chosen that as the best place to land. She crouched down and listened, trying to hear any sounds coming from the interior of the penthouse flat. The mechanical rumbling of the air conditioner made her exceptional hearing nearly useless in this situation. Normally, she would be able to hear a conversation clearly, but thanks to the clamorous machine, Jordan could only vaguely make out a voice speaking in a very sharp tone.

"Something's going on. I can hear an upset tone, but nothing else," Jordan murmured over her com. The small device used vibrations in the wearer's mastoid bone whenever they spoke to detect what they were saying instead of a traditional mike. It was able to detect even sub-vocalized speech so that the wearer wouldn't give their position away. In addition, any loud environmental noises wouldn't interrupt the channel, allowing for clear transmission even in the din of a gun battle.

"Lead, this is Seven. The two smokers are heading back inside. Still clear here, but the traffic is starting to pick up some."

Briar Young's voice responded over the communications net. "Lead, this is Four. I'm at position six, all clear here."

"Understood. We are moving to second phase," Jordan responded and visualized Briar standing near the heavy steel mailbox that they had labeled as position six. He would have a good view of the building's entry as well as the streets nearby. She felt confident that the man would have spotted any observers lurking around the area, so she nodded to her partner, signaling him to go.

Douglas returned the nod and waited for the camera to pan past their position before he darted up and towards the side of the building with the balcony. He dropped over the edge of the building quickly and vanished from sight. In moments, he reported back over the comnet in a calm and steady voice. "Lead, this is Three, clear out here. They have the curtains pulled, but someone sounds really pissed off in there. The door is secured and I have no visual on the interior."

Jordan frowned as she heard the report from Douglas. It was possible that the Russian metamorphs were interrogating Brian, but it was equally possible that Brian was arguing with someone. Normally, Jordan would trust her instincts to determine which it could be, but her concern for Brian's safety overpowered them. *I'm too close to this. I should have stayed home,* Jordan chided herself. Shaw had said the same thing to her, but she insisted on coming despite his concerns. *Too late for regrets now, girl, time to work.* "Control, this is Viper Lead. We are a go."

"Copy, Viper Lead. You are cleared for action. Confirm and execute."

"Confirming cleared for action. Viper to team, execute on three," Jordan replied and crouched down on one knee with her knuckles resting on the rooftop. She focused and willed herself to vanish from sight. Psionic waves immediately saturated the area for blocks around the building and in the minds of everyone in the radius of her powers, Jordan ceased to be. Anyone who looked at her would simply fail to register her existence in their mind, including whoever was watching the camera that monitored the roof if they were close enough.

The action only took a moment of concentration and then Jordan vaulted high into the air. She flipped in a slow arc and came down with her booted feet aimed towards the flat, angled glass of the skylight. The ebon-haired agent reappeared just as she crashed through the skylight feet first. The weight of her body combined with the momentum of her fall sent glass streaming to the floor below her.

Simultaneously, the balcony door wrenched open in a screech of metal as the lock broke and popped free of the handle. Douglas stormed into the room, using one hand to sweep away the beige curtain that had obscured his vision. He charged inside, ready to take on a room full of the shark metamorphs, but his expression turned from fierce to amused as he stared at seven shocked faces.

Both operatives had been expecting the worst but what they found was far from it. Brian, Lina, and the rest of the ambassadorial staff were sitting around the living room with coats off and ties undone. Next to each one of them was a laptop and numerous manila folders stuffed with documents. Several alcohol bottles sat empty on the coffee table along with glasses and numerous white take out boxes covered red Cyrillic writing.

Count Brian Agincourt, trade ambassador to Russia, stood with one foot on the coffee table and the other planted on the floor behind him, both hands gripping the front of his shirt like the lapels of a jacket. He had a dishtowel over his head in a mockery of the white powdered wigs that were worn in the British Parliament. Like the other members of his staff, he had a shocked expression on his face, but he recovered quickly and motioned to where Jordan stood in a defensive stance amongst the broken glass of the skylight. "Ladies, gentlemen, my future wife, the lovely and talented, Jordan Law."

The Count's words were slightly slurred and all of the members of his staff looked like they had been awake for too many hours and had far too much to drink. Red eyes and tired faces stared back at the two operatives, though Lina shook her head disapprovingly.

Douglas quickly checked the adjoining rooms and then gave Jordan the all clear. He walked back over and closed the curtains just in case they had missed any observers. Busting in to the meeting had been embarrassing, but it wouldn't be anything compared to the embarrassment of a sniper killing someone because of carelessness. Douglas figured that whatever embarrassment he was feeling, Jordan had to feel two-fold.

There was no doubting she was emotionally compromised, but Douglas had backed her request to join the mission team anyway. SOS7 lacked the heavy hitters it needed to deal with the metamorphs in close combat. Jordan and Douglas had strength and resilience, and Chance had his luck. The rest of the team would have needed heavy firepower to deal with the sharks. Heavy firepower needed equally heavy authorization, and if past operations with the Russians were any indicator, that meant time. Nobody was certain if time was a resource they had when dealing with the metamorphs. Douglas was certain they had made the right call, but he was sure Jordan was already berating herself for overreacting.

Jordan felt her cheeks flush red both with anger and embarrassment as she spoke over her com. "Control, this is Viper Lead, we are clear inside." The tall woman didn't wait for mission control to respond before she strode over to the coffee table and picked up Brian's cell phone. She thumbed the flip cover open and looked at the display. It had over thirty missed calls and the speaker icon on the display had diagonal line through it indicating that it had been silenced.

Brian gazed up at the skylight opening that was over three meters high and then looked at his soon-to-be wife. "How the hell did you do that, love?"

In a tone that belied her current state of embarrassment and anger, Jordan addressed the rest of Brian's staff, "If you'll excuse us a moment, please. My partner will escort you back to your rooms and explain the situation." Jordan turned and strode past Brian towards the bedroom. "We need to talk."

Douglas inclined his head to Brian and walked towards the members of the ambassadorial staff with his arms out to his sides like he were herding a tour group. "If you'll excuse us, Your Lordship. Come on then, people. This way, please."

* * * * * *

The bedroom felt far too bright for Jordan's liking. It wasn't the intensity of the light in itself but the fact that she couldn't hide the blush from her cheeks. She was embarrassed that she made such a rookie mistake due to her lack of patience. The fact that Brian had also ignored her calls because he was too busy carousing rankled her. Jordan was thankful that Brian was safe and any embarrassment was a small price to pay for that.

Brian came up behind Jordan and placed his hands on her shoulders so he could turn her to face him. "How did you jump through the skylight like that? You don't have any climbing gear on."

Jordan's eyes focused on Brian's face as she dodged the question. "There's been a threat on your life. We need to get you and your people out of here right away. My team was sent here to get you out."

The urgency in Jordan's voice caused Brian to hesitate for a moment. "You're serious, aren't you?" He said and then brushed her cheek with the tips of his fingers. "I've never seen you worried like this. Who's made the threat? Is it because of the trade deal I've been working on?"

"It's very serious. There have already been other casualties. I can't provide details in an unsecured environment," Jordan replied in a quiet voice. Her eyes closed at Brian's gentle touch and she took a few seconds to enjoy his presence. It had been months since they had seen one another and even this fleeting moment made her feel a certain level of contentment.

"I can't leave right now, Jordan. There's a big function tomorrow so that the Russian trade minister and I can finalize the deal I've been negotiating. There's too much riding on it for me to just disappear. I'll just ask for more security from the embassy." Brian said confidently.

Jordan's eyes snapped open and she stared into Brian's with a mix of worry and aggravation. The look in his eyes was typically stubborn, but Jordan pressed on "Embassy security can't handle these people. They're too well trained."

"The FSB will have people all over the place and so will the police. This is going to be a big affair with press coverage and all the usual pomp and circumstance. I'll be fine," Brian tried to reassure Jordan.

"No, you won't. Not if these people follow through."

Brian shook his head. "Jordan, I've put a lot of time into this deal. It's going to mean millions of Euros for the economy, not to mention easing some of the tensions we've had with Russia since the Cold War. This is good for the United Kingdom, good for the world. We could use a lot more peace and prosperity."

She expected this reaction from Brian and had informed Director McIntyre that the likelihood of getting her fiancé to leave was very small. McIntyre had reluctantly agreed that if Brian refused to go that she and the other members of the team could stay and provide security. The Director hadn't been any more enthusiastic about her presence on the mission team than Shaw had been, but he understood the necessity. "I agree. I also thought you'd be stubborn about this. My team and I are going to stay as your protection detail."

"We have an arrangement then," Brian replied playfully in an attempt to offset Jordan's displeased look.

The attempt failed and Jordan's worried expression remained in place. "This isn't a game. These are very dangerous people."

"Fine, Jordan. You're the expert here. At least tell me how you pulled off that trick with the skylight," Brian replied.

There was no easy, mundane answer to give Brian about how she had managed to drop three meters without injury. Jordan had never hidden that she was very athletic and strong, but Brian wasn't going to believe that she had just gotten lucky. It wasn't the movies after all, and crashing through a skylight usually resulted in injury. Jordan was tired of lying to Brian, so she decided to go with the truth. "That's it, then. Sit down."

Brian took a seat on the edge of the bed and watched Jordan curiously while she pulled four small disk shaped devices out of her suit pocket. She quickly attached them to the windows of the room and then pressed a button at the base of each. The button press activated small green light emitting diode at the center of each device. After each disk was placed, she drew the blinds shut which darkened the room considerably. Once that was done, Jordan walked into the bathroom and turned on both the shower and the sink which filled the quiet of the bathroom with the sound of rushing water.

"That's a serious bit of work you're doing, love," Brian commented as he watched Jordan work. "What are those disks for?"

"They're anti-surveillance devices that vibrate the window enough to prevent laser microphones from working. They also emit both ultra-high and ultra-low level white noise that will jam any bugs in this room. The water running is to prevent anyone outside the door from hearing what I'm going to tell you," Jordan replied and walked over to lock the handle. "What I tell you can't leave this room. Promise me."

Any hint of playfulness dropped from Brian's tone and his expression became wary. He studied Jordan intently before responding to her demand and realized that her entire demeanor was out of the norm. "I promise."

A nod of her head is all Jordan provided before she delivered the answer to Brian's question in blunt fashion. "To put it plainly, I'm a super-human."

Brian made a sound that was half-snort and half-chuckle. "A what? Come on now, there's no need to have a go at me."

"I'm not having a go, Brian. I'm serious. Pay close attention," Jordan said and then willed herself to vanish from sight.

The sudden disappearance made Brian leap to his feet with a wide-eyed expression on his face. He felt around in the empty space in front of him and blinked in shock.

Jordan stepped back out of the space Brian was searching and moved to sit on the bed next to where he had been before she dropped her veil of invisibility. "Believe me, now?"

Brian nearly tripped over his feet as he spun around to face Jordan. "How did you do that?"

"I simply think about it and I turn invisible. It took quite a bit of time to learn how to control it, but I used to use it to sneak into class late," Jordan replied and gave Brian a hint of a smile. "I can do quite a bit more than that though."

The shocked look on Brian's face didn't waver and he slowly ran a hand through his hair as he digested what Jordan had just shown him. "I'm almost afraid to ask."

"Yet you will, anyways. Still, seeing is believing, yeah? Would you have accepted it if I had just told you what I could do?" Brian shook his head mutely and Jordan continued. "I can lift several tons and my reaction times and speed are roughly five times faster than those of a normal person," Jordan said and rose to her feet which caused Brian to take a step back. A tightness formed in her chest as Jordan recognized a look bordering on fear in Brian's eyes. "I won't hurt you, Brian."

"Why didn't you tell me about this before, Jordan? This isn't a small thing, you know," Brian said and searched Jordan's eyes for an answer.

Jordan hesitated for a moment, her head shaking lightly. "It isn't something you go telling everyone about. What was I supposed to say? Oh, I had a lovely time tonight, Brian, but I should tell you that I can pick up your Jag and carry it down the road? No need to drive, I'll just jump us home, auto and all."

A hint of a smile appeared on Brian's face. "So, when you asked for help opening that bottle of wine on our first date that was for my benefit, wasn't it?"

The dark haired agent smiled at Brian warmly and rolled her shoulders in a slight shrug attempting to look as innocent as she could. The result was a welcome laugh from Brian that shattered the remaining tension in the room.

Brian moved over and took Jordan by the arms just before he kissed her passionately. The two lingered like that for a while before Brian leaned back and looked down into Jordan's eyes. "This is going to take some getting used to. Do you fly, too?"

The response from Jordan was a snicker and a roll of her eyes. "I wish. It would make life far easier if I could." The smile that she favored Brian with lit up her eyes and made him smile in response. "I'm sorry I never told you, Brian. I was afraid of it getting out. I knew I couldn't be the only one with these sorts of abilities, but I didn't want to be the first one to be found."

"I can understand that. I doubt it would be as glamorous as the comic books make it look," Brian said quietly. "How did you get these, what do I call them, powers?"

"I was born with them. They gradually grew stronger as I got older."

"Christ, Jordan, how hard was that? You've been hiding them all your life?" Brian asked and cupped Jordan's cheek gently. His eyes filled with compassion as he stared into hers. "Do your parents know? What about your sisters?"

Jordan smiled and felt light after unburdening herself. She was always impressed with Brian's ability to adapt and deal with situations and this time appeared to be no exception. "I can't answer twenty questions all at once."

"I'm sorry, Jordan. It's just a lot to process."

"I know the feeling, and I'll answer what I can later."

Brian nodded towards the living area. "So, your friend out there, he's got these powers to?"

"Yes. I'm not the only person with these abilities. We need to talk about that."

"So, these people after me have powers, like you do," Brian deduced. "That's why you're here and not the FSB or someone else."

Jordan didn't miss the concern that entered into Brian's voice. She was glad that he was taking the situation seriously now. "Yes, they have powers. They aren't after you, specifically. They're after me."

A stormy look entered Brian's eyes and he set his jaw, "You? Why are they after you?" he asked and held Jordan a bit tighter.

"We're not certain, not entirely. They took a photo of me on an operation we recently conducted. I killed one of their people and that's the only reason we can think of for their interest in me," Jordan replied and rested her chin against Brian's shoulder. She felt safer being here with him.

The logic of it was absurd. Brian wasn't a trained operative and he didn't possess any special abilities like she did. Yet, Jordan knew Brian would do whatever it took to see that she was safe, and it comforted her.

"My God, Jordan. What is SIS doing about this? How are they working to find these people? I'll make some calls and get some extra help here," Brian replied and disengaged himself from Jordan. He was springing into action as he normally did whenever things needed doing.

Jordan gripped Brian's arm and pulled him back. "This isn't something your people can handle, love. These are metamorphs; they turn into shark-like creatures that are immensely strong and damn hard to kill. The agency I work for can handle it, but it's going to take time."

The explanation seemed to stun Brian and, for the first time since they had met, he looked as if he were out of his depth. "How the hell has all this not come out in the press? People running around turning into sharks, women lifting cars? This has to be a cover up on an epic scale."

"It is. There are multiple governments that know of the existence of Awakened humans. Most run programs that see to the protection of the populace from Awakened beings that violate the law. You need to keep this between us. Period. Imagine the mass panic that would ensue if the population at large found out about people like me," Jordan said earnestly.

Brian's response was immediate and convicted. "There are ways it could be done properly, Jordan. This isn't something that should be hidden from the world. It isn't right. People have a right to know that these beings are out there, beings that can't be stopped by normal means. This sort of government secrecy allows people to be used, to be abused, and no doubt killed, in the name of national security."

Cautiously, Jordan extended a hand to touch Brian's chest. He was worked up now and needed to be grounded before he launched into some sort of action. "Do you trust me?"

The question caught Brian off guard and slowed down his building ire. "Of course, I do, Jordan."

"Then trust me to be right, for the moment," Jordan replied in a soft, but firm voice.

* * * * * *

Doctor Elgen Spears casually exited the executive elevator and walked into the expansive living area of his building. The opulent open-air space occupied the three top floors of the tallest building in downtown Los Angeles. The building was owned by Spears, personally, and he leased space to his company ImaGen for an exorbitant amount of money. He was the only employee to call the building his residence, but in his mind it was a palace, a display of his influence and power. Spears knew it was a vain, petty, thing to throw his wealth in other people's face but he really didn't care. Showing them his power, that was a different matter entirely. What good was power if you never used it?

Long ago, Spears had learned that visual displays of the power he possessed were almost as useful as actual application of said power. His enemies were kept at bay by the fear that Spear's would turn his considerable resources on them. Fear made them weak and overly cautious.

Of course examples had to be made from time to time. Humans had short memories and they had to be reminded from time to time. Over the years Spears had destroyed three different competitor companies by convincing politicians to block their construction projects and destroying their brands. Wielding the news media like a sword, he cut their reputations apart and made the public question every action they took. Soon activists swarmed their corporate campuses and turned the masses on the internet against them. In the end, he selectively hired their best corporate officers and researchers, and purchased their best research projects. He had made millions as a result, but the money was nothing compared to the feeling of accomplishment that destroying an enemy gave him.

Spears tossed his keys and code card into a brass dish near the door as he strolled down the entry stairs into the sunken living area. The room had a large sectional couch that was covered in brown leather which surrounded a low coffee table that had been grown from clear synthetic crystals. The table had compatriots in similarly crafted floor lamps, and a table that ran behind the sectional couches.

All of the furniture sat on an expensive dark wood floor that had been hand made from oak. Spears had considered putting a fish tank in the floor at one time. Perhaps stocking it with some of the genetically enhanced fish species he had designed. That idea was cast aside quickly once Karen mentioned that it was something that a mad scientist from a James Bond movie would do. He knew that she wasn't mocking him, but the thought of someone else doing so because of the floor angered Spears. Instead, he had opted for something more mundane, less spectacular, but far more sentimental.

Along one wall were numerous pictures framed in brass, nearly thirty in all. They were of different sizes but all of them depicted groups of children from various countries where life was hard on the young. Most were from places in Africa or South America, but a few were Russian or Chinese. Spears had met each one personally and had spent a considerable amount of time going to their villages and towns to provide much needed medical assistance. He had personally donated the money to build modern schools and medical clinics in most of the areas he visited.

The world had rushed to heap laurels on him for that. Spears had graciously accepted all of the humanitarian awards and recognition, but reminded everyone how important caring for those who couldn't help themselves was. They were so short-sighted. Spears had done far more than raise the children up from the squalor that dominated their short lives. He had given each and every one the chance to reach their ultimate potential.

Without taking his focus from the display wall, Elgen Spears called to his AI, Jenna. The supercomputer managed nearly all of his lab operations as well as building operations and global communications for ImaGen. "Jenna, lights, also, some Tchaikovsky."

There was no response.

A look of consternation formed on Spears' face and he turned to look in the direction of the ceiling mounted optic that Jenna used to watch the living room. "Jenna, status?"

"Your toy won't hear you, Fourth Caste Vandre," a voice intoned as if it were speaking to a child.

A shiver ran down Spears' spine as the familiar voice brought back memories long buried by time. He looked away from the picture wall as a tall and very gaunt man who looked of African descent walked into view from the dining area. The man had a clean pate that bore an elaborate tattoo that looked like bolts of lightning along the left hand side of his head. There was absolutely no facial hair except for two thin black eyebrows hung low over very pale grey eyes. An off-white suit clung to his tall, lanky frame and the cut of it only made him look taller and thinner.

Behind the first man stalked a second who was muscular like a bodybuilder. He appeared to be Germanic, complete with well-trimmed blonde beard and long hair pulled into a ponytail. The dark suit he had managed to squeeze into contrasted sharply with the white suit of his companion.

Spears quickly composed himself, despite the sudden triggering of his fight-or-flight instinct. "Third Caste Talmad, you and your Second Caste stand out like a Dassk at a late season festival."

"I'm surprised you remember our ways, or our celebrations, Vandre. It's been a considerable amount of time since you were among your people," Talmad replied. His tone was as disdainful as his expression. The tall man drifted over to pick up a heavy brass statuette from one of the bookshelves in the room. "I see you have disobeyed your orders and this species flourishes. Here, we thought you and your fellow technicians had perished."

Scrambling for an explanation, Spears walked over to the bar near the large windows that overlooked downtown Los Angeles. He didn't miss the hostile look that Talmad's bodyguard gave him and poured a large measure of scotch into a tumbler with shaking hands. Talmad was a member of the third caste of his people, the Jenagyr, his direct superior, and one of the Genemasters of the Jenagyr scientist cast. Spears, or Vandre as he had been known amongst his own people, glanced at Talmad. "Did you want some?"

Talmad inclined his head in the affirmative so Spears filled a second tumbler half way and brought it to him. It took all of his will to steady his hand, which filled Spears with rage. He had thought himself long past the subservience to the upper castes of his homeworld. The large bodyguard from the Second Caste intercepted the glass and sniffed at it once before he passed it to Talmad who watched Spears with his cool grey eyes. The Jenagyr science master sipped the amber liquid, but gave no sign if he enjoyed the human alcohol. Instead, he kept his gaze fixed on Spears and waited.

As soon as the drink was delivered, Spears walked over towards the bar and collected his own drink again. He ignored the overtly hostile look from the bodyguard took a long pull from his scotch before he spoke. "I'm surprised you brought only one of the warrior caste with you, Lord Talmad. How goes the war?"

The Science Master quirked a thin eyebrow and seemed to consider his response for a moment. "The war has been in stalemate for the last three thousand years. We strike the Incarna and they strike us. Our initial gains were great, but the

Incarna have had several of the other races take their side and provide materials, safe haven, and intelligence."

"I see. I have seen no sign of their return here. My people know what to look for and I monitor all local communications for any indication of their reappearance," Spears said in a diligent tone.

Talmad's face remained impassive though the slight tightening of his eyes suggested impatience. "I've noticed that these, *humans,* have built quite a civilization for themselves. They're very war-like, very destructive on a planetary scale. I trust this is your team's doing, Vandre?"

"Unfortunately, my team perished when the drive shielding fragmented. I was in the observation pod preparing to detonate the bio-weapon we had devised to eradicate the Incarna's pets. As you can, see after the accident I refrained from doing so. I was stranded here and I thought that I may still be of service by trying to complete your work. The humans could still be a viable army, Lord Talmad," Spears said as he improvised a plausible falsehood.

"Yes. So the evidence would suggest, Vandre. Or should I refer to you as "Elgen Spears"? I find it odd that a technician would take the name of a weapon as a means of disguising himself. It is, at best, insulting to our Second Caste," Talmad mused.

The large warrior from the Second Caste made a sound that was reminiscent of a growling tiger. "It is more than that, Science Master. It is against our laws! This low caste should be executed."

Spears saw the tension building in the Second Caste's body and briefly wondered if he could survive a fall from ninety-eight stories. He might be able to make it through the window before the large warrior could catch him. The Second Caste was the frontline warriors of the Jenagyr and, as with everything from his people's culture, strict rules surrounded the use of names and titles. He had chosen the name as a slight to the strict caste system of his people. Here on Earth, he was a lord, a member of a high caste. He cursed himself for not destroying their vessel outright. If there had been nothing left of it, they would have assumed it, and he, had been a casualty of their on-going war with their blood enemies the Incarna.

"You are quite correct, Second Caste, quite correct. However, we must investigate the matters surrounding Fourth Caste Vandre's failure to eliminate the beings that populate this world. Technically, you do have the right to carry out that punishment now; however, I would council patience in this matter. There could be more crimes to address that could merit far worse punishments than death," Talmad said and glanced up at the massive warrior.

Spears did his best to avoid the gaze of the Second Caste warrior who was poised to launch himself across the room. He downed the rest of his drink and sat the tumbler down. As he did so, his hand brushed against the remote control that rested on the bar which made it spin slightly. With Jenna offline, he wasn't able to have her activate the defense systems inside the residence. However, he could do so with the remote if he were given time. Time was something the warrior wouldn't allow if he sensed that Spears was trying to take an aggressive action, and Jenagyr warriors were well known for their battle sense.

Spears forced his voice into a rock steady cadence as he took the remote in one hand. "With all due respect to both the Second Caste and yourself, Science Master, I ask that I be allowed to explain my actions and how they were for the betterment of the Jenagyr."

Talmad rose to his feet smoothly, gesturing towards Spears with his free hand. "Speak briefly."

A well-concealed exhalation escaped Elgen Spears as he turned towards the wall where a large black marble mantle sat. "Allow me to show you something of this world." He thumbed the remote and summoned an eighty inch television from the ceiling. Spears changed it over to the History channel and raised the volume. The screen suddenly filled with images of World War II, rendered in high definition black and white. Thunderous explosions and the pops of firearms mingled with the clanking and rumbling of tanks and armored vehicles. Spears let his 'guests' absorb the sounds and imagery for several moments before he turned and took a position so that he was standing in the middle of the screen. "This is humanity. Gone are the days where they peacefully farmed and only fought skirmishes over food or females. They fight on a global scale for resources, for territory, for power. Nearly every invention of note has either sprung from warfare or been turned to that purpose later."

Talmad and his Second Caste bodyguard both watched the images flashing by on the screen and, for the first time, their interest was piqued. The Jenagyr were a war-like species. Conquerors. Their own media were little more than training tools and this sensationalized version of violence resonated deeply with them, just as Spears had hoped.

Technician Fourth Caste Vandre smiled faintly as he watched his fellow Jenagyr become enraptured with the display of human violence. He brought up his empty hand and gestured to the screen in order to keep their attention focused away from him and on the images and sounds. "*I* have helped guide them down this path. We sought to Awaken their inner power, their genetic legacy gifted to them by the Incarna. Yet, in the absence of that power, they have learned to make a new power of their own. With their hands and their minds! I have taught them now to work the atom, manipulate magnetic energies, and soon they will harness zero point energy and *that* will make them able to fight on a galactic scale."

Spears discreetly worked the remote control he held using his thumb. He knew that he only had one chance to deal with the Second Caste warrior. The Second Caste had been bred for war for over twenty thousand years. Though all Jenagyr had to test for position at the age of adulthood, those families that had long been warriors seldom were anything but First or Second Caste. The grueling mental and physical challenges ensured those with the genetic edge would place in an upper caste while those from so-called inferior stock were seldom able to rise above their parents' own caste. It had created massive labor and technician castes that generally had less wealth, status, and influence than those of the ruling, warrior, or science castes. A side effect of the tendency for lower castes to breed only within their caste had positioned certain Jenagyr Houses at the top of the power structure while others toiled thanklessly to support their empire.

Long ago, the First Caste's overlords had created indoctrination programs to help keep the masses in their place and those who showed too much dissent were sent into battle as fodder, or simply placed in mines or on foundry worlds where the normally long Jenagyr life expectancy was cut brutally short by the working conditions. Technician Vandre had gotten lucky when he was assigned to the Terra expedition.

He had escaped life in the science labs where he would answer to Science Masters like Talmad. The technician caste was the ones who handled all of the mundane duties like cleaning, performing follow-up experiments, and overseeing maintenance on the lab equipment. Those unlucky souls who constantly scored low on their weekly performance evaluations were often used as test subjects and seldom seen after their third or fourth consecutive failure.

Spears chuckled inwardly and wondered if the science masters even understood how many of the lower castes hated those above them. Only the power of the First Class and Second Caste had prevented civil war from breaking out.

Like many of his Caste and those below, Spears had been unhappy with his lot, but unlike the others, he had acted on it. He had conceived the plan to fake the deaths of himself and the team that had been left to destroy humanity when it was still in its infancy. He had been the one to take the courageous first step and kill the lower ranked Science Master that had been placed in charge of the technicians. He had been the one to lay out the plan for uplifting humanity and taking a position of lordship amongst them when they were of sufficient power. Most of his fellow technicians had lost their courage over the years and had to be dealt with. Now, only a scant three of them remained and only Spears had possessed the conviction to continue with their plan to Awaken humanity. They would create their own empire, one that would place them above all.

Methodically, Spears continued to program the targeting parameters of his home's internal defense system while his fellow Jenagyr were distracted by the images of war that called to their genes. "By our standards, they are still primitive and undisciplined, but that will change once we begin to indoctrinate them. Once we train them and supply them with arms, we will have *seven billion* soldiers, laborers, and lower caste slaves that will provide us with what we need to crush the Incarna! I did this for the glory of the Jenagyr, for the power of our entire race!"

Talmad regained his senses long enough to look at Spears with new eyes. "You have exceeded your station, Vandre. Though I must admit you have done, well." The suddenly flash of a nuclear detonation on the screen pulled Talmad's attention back to the television. "These humans will make excellent slave troops."

The images behind Spears had changed to show several nuclear detonations from varying angles and gradually changed from black and white images to full color displays that bathed the room in hues of fiery oranges and reds. The two Jenagyr were still focused on the display when Spears completed the final command. With his thumb hovering over the enter button Spears fixed his gaze on Talmad. "Oh yes, Science Master, they will serve *me* well!"

That drew both of the Jenagyr's focus away from the blossoming nuclear fire on the screen to Spears who had a smug look on his pretty human face. "Fourth Caste Technician Vandre is dead, just like you."

Spears viciously stabbed his thumb down on the remote's enter key and grinned as arcs of incandescent blue energy shot from the corners of the room and enveloped both Science Master Talmad and his Second Caste bodyguard.

An agonized scream tore from Talmad's throat as a web of coruscating blue energy wrapped across his body, burning everything it touched. His pristine white suit ignited and the Faceshifter device he used to hide his true appearance shorted out. Talmad's agonized features started to revert to their natural state but any detail was quickly consumed by black ash.

Within moments both figures were reduced to charred corpses that lay in twisted positions that spoke of the agony of their deaths. Each still smoldered as the intense heat that had converted them into carbonized ash gradually dissipated. The entire room smelled like ozone and burned meat which caused Spears to lament having to replace the décor for a moment. But only for a moment.

Triumphantly, Elgen Spears raised his arms aloft and thanked the Creator of All for his fortune. This had been a close call. He would, of course, have to find the Science Master's vessel and deal with that before any automated signal could go out. He wouldn't waste this triumph. With a broad smile still on his face he pulled his PDA out and tapped in a twelve digit code.

Thirty seconds passed and then a response was returned by Jenna's mainframe. "Doctor Spears, I seem to have gone offline. I'll run a diagnostic immediately."

The AI's voice was distressed at its inexplicable shutdown and Spears did his best to soothe her. "It's not your fault, Jenna. We had some uninvited guests. I'll need a cleanup team to sanitize my residence. Oh, and the two bodies, have them moved and coated with a protectant. I think I will keep them as mementoes."

"Of course, Doctor." Jenna replied in quiet tone. "I'm sorry I failed you."

That made Spears smile even more broadly, "My dear. You haven't failed me, quite the contrary, in fact. I'll be making some upgrades to your systems in a week or two. First, however, I need you to run a global scan for Jenagyr magnetic resonance signatures. Secondly, have Karen prepare my flat in London. I'll have to take my trip a little earlier than planned while this mess is cleaned up. Oh, and make sure you remind her to free up Ms. Lancaster's time. I'm in the mood for some company."

"As you wish, Doctor," Jenna replied. Her advanced neural net processor allowed her to make the appropriate changes to schedules, flight plans, and dinner reservations all at once. It even allowed her to run a diagnostic to see how exactly she was shutdown. She knew Spears would check himself, but she felt it was her duty to make sure she was one hundred percent functional. After all, she had an empire to run.

CHAPTER 17

The clamor inside the Ararat hotel was starting to die down after several hours of joyful celebration by the participants of the trade negotiations. The entire hotel had been swarming with various government officials and the corporate elite that would benefit from the agreement reached between the United Kingdom and the Russian Federation. All manner of journalists were interviewing anyone who had been involved in the negotiations, as well as several business analysts that had made the trip to Russia for a few moments of face time on international television. The five star hotel's large open-air courtyard still echoed with laughter and the clank of dishware and glass as the remaining party goers finished off their deserts and drinks.

Jordan blended in well with the rest of the guests. She had managed to get a hold of a nice dark blue gown that flattered her sleek shape well. The soft silk shimmered and caught the light just right and the backless design had been a hit with Brian. He hadn't been the only one, she noticed Briar watching her again. She ignored it. As long as they were in the middle of this mission she wouldn't act on Briar's unprofessional behavior. Not unless it jeopardized the operation. Jordan kept her focus on the nearby area and smiled prettily as Brian chatted with a member of the Russian trade delegation.

The place was packed and it was an ideal place for someone to make a close ranged hit if they didn't care about being caught. Jordan was the quickest and most likely to be able to intercept any attacker before they could cause any harm.

Douglas stood guard over the couple, and Jordan was grateful for his support. Though she had only been on the team for a short time, she and Douglas had fought together and that had given them the beginnings of a strong bond. Douglas' character was solid and Jordan knew that he would never leave Brian's side if she were taken out.

As Jordan swept her gaze around the area she saw Briar Young casually making his way around a large ice sculpture. She wasn't pleased he had been sent with the team. His skills weren't in question, just his character. Young was self-serving and his participation in SOS7 had been coerced. Jordan had memorized his file and the former thief had been given the choice of working with the team for the length of his fifteen year prison term or being tossed into the darkest deepest hole that could be found. That made his reliability tenuous at best in Jordan's opinion, and she wouldn't trust Brian's safety to a man like Young.

Jordan wished that Chance were with them instead. In training, Chance had shown that he was steady under pressure and possessed the combat skills to back up any bravado he displayed. Having another hand in case things went sideways was always welcome, especially when luck always seemed to be on their side. Chance had returned to the jet after a mysterious call from one of his contacts. He had assured the team that this contact would pay off, so they agreed to manage without Chance's presence.

A beep from Jordan's small handbag drew her attention. She casually pulled her phone from inside of it and read the text message.

All clear. L

The message was from the only other member of the team with them, Brady Lincoln. Lincoln was brought in to make the fourth man on their team and was stationed outside in Brian's car to keep an escape route clear, should they need it. Jordan wasn't close to Lincoln, but she was relieved to have him instead of Briar guarding their exit. One, he could be trusted. Two, his enhanced reflexes and reaction times made him a better driver than the thief.[WU1] Young was roaming the glass and brass interior of the hotel looking for anything or anyone out of place. He was in charge of perimeter security, or the green zone, which let him check hallways, bathrooms, and other areas of the hotel not being used by the trade delegations. Jordan and Douglas were sharing the red zone physically though Douglas was watching the middle, or yellow zone.

"If you'll excuse me, I'm going to get us a refill," Jordan said and waggled her empty wine glass. She smiled at Brian and took the glass from his hand as well. Using a kiss to the cheek as a pretense Jordan whispered in Brian's ear, "I'm going to check on Briar. Be right back."Brian ran his hand along the small of Jordan's back and smiled at her warmly, "Don't be too long."

"I won't be," Jordan replied, smiling a bit brighter after the caress. As she turned to go Jordan made eye contact with Douglas and then looked towards where Briar was between the buffet and the six piece orchestra. She proceeded across the crowded room towards where the Briar had posted himself. The flash from a camera momentarily blinded her and by the time she blinked away the motes of light from her vision Briar was nowhere to be seen. Cursing under her breath Jordan proceeded through the crowd to where she last saw Young standing.

Thankfully, the event was winding down, because Jordan was thoroughly fed up with her rear being pinched, patted, or groped by drunken corporate officers and politicians. Crossing the floor in the alluring dress was like throwing a fillet mignon to a pack of dogs. With her best smile in place Jordan moved through the crowd paying no mind to the subtle, and not so subtle, touches. She pressed on until she reached a table where several glasses of champagne were stacked in several neat triangles. She sat the two spent glasses down and selected two full ones from the arrangement. Jordan sniffed at each discreetly, the way the bubbles tickled her nose made her nose wrinkle. Satisfied there wasn't anything dangerous in either glass she turned and looked for Briar again. *Where the hell have you gotten off to?*

After a sip from her glass Jordan shook her head. She was glad that she had been able to talk Brian out of attending the dinner after the luncheon. The dinner was taking place at a large estate outside of Moscow which would have been much harder to secure on short notice, especially with only a handful of operatives.

Jordan was unexpectedly pulled from her musings by a firm grip on her rear. Her immediate reaction was to glance backwards though she desired to precede the look with a hard elbow thrust. A grinning Briar Young moved up next to where she stood by a large decorative planter, his hand tracing the arch of her buttock.

"You'd best move that hand before I break the arm it's attached to," Jordan said and schooled her expression into one of congeniality.

Briar's expression transformed into a more subdued look of amusement, "Where would you like me to place it next? I can offer a few suggestions."

One of Jordan's slender black eyebrows arched, "My patience with your games has limits."

The smile faded from Briar's face as the sincerity of Jordan's terse response sunk in. "Alright, alright, just havin' a bit of fun, love. The parking lot looks clear. Did you still want to move him out the side entrance?"

Jordan's gaze swept to where Brian stood. He had moved on and was chatting up the Russian Trade minister and his assistant. As he spoke Brian adjusted the lapel of his dark grey Dolce Gabana suit. He continued to wear a charming smile as he had done most of the day, looking just as dashing as always. Jordan noted that Lina had joined the small cluster of people her dark suit and skirt contrasting with the high cut gold gown the trade minister's assistant wore. Nearby Douglas was watching over his charges looking dangerous and intense. "Yes. Once we manage to get him away from his fans."

"That one likes to talk, alright. He's been working the entire room like a pro. Never trusted blokes like that myself," Briar replied and drifted off. "I'm going to make another sweep, starting with the loo."

Jordan remained where she was and watched Briar cross across the room to the buffet area. He snatched a piece of shrimp from a plate and munched it as he continued out of sight near the restroom. A quiet sigh escaped Jordan and she found herself questioning Director McIntyre's judgment. She wondered what McIntyre could have been thinking in bringing Young onto the team.

* * * * * *

Brian Agincourt excused himself and headed away from the trade minister after a quick handshake. He had seen Young head into the bathroom and headed for it with Douglas in tow. "I'm going to hit the loo."

Douglas nodded in response. "Let me go in first to make sure it's clear, Ambassador."

"Of course," Brian replied. "I do get a bit of privacy when I'm in there, don't I?"

"I'll make certain of it," Douglas replied.

Brian nodded and walked over to the door. He gestured for Douglas to do his work and stepped off to the side to wait. Brian noticed Jordan watching them from across the room and smiled at her. When she returned the smile Briar grinned and looked at Lina, "I'll be right out. You may want to make a run. I don't think our security contingent is going to let us stop until we get to the plane."

Lina smiled and turned for the nearby women's restroom, "Good point. I won't be a moment."

Douglas waited for the two to finish before he pushed the bathroom door open with one hand. When he saw Young standing in front of one of the urinals, he nodded towards the man, "You the only one in here, Briar?"

"Yeah, just finishing my business, as it were."

"Good, the Ambassador will be right in so take your time washing up. You *do* do that, right?" Douglas said and cocked his head quizzically.

"Ha, fucking ha."

Douglas smiled and turned to where Brian stood. He gave Jordan a nod, noting her new position across the room. "You're all clear, Ambassador."

"Thanks," Brian replied and went into the bathroom. "I may be a few minutes, and I do want the privacy."

"You've got it. I won't let anyone in," Douglas replied and pulled the door shut.

Young was at a sink, washing his hands at a leisurely pace. He didn't spare more than a glance at Brian and continued washing.

Brian walked in with purpose and moved up to the sink right next to Young's. He turned on the water and begun washing his hands, his eyes settling on the other man.

Young felt Brian's gaze on him and looked in his direction, "Ambassador."

"Young, isn't it?"

"Yes, sir, Briar Young."

Brian inhaled and washed his hands thoroughly. "Briar Young," he said, committing the name to memory. "Do you mind if I call you Briar?"

"No," Young replied suspiciously and pulled three paper towels from the dispenser to dry his hands. After he finished drying his hands, Young tossed the used towels in the garbage can and admired his reflection in the mirror over the sink. He patted the sides of his hair lightly; making sure everything was in place.

"Good," Brian pulled a handful of paper towels from the dispenser himself and took his time drying his hands off. "Briar, I'm only going to say this once, so open your ears. If you *touch* my fiancé again, I'm going ruin you."

Briar's primping instantly ceased and he fixed the ambassador with an incredulous look. "Excuse me?"

"I saw your little maneuver out there," Brian said with a calm intensity. He crumpled up the towels and nonchalantly tossed them in the trash, "If it happens again, I'm going to break your fucking neck."

The thief was taken monetarily aback. He gave the ambassador a slick smile and shrugged his shoulders. "You don't know who I work for, mate. You can't touch me."

"I don't care who you work for," Brian said quietly. He stared into the shorter man's eyes without flinching. "If you touch Jordan like that again, I'll activate whatever dental policy your little secret organization provides you."

It only took one look into Brian's eyes to realize that he was willing to back up his words here and now if needed. The former thief was also certain that McIntyre would be more than a little brassed off if he and the Ambassador mixed it up. Maybe even enough to terminate their arrangement and send him back to prison. He gave Brian a contrite look and stepped back. "Hold on now. I was just having some fun with her. It won't happen again, you've got my word on that."

Brian nodded but said nothing as he moved for the door. He also made no effort to avoid Young which forced the agent to step around him. Brian waited and let his anger subside some before he joined Douglas outside. "Let's get going."

"Of course, Ambassador," Douglas refrained from smirking. He wasn't going to ask what happened. He had a theory, however; which he kept them to himself as he escorted Brian back towards the main room.

* * * * * *

The long hall reverberated with the merriment of the party goers. Their laughs and murmuring voices filled the empty space with a river of white noise. The further Briar Young got from the main hall the less detail he could pick out in the conversations and soon it was just a distant clinking of glasses. He was thankful for that. If he had a suitcase of Semtex he would blow all of them up; the rich and powerful, the government politicos and the military establishment types. He hated them all and his encounter with Brian Agincourt had just reinforced his opinion of them.

Even the passage of twenty minutes couldn't dampen the anger Briar Young felt. Agincourt was just like every other person of means Briar had ever met. He was arrogant and had no problem using his influence to destroy someone who pissed him off. One look in the ambassador's eyes told Briar everything he needed to know about the man. For a moment Briar wondered if his own father had seen the same thing the day he was fired from the plant. He wondered if the corporate executive that had let all of the workers go felt that sense of self-assured invincibility. After all who did the serfs and peons think they were to want an honest wage that could provide for their families. How dare they stand in the way of progress.

Briar would never forget the sight of his father lying against the living room wall weeping. He was only twelve at the time but Briar knew losing his job of nearly twenty years had broken his old man. It was only a year after that when Briar's mother left to shack up with some cop who could provide for her.

Any further reflection was abruptly halted as Briar's shoulder collided with a passing waiter. The impact almost sent him to the floor though the waiter barely moved. The tray waiter was carrying was knocked from his hands sending it and the utensils that were piled on its surface clattering to the floor.

The waiter didn't waste any time in stooping down to scoop up the assortment of silverware, "Excuse me." The man avoided eye contact as he quickly worked to gather up the scattered silverware.

Briar started to reply but stopped as he noticed a shark's tail picked out in black ink on the man's wrist. He couldn't see the entire tattoo but he didn't believe in coincidences. Without a word Briar crouched down and started to help the man pick up the scattered utensils, "Sorry about that mate. I wasn't paying attention."

The waiter nodded but said nothing as he quickly placed the silverware back on the tray. As he reached for the last wood handled steak knife his sleeved slid up his arm enough for Briar to see the entire tattoo. It was old and faded as if it had been inscribed years ago, a simple black shark with a tattered American flag in its mouth.

"Nice Tat. Guess the Spetsnaz hand those out like candy huh?" Briar asked matter-of-factly and looked into the waiter's eyes.

"You should have kept going," the waiter replied in English absent of any accent. In a flurry of motion he lunged for Briar and slammed his forearm across the smaller man's chest. Using his extra four inches of height and sixty pounds the Vodnik soldier drove Briar back into the wall sharply. Light flashed off of the knife's aluminum blade in the man's other hand as he positioned it to stab Briar in the heart. Then he froze in place.

Briar smiled darkly and gripped the man's forearm, "Thought you were going to just walk through me huh?"

The Russian grunted with effort as he tried in vain to move. Briar chuckled and reached over to open a nearby door with his other hand. After a quick check to make certain the laundry closet was empty Briar hauled the mercenary inside and shut the door with his boot. Keeping his grip on the man's forearm Briar started searching his pockets for anything of use. A cell phone, combat knife, and wallet later Briar smiled. He placed the knife and phone on a shelf of cleaning supplies before he flipped the brown leather wallet open. He read the name off of the diver's license, "Anton Kotko huh?"

The only response the Vodnik could give was an angry grunt. His brown eyes were murderous as they looked at Briar. There was little doubt in Briar's mind that the Russian would kill him if he could.

"I want to speak to your boss," Briar said and dropped the wallet on the shelf. He flipped open the phone and started cycling through the numbers in the device's memory. There were several that had been dialed within the last twenty four hours though two had been called repeatedly. Briar smiled and tucked the device into his jacket pocket, "You see I'm looking for a promotion, a position with good benefits and travel. Of course the compensation has to be top notch but I'd make some concessions if I can start right away."

The waiter suddenly found himself able to speak. Whatever force that had prevented him from doing so was gone though it continued to hold the rest of body in thrall, "Why would I give you anything? You're going to kill me so I don't see anything to gain by helping you."

"From what I understand you bastards are hard to kill. You help me, I help you," Briar said and picked up the man's thick bladed combat knife. He admired the edge for a moment and then looked at the helpless mercenary, "I'm going to give you an e-mail and you're going to give it to your boss. That's all you have to do."

"What's to stop me from killing you?" The man retorted.

"This," Briar replied calmly and turned the man towards a laundry cart parked in front of the laundry chute. There was little preamble as he lifted the blade beneath the man's sternum and into his heart. Without a second thought he shoved the Vodnik into the waiting laundry cart.

The mercenary twitched and gurgled as his heart stopped circulating blood. Briar grabbed the man's wallet and pulled a thick sheaf of bills from it, folding and tucking them into his pants pocket. He pulled a pen from inside his coat and quickly scribbled an e-mail address down on a piece of paper inside the wallet. With a casual flick of the wrist Briar tossed the wallet into the cart with the man, "Don't forget to give this to your boss."

Unceremoniously Briar pulled the knife from the man's chest so he would heal. He dropped the weapon into the cart next him and immediately began tossing clean towels from a nearby rack on top of the man. He continued until the mercenary's body was no longer visible before upending the cart dumping its contents into the laundry chute. Briar chuckled as he heard the man's body thump against the walls of the chute but he didn't dwell on it for long.

After checking himself for blood Briar walked back into the hall and collected the tray of utensils. He proceeded down the hall back towards the party and dumped the tray into a nearby garbage can. Briar gave his suit one last check before heading back into the party with a spring in his step.

* * * * * *

The way Young swaggered across the floor made Jordan curious. She wondered what could have possibly happened that gave him cause to walk around like he owned the world. Jordan considered that her dislike of Young might be coloring her perceptions. She didn't care. Jordan glanced up at Brian and then caressed his wrist with her hand, "We're going to miss our flight."

Brian glanced at his watch and nodded, "You're right." Jordan had given him the code phrase that morning. He wasn't quite ready to go but he wasn't about to push Jordan's patience. Just seeing her in the silk gown was worth leaving early. Brian smiled at the trade minister and extended his hand, "Minister, again, thank you for everything. I look forward to seeing you in a few weeks after I report to parliament."

Minister Artur Bobrov shook Brian's hand vigorously and gripped his shoulder, "Of course, Ambassador. When you come back, you and your lovely fiancé must come to my house for dinner."

"We would love to, Minister," Jordan replied earnestly.

The older Russian man took Jordan's hand and kissed the back of her knuckles gently, "Excellent. We will see you in a few weeks then."

Jordan slipped her arm back into Brian's and smiled in a way that lit up her eyes, "I'm looking forward to it."

"Artur, give my best to your family," Brian said, still smiling at the man warmly.

Bobrov chuckled, his rich voice full of amusement, "I'll will. Have a safe flight."

"Thank you, Minister," Brian replied and started to guide Jordan towards the designated exit.

As the entourage moved towards the exit Young turned and headed down the hallway leading to it.

Jordan followed Young towards their planned exit route. She placed a hand on her handbag and the Russian made GSh-18 nine millimeter semi-automatic pistol that Brian had procured. She didn't particularly care for the weapon as it had less stopping power than her .45 ACPs and it felt fragile. The

GSh was half-polymer and half-steel so Jordan thought it would hold up well enough, though she had heard reliability was a problem with it. It would fit in her handbag though, and it was better than nothing.

Despite all of her powers, Jordan liked being able to engage a target at range if possible. It was much easier to extract yourself from a situation when you could move and strike back. Getting too close to a target meant that you had to avoid everyone else's gunfire to stop them and, truthfully, being shot hurt.

The small procession filed down a long hall with only a few doors on either side. Jordan watched those doors warily as they walked towards the twin glass doors at the end of the hall. She concentrated for a breath and let her hearing expand outwards. Behind the doors to the left she heard the sounds of the kitchen staff working on cleaning up the mess made by the party guests. The clattering of plates and silverware being washed blended with the sounds of the staff's voices as they gossiped about the guests in Russian.

Satisfied that nothing was amiss there, Jordan cocked her head and focused on trying to hear anything coming from the right side of the hall. There, she heard only the sounds of laundry being washed by several whirring machines. The consistent droning of the washers and the sloshing of water made for a terrible bit of white noise. She furrowed her brow and willed her hearing back into normal ranges. She was still learning exactly how her physiology allowed her to control her hearing range and distance, but thanks to Doctor Lindon's lessons, she was gaining more control over it.

Discreetly, Jordan made a slight flicking gesture towards the right side of the hall. It was an indicator that she couldn't determine if there was a threat from that side or not and she trusted her teammates to follow that warning accordingly. She heard Douglas call Lincoln over the radio and the operative replied with the proper code phrase that indicated he was all clear.

There were only two types of operatives that trusted that the person on the other end hadn't been coerced to speak the proper phrase: the dead and the soon to be so. Keeping that in mind as she exited through the glass doors, Jordan looked around the exterior. There were numerous cars parked in the lot, all of which could have dangers hidden in or around them. Gunmen, explosives, even the potential of being struck by the car itself were all possible dangers when moving the principal, in this case Brian, through such an area.

Jordan allowed her perceptions and mental acuity to gradually ramp back up to their highest levels. Everything around seemed to slow and distort as her mind entered that state of alacritous existence. It only took moments for Jordan to visually search every nook and cranny of the parking lot that lay in her field of vision. She then methodically surveyed the tall buildings that filled the area for any unusual flashes, loiterers on the rooftops and the like. However, a good sniper wouldn't be in the window so much as they would be in a room with an open window a few meters away from it. Those were the ones that you wouldn't see until it was too late. Jordan held her hand behind her back to signal that the others stop inside the building's entrance.

With well-timed precision Brady Lincoln pulled the black Mercedes Benz sedan up to the side entrance and left the engine rumbling. Jordan recognized Lincoln's face through the partially open passenger window and met his gaze. She didn't see any alarm in the man's brown eyes, so Jordan gave him the briefest of nods in recognition that they were clear. Moving quickly, Jordan opened the rear passenger side door and swept the interior visually before she gestured to bring the others forward. As soon as Brian got to the car, Jordan slid in and over to the far side of the back seat. Brian and Lina came next, followed by Douglas, while Young darted around the rear of the idling car so he could climb into the front passenger seat. The whole process took seconds, but in it felt like a lifetime to Jordan.

As Young closed the door, Lincoln accelerated away from the building and pulled the powerful luxury car out into the late afternoon traffic. Rush hour was already in full swing so Lincoln eschewed the busy highway for the back streets, using the route he and Jordan had planned out the night before.

The occupants of the vehicle remained silent for several minutes as they cleared the area around the hotel. The hum of the engine was distant, thanks to the vehicle's normal sound proofing, which ensured that only the occasional thumps of the vehicle traversing rough spots in the road were heard. The four agents focused on looking for vehicles following them or any signs of ambush while Brian sat with his hands clasped.

Eventually, Brian broke the silence. "That went exceptionally well." He took Jordan's hand in his so he could squeeze it and smiled at her fondly. "It was interesting seeing you in action. If I didn't know better I would have never thought that you were part of the security contingent."

"Thank you, love. I think a large part of my success is owed to this gown," Jordan replied. She refrained from mentioning that this wasn't the first time that she had posed as someone's date on a mission.

Lina exhaled, "I'm glad we're done. I've never felt so tense in my life."

Jordan instinctively went to pull her hand away from Brian's, but stopped herself. "It's not over yet. Until we have you on a plane back home, we need to keep our guard up, and hands free." She followed the mild chastisement with a soft smile and traced her thumb over Brian's.

While Brian and Lina both had their attention focused on Jordan, Douglas mouthed the words *how adorable* and grinned.

The smile on Jordan's face grew wider in response which only encouraged Brian to lean in and kiss Jordan rather passionately. She placed her fingers on the side of his cheek and allowed herself a brief break from discipline.

It was Briar Young that spotted their tail first. "We've got a rider."

His tone was all business and prompted Jordan to abruptly break off the kiss and look out of the tinted rear window. Several car lengths behind them prowled a blue BMW sport bike with a single rider dressed in black leathers.

"He's made the last two turns with us," Young said and looked into the back seat. "I can't tell if he's armed, but he's definitely tailing us."

Brian's expression returned seriousness as he joined Jordan in looking back at the motorcycle. "What's the plan?"

Douglas reached up and pulled the knot out of the tie he had been wearing, discarding the accessory on the back deck of the Mercedes. "We do our job, Ambassador."

"Both of you keep your heads down and stick with William," Jordan added and reached beneath the seat in front of her to pull out a slim black combat vest with thin black armor plates attached all over the front, back and sides. "Put this on."

Brian did as he was told and put on the vest while Jordan secured the closures. "I've never seen a bullet proof vest like this before."

"It's new, Ambassador," Douglas said and pulled a similar one out from the other seat for Lina. "You can take an RPG in this and be ready for a polo match the next morning."

Lina took the vest from Douglas and shrugged into it. "This is going to be a bit snug. My assets are somewhat of a hindrance."

Jordan shot a hard look at Briar Young before he could comment. "We've expanded this one as much as possible. It won't be comfortable, but it's better than being shot without it."

The younger woman nodded and proceeded to fasten the vest down on her own. She pulled the front piece across her body from right to left and exhaled as she snugged it into place. The exaggerated expression she made as she clicked the plastic buckles closed was almost comical. "Yes, you're right about that first part."

While Jordan and Douglas prepared their charges, Young was speaking into his com unit alerting Chance and mission ops of their situation. The exchange was brief and once done, he pulled out his pistol. Young scanned the sedan's mirrors. "This thing isn't bulletproof, is it?"

"No," Brian replied in a surprisingly calm tone. "I've never needed a bulletproof car before."

"We may need one soon," Jordan retorted and glanced out of the side window, noting what had prompted Young to draw his weapon. She frowned as she caught a glimpse of another motorcycle pacing them. "There's another one, running parallel to us on the street over to the west."

"There's construction up ahead," Lincoln said. His voice was surprisingly calm.

They had checked for construction in their route planning and specifically chosen to go around it. They were at their most vulnerable when stopped and Jordan's instincts said that what awaited them up ahead must be a trap; Jordan made eye contact with Lincoln and pulled her pistol free the handbag.

"Everyone, hold on," Lincoln jerked the wheel hard to the right and slewed the Mercedes past the oncoming traffic. The car's tires squealed as he mashed the accelerator with his foot and tore off down the two-lane road. He expertly swung the sedan around a battered delivery van that was parked in the street and ignored the driver who screamed at him furiously in Russian. Lincoln wasted no time in accelerating once more and sped off down the road.

"Bollocks!" Young growled. "There's fucking lorry cross the road ahead. Turn, turn, turn."

Looking past Briar and Lincoln, Jordan could see a long tractor trailer parked across the road with several men unloading furniture from it. It was still several blocks ahead of them, but as they passed another street on the left she saw cars parked in both lanes of the street. Jordan quickly looked down the opposite road and saw that it was open and unblocked but the next two streets had some sort of blockage on either side as did the ones after that. "They're herding us."

"What?" Lina and Brian's alarmed voices chorused back.

Douglas nodded grimly and to the two motorcycles speeding up behind them. "She's right. We need to break the net now or we're assed."

"Lincoln, whatever it takes," Jordan said in a calm but emphatic voice. She glanced back once and then rolled the window down, "Do it."

Lincoln glanced in the rearview mirror and calmly sent the sedan into a long, arching turn to the right. The car slid onto a side street that was blocked by a garbage truck and careened onto the sidewalk. The passenger side fender exploded in a spray of sparks as the Mercedes clipped a brick building in its mad rush to escape the developing trap. All along the sidewalk, people screamed and dove out of the way of the speeding sedan as it plowed through nearly a block's worth of garbage cans leaving a wake demolished cans and refuse in its path.

The two motorcycles still came on, their riders avoiding the swath of destruction easily. One of the quick machines moved to the left of the Mercedes as it leapt off of the sidewalk back onto the street while the other stayed to its right. Both of the riders pulled compact Heckler and Koch MP5K submachine guns from behind their backs and accelerated towards the speeding sedan.

Suddenly, Jordan popped out of the left side window and fired two shots from her GSh-18. Both bullets tore through the faceplate of the rider's helmet and lodged in his brain, killing him instantly. With its rider now dead, the bike tore off at an angle and slammed into the back of a parked car sending both the rider and machine spinning over the top of it. By the time the wreckage came to rest, both the Mercedes and the other motorcycle were far down the street.

The second rider took the death of the first as a cue to begin more vigorous evasive maneuvers and started to weave randomly from right to left as it closed the distance. The rider tried to steer his machine alongside the driver's side of the car, but the Mercedes lunged towards the rider and forced him back.

"Take the next left!" Young shouted and looked back at where the rider was once again trying to get position on the driver's side of the vehicle.

Lincoln was already on it and pulled the Mercedes into a hard slide which carried it onto another street. At the speed they were traveling the car should have rolled but Lincoln's reflexes allowed him to make minute adjustments that kept it on the road. He had a determined look on his face as he took another turn at the same breakneck speed. This time the tail end of the luxury sedan smashed into a parked car as it passed which crumpled the rear quarter panel and ruined the fender. Lincoln smiled and hazarded a look in the rearview mirror. The motorcycle that pursued them didn't even try to make the turn, "Surprise, you bastard."

The rider gunned the machine and sped by the street entirely, his helmeted head turning to watch the escaping sedan.

Jordan looked out of the back window, "He's going to come round on us and try to cut us off."

"No need for that," Brian said in alarmed voice and pointed down the street where four more motorcycles waited along with three black American-made SUVs.

A lone man leaned out of the passenger side of one of the Cadillacs with a rifle that Jordan was all too familiar with raised to his shoulder.

Arkadi narrowed his dark eyes and sighted down the scope of the Accuracy International Arctic Warfare. The speeding Mercedes was already preparing to turn and the driver swung the car out wide so he could take the turn at high speed. As the vehicle cut to the left, Arkadi squeezed the trigger and fired a single 7.62x51mm bullet towards the sedan.

Jordan saw the muzzle flash and realized immediately that there was nothing she could do from the back seat of the car. She could see the waves of distortion radiating from the bullet as it sped towards them. At the moment, it was only a small dot that gleamed brightly as it reflected the rays of the summer sun. That far out, there was no way to determine who it was aimed at so Jordan took the only option she could.

Reaching forward with one hand she grabbed the back of the front passenger seat and pulled hard. The entire seat shuddered as the mechanism that locked it upright snapped under the force of Jordan's strength which pitched Briar's upper body backwards.

Without waiting, Jordan leaned her upper body across Brian and met his eyes. She was moving so fast that neither man had time to register what she had done, let alone react to it.

Just as the Mercedes reached the apex of its turn, the front passenger side window suddenly shattered. The high-powered round easily smashed through the glass, cut through the air where Briar Young's head had been, and slammed into the side of the Lincoln's head with the force of a sledgehammer.

Sergeant Brady Lincoln was dead before the car had fully crossed the halfway point of the turn. Without his steady hand on the wheel, the tremendous energies of the speeding Mercedes were uncontrolled and the vehicle's momentum carried it sideways towards an old brick apartment building. The occupants of the vehicle were suddenly sprayed with blood and bone and Lina's scream of horror filled the cabin.

"Young, get the wheel!" Jordan shouted over the sounds of Lina's terror and squealing tires. She quickly looked out the back window and saw the Russians already accelerating away from their makeshift blockade, towards the stricken sedan.

Briar Young's will to survive was one of his best traits, or so he thought. He immediately brought his leg over the console that separated him from the driver and stomped on the top of Lincoln's lifeless foot. The accelerator mashed to the ground and Young grabbed hold of the wheel with one hand to steer. The vehicle's engine roared as Briar fought to get the Mercedes under control, but his reflexes weren't up to the task. The back tires lost traction causing the rear end to swing out wide and slammed into the apartment building with a bone-jarring crash.

The sound of tortured metal and crunching plastic filled in the inside of the vehicle's cabin as the car slid along the side of the building for several feet. Sparks flew into the air as part of the vehicle's left side quarter panel and fender ripped free leaving pieces of metal, fiberglass, and multi colored plastic from the taillights in strewn all over the sidewalk.

"Somebody cut the seat belt!" Young screamed over the racket made by the disintegrating car. "I can't bloody drive this thing from the passenger seat!"

Jordan produced the carbon steel commando knife she had tucked in her boot and sliced Lincoln's shoulder belt free. Without hesitation she reached forward around the driver's side seat and released the lap belt's latch. "Go!"

A horrified expression appeared on Brian Agincourt's face as Jordan's hands hurriedly performed their work. "Wait! What are you doing?"

In the front seat, Briar Young contorted his body so he could reach across to open the driver's side door with one hand and place the other on the wheel. "Sorry, mate."

Brian made an attempt to grab Young before he could eject Lincoln's body from the car, but Jordan intercepted his wrists and held them firmly. "It has to be done."

"Jordan, that man's part of your team!" Brian exclaimed and tried unsuccessfully to free his hands from Jordan's grasp. His eyes flared with anger and searched Jordan's for any sign of compassion.

"I know," Jordan said softly. She clutched Brian's wrists as tight as she dared and held his gaze. "Do it."

Without any further ceremony Young pushed Lincoln's body out of the speeding Mercedes and slid into the blood covered driver's seat. Young glanced behind them as he slammed the door shut ignoring Lina's horrified gasp in the process. "Jordan, you need to stop wrestling with the Ambassador back there and deal with our friends."

Grim faced, Douglas looked out the back window. "We better do something quick. They're gaining on us."

"Douglas, give me your weapon," Jordan said and slammed a fresh magazine into her pistol.

Reluctantly, Douglas handed over his own GSh-18 and the three magazines he had for it. "What are you planning, Jordan?"

Jordan passed the magazines to Lina and checked Douglas' weapon before she released her own seatbelt. She kicked off her high heels and then tore the slit of her dress so that she could move more freely, "I'm going take care of this situation." Jordan took the magazines back from Lina and tucked them into the back of the gown.

Brian suddenly gripped Jordan's forearm. "What are you going to do? We just need to wait for the police to catch up to us. They can't have missed what's going on."

"The police aren't that expensive to buy here, Brian. If we don't end this now, we're either going to crash, or they're going to hit someone else. I'm just going to give them what they want," Jordan said in a harsh tone she immediately regretted.

Reluctantly, Brian released Jordan's arm and watched her with a pained expression. "What's that?"

"Me," Jordan replied and grasped the top of the door with one hand. She ignored Brian's startled shout and pulled herself out of the window. Jordan used the momentum of her exit to throw herself in a backwards arc so that her body would come up and over the roof. Twisting in mid-swing she pivoted around and landed on the roof of the speeding Mercedes, facing their pursuers.

Jordan moved into a low crouch on the roof, her dark hair whipping across her face. As she drew her own pistol from its holster, she released the restraints on her perceptions and reflexes, fully entering a state of hyper acceleration. She felt unchained, her body and mind unified in purpose and synchronized in movement. With a weapon in each hand, Jordan sprang high into the air, the twin 9MM pistols barking out shots so quickly they seemed to be firing on full auto. Her arms outstretched, the dark haired agent looked like an angel of death as she leapt the three car lengths that separated the sedan from the pursuing SUVs. The pistols spat fire and riddled two of the pursuing motorcycle riders with bullets as Jordan swept the weapons in a wide arc. She continued to track the weapons in an ever narrowing cone as she landed on the hood of the first SUV on one knee.

The lead SUV's driver still had a stunned expression on his face when four well-placed shots struck him in the heart. In the last moments of his life, the passenger of the SUV couldn't rid his mind of the terrible cobalt stare that the dark haired woman gave them just before she sprang away.

Keeping her body extended, long and straight, Jordan spun in a three hundred and sixty degree rotation several times. She kept her arms tightly folded across her chest through six rotations until her path and the second Escalade's crossed. When the toe of her right foot touched the front of the SUV's hood she extended her left leg and arms out to gather more momentum. At the pinnacle of her turn, she hurled both of the GSh-18 pistols in different directions.

The first pistol whirled like a pinwheel and embedded itself in another of the mercenary's motorcyclists' back. The man's body flew forward over the handle bars of his machine, transforming him them into a wildly tumbling ball of flesh and metal.

The second weapon crashed through the windshield in an explosion of glass. The driver threw his hands up to shield his face, but the presence of his hands did little to protect him from the spinning piece of metal and polymer. His cry of pain evaporated in the moment it took the weapon to connect with his skull.

Jordan brought her left foot down and dropped into a crouch where she perched on the front of the SUV's nose. She pushed off and threw herself into a flip just before the motorcycle and its deceased rider slammed into the front of the speeding Cadillac. The large sport utility lurched as the bike and its rider's body disappeared into the SUV's front wheels. The passenger side wheel locked up as the motorcycle's remains caught in the fender well and sent the vehicle into a sideways roll.

The dark-haired agent seemed to defy gravity as she hurtled over the second SUV's bulky form toward the remaining two vehicles. As she came down on the hood of the last SUV, the fourth motorcycle rider brought up his compact submachine gun and opened fire. Before the first shot had even left the barrel, Jordan dropped forward and planted her palms on the hood. She snapped her foot out and kicked the rider's wrist with her bare heel putting his weapon in line with the driver's side window. The hail of bullets struck both the screaming driver and the bald man sitting in the passenger seat.

For the first time in over a decade, Arkadi Malyev felt fear. True fear, cold and raw. It was an instinctual. Knowledge that what confronted you could extinguish your life. It was the fear of a death he had no means to stop. Mercy was absent in the dark-haired woman's blue eyes as she crouched on the hood. In her own way, Jordan Law was as much a predator as he was. At last, he understood why Konstantin was willing to pay such a high price to possess her. Amongst superior beings such as him and Konstantin, she was an equal.

The driver's body jerked violently as the hail of 9mm bullets ripped into it, spraying the cabin with blood. The motorcycle's rider was forced to drop his weapon in order to keep his machine upright and Jordan took the opportunity to launch herself into the air once more. She sprung out away from the SUV like an arrow and grabbed onto a nearby light post. Jordan spun around the post once, her gown trailing blue silk behind her as she tucked her legs up. As she reached the apex of her spin Jordan kicked her legs outwards and used the momentum to catapult herself towards the back of the last motorcycle. She landed gracefully on the back of the machine behind the rider just as he pulled away from the now out of control SUV. The man barely had time to glance back before Jordan seized him by his jacket and pitched him from the speeding bike.

Leaning forward Jordan gripped the motorcycle's handle bars, using them to pull herself forward on the seat. She stomped her feet down on the foot pegs and twisted the accelerator back making the bike's engine roar powerfully. A slight smile appeared on Jordan's lips as she felt the power of the bike flow from its engine, to the drive train, and then to the rear wheel. That smile only widened as the motorcycle accelerated like a rocket and tore down the wreckage strewn street past burning remains of the three SUVs.

Jordan guided the bike towards the battered sedan she had vacated less than a minute before. All three of the back seat's occupants looked at her with stunned expressions and, with adrenaline singing in her blood, Jordan winked at them.

CHAPTER 18

A grim expression had affixed itself to Konstantin Tretyak's face as he listened to Arkadi describe the attempt to capture Jordan in Moscow one more time. With arms folded across his broad chest he stared out the window at the people who went about their business on the packed London streets below. They were normal humans. Weak, frail, undisciplined. They went about their lives serving whatever corporate master they had tied their fates to. They were prey.

It had always been Tretyak's opinion of most humans. Jordan Law was different, and every time Tretyak looked at her picture, he felt his blood stir. Despite his desire to have Jordan, the cost of acquiring her was growing rapidly and his more practical side wondered if she was worth it. They had spent almost one hundred thousand dollars subcontracting mercenaries, bribing police, and acquiring the equipment for the operation. Fortunately, Arkadi had been the only member of the Vodnik on the mission, otherwise the cost would have been much higher.

"I have never seen anything like it. Like her," Arkadi rasped painfully. "I understand now, my brother. I understand why you want this woman."

The Crimson Shark turned and looked at his longtime friend and lieutenant. The entire left side of Arkadi's body was a mass of purple and red burned flesh that pulsed unnaturally. His regeneration was struggling to repair the damage caused when the SUV he had been in crashed and caught fire. Arkadi's body had long expelled the bullets that he took during the encounter, but the damage caused by fire was much more difficult to heal.

The destruction the cell's ability to reproduce meant that Arkadi's body had to reconstruct those missing pieces from scratch and that took a long while to accomplish. His body also had to repair a damaged eye, and ear, not to mention all of the organs that had been injured when the Escalade had smashed into the wreckage of the one in front of it. It was only through Arkadi's stubbornness that he lived. Tretyak reached out and gave his lieutenant's uninjured shoulder a firm squeeze, "I am glad you survived, brother. I'm willing to spend much to possess this woman, but not your loyalty, or your life."

Arkadi laughed. The sound was hoarse and wet. "Stop worrying like an old woman. This little injury is nothing. You gave me the gift of your power and saved my life in doing so. How can I refuse you this thing you want so much?"

"Afghanistan was a shit hole, wasn't it?" Tretyak said thoughtfully. He remembered the ambush that had nearly killed them both. Despite his powers, the Mujahidin fighters had overwhelmed the Spetsnaz team that Arkadi and he had lead into the Hindu Kush mountain range. Arkadi had been mortally wounded by an RPG blast and Tretyak had given his own blood to his friend in an attempt to save his life. It had done so, turning Arkadi from a normal human into a metamorph like Tretyak, himself. He had barely survived the process due to the seriousness of his wounds, but in the end, Arkadi's will won out.

Arkadi laughed, but was wracked by coughs as the air irritated his burned lungs. He closed his eyes and settled back into his bed, letting the episode pass. "It was. Let the Americans deal with it now."

"Get some rest. I should have handled this myself," Tretyak said and looked down at his friend. "How can she respect me if she never has to face me?"

There was no reply from Arkadi. Once again, he had succumbed to his body's need for rest, which caused him to fall into a coma-like sleep. Tretyak watched his friend for a moment before he turned and left the room. Outside the door, a small balding man in his sixties waited. He was wearing an out-of-date grey suit and silver framed eyeglasses that perched unevenly on his nose. The man grabbed his briefcase from where it sat next to him on the floor and hurried to keep pace with the taller Tretyak.

"You have the results?" Tretyak said without looking at the man.

The little man looked up at Tretyak as they walked. "Yes. It was difficult to run the tests from what little DNA we found. However, the car they abandoned had a few strands of her hair and I was able to create several models."

Tretyak fixed his dark gaze on Doctor Yeltin. "And?"

"It will work, *if* we use a direct spinal infusion. Your blood and flesh are teaming with the microbes that pass on your abilities. However, as you well know, successful transmission is not always assured. If I take a sample of your spinal fluid and transfuse it into her spinal column, it will very effectively overwhelm her regenerative abilities. I have very little doubt that her transformation will be quick, though probably very painful," Yeltin said between breaths as he struggled to keep up with the Crimson Shark's determined pace.

"When will you be ready to take the sample?" Tretyak asked as he pushed the double doors to his office open. He crossed the large room and took a seat an oversized leather chair that sat behind a black desk made of wood and metal.

The doctor held the handle of his briefcase in both hands and watched his employer. "Why, right now. My lab is ready. I can maintain the sample's viability indefinitely. I overheard your men mention the difficulty you're having in acquiring this particular subject, and I want to assure you it will be ready when you are."

Tretyak's expression turned dangerous and he settled his dark eyes on the smaller man. "Cost?"

The doctor inhaled and marshaled all of his courage. He was terrified of this man, and was already regretting the arrangement. "One million pounds, in bonds. Half when I take the spinal fluid from you, the other when I infuse the subject."

"Deal," Tretyak replied and pulled open a desk drawer. He pulled out a photo of a middle aged woman with long brown hair and a young girl who was no more than five or six years old sitting on a warm, sunny beach. Both were wearing swimsuits and smiling as if they hadn't a care in the world. The Crimson Shark casually tossed the picture onto the desktop so that it landed where the doctor could see it. "Once it's done, I will return your daughter and granddaughter to you, Doctor Yeltin."

"Oh, my god," Yeltin's voice cracked, fear making his voice barely more than a whisper. His hand trembled as he picked the glossy eight-by-ten from the desktop and stared at the smiling faces of his family. "W-why? There's no need for this."

"Insurance. I've heard that some of your experiments don't turn out well," Tretyak said as he leaned back in his chair. The little man's scent was laced with fear and anger, but beneath it all, there was helplessness. As usual, Tretyak kept the smile from his face. "They're currently enjoying an all-expense paid vacation. However, I understand that this beach has a problem with sharks."

* * * * * *

The sidewalk in front of the Carmichael Building was teaming with people as the lunch time crowds rushed about to get their mid-day meals. All around, there were men and women dressed in suits and professional outfits with cups and takeout boxes in their hands. Several talked amongst each other and discussed the comings and goings of their respective businesses while others spent the noon hour talking to loved ones via wireless phones.

Doctor Thomas Lindon always marveled at the way humanity adapted to their circumstances. Society had gotten busier and busier, so they had invented fast food and wireless phones. They were plagued with disease, so they made vaccines and treatments. They needed more food, so they invented hydroponics and cloned animals. All in all, humanity was an amazing thing.

Just as Lindon reached the main entrance, the door burst open and a rather upset-looking man in his sixties came rushing out. The man's briefcase clipped Lindon's arm which made the smaller man lose his hold on it. The aluminum covered case tumbled to the ground at Lindon's feet with a clatter.

"Watch out!" the older man barked angrily.

Lindon responded with a friendly smile and stooped down to pick up the case. "Sorry, my friend, I didn't mean to block your way."

The shaken looking man snatched his case from Lindon's hand hurried off down the busy sidewalk. Doctor Lindon shook his head and watched the man until he disappeared into the throng of lunch goers. Dismissing the man from his mind, Lindon pulled the glass door of the Carmichael Building open and stepped inside.

The entry of the building was spacious and decorated in black and grey granite from wall to floor. There was minimal artwork about, only a few brass planters and a large glass sculpture of the Greek god Poseidon rising up from the waves. To either side of the statue were two sets of brass elevator doors that had been crafted with a wave-shaped facing. Lindon turned and headed to the west side of the building where one of the business district's trendiest cafés sat.

The brass sign above the café's entrance read Eternity and was back lit with a soft red light. Lindon smiled and considered how presumptuous the name of the place was considering how fragile the world was. Even from outside, he could see that the place was packed with people wearing expensive suits and other business attire. As he neared the café, the scents of braised sirloin tips, roasted chicken, and steamed vegetables filled his nostrils.

The pleasing array of smells brought a smile to Lindon's face and he swept by the pretty hostess with a dip of his head and jaunty wave. The woman was quicker than she looked and she stepped in front of Doctor Lindon like a well-dressed guard dog. "Excuse me, sir. Do you have a reservation?"

Lindon blessed the woman with a charming smile and followed her gaze down to the bright red Converse sneakers he wore. "I know, dress code and all that. I'm here to meet Doctor Elgen Spears. He's a cranky, arrogant sort of chap that doesn't like to be kept waiting."

The woman's expression became more congenial. "Doctor Spears is expecting you, Doctor Lindon. This way, please." She gestured towards an area that was slightly raised and provided a view of the rest of the café.

Still smiling, Lindon followed the hostess across the busy restaurant. He ascended the two steps that lead up to where

Spears sat in one bound and dropped into the seat across from his host, "Doctor."

Spears inclined his head in Lindon's direction and waved the hostess off dismissively. He reached into the inside pocket of his expensive suit and placed a gold pocket watch on the table. Using his thumb, Spears flipped open the face cover and then picked up the glass of whiskey in front of him. "Our conversation won't be overheard, Lyhonon."

The smile instantly vanished from Lindon's face and was replaced by a grimace. "I don't go by that name anymore, Vandre. Unlike you, I'd rather forget those days, that life, and enjoy a casual existence of study and observation."

"Oh, I very much would like to forget those days, my friend. It doesn't seem that either of us will be given that opportunity."

Lindon picked up the glass of water that sat in front of Spears untouched and took a drink from it. "What do you mean, Elgen?"

"Talamud and a Second Caste paid me a visit," Spears replied and gave Lindon a meaningful gaze.

The second Jenagyr's expression changed to one of poorly concealed shock and he slowly sank back in his chair. Any reply he could have mustered at the moment was lost in thoughts of the homeworld and his former life as a Fourth Caste genetics technician.

"You can thank me later for dealing with them, Lhyonon. I also recovered their vessel and dealt with another Second Caste that was left to guard it. We don't have much time left." Spears' voice had a certainty in it and his eyes were as serious as Lindon had ever seen them.

They had known each other for the better part of seven thousand years and that was what made Lindon the most uncomfortable. Spears was seldom concerned about anything other than his work and the very fact they were meeting after a decade of avoidance highlighted his former friend's level of concern.

Lindon downed the water and set the glass in front of him. He studied the multifaceted crystal that the container had been formed from, admiring the way the light reflected off of its surface. "Did you get anything from them?"

"What do you think? They displayed their usual contempt for a lower casteman. Their arrogance allowed me to kill them," Spears replied contemptuously.

"Is there a reclamation battalion coming?" Lindon asked in a quiet voice.

Spears' head shook slightly. "No. Their scout ship's communications log showed that they were dispatched to investigate a micro-singularity a few light years from here. Normally, I wouldn't be concerned. Their disappearance could easily be explained on navigational error, an Incarna attack, even pirates."

"But?"

"They're from the Eighty-Third Warhost." The horrified expression on Lindon's face drew looks from the occupants of the nearest table and Spears acted quickly to get Lindon under control. "Get a hold of yourself, Lyhonon. I took care of them. Even the mighty Lord Dominous won't look for the ship."

Doctor Lindon's shoulders slumped. "The Eighty-Third. You know as well as I do what horrors Dominous would inflict on this world. Humanity would cease to be. At best, they would be slaves. At worst, he would use an orbital strike to irradiate everything on the planet simply because it amused him."

Spears leaned forward and slammed his palm down on the table rattling the silverware. He ignored the other patron's looks and hissed angrily at Lindon. "If you had worked with me to Awaken these primates, we would have an army that even Dominous wouldn't be able to defeat! Instead, you've squandered your long years on observing them, studying their behaviors. You've wasted your superior intellect, Lhyonon. Wasted it. *If* for some reason, Dominous chooses to come to this backwater, insignificant world, the human's deaths will be on your head. We have been here for twenty thousand years, and I have asked you time and time again to join me in my work. Every time you refuse. Just like the others did, all of you thinking you're human. All of you equally pathetic!"

Lindon's expression grew dark and he fought his desire to respond to his former friend's baiting with anger. After a deep breath, the Jenagyr that had once been known as Lhyonon fixed his gaze squarely on Spears'. "I haven't changed my views on this subject, Vandre. If we subjugate humanity, how does that make us any better than our own upper castes? All we're doing is replicating a bad idea and condemning another species to servitude. These are living, thinking, loving creatures. Not so unlike us, in our early days. Our people feel war in their blood; we thrive on conflict far more than any other species we've encountered. Humanity does as well. Look at their entertainment. Do you remember the games in Rome? The pit fights in Gaul? What about all of the underground fights you attend even now, Vandre? Somewhere in the human psychology, they have learned to rein in these tendencies. It is a constant struggle for them, yet they are slowly evolving as a society, as a species."

A harsh alien sounding chuckle resonated from deep inside Spear's throat. "Evolving? Peace? They kill each other as readily as our own people have. When is the last time you've been in Africa or The Middle East? Watched the news lately? They are violence channeled, fueled by greed, fueled by a lust for power. All they need is a strong hand to guide them as a species, to direct their capacity for innovation, adaption, and violence to a greater end. Imagine what seven billion Awakened humans could do to our former masters? We could free our lower caste brethren and put ourselves at the head of the Jenagyr Empire!"

"All of your proselytizing will not change my mind. It hasn't in thousands of years, why do you think now is any different?" Lindon retorted.

Spears balled his hand into a fist and for a moment it looked as if he were going to strike Lindon. Slowly, he lowered it to the table, his voice still filled with a quiet malice. "You're a fool, Lhyonon, a fool and genetic deviant. Even without your help, I will break the genetic locks the Incarna placed on their forgotten children. I will take this world, and I will use the genetic spawn of our greatest enemy to free our brethren and to destroy their very own creators."

Pity filled Lindon's voice as he slowly rose from the table. "Who's the fool here Vandre? Is it you or I? I see the folly of subjugating another sentient people to free our own oppressed caste. Assuming you succeed in all of your grand plans, when do you expect your Awakened human army to rebel against you? Will it be your own technical servants that foment it? For all of your scheming and bluster and, indeed, actions, you have shown me nothing different than a First Caste would. You plan to have servants, and sycophants, and harems of exotic females just as any First Caste. You create weapons of destruction and plan to use them without restraint. Any hand of friendship is slapped aside so you can better hold onto your own power and envisioned genetic superiority. All you seek to do is place yourself in their company, to rule in their place."

Silence was Elgen Spear's only reply to his former friend and colleague. His narrowed eyes virtually blazed with the rage he was struggling to keep in check.

After letting the silence hang between them for a few moments, Lindon's normally contagious smile returned and he bowed to Vandre as if he were a triumphant general accepting the surrender of an enemy commander. "Good day, Doctor Spears."

It took every ounce of Spears' considerable willpower to refrain from leaping up and strangling his fellow Jenagyr technician. Lhyonon had always been an insufferable idealist, and particularly expert in rubbing those ideals in everyone's faces. As he watched Lindon maneuver his way out of the busy café, Spears swore that he would make certain his former friend lived to see the moment of his victory. He would provide a front row seat so that the insufferable man would see former Fourth Caste Technician Vandre become the ruler of humanity and the savior of the Jenagyr lower castes. Then, once that was complete, once he had everything he had always dreamed of, he would strangle the life from Lyhonon with his bare hands. .

* * * * * *

The way Shaw watched Jordan made her nervous. He was harder to read than her father was though she expected Shaw's response was about to be similar to one of the dressing downs she received during her teenage years. It had been two days since the team touched down at Heathrow with Brian and his people in tow. They had all been through debrief, though Brian and Lina got an especially thorough grilling, thanks to Jordan using her powers in their presence.

Director McIntyre hadn't even spoken to her and that made Jordan nervous. She expected to be punished in some manner, perhaps even expelled from the agency for violating one of its principle tenants, but she wanted to at least defend herself. There was no doubt in her mind that she made the right call. They would have never escaped the Russians if she hadn't acted.

"How do you think you did?" It was *just* like one of her father's lead-ins. The tone Shaw utilized was even and calm, not accusatory in the least. She wondered if, like her father, Shaw was going to make her incriminate herself.

Jordan mulled over her response, just as she would do with her father. "I did what it took to save the lives of my mission team and my principal."

Shaw raised an eyebrow. "Principal? You mean your fiancé?"

"Of course."

"Let's not mince words, Jordan. I'm not looking to find a scapegoat. This is an honest mission review. You were the team leader, you made the calls. We need to walk through them so that we both learn from the operation," Shaw replied casually.

"Yes, Colonel," Jordan said and searched Shaw's eyes for any sign of a trap.

"You chose to break our number one rule; public power use in an uncontrolled environment. I've read the reports, but I want to hear your thoughts on it. Why did you opt to exit the vehicle and go after the pursuit team?" Shaw asked in that same inscrutable tone.

"We had entirely lost the initiative. We were on the run in an area we were only familiar with on paper and, at the time, we had already had one casualty. The vehicle was badly damaged and I realized that if I didn't do something we weren't going to be able to extract," Jordan explained. She continued before he could interject anything else. "I considered our current weapon load out and the lack of any reinforcements and realized we weren't going to get out of the situation without a more aggressive response."

"Douglas agreed with you. That's not surprising. You and he seem to have bonded."

Jordan tilted her head slightly, and was more than a little angry at the comment. "Are you suggesting he's covering for me, sir?"

"Not at all, he wouldn't do that if you had really bodged it," Shaw said and rubbed his chin. "Briar said you made the right call too. That's pretty good, considering how well you two get on."

"I guess saving his ass earned me some good will," Jordan said dryly.

Shaw shrugged. "Maybe. Young is many things, but he recognizes the reality of a situation that some of us military types miss. We tend to put our head down and charge even when we could step to the side and avoid something altogether. He looks after his own skin, so he doesn't engage in unnecessary conflicts. If he's backing your call, then he didn't see any other way out of it either."

Jordan replied honestly. "I'll try and keep that in mind, sir."

The response was a nod and Shaw continued on with the debrief. "So, why you, Jordan?"

"Excuse me?"

"Why did you exit the vehicle? Why not Douglas? He's nearly impervious and he's stronger than you are by far, "Shaw queried and watch Jordan's eyes.

"He's stronger, yes, invulnerable, yes, but he's not as agile, or as accurate as I am. If he had missed one jump we would have been down a team member," Jordan explained.

Shaw countered quickly, "What if you had missed?"

"I'm faster than he is. I could have re-engaged with a little creativity."

"So you didn't have any reservations about leaving Brian?"

Jordan's response was all business, but emphatic. "Of course, I did. I know I was emotionally invested in the outcome, but I was the best choice to stop the pursuit. Our best play was to keep moving. If we had stopped to try and engage them we would have been surrounded and overwhelmed. I was unquestionably the best choice to go on the offensive because I'm better on the move and had the powers to back the action."

A smile finally broke Shaw's mask of neutrality. "Good enough. What mistakes did you make?"

"Mistakes," Jordan said and let the word hang in the air. She wasn't used to making mistakes, but she knew she had made a few this time. "I should have waited for satellite coverage so that Brian's apartment could be thermaled. I rushed and called an entry when I wasn't certain, or even reasonably sure, what I would find inside. I let my emotions get the better of me. My fear of losing Brian compromised my instincts. As a result, I acted when I should have waited."

Colonel Shaw seemed satisfied with the response. "Correct, on all counts. Do you have anything else to add?"

Jordan shook her head. "Do you?"

"Don't beat yourself up about this, Jordan," Shaw started. "We had to play this hand. If I had a choice, you would have sat this one out. As it was, we needed our heaviest hitters on this operation and that's you and Douglas. Honestly, this showed one glaring fault in our team make-up. We don't have enough power-based damage output or resilience. We can handle the ones and twos but a team of hyper-physicals puts us at a massive disadvantage. These metamorphs are a game-changer for us, we're going to have to adapt."

There was no doubt in Jordan's mind that Shaw was correct. The encounters with the Vodnik hadn't been victories. So far, SOS7 had come up nil and had only saved its own skin in every conflict. The thought made Jordan worry for her family who were currently in protective custody with the team's non-powered operatives. "What are we going to do about it in the short term?"

Shaw smiled at Jordan like a predatory cat. "Oh, we've got a few tricks up our sleeves. You better go get dressed so that you don't keep Chance waiting. He's been chasing this contact down since Saint Petersburg so he's probably in a mood already."

* * * * * *

Rain deluged London, as was often the case, without warning or mercy. Every surface echoed with the resonance of the corpulent drops of water as they struck, creating a pleasing array of natural sounds. The hollow metallic accompaniment of water spilling into the street drains added a back rhythm to the evening environment and made conversation outside of a few feet almost impossible.

Jordan and Chance strolled down the street arm in arm. Both were clad in stylish club-going clothes beneath the long black trench coats they wore to keep themselves dry. Jordan felt very self-conscious in the skin-tight leather pants and half top she wore; it wasn't her usual dress and it did nothing to keep her warm in the cold British weather. As they walked, Chance frequently adjusted the dark blue brollie, in his left hand to keep Jordan as dry as possible. The rain did its best to defeat the protection of the umbrella by coming down at a slight angle.

Walking so intimately with anyone aside from Brian made Jordan feel odd, but she and Chance were trying to blend in amongst the other late night pedestrians. They were near several clubs and it made sense for a man and woman to be walking as a couple instead of alone in streets that were frequently dangerous.

"You need to relax, Jordan," Chance said just loud enough for Jordan to hear. "It's not like you're cheating on him."

"I see you've added mind-reading to your repertoire," Jordan said in a good natured voice.

Chance chuckled and discreetly pulled Jordan a bit closer. "I am a man of many talents."

Jordan smiled and leaned into Chance, taking his bicep with both hands. She forced herself to relax her posture and rested her head on his shoulder. "Better?"

"Definitely. In a platonic sense, of course," Chance replied. "How's Brian going to take all this running about with other men anyways?"

"Now that he knows what I do, I think he'll be ok with it. To a point. I'm glad that Ethan allowed him to remain at the office," Jordan said mentioning the Director by first name just in case anyone could overhear what she was saying.

Chance nodded. "He's a good bloke, our boss. My guess is that he assumes Brian will be easier contained and protected at the office. Besides, Ms. Cat-out-of-the-bag, you've shown him all of your goodies now haven't you?"

Jordan laughed quietly. "I suppose I have, at that."

"We're almost there, now. His flat is right above the butcher on the corner," Chance said quietly and indicated the shop with a nod of his chin.

"Right. You're sure he can be trusted?" Jordan replied and swept her gaze over the shadowed streets methodically. Most everyone was dressed in similar fashion with club outfits beneath rain wear.

Across the street, the sidewalk was packed with a line of club-goers waiting to get into The Veil. It was a trendy Goth club that catered to the crowd that favored black clothes and lots of make-up though it had a reputation for being little more than an S&M club that had been dressed up.

"No. His information is usually good, though and we don't have too many options." Chance replied and paused in front of a worn steel door that was covered in chipped blue paint. Next to the door was a battered intercom with a speaker at the top and a white buzzer button which he pushed with his thumb. Chance released the button after a few seconds.

A voice with a Russian accent issued forth from the speaker a moment later. "Got the money?"

Chance glanced around to make sure nobody was near enough to overhear, "Yeah, plus a bonus if the information is exceptionally good."

The buzzer sounded again and the door's heavy lock clicked open. Chance grabbed the metal handle and hauled the metal door open. He looked up the stairs briefly and then motioned for Jordan to enter while holding the door open for her.

The staircase consisted of old wooden stairs surrounded by white walls, graying from age and inattentive housekeeping. There were very few features except the old, incandescent light that cast the interior in a pale yellow glow. Cautiously, Jordan walked inside and triggered her powers. As expected, everything seemed to slow to a crawl around her. Each step made the old staircase creak in protest and Jordan avoided grabbing the metal railing that ran along each side of it. Lots of nasty surprises could be connected to or inserted in a conductive metal object, the least of which could incapacitate an unsuspecting person. Jordan did a quick search for any signs of tampering, just in case she needed to make use of the railing at some point. When she found none, she continued up the staircase and paused in front of another steel door.

At the bottom of the stairs, Chance made the pretense of shaking water off of the umbrella by opening and closing it. He diverted his attention between Jordan and the street and waited for her nod before he stepped inside and allowed the door to latch shut. Much like Jordan, Chance avoided the hand rail as he jogged up after his partner. As he reached the door, he rapped on its metal surface four times in quick succession with the handle of the umbrella.

Three metallic clanks resonated through the door as it was unlocked from inside the apartment. It didn't take long for the door to swing open. Behind it, stood a decidedly ugly, balding man in his late fifties dressed in a pristine white tank top and a pair of black slacks. He was no more than five foot five and his compact muscular form displayed the hard won mileage of a rough life. His arms were decorated with a myriad of scars, many of which looked like they had been inflicted by shrapnel, though a distinct series of five white lines ran from his right shoulder to his forearm.

"You bring a lovely woman to my home, Chance. What you want must be worth a lot of money," the man half-slurred.

He spoke with a thick Russian accent that Jordan found to be so theatrical it made her doubt its validity. Grinning broadly with a mouth full of stained teeth, the little man bestowed Jordan a lascivious look that made her skin crawl. He let his brown eyes wander her body openly, but Chance smoothly stepped in front of Jordan to block his view.

"She's with me, Dimitri. You've got money, go buy yourself a woman if you can't find one that will put up with your ugly face."

The worn little man grinned up at Chance in a friendly manner. "And here I thought my bonus would be a night with this amazing creature. My luck has never been so good, I think. Come in, my friends. Let us talk."

Jordan and Chance followed the man into an apartment that reeked of clove cigarettes, vodka, and greasy takeout. It wasn't much to look at either. The walls had once been white, but were faded and stained yellowish from cigarette smoke and general neglect. The sparse furnishings were all old and worn as if they had been pulled off the back of a donation truck. There was no rhyme or reason to the colors, and most had off-color patches. A large flat screen plasma TV stood out from the rest of the apartment's trappings and an assortment of American and Russian DVDs sat next to a compact silver disc player.

Dimitri motioned to the TV casually as he picked up a wiry old tabby cat from the couch and gently sat it on the floor. "I like football." The cat hissed and padded past Jordan and Chance towards a door that was cracked open just far enough for it to slip through. Dimitri motioned to the feline. "Ignore Babba, she's older than the furniture and not good with people she doesn't know."

Dimitri nodded towards a kitchenette set with a pink table and three blue chairs. "I'll get us something to drink."

Chance and Jordan remained standing with the former shaking his head. "No, thank you. We'd like to get down to business."

"You know, that's the problem with people these days. No time for pleasantries. No patience for small talk," Dimitri observed as he walked into the kitchen and pulled three tumblers from the cupboard. As he passed a half full bottle of Stolies Vodka sitting idle on the counter, he grabbed it with one hand and placed it, along with the glasses, on the kitchen table. Dimitri pulled out one of the old wooden chairs that sat at the table and deposited himself in it. "You have lots of questions, yes? If so, sit. Be comfortable. If I wanted to try something, I wouldn't be doing it here. Not when you have people outside watching us."

Jordan acquiesced and took a seat in the chair next to Dimitri. She folded her hands in front of her on the table and lightly tapped one of the glasses with her fingernail. "Are you pouring or talking?"

"I like this one, Chance. She's very direct," Dimitri said with a Cheshire-like grin.

Chance took the seat immediately across from Dimitri and looked the man square in the eyes. "She's a handful, though. She's very demanding."

"I like a demanding woman. They're generally very good in bed, yes? They love to get rough and dirty. They also go all night long and demand more in the morning." The Russian filled the three glasses and smiled at Jordan in a suggestive manner.

The expression on Jordan's face was playfully suggestive though her eyes never managed to capture the sentiment. They were icy and cool as they returned the Russian's look. She reached into her coat and produced a laminated picture. A scowling bald man glared out from the flat piece of paper as she placed it on the table in front of Dimitri. It was a computer reproduction based on Jordan's description of the bald man that had been on the Russian hit team. It wasn't perfect, but it seemed to strike a chord with Dimitri.

The suggestive expression evaporated like it had never been as Dimitri stared down at the picture. His scarred right hand hovered over the edge of it, not quite touching it as if he were afraid it might burn him. He made a deliberate effort to pick up the picture though he never lifted it more than a few inches from the table.

"It seems our first question has been answered," Chance said after taking a drink of the vodka.

Jordan nodded and flicked her eyes to Dimitri. "We need to know everything about this man. Who works for him, who he works for, *everything*."

Dimitri dropped the picture on the table and grabbed his glass. He downed the contents of it like water and sat back in his seat. Unconsciously, he brought his left hand to the five white lines that marred the flesh of his right shoulder and massaged the skin. "This will cost double."

"Double is fine if we get good information," Jordan replied before Chance could speak. The latter sat back in his seat and watched the Russian with wary eye.

Nodding, Dimitri refilled his glass and downed it again. "This man is your enemy, yes?"

"He appears set on it," Jordan said and took a sip from her own glass. She held the liquid in her mouth for a few moments before swallowed it. "Who is he?"

"A bad man to have as an enemy. An evil man," Dimitri replied and leaned forward to pick up the vodka bottle again. He quickly filled his glass and sat the near empty bottle down. As soon as the glass was full, Dimitri drained it to half capacity and swirled the rest of the contents around.

"This man, this enemy of yours, is a monster, a murderer. Inhuman. This is what he looked like when you saw him?" Dimitri asked.

Jordan nodded and drank from her glass again. She could smell the acrid stink of fear emanating from the Russian. He was terrified but doing his best to conceal it. "We know *what* he is. We need to know *who* he is."

The Russian rose to his feet and shuffled over to the kitchen. He crouched down and lifted a section of tile near the battered white stove that sat against the wall. When he stood back up he held a steel strong box in both hands. It had a thick coating of dust on its surface, which he blew off, sending it wafting into the air. He waved his hand through the cloud to disperse it and returned to his seat at the table. He let the box lie for half a minute before he pushed the lid up with both hands.

Inside, there were several worn envelopes and a stack of photos bound together by a thick rubber band. Dimitri hesitated for a moment before his calloused hand reached into the box and pulled the bundle out. He placed the stack in front of him and worked the band off, the aged rubber snapping in the process. He set the remains next to the box before he began to flip through the photographs. After a few moments of searching, he selected one five by seven photo and placed it in front of Jordan and Chance.

The photograph was worn around the edges as if it had seen as much living as its owner. The colors were pale and desaturated, marking the picture as something taken with a low quality camera on film that was made decades ago. It depicted fifteen young men, hard eyed and grime-covered, all dressed in khaki fatigues and loaded down with Soviet-era military equipment. They looked like they had been in the field for some time, though many had smiles on their dirt-streaked faces.

Jordan immediately recognized the bald man who scowled in the direction of the camera as if he were trying to kill the photographer with a look. Next to him was a larger man who had short dark hair and rugged features. His face, though attractive, held little emotion and his dark eyes were as unforgiving as any Jordan had ever seen.

Dimitri tapped the bald man's face. "That is Arkadi Malyev. He was the second in my Spetsnaz unit. Back then, we thought we were unstoppable. We were killers, ghosts in the night. Arkadi was one of our most ruthless and one of the most skilled. We all feared him, but we knew he would see us through the war. Still, nobody liked him. He killed women, children, whomever he felt like. He even killed an infantry lieutenant once because the man refused to provide support for one of our teams."

"Who's this other man?" Jordan asked and placed her index finger above the dark haired man.

"That is Colonel Konstantin Tretyak," Dimitri replied quietly. "He was our commander. If anyone is holding your dog's leash now, it's him. He was the only one who Arkadi respected enough to listen to. Tretyak was one of the best Spetsnaz officers I had ever seen back then. He was loyal to his men and an excellent tactician. He is also a thing, a creature. I don't know what he is exactly, but he isn't human." Dimitri paused to light up a cigarette. He looked down at the photo as he took a drag from it. "I saw him change once, in the middle of a battle with the Mujahedeen. He looked like some sort of demon, half-shark and half-man. They shot him again and again, but nothing stopped him. He tore into them with his teeth, his claws. There was nothing left of them but bloody rags and bits of flesh. Then he came for me. It was as if he didn't recognize me."

The Russian massaged the shoulder where the five white scars marred the flesh and his voice took on a distant tone as he relived the experience in his mind. "I tried to run, but he grabbed my shoulder and lifted me off the ground like I was a pebble. His breath stunk of blood and flesh, and I pissed myself right there. What sane man wouldn't? I looked into his eyes; they were like a shark's. You've seen them, yes? Black, no compassion or remorse, nothing but purpose and hunger in them. I thought I was going to be devoured, but then he- *it* stopped. It dropped me on the ground and stalked off into the smoke of the battle. The next time I saw Tretyak was back at the base days later. He just looked at me and nodded, like nothing had happened. He may have been human then, but his eyes were the same. I never said shit to anyone about what happened."

The Russian lapsed into silence and drained his glass. His hands were shaking badly and he wrung them a few times in an attempt to stop himself. Once that failed, he took several puffs from his cigarette and looked up at the two agents with watery eyes.

"Where is he now, Dimitri?" Chance asked. "We need everything you've got on these blokes."

Dimitri refilled his glass and took a healthy drink from it before he spoke again. His voice was quiet and his eyes were cast down towards the tabletop. "After Afghanistan, Tretyak and fifty other Spetsnaz operators were hand-picked for some special KGB project. You know the type, it doesn't exist, none of the people in it exist and all that bullshit. The KGB scrubbed their existence entirely. They purged medical records, service records, everything. Those of us who knew them were told that it would be very unhealthy to remember them. Some KGB slug came in and took anything that we had that showed or mentioned them; photos, journals, anything that referenced their names or images. I managed to keep what I had only because I sent most of this stuff home to my sister when I left Afghanistan instead of bringing it back with me."

Jordan gave Dimitri a nod, indicating he should continue, though she paid close attention to the fearful tang of his scent.

The weathered Russian rubbed the scars on his shoulder again and took another drag from his cigarette. "Truthfully, I don't know what they did with those men. There were rumors, of course, but nothing that was ever substantiated. Some said they were part of a program to create super soldiers, like some fucking comic book. But they were just rumors, who would believe that? After a while I just pushed that shit out of my mind. In the old days, it wasn't healthy to have a good memory."

Dimitri glanced between Chance and Jordan again and continued. "A few years ago, Tretyak surfaced in the underworld going by the name Crimson Shark. He did some wetwork for a former KGB official, then some more for the Americans. An old comrade of mine said he's running a merc unit called Vodnik that specializes in hard-to-accomplish tasks. My friend said that the men were all like Tretyak now, demons, monsters, whatever you want to call them. I just know that I never want to see any of them again. As far as where they are now, who knows? You should check with Rene Artis to see if he can make that connection."

"Thanks, Dimitri. Artis is in a prison in China. We probably won't see him again," Chance said and reached into his jacket pocket slowly. "Maybe you should get out of town for a while. These guys have been working round here." He withdrew three bundles of bills and placed them in front of Dimitri. "That's triple what we agreed on. I just want to take a scan of that photo for the extra bit."

Dimitri waved his hand and stood up. "Where am I going to go? Tretyak's people are specialists in espionage and black ops, they'll find me if they want. I'm not going to go live in some hovel down in South America or Africa. Fuck that. I'll be fucked if I'm going to end up in some Chinese prison, either." He collected the bundles of money and walked over to place them in a black satchel. "Just keep this between you and I, you don't say anything to Tretyak or his people about me and they have no reason to look, eh?"

Jordan pulled out her agency phone and turned on the scanner feature of the camera. "Don't worry, we aren't going to mention you." She held the phone over the photograph and let the device scan the image. Once the phone was done, Jordan examined the image on the screen of her phone and then tucked the device away. "We appreciate the information, Dimitri."

"And I appreciate the money," Dimitri responded. "If you go after them, you better make certain you got your life insurance policy updated. They don't screw around."

Chance smiled broadly and rose to his feet. "I'll make sure to pick up a few insurance policies, preferably of the anti-tank sort."

Dimitri chuckled darkly. "You may need more than that, my friend."

"We'll be careful," Jordan added and stood. She pushed her bangs back and walked towards the door along with Chance.

"Good. You two pay well and I don't mind a pretty face stopping by from time to time," Dimitri retorted as his former demeanor returned. "Next time, leave Chance at home and I will make you a very good breakfast. I'll even make sure to get some kippers from the market. I hear you Englishmen like them."

Jordan laughed softly. "Tempting, but I'll pass."

Dimitri gave Jordan his best disappointed look. "That's too bad. An old dog like me could show you a few new tricks, I think."

The vibrating alert from Jordan's phone drew her attention and she pulled the compact device from her pocket. The display flashed showing a new text message and she ran her thumb along the lock icon on the screen to access it. The message instantly popped up with an emergency alert verification code appended to it.

Jill's off the reservation. Not sure where she's gone yet. Tristan.

Chance gave Jordan an inquisitive look which she put off with a slight shake of her head.

"Keep your head down, mate. We have to get back to the office," Jordan said and proceeded down the stairs. She heard the door shut behind her, but she continued out onto the street after checking the area from the doorway.

"What's going on, Jordan?" Chance asked as he hurried to catch up to his companion who had turned to head back to where they left the car.

"My sister, Jillian, has done something foolish," Jordan said wearily. "Again."

Chance nodded and took Jordan's hand so that the illusion that they were a couple would remain intact for any onlookers. "Wonderful. Care to elaborate?"

"She's left the estate and managed to elude the security teams," Jordan said after a brief look at Chance. "I've got to find her before this Crimson Shark does."

CHAPTER 19

The warmth of the summer sun cast its light down on the busy Covent Garden shopping district and the throngs of tourist shoppers that plied its streets and walks. The locals were also out in force, though they were easily picked out from the tourists by the presence of various sizes and styles of umbrellas that they carried. The unpredictable weather in London meant that a shower could hit at any time, and today was no exception.

The pavement and roofs of the shopping district still had small tendrils of steam rising from them from a strong rain that had occupied the early morning hours. It had cleaned the air in preparation for delicious scents that issued from the various cafes and eateries that lined the area. Numerous street performers dressed in brightly colored costumes danced, juggled, and cavorted about, entertaining the tourists that had come from all over the world to see the renowned district.

The sight of so much happiness brought a bright smile to Jillian Law's face. She caught sight of her reflection in the window of Starbucks and paused to fuss with her hair. Jill was the youngest of the Law sisters and, unlike the rest she was on the shorter side at five foot five. She shared her father's blonde hair which she wore in what she thought was an adorably cute pixie cut. Jill's expressive eyes were also blue, like her father's, and as she looked at her face, she realized she didn't much look like her sisters at all. That was ok; she was fine sticking out from them and could live with being adorable as opposed to Amazonian.

The only sister that resembled her at all was Marisa. She was also blonde and had similar eyes, though she was taller and more slender compared to Jill who was a very curvy seventeen year old young woman. The tight pink and white baby doll shirt she wore had the picture of a white cat wearing battle armor with a very large machine gun on it. She also wore a pair of tight blue bell-bottomed jeans, a pair of black and pink tennis shoes, of which she owned no less than six pairs.

Jill took a sip from her trademark venti five-shot caramel macchiato before she wandered off down the sidewalk toward one of her favorite boutiques. She couldn't help but feel satisfaction at the fact she had escaped her sister's government goons by using the family's pet Wolfhounds to distract the heat sensors and guards that patrolled the property. Fortunately, they were too busy verifying that the dogs were just dogs to notice her using an old escape tunnel to get off the property.

"All too easy," she commented to herself and smiled. The impact of a large, well-dressed man bumping into Jill shook her out of her brief moment of mental glory and made her work to keep from dropping her coffee.

"Excuse me," the dark eyed man said in a friendly manner. "My apologies."

Jill nodded and looked up at the man who towered over her. "No worries. Sorry 'bout that," she replied and smiled at him.

The man inclined his head politely and continued on. "Have a good day."

"Pretty tasty," Jill said to herself and turned to watch the man walk away. A grin blossomed on her features and then she turned to continue on her way. By the time she reached the shop, she was thinking about what she should buy and a pair of red high-heeled boots sitting in the window caught her attention. When the shadow fell over her, Jill scarcely noticed it, but the presence that it belonged to was all too familiar. "Shit."

"Language, Jillian," Jordan intoned from behind her sister.

Jill turned to face her sister and gave her an innocent smile, "Coffee?" She extended the cup towards Jordan and smiled brightly. "It's very tasty."

Jordan, still dressed in the same clothes she wore the night before, placed her hands on her hips and watched her younger sister through the emerald lenses of her sunglasses. "Everyone's worried *sick*, Jillian. What were you *thinking*?"

The smile vanished from the blonde's face. "I was thinking that it was terribly boring being a prisoner in my own house."

"It isn't the best situation, but it's necessary to keep everyone safe until we can deal with what's going on," Jordan said in a sympathetic tone.

"Brilliant, when's that going to be, huh?" Jill retorted and met her sister's gaze.

"I don't know," Jordan said honestly. "I'm sorry that my work has crossed into your life, Jillian, but there's little I can do about it now except to deal with the problem. I am trying to take care of it as quickly as I can, but this isn't a simple matter."

Jill made a hissing sound. "Jordan, you guys are always getting to dictate my life to me. God, between you guys and Mom and Dad, I feel like *I'm* in the fucking military. I have friends, and a life, and school. I can't sit locked in the house like a criminal while you do whatever it is that you do!"

"Keep your voice down," Jordan said in a low tone and took Jillian's arm firmly to guide her down the street and away from the main crowd. "This is a life and death matter, Jillian. The men that are looking for me are very dangerous."

"Looking for *you,* Jordan, *you*. Not me. Hell, I don't know where you are ninety percent of the fucking time!" Jill growled. "I had a date and it totally got jobbed by your friends. They scared Marty so bad that he about pissed himself. He won't return any of my texts now. I *liked* him, Jordan."

"I'm sorry for that, Jill. I truly am, but you needed to be picked up right away," Jordan replied and eased up her grip on Jill's arm. "I would never ruin something for you if there wasn't a good reason for it."

Jill's expression softened slightly. "Jordan, look, I can take care of myself. Dad's shown me the self-defense stuff he's shown all of you guys. I'm actually better at it that Ryan and Alessa. You guys worry about me too much."

Jordan nodded slightly and sized control of the conversation. "I know you can, Jillian. This isn't a negotiation, however. We're going back to the house and you're going to *stay* there this time. Your other option is a cell somewhere, if that's what it takes to keep you safe."

"Are you serious?" Jill exclaimed incredulously.

"Very."

"Fuck," Jill growled angrily and turned to look in the nearest shop's window. "This isn't *fair*."

"I know," Jordan said and placed her hand on Jill's shoulder. "Life frequently isn't, Jillian. I'll do my best to end this so that you can get back to living your life. I love you and I'm not going to let anyone hurt you, even if it means causing you some inconvenience."

Jill continued to look into the window for a good minute, leaving a large silence between her and Jordan. The feisty blonde wanted her older sister to feel the irritation that she felt and folded her arms. Eventually, reason won out and Jill exhaled. "Fine, but you owe me for this. You owe me big. I'm going to miss my graduation ceremony if you don't sort this out in a week. I refuse to miss that."

A smile formed on Jordan's lips as Jill relented and she gave her sister's shoulder a firm squeeze. "I'll make this up to you, Jillian. I promise."

Without warning a large hand seized Jordan's wrist with inhuman strength and held it. "You are a very difficult woman to track down, Jordan Law, but well worth the effort."

Jordan cursed herself for allowing Jill to distract her to the point that she lost her situational awareness and turned her head to look into the eyes of the man that had hold of her. She immediately recognized the Crimson Shark's face; the hungry intent in his dark eyes terrified her. He wasn't alone either; three other men were next to the Shark, trapping Jordan and Jill against the wall. A quick scan of the area revealed at least three more in the nearby vicinity. "I see you finally decided to come after me yourself, Tretyak."

"You know who I am, very good," the Crimson Shark said in a pleased tone. "Then you know what I can do, as well. If you come along peacefully there won't be a need for violence."

"I'm sure that disappoints you," Jordan replied in a wintery tone. She wrinkled her nose as a musky smell caught her attention. The Crimson Shark's scent was laced with lust and satisfaction, but there was something else backing it that was starting to make Jordan feel disconnected from herself, pliable.

"To a point, yes, however; there will be time for foreplay later," the Shark replied and gave Jordan a predatory smile. "After you've become one of us."

"Become one of you?" Jordan replied softly. She was having trouble focusing on anything besides The Crimson Shark's voice. She felt intoxicated, but it was more than that. It felt like every instinct was telling her that she needed to obey him.

The Crimson Shark laughed dismissively. "Yes. You didn't think I was going to all of this trouble to satisfy some petty need for revenge, did you?"

"Why?"

"Isn't it obvious? I need an equal. A mate, "Tretyak said. He released his grip on Jordan and lifted the hand to cup her cheek.

Warmth spread through Jordan's body and her eyes slowly closed. Yes, she wanted what he was offering. She was certain of it. There was someone she *should* be thinking of, but Jordan couldn't remember his name, or his face. All she could think of was Tretyak, he was her world. The Crimson Shark's touch thrilled her. His black eyes drew Jordan closer and she moved to place her hands on his chest. "Yes."

"Jordan!" Jill shouted suddenly. "What are you doing?" The younger Law sister grabbed Jordan's arm and jerked her away from Tretyak's embrace. "Get the fuck off of her, you wanker."

Tretyak's eyes filled with fury and his hand lashed out so quickly Jill didn't see it coming. She felt the impact against her cheek and the blow drove her to the ground against the wall. Jill's head was swimming and she looked up at Tretyak fearfully. The wrath she saw in them terrified her. He was going to kill her, Jill was never more certain of anything in her life. She was too scared to move as Tretyak reached for throat with one of his massive hands but his wrist was suddenly grabbed before he could reach it.

"Leave her alone," Jordan growled and snapped her foot up to catch one of the Crimson Shark's thugs in the jaw. The force of the blow sent the large man spinning end over end out into the street. His flight was halted when he slammed into the side of a delivery truck so hard that the cargo area crumpled like paper. The vehicle went out of control and crashed into a parked Mini Cooper, triggering the vehicle's alarm.

Jordan used the hold on Tretyak's wrist to swing herself to the opposite side of The Crimson Shark's body and kicked the other two thugs in the chest hard enough to knock them to the ground. "*Run*!"

The younger Law sister didn't need to be told twice and darted through the opening that Jordan created. She tore off down the sidewalk as fast as she could, but one of their attackers lunged at Jill from the open door of an SUV. Jill spun out and away from the man's grasp, hurling her coffee cup in his face and splashing him with the hot liquid. Jill looked back as she ran down the street and saw that the man that held Jordan had wrapped both arms around her body in an attempt to subdue her.

Unable to use her arms, Jordan threw her weight back into the Crimson Shark and drove him into the shop's window. The glass wasn't strong enough to bear the weight of such a large man in addition to Jordan, and broke with a loud crash. The scent of blood reached Jordan's nose and she felt Tretyak's grip on her loosen just enough for her to worm free.

Immediately, another of the Shark's thugs came at Jordan and struck her in the stomach, knocking the wind from her. The man made the mistake of grabbing Jordan's shoulder instead of striking her again and she capitalized on the error. With both hands, she grabbed his hand and wrist, levering his limb so that he lost his grip on her. In a flash, Jordan brought her knee up and pushed the man's extended arm down so that his elbow took the full force of her knee strike.

The bellow of pain couldn't disguise the sound of bone and muscle rending in the thug's arm. Keeping her hold on the man's extremity, Jordan spun on her heel and smashed the wounded mercenary into one of his fellows. She let go at the last second and let momentum carry both men down the sidewalk where they fell, tangled together.

Jordan felt a rush of pain in her back as something struck her from behind and drove her into the sedan parked in front of the shop. The passenger side window shattered as Jordan's arm crashed into it and she could smell the tang of her own blood in the air. The familiar sensation of something warm and wet spread across the skin of her forearm as blood spilled out of the wound.

Without hesitation, Jordan rolled towards the back of the car, narrowly avoiding the Crimson Shark's follow up blow. His large fist shattered the back passenger side window and sprayed glass into the car's interior. Despite his bulk, the Crimson Shark was *fast*. Before Jordan had finished her evasion, the Crimson Shark's booted foot struck her in the stomach and sent her tumbling over the back of the car's trunk. Jordan tumbled on to the ground on the other side of the car and was left gasping for breath.

"I'm glad you decided to put up a fight." The Crimson Shark grinned. "It will make your surrender all the sweeter."

Jordan's gaze hardened as she rose to her feet. "I won't surrender to you."

"Then I'll have to break you," the Crimson Shark promised darkly.

The words made Jordan's skin crawl. There was a certainty in Tretyak's eyes that made her realize she was in the most danger she had ever been. This man wasn't going to stop until he had what he wanted or he was incapable of getting it. She wanted to ask him what made her so special, why was she worth so many lives, but Tretyak was already moving towards her to fulfill his promise. Jordan quashed the fear she felt gnawing at her resolve and launched herself across the trunk towards Tretyak.

She was moving as fast as she could, a nearly invisible blur to the crowd of stunned onlookers that were gathering at the edges of the combat. Jordan used the edge of the trunk to flip herself high into the air, her upper body pointed at the ground. She pulled the twin .45 pistols from the small of her back and squeezed the triggers as fast as the weapons would allow.

To Jordan's surprise, Tretyak actually appeared to be moving when every other person in the area was almost statue-like. The Crimson Shark didn't bother to avoid the bullets, instead he hunched over so that all of the projectiles struck him in the upper back and shoulders. Blood splattered as the heavy rounds struck him and ruined the expensive suit he wore. The force of the high caliber rounds' impact slammed him against the back of the sedan, but he managed to retain his feet.

Jordan landed gracefully on the ground and lashed out at Tretyak with her booted foot. She felt The Crimson Shark's sternum crack from the force of the impact and his body went spinning over the car. The Crimson Shark spun head over heels and crossed the one hundred foot distance between the two sides of the street in the span of a single breath. His flight was suddenly, and painfully, arrested as he crashed through the brick wall of a bookstore which sent a cloud of dust into the air.

The crowed suddenly erupted in cries of fear and Jordan saw them pointing in her direction. Jordan looked over her shoulder and saw one of Tretyak's men transforming into the massive bestial shark form they possessed. The hulking creature charged at Jordan as soon as its transformation was complete. The sidewalk shook beneath Jordan's feet as Tretyak's soldier came at her and she prepared to jump out of the way when a dark form leapt down at the creature from above.

Douglas' fist slammed into the side of the creature's head hard enough to send it crashing through a police box and into the back of a large rubbish hauler. The mercenary staggered forward, blood running from his tooth filled maw and Douglas started towards it. "I've got this one, love. Go find yourself a new playmate."

The smile on her face died as Jordan looked around the street. Now that one of the mercs had chosen to reveal himself, the rest of Tretyak's men followed suit. The mercenaries' human bodies quickly grew and distorted as they took the nightmarish form that was half-shark and half-man. Each was well over two meters tall; and all of them were nothing but muscle, claws, and razor sharp teeth, honed by cold instinct and driven by the intellect of men.

"Bollocks," Jordan breathed.

The mercenaries' transformation drew gasps and fearful cries from the crowd of people either too foolish, or too scared to flee. Several people had taken their phones out and were taking pictures of the combatants, but even they were momentarily stunned by what they were witnessing.

The shark men started towards Jordan and Douglas just as the latter tossed his opponent into the middle of the street. The nearest of the transformed mercs shoved a parked car out of his way, sending the vehicle smashing into the Mini Cooper with the blaring alarm. The two vehicles compacted as they met and the alarm ceased.

Jordan glanced at her friend and tucked her pistols away. "I hope you're not tired."

The former Royal Marine had a determined look on his face as he watched the approach of the large creatures. "Not even close. You?"

"I'll be fine. You take the five on the left. I'll take the five on the right," Jordan said grimly.

The thunder of turbine engines roared overhead as the SOS-7 jet thundered into view above Covent Garden. The powerful engines switched to standby as the craft began to orbit the area using its magnetic drive. On either side of the craft the personnel doors slid open and black clad soldiers leapt out. Each man wore a magnetic ascender belt to slow their fall as they took up positions on the tops of the roofs.

The mercenaries looked up and a chorus of challenging snarls came from them. They began to tear off hoods and doors from the cars in the area, while some tore out parking poles or other implements they could use as weapons. Three of the shark men charged towards the building that the main formation of SOS-7 soldiers had landed on. They leapt onto the side of the building and began to climb up towards the roof using their claws to dig into the brick and stone of the buildings.

As the sleek jet made another orbit three more men launched themselves from the doors of the craft and landed near Jordan and Douglas. Jordan immediately recognized Tristan, Portsmouth, and Chance and gave them a tight smile. "Nice of you to join us."

"Can't let you have all the fun, love," Tristan replied smoothly.

Portsmouth frowned at the two and brought up the rifle he carried. "Flirt later." The hard-bitten soldier took aim at the approaching creature and opened fire. Several glowing blue energy bolts flew from the barrel of the gun. They made the air sizzle as they came at the creature but it dropped to a very low crouch to avoid the tightly grouped blasts.

The mercenary sprang towards them like a leaping tiger. Douglas intercepted it in mid-air and the impact sounded like a car wreck. The smaller man managed to overpower the creature and both of them tumbled to the street unceremoniously. Both combatants rose and began trading blows immediately.

Chance charged up to one of the parked cars and braced his own rifle on it as he opened fire on another of the creatures. This one was less quick than its fellows and the energy blasts stitched a path along its side. The scent of burning fish wafted into the air from the patched of charred skin that the mercenary now bore. Yet the metamorph still came on, heedless of the painful wounds.

Another salvo of energy bolts struck the creature as Tristan moved to help his brother. "Spread out, teams of two!"

With only Portsmouth near her, Jordan moved to his side. "Cover me. I'm going to see if their leader is down for good."

The older man nodded his head and triggered a burst from his weapon at the merc Chance and Tristan were firing at. "Go!"

Jordan darted across the street like a bullet. As she crossed the path of one of the mercenaries he swept his arm around in an arc, trying to eviscerate her with his talons. The dark-haired operative leaned back and let herself fall into a slide so that the blow passed cleanly over the top of her head. She slid between the creature's legs and came out behind it.

The merc roared in pain as Portsmouth placed a tight group of blasts in the center of its broad chest. Another volley of rounds struck the creature in the same location as Portsmouth continued forward, firing his rifle.

Capitalizing on her momentum, Jordan turned her slide into a roll by throwing her weight to one side. With the grace of a cat, she came up out of her roll at a full run, her legs and arms pumping as she hurried to cross the street. There was blood on the edges of the wall where Tretyak had broken through and, momentarily, Jordan felt a surge of hope.

That hope vanished as soon as Jordan saw two massive, clawed hands grasp either side of the ragged hole. She skidded to a stop several meters from the damaged wall and dropped into a defensive stance. Jordan's eyes widened in shock as a transformed Tretyak stepped out onto the sidewalk.

The Crimson Shark rose to his full height and stared down at Jordan with an unreadable expression. At three meters tall, Tretyak's monstrous form dwarfed even his own men. Hard muscle flowed beneath the blood-red flesh that covered Crimson Shark's body. Like his men, Tretyak's combat form had the head of a shark with a mouth full of triangular, serrated teeth and heavy black claws on his hands and feet. It also had a massive, angular fin just behind the head and four gill slits on the side of its thick neck. Unlike the rest of his men, Tretyak's transformed body had a long, powerful, shark's tail that methodically moved from side to side.

With a voice that reminded Jordan of the roar of a blast furnace, the Crimson Shark taunted her. "Come, show me your power, woman. The time for games is over. You and I will come to an understanding of one another."

Jordan swallowed her fear and gazed back into the Crimson Shark's black eyes. "I understand you more than I care to." Calling upon all of her speed Jordan made a short leap and drove her fist into Crimson Shark's jaw. The blow sounded like a gunshot when it struck, but, to Jordan's surprise, all it accomplished was jerking Tretyak's head to the side. She followed up with a kick to his chest and several punches to his torso, but it was like hitting a steel wall. His skin was rough, almost like sandpaper, and it abraded Jordan's knuckles with every strike. At the end of the assault, her hands were covered in her own blood and painfully sore.

The Crimson Shark seemed unphased by the attack and drove his fist into Jordan's side with an incredible speed. A sharp cry of pain tore its way out of Jordan's throat as she felt two of her ribs snap. The force of the impact was nothing like Jordan had ever experienced and before she knew it she was tumbling across the ground, gasping for air. Every breath sent a spike of pain through Jordan's side, and as she struggled to regain her feet the Crimson Shark struck her again.

The kick hit Jordan square in the stomach and tossed her back into one of the parked cars. She heard the sound of metal failing as she dented the vehicle's door inwards. Again, pain washed over Jordan and she shouted out in agony. Instinctively she placed a hand over her ribs to protect them from further assault.

Reaching down, the Crimson Shark grabbed Jordan's short black hair, jerking her head up so that she could see his eyes. The pained expression she wore made him feel a certain level of satisfaction and he knew it wouldn't be long before she was begging him to accept her. "Do you see the power of the gift I offer you?"

"If you're talking about the bad breath, I think, I think that I'll pass," Jordan responded as she struggled to fill her lungs with oxygen.

"Apparently, the lesson must continue," Crimson Shark replied calmly. He grabbed the front of Jordan's top in one hand and flung her casually away from him.

Jordan's world exploded in stars as she slammed into an iron light pole fifty feet away. The resonate sound of the hollow pole stopping her flight was the last thing Jordan was aware of before the world dimmed around her.

* * * * * *

Jill was still scared out of her mind. Despite all of her bravado and tenacity, she had never been in anything more than a fist fight. Now she was surrounded by creatures that shouldn't exist, and they were far worse than anything shown in a movie or video game. Jill's heart raced so fast that her ears pounded with blood. She peered out of her hiding spot down the street just in time to see her sister's body strike the light pole. When Jordan didn't get up, Jill felt tears streaming down her face and watched in horror as the red skinned shark stalked towards where her sister fell. *This is my fault. Jordan wouldn't even* be *here if it wasn't for me!*

Fear gripped Jill's heart as she saw the red skinned shark man reach down and pluck Jordan's limp body from the ground. There was no sign of movement from her sister and the creature handed Jordan to one of its friends. *You take care of your own.* The family's informal motto wasn't hard to remember, but until now Jill had never really taken it seriously.

Jill wiped at her eyes with the back of her jacket's sleeve. "Fuck this!" The youngest Law sister broke from cover and ran towards the only weapon she could see. She wasn't going to let these creatures kill her sister without doing something. "I'm coming, Jordan!"

* * * * * *

Portsmouth had been in more battles than he could remember. He had served the United Kingdom for over fifty years, thanks to his gifts. But he had never felt as old as he did right now, nor as overwhelmed. Most of the operators that the team had brought with them were holed up on the top of a building, trying to hold back the Vodnik. The plasma cartridge rifles, or PCRs, were definitely more effective than standard munitions against the Vodnik, but not enough. It would take an entire magazine, if not more, to burn one of the shark men down and even then, out of the five they had "killed," two had gotten back up. Douglas seemed to be the only one that was truly effective against their opponents and, despite all of his strength, he was only one man.

"Jordan's down," Chance said as he dropped behind the car that Portsmouth was using for cover. "The big red one's passed her off to one of his mates."

"I saw," Portsmouth replied gravely, his eyes flicking to the younger man. "I'm going after her. You stick with your brother and keep working on these bastards."

Chance nodded and took a deep breath. "Give me some cover, old man."

Portsmouth popped up over the car and opened up on one of the mercs that was assaulting the position Tristan had set up on the corner of the block. His weapon spit three of the plasma rounds at creature which struck it in the spine with little effect.

"Wish me luck!" Chance said and lunged to his feet. He sprinted towards his brother's position, headless of the fact that he would have to pass two of the Vodnik soldiers. One of the mercs tried to grab Chance as he neared, but the large creature inexplicably tripped over a discarded car door and went face down on the ground. The merc had a shocked expression as Chance hopped up and used its head for a stepping stone. With a cocky smile on his face, Chance ran by the second creature that Portsmouth was firing on and lofted a grenade at it.

The spherical weapon promptly thumped against the Vodnik's chest and landed in its open hand. The mercenary blinked in surprise and looked down, just as the device detonated. The creature's hand disappeared in a burst of fire that covered its face and torso with burning gelatin. A pained roar issued from the immolated Vodnik soldier and it fell against an abandoned balloon cart. The flames were contagious and quickly spread to the cart and its contents. The mercenary thrashed about in a futile attempt to get the burning chemical gel off of its body.

"Cheeky bastard," Portsmouth commented as he watched Chance dart over the car to his brother Tristan. Both men popped back up and fired on the burning creature until it ceased moving.

Looking around briefly, Portsmouth spied the creature that had Jordan making its way quickly up the street towards the alarmed crowd of onlookers. Meanwhile, the Crimson Shark covered the retreat by tearing chunks of cars off and hurling them at the SOS-7 soldiers' positions. Portsmouth changed the magazine on his PCR and broke cover. He ran towards the creature carrying Jordan as fast as he could manage. As he closed the distance, the old soldier brought the rifle to his shoulder and fired a burst into the back of the Vodnik's knee.

The creature stumbled and went down, howling in pain and lost its grip on Jordan. Her body tumbled free and came to a stop next to a half-full bicycle rack. Portsmouth continued forward, pumping round after round into the creature's body until he came around to its head. With a grim look of satisfaction on his face Portsmouth put the PCR up to the creatures' eye and fired the remaining three rounds into it. The plasma rounds exploded inside the Vodnik's brain cavity, causing smoke and flame to pour out of both eye sockets and its gill slits. The mercenary twitched several times and then went limp as its life came to an end. Portsmouth reloaded his weapon and watched the creature for a moment, prodding it with the toe of his boot. Satisfied that it was dead, Portsmouth knelt down and carefully turned Jordan onto her back.

The dark haired woman wasn't moving and Portsmouth couldn't tell if she was breathing. Swearing under his breath he pulled off the glove on his left hand and then pressed his thick fingers to the side of Jordan's neck.

"Come on, girl," he said in a firm voice. "Don't give up yet." A rare smile formed on Portsmouth's face as he felt the pulse of a vein beneath his fingertips. Just then, Jordan's eyes slowly opened and the old soldier schooled his expression into a serious scowl. "There we go. Rest a moment, Law. Let your body heal."

Portsmouth's scowl was replaced by a shocked expression and pain exploded along his spine. The rifle in his hand fell from his grip clattering to the sidewalk next to Jordan. Grimacing as the pain intensified, Portsmouth looked behind him into the soulless black eyes of the Crimson Shark.

"She's mine," Crimson Shark intoned and flexed the fingers of his hand causing the sharp five inch claws to drag through soldier's flesh. The act wrenched a shout of pain from the man so the Crimson Shark did it once more. The old soldier reached back and grabbed Crimson Shark's hand in a surprisingly powerful grip and tried to pry himself free.

"You're weak," Crimson Shark said with disdain and spun on his heel. He slammed the old man into the wall next to them with enough force to crack the stone. Tretyak could hear the breaking of bone and smell the scent of blood, but the soldier was still trying to break loose from his grasp. Drawing back the British operative, the Crimson Shark drove him into the concrete sidewalk. The surface fractured and spider webbed beneath the soldier, leaving him bloody.

The Crimson Shark released the man and looked down at him. "Like most of these men, you're just prey." Then, the mercenary leader brought his fist down towards the old man's head, but a hand caught his fist and stopped the death blow from falling.

Jordan strained to keep the punch from connecting ignoring the painful protest of her healing ribs. "Remember me?"

Gripped in her other hand, Jordan held Portsmouth's discarded plasma cartridge rifle and she jammed the barrel up into the Crimson Shark's armpit. She squeezed the trigger and poured several rounds against Tretyak's skin.

Crimson Shark roared in pain as the plasma bolts tore through his flesh and burned vital organs. Snarling like a wounded beast, the leader of the Vodnik lashed out with his clawed hands, driving Jordan back several steps.

Undeterred, Jordan kept the trigger depressed and emptied all fifty rounds from the PCR into the Crimson Shark's body. Smoking and charred, the mercenary leader fell to his knees, down, but not out. Jordan took the rifle's stock in both hands and spun around on her heel. As she came back around to face the Crimson Shark, Jordan smashed the PCR across the top of his head shattering the weapon. The impact pitched the Shark into the sidewalk face first and drove the oxygen from his lungs.

Sluggishly, Tretyak tried to lift his monstrous bulk from the ground. His torso was savaged from the PCR's fire, but the Russian metamorph seemed determined to continue the fight. Before he could stand, Jordan grabbed the end of the Crimson Shark's tail and spun with all of her might. The Shark's body lifted into the air and made two revolutions before Jordan drove him into the stone wall of a bank. Fragments of stone exploded away from the wall, some powdering into dust from the force of the Crimson Shark's impact.

Jordan ignored the sensation of her barely knitted ribs snapping again and swung Tretyak's body into the wall on the other side of her. She repeated the action two more times sending fragments of masonry and dust into the air. Jordan dropped the Crimson Shark's body to the ground near the building and staggered back away from him. Panting and holding her side, Jordan walked over and tore the bike rack from the ground. She wrapped the metal structure around Treyak's torso and twisted the ends together to imprison him. She wasn't sure it would hold Tretyak for long, but it was better than nothing at all.

Exhausted, Jordan dropped to the ground next to a car and clutched her side. She could feel her body working to heal the many injuries she had, but realized that it would take days for all of them to mend. Nearby, the sounds of weapons fire and cries of pain were starting to die down, but they weren't out of danger yet. Closing her eyes, Jordan focused on her body's healing, but a pained groan from next to her made Jordan almost jump out of her skin.

Portsmouth rolled onto his side and looked at Jordan through the eye that wasn't swollen shut. His face was streaked with blood, though the gash that it had come from was slowly closing up. "About time you dealt with that wanker."

A faint smile appeared on Jordan's face and she looked into Portsmouth's good eye. "I thought you had him."

"That makes two of us," Portsmouth replied and pushed into a sitting position. One of his legs was still at an odd angle so the old soldier pushed the damaged limb back in place with a loud pop. With obvious effort, Portsmouth hauled his wounded body along the ground and sat next to Jordan with his back against the car. "The big one snuck up."

"He's apparently good at that. I've put a ringer on him though, so that should be done for a while."

Portsmouth nodded and looked at the mass of metal that Jordan had wrapped around the Crimson Shark's unconscious body. "Nice piece of work, that."

"Thank you, Sergeant," Jordan replied and rested her head against the car door's cool surface. She grimaced and turned her head so she could look at Portsmouth, "I owe you one, don't I?"

"You don't," Portsmouth said firmly and turned his head so he could look at Jordan in turn. "That's what teammates do for one another, Law."

With effort Jordan nodded, "I'll remember that."

"See that you do, girl," Portsmouth said wearily.

Heavy breathing from behind them made both Jordan and Portsmouth look up. Standing on the other side of the car was another one of Tretyak's shark men. He was battered and bloody, but looked like he had more fight in him that either them could manage in their current states. The Vodnik soldier's expression turned into a savage smile as he saw the two wounded operatives nearly helpless before him. Jordan pushed herself away from the car and staggered to her feet. Weaponless and wounded, she prepared to go down fighting when the roar of a diesel engine and the sound of an air horn drowned out the pounding of her heart.

The shark man turned to face this new challenger, but was crushed beneath the wall of green metal that was the rubbish hauler. The vehicle kept going, pulling the Vodnik beneath its six wheels as it collided with a parked delivery lorry a few feet away. The impact caused a chain reaction several cars long. The line of vehicles was crushed together by the weight of the rubbish hauler, but managed to stop it from going any further. The vehicle's engine sputtered and died as the driver stalled it out, but the lorry had served its purpose. The Vodnik's body was torn in half by the truck's wheels, though its upper body was sticking out from the side of the vehicle. Jordan blinked in disbelief and glanced at the streak of blood that had been the mercenary's lower body prior to the introduction of the truck when the driver's door flew open.

Jill jumped down from the cab and grimaced at her handiwork. The youngest Law sister side-stepped the creature's remains gingerly and darted to where Jordan was.

* * * * * *

Douglas tossed another of the unconscious Vodnik mercenaries down next to his comrades and nodded to Tristan. "That's the last one down here. Looks like Jordan's got a couple up the street."

Colonel Shaw glanced up where Jordan was talking with her sister, "Including the Tretyak. Containment will be here in ten minutes, Douglas. Make sure you keep these bastards down if they wake up."

"Righto, Colonel," Douglas said flippantly. "Not a problem in the least."

Both men turned as Chance and a couple of the team's operators walked up from where Laird, Young, and Deckard were containing the civilians.

"How did we do, Chance?" Tristan Shaw asked and watched his younger brother's dark expression.

"We lost nine men. Fourteen are injured. Deck's shoulder is dislocated and Laird's got a nasty gash along his thigh," Chance said.

Tristan rubbed his chin and looked towards where Portsmouth and Jordan were sitting. "They look like hell, too. What about civilians?"

"So far, eight dead, at least thirty injuries and all of them are scared out of their minds. We've confiscated all the phones and video cameras, but this area had hundreds of people in it when all of this started. My guess is that we'll be seeing this up on YouTube in an hour if it isn't there already," Chance replied and watched his brother's reaction.

Tristan made a helpless shrugging gesture. "Not much we can do about it. Call command and make sure they're aware so they can start trying to shutdown the footage."

Sergeant Douglas folded his arms across his chest and nodded his chin in Jordan's direction. "I'm going to go check on them and bring back their catch."

"Alright, just don't take too long. Who knows when these blokes are going to start waking up," Tristan said. He watched

Douglas jog up the street and then turned back to his brother. "The old man is going to be furious."

"That's an understatement," Chance replied in an unusually thoughtful tone. "We just changed the world."

* * * * * *

Jordan shook her head as Jill rushed over and threw her arms around Jordan's torso. A shudder of pain shook Jordan's body and Jill loosened her grip. "I thought you were *dead*!"

"And I thought I told you to run," Jordan replied and put her arms around Jill carefully. She held Jill close and rested her chin on the top of her sister's blonde head. Relief flooded her as she noticed that her younger sister was completely unharmed.

Jill's response was excited and almost incomprehensible, "IdidandthenIsawyoufightingandyougotsmashedintothepole!"

Sore and exhausted, Jordan smiled fondly at her sister and led her over to the car where Portsmouth sat. She dropped to the ground next to him and looked up at the smiling face of her youngest sister. "You did well, Jillian."

Jill crouched down and brushed the sweat and blood soaked bangs from Jordan's face. "I did?"

"You did," Jordan reiterated and smiled.

"We need to get you to a hospital, Jordan, your friend too," Jill said and gave Portsmouth a warm smile.

Even though it hurt to move, Jordan shook her head. "No. I'll be fine. I just need time to heal and my friends will see to me."

"You're really hurt though, Jordan. You're ribs are broken, you've got internal bleeding, contusions, and a concussion," Jill exclaimed excitedly and then covered her mouth.

Jordan raised an eyebrow and watched her sister. "How do you know what injuries I have?"

The girl who was seldom nervous suddenly was. "I, um, well, I, can *see* it. I can just tell. I know when things are sick, or hurt. I've got powers like you, Jordan. Though yours are really cool, like that super speed thing and you're really strong! Can you fly? Can you shoot beams out of your hands? What about breathing fire or ice?"

"Jillian, focus, how long have you had these abilities?" Jordan asked in a softer, but serious voice.

"For about a year," Jill replied sheepishly. "I was afraid to tell anyone."

"You shouldn't," Portsmouth added. "Keep it quiet."

"He's right. For now, just keep it to yourself," Jordan said and reached out to touch her sister's cheek.

The seriousness on Jordan's face made Jill's smile wane. She nodded her response and took a seat next to her sister. "I won't tell anyone."

"I know you won't," Jordan replied and put her arm around Jill's shoulders. Her ribs provided her a painful reminder that they were still there and still healing from the second break so Jordan relaxed the muscles a bit. "So, what made you think of using that truck to run down that metamorph?"

Jill grinned, "A game. I think someone owes me an apology for saying that video games served very little real life purpose." Jill finished the last part of the sentence with her Jordan impression.

Both Jordan and Portsmouth chuckled and the former gave Jill another hug. She held this one a bit longer and smiled. "Perhaps, I do."

CHAPTER 20

The operators of Special Operations Squadron Seven exited the briefing room in a quiet, orderly fashion. All of them had been through medical checks and hours of debrief, so the two days of downtime hadn't been very restful for most. The men all wore different expressions as the pitched battle had had different effects on each of them.

Deckard, who was still recovering from a dislocated shoulder, was reflective and hadn't said too much. Laird, who was on crutches, was talkative, and he and Chance were discussing where they were going to go pubbing. Young, who managed to escape the battle entirely injury free, was in good spirits, though he did give Jordan a smug look when she and Douglas were asked to stay.

Jordan knew that Young was taking pleasure in the fact that she was being blamed for outing Awakened beings. Not just by their Director, but by every official that had access to the footage of what was being termed The Covent Garden Incident. She looked in Douglas' direction and felt no small measure of guilt for his situation. He had been present both times that she had to very visibly use her powers and, as a senior operator, he was expected to rein her in. Now, he sat in the hot seat with her.

The cocky sergeant smiled reassuringly and nodded his head as if he had everything under control. William Douglas looked back towards the front of the room where Director McIntyre stood with Colonel Shaw and Sergeant Portsmouth and folded his hands to wait.

It wasn't long after the briefing room's door shut when the three men looked in Jordan and Douglas' direction. Portsmouth gave Jordan a nod of acknowledgement and continued to lean against the section of wall that he usually claimed during meetings. He still looked like hell. The older man's face was swollen and bruised still, though both eyes were now open and the fractures in his cheek had mended. One arm was still in a cast and Portsmouth needed a cane to move around effectively. The wheelchair he was supposed to be using sat nearby. Portsmouth's healing factor was far less effective than Jordan's, though it had still saved his life. It also made certain he wouldn't spend the rest of his life as an invalid.

Shaw was much harder to read. His face was schooled into a semi-stern expression and he stood with his arms folded across his chest. He hadn't said much in the final debrief of the team as a whole, nothing that could be counted as an opinion of the team's actions in regard to openly using their powers. Tristan had methodically given the team the cost of the battle in both lives and collateral damage and then congratulated them for bringing the mercs down. Every member of Special Operations Squadron Seven said that it had been one of the most difficult fights that the team had been in so far.

Jordan sighed inwardly. The Squadron has lost nine men, with fourteen injured. Out of those fourteen, three would never be able to work in the field again, and one was an invalid. The civilian cost was much higher. Eight had died during the battle and a further five more had died of their injuries. Over fifty people had been hurt, some minor, but some were still on life support. While Jordan had been fighting the Crimson Shark, his Vodnik had intentionally attacked the civilians in order to draw the SOS-7 team out of cover and force them to engage close range. The team had fought bravely and their sacrifice had reduced the number of civilian casualties. Sadly, they would never be publically recognized for it. Their families would be well-compensated, though that did nothing to assuage Jordan's self-imposed guilt.

Before Jordan could dwell on it any further, Director McIntyre walked forward to stand in front of the podium. His eyes still held anger, though it was controlled and focused, and that tension seemed to fill his entire body. McIntyre leveled his gaze at Jordan and Douglas. "I'm half-tempted to eject you both from the agency." McIntyre glanced at Shaw and Portsmouth momentarily and paused. "Others think that would be a waste of material."

The Director let Jordan and Douglas have several moments to absorb the weight of his words before he continued. When he continued his tone changed, it became harder-edged and dangerous. "In the future, you may not find me as generous. The two of you compromised the secrecy that a dozen agencies around the world have been bleeding to keep for decades. The damage you've caused is irreversible at this point. Videos of you using your abilities have been posted all over the internet. Somewhere, somehow, you've earned fortune's favor because nobody has a clear picture of your faces."

Douglas started to speak, but McIntyre silenced him with a single look. "What *is* clear in those videos is people turning into bloody walking sharks and tossing cars about like they were a potted meat tin. Every news channel in the world is playing this footage. There *is* no other story right now."

The Director paused to rub the bridge of his nose and let his breath out in a futile attempt to decrease the tension in his body. Douglas and Jordan exchanged brief looks, but the sound of the Director's voice snapped their attention back to him. "Doctor Lindon feels that this incident is only going to encourage Awakened humans to emerge from the shadows and start acting openly. Robbing banks, holding governments hostage, killing, and those are just going to be the start. Every normal human will live in fear."

"Why?" Every set of eyes in the room turned in Jordan's direction as she spoke. She felt very self-conscious, but pressed on despite of it. "I'm quite serious. There's nothing to be done about what's happened. Everyone knows it, that's why you're all so angry. The way we react to this today, tomorrow, a year from now, will determine Awakened humanity's future if not humanity's future as a whole." Jordan's tone became passionate as she spoke, her eyes meeting each man's in turn finally settling on the Director.

Her sense of trepidation vanished and was replaced by determination. "The time for all of this cloak and dagger rubbish is *gone*. We can use this as an opportunity to, not just protect people, but *inspire* them. We can show them that there are men and women there to protect them. Show them that there are dedicated people to stand between them and all of the murderers, rapists, and psychopaths of this world. Because we all know very well that some of those very same murderers, rapists, and psychopaths are exactly like us, Awakened."

* * * * * *

The room was silent except for the clicking of the crystal glasses that Ethan McIntyre retrieved from his bar. He placed them both on the desk and filled a measure of scotch in each. He didn't bother to cap the bottle as he nudged one towards the man who sat across the desk from him. McIntyre sat and then hoisted his drink. "Cheers."

Cassidy Law raised his own drink and downed nearly half of it before he sat the glass back on the desk. He glanced to the side and caught a glimpse of his own reflection in the window. His blonde hair was longer, his blue eyes more distant, but he didn't look so different than he did in the picture of the old team that Ethan McIntyre kept on his den wall.

The old team was all smiles back then, full of confidence and determination. Most of them were either dead or retired, or on to other pursuits. He and Ethan were more or less it, though they were different from their contemporaries on SOS7's former incarnation. Cassidy though his reflection looked as angry as he felt. No, anger was a poor choice of words. He was furious.

"Out with it Cass," McIntyre prompted, "You aren't here for the scotch."

"If you *ever* use one of my daughters as bait again, I'll kill you," Cassidy Law said plainly. His Scottish accent wasn't thick, but he had been using it for so many years that it had become a part of him. It wouldn't have mattered which accent Cassidy used, or which of the many languages he knew. The anger in his voice was as plain as day. It pervaded him and showed in the set of his square jaw and the flash of his blue eyes.

"I did what I had to do. I thought Jill would rabbit if she had half a chance and she did. The Shark wanted Jordan and it was pretty clear he was going after loved ones to draw her out," McIntyre replied unapologetically. "I used his own trap to catch him. In the old days, you would have made the same call. Besides, my people were watching her the entire time. It was a calculated risk and it paid off."

Cassidy frowned at his longtime friend. "I'm serious, Ethan. Never involve my family in your shite again. Not like that. Jordan can handle herself, but Jill's not the same sort of spirit. You put her in a position where she had to kill someone and now she has to carry that with her."

McIntyre raised an eyebrow but remained on course. "Her mother said she's been her typical self. No obvious change in personality or demeanor. Maybe you need to give her more credit. She tough, just like the rest of your family. "

The sound of Cassidy's hand slamming against the top of McIntyre's desk was unusually loud. His anger was getting the better of him and it was all he could do to keep from reaching across to drive McIntyre's head into the desktop. "It hasn't sunk in yet, and when it does, she's going to be devastated. You stole her innocence and I can't forgive you for that!"

Silence reigned between the two men for a time. Cassidy glared and McIntyre looked introspective. Finally McIntyre spoke. "I'm sorry for that, "he said sincerely, "but I would do it again if I had to."

"I'm a man of my word, you know that. You better keep that in mind next time," Cassidy threatened. "My children aren't part of this war."

"Do you think she can avoid it? Do you think any of them can? The Jennies aren't going to leave Earth alone forever. We know that Lindon isn't the only one here, but he's been good covering his tracks and so far he hasn't led us to any more of them," McIntyre said and watched Cassidy's reaction.

The patriarch of the Law family responded by downing the rest of his glass. McIntyre refilled it and then topped off his own again. "You chose to retire. I can respect that. You've done more for our people than I have and you deserve the rest. "

"But?"

"But we need to keep our numbers up. Humanity is Awakening and we need to steer them in the right direction. Jordan can help do that if she's half the leader you are. She's already got the charisma. I'm giving her the experience," McIntyre elaborated.

Cassidy took another drink and shrugged. "I'm not happy about any of this, Ethan. Why didn't you tell me you were going to recruit Jordan?"

"Because I knew this would be your reaction. Even if you've decided to leave the war, the war hasn't left you. I needed her. I need her skills and her powers. I'm going to root out the Jennie cells and she's going to help me, "Ethan said intently.

"These aren't humans. The Jenagyr don't think like humans, or even us for that matter. She doesn't know anything about fighting the Jenagyr, how can you expect her to do any better than the rest of your team?" Cassidy replied angrily.

McIntyre gave Cassidy a sly smile, "How? She's your daughter. She's got the heart of a fighter and she means to use it. Let me worry about educating her."

"After what you pulled I'm not sure I trust you anymore, Ethan," Cassidy said and rose to his feet. He gave McIntyre one last hard-eyed look and headed for the door. "I'll be in touch."

McIntyre watched Cassidy stalk from the room and finished off his drink. He smiled and sat back in his comfortable chair. The relationship between him and Cassidy would never be the same. He regretted that. They had been friends since they were children, but there was a war to win. The war was bigger than either of them, bigger than Cassidy's family, and bigger than Earth.

CHAPTER 21

The flash of cameras was nearly blinding as Doctor Elgen Spears trotted jauntily down the stairs of the CNN building in Atlanta. His assistant, Karen, was still furious that Spears had decided to leave by the very public front entrance instead of utilizing a more discreet means of departure. Still, she was doing a very admirable job of deflecting all of the questions that the throngs of reporters were tossing his way. Not one to disappoint, Elgen paused and smiled charmingly for the cameras, even taking a moment to wave. *That's front page on every paper by morning,* Spears mused.

He put off the questions by raising his hands and silencing the crowd. "Friends, friends, I know you all have more questions. Don't we all? I know I do. Questions like, how many years have the governments of this planet been hiding the presence of metahumanity? What can these people do? How dangerous are they? Do they need our help? I can assure you, I am demanding these answers from my politically inclined friends. I also assure you that I am willing to help *any* metahuman that comes to me. I will do everything in my power to see that they are able to live a healthy, happy, and safe life, so that we can all have the same opportunity. I, and my company ImaGen, stand ready. Right now, we are preparing our San Bernardino facility to house and assist any individuals with these superhuman abilities. We want to examine them and make certain that there aren't any dangerous genetic side effects that could impact their quality of life."

Spears smiled warmly at the cameras and continued on. "The game has changed. We've got to change with it. Our fellow humans *need* us, even if they don't know it yet. No doubt, our brothers and sisters have been living in the dark recesses of society for years, outcasts, afraid, alone. *Used*."

The well-dressed man made a stabbing motion with his finger and let indignation creep into his tone. "How many of our sons and daughters have been virtual slaves to the government's more shadowy organizations? All in the name of what? National security? Preventing fear? Preventing mass panic? Or is it that they wanted to hold onto a powerful resource that lets them keep control of us? Abusing other human's rights so that they can keep power for themselves?"

"We all know about Gitmo, about Tuskegee, and the Holocaust. How many of these atrocities, these crimes against humanity, have been hidden from us? We cannot hate these gifted individuals. No, we must embrace them. Genetically, they are the future of us all. There could be a child out there right now whose genes have the cure for cancer, but that child could be in the hands of evil men. Evil men that want to use his gifts to further their own goals."

The smile returned to Elgen Spear's face and his voice burgeoned with warmth. "Friends, our world, as we have known it is much bigger than we ever dreamed. Only by extending our hands out to metahumanity can we all make that world a better place, a safe place for all us. Who knows, perhaps one day, *all* of us will be able to fly."

Spears paused dramatically and let his words permeate hearts and minds of the millions, if not billions, who were watching or would watch this impromptu interview. The reporters were largely silent, only the clicking of cameras and the excited breathing of the many humans gathered on the stairs could be heard. "Now, if you'll excuse me I need to get back to work," Spears said and proffered another charming smile to the cameras as he hurried down the stairs into the waiting limousine.

As the door shut behind him and Karen, the hastily shouted questions from the reporters were silenced. Only the faint sound of the limo's engine speeding them away down the street was audible. Spears took a moment to soak it all up, before he looked over at his assistant expectantly.

The pretty blonde quickly worked the controls of her tablet pad. "You're trending up on Twitter by forty-three percent over yesterday, and ImaGen's stock has gone up nearly 280% since Revelation Day," She said and fought to keep the smile from her face. "I have eighteen more requests for interviews and the Prince of Saudi Arabia wants you to come for dinner at the end of the month."

"Arrange half of the interviews and tell the Prince that I'd be happy to come speak to him," Spears said in a casual tone. "Revelation Day. I have to admit that was a stroke of genius on my part. How are the other terms I've been using coming along?"

Karen swiped her hand across the screen of her tablet and studied the information for a moment. "Honestly, your terms are becoming *the* terms. Data mining's report shows that nearly every talk show host, politician, and internet blogger have been using the terminology you presented in your first interview."

"Excellent," Spears said, with a wide, pleased, smile on his lips. He was once again shaping humanity and, soon enough, he would have everything he needed to unlock the secret of Awakening.

The sound of Spears' cell phone ringing banished the momentary silence. He plucked the device from his pocket and smiled as he saw the number resolve from Unknown to a series of numbers

"My dear, Whip Scorpion, I trust you are the bearer of good news today?" Spears said in a good natured voice.

The reply was all business, though the voice on the other end was distorted by some sort of voice masker. "Yeah, we've got your order. Delivery will take place on schedule."

"That *is* good news. Apparently, you're quite the fisherman. Good work." Spears hung up the phone and tucked it back in his pocket. "Karen, who's that lovely reporter from MSNBC that I interviewed with last week?"

"Mia Strong," Karen replied and looked up from her tablet.

"Mia, yes. Invite her to dinner her tonight. I might be persuaded to do an impromptu interview. Tell her I'll send my private jet to collect her and we'll have dinner in Monaco," Elgen Spears said and sat back to make himself comfortable. "Tell her to pack a bag."

Epilogue

"Countess Agincourt, are you planning on coming back to bed?" Brian asked from where he lay reclining on the large four poster bed. He smiled at Jordan fondly and swung his legs over the side of the bed. "You may have ten times the stamina I do, but I'm feeling very invigorated."

The smile on Jordan's face was inadequate to describe what she was feeling inside. Their wedding had been three days ago, but Jordan was riding the high from it still. It had been a wonderful affair with family and friends in attendance and her stoic mother had wept with happiness. Brian's family had even warmed up to Jordan at the reception and that had made it all the more special. They had escaped to the small cabin in Gstaad Switzerland the same night, bidding friends and family farewell so that they could start their marriage off properly.

Brian came up behind Jordan and slipped his arms around her waist, his fingers teasing the bare skin of her hip. "How many times are you going to look at it?"

Jordan smiled and brushed aside the tress of her wedding gown to reveal the armored case sitting on the table below where she had hug the bulky garment. Inside the open polymer container, sat a neatly folded black suit, a pair of armored plated knee high boots, matching gauntlets and a small curved mask. "I'm just getting used to it."

"Mm, well get used to it later, when I'm sleeping or something. You can play Batgirl later," Brian urged gently, though he did pull out one of the drawers which revealed an assortment of hi-tech items including knives, miniature grenades, and a variety of devices he didn't recognize.

"Deal," Jordan said and nudged the drawer closed with her hand. When she tried to close the top, Brian placed his hand over hers and stopped her.

"Bring the boots," Brian said firmly," and the mask."

About the Author

Garth Reasby was born and raised in the Pacific Northwest and currently lives there with his wife Heather Reasby, also an author, and their menagerie of animals. Over the years Garth has done a variety of work besides writing. Everything from making tools in a small tool shop to bodyguarding religious figures, to his current job as a project manager for a telecommunications company.

All of his life Garth has enjoyed creating and has channeled those energies into art, music, prop making, and writing. In college he was told frequently that he should look at writing professionally though at that time his passions lay in music and drawing. After being put in a collaborative environment with other writers, working book covers and editing, Garth was bitten by the bug again and dove back into writing.

Currently, Garth has his first book "Awaken" out and is working on two additional novels in the series. In addition he is preparing to write a fantasy series as well as writing stories for a soon to be released anthology with several other authors including his lovely wife, Heather.

When Garth does find time to relax he enjoys reading, comic books, video games, music, going camping and off-roading, as well as putting a few hours in at the range to keep up his firearm skills.

Garth Reasby can be contacted via the following methods:

Website: www.thermalscorpion.com

Twitter: @GarthReasby

Email: ThermalScorpion@Gmail.com

Look for the second thrilling book in the Children of Divinity series, *Evolve*.

Coming in 2012!

Made in the USA
Charleston, SC
01 February 2013